Big Trouble

Marianna Jameson

A SIGNET ECLIPSE BOOK

SIGNET ECLIPSE
Published by New American Library, a division of
Penguin Group (USA) Inc., 375 Hudson Street,
New York, New York 10014, USA
Penguin Group (Canada), 90 Eglinton Avenue East, Suite 700, Toronto,
Ontario M4P 2Y3, Canada (a division of Pearson Penguin Canada Inc.)
Penguin Books Ltd., 80 Strand, London WC2R 0RL, England
Penguin Ireland, 25 St. Stephen's Green, Dublin 2,
Ireland (a division of Penguin Books Ltd.)
Penguin Group (Australia), 250 Camberwell Road, Camberwell, Victoria 3124,
Australia (a division of Pearson Australia Group Pty. Ltd.)
Penguin Books India Pvt. Ltd., 11 Community Centre, Panchsheel Park,
New Delhi - 110 017, India
Penguin Group (NZ), cnr Airborne and Rosedale Roads, Albany,
Auckland 1310, New Zealand (a division of Pearson New Zealand Ltd.)
Penguin Books (South Africa) (Pty.) Ltd., 24 Sturdee Avenue,
Rosebank, Johannesburg 2196, South Africa

Penguin Books Ltd., Registered Offices:
80 Strand, London WC2R 0RL, England

First published by Signet Eclipse, an imprint of New American Library,
a division of Penguin Group (USA) Inc.

First Printing, May 2006
10 9 8 7 6 5 4 3 2 1

SIGNET ECLIPSE and logo are trademarks of Penguin Group (USA) Inc.

Printed in the United States of America

PUBLISHER'S NOTE

This is a work of fiction. Names, characters, places, and incidents either are
the product of the author's imagination or are used fictitiously, and any resemblance to actual persons, living or dead, business establishments, events, or
locales is entirely coincidental.
  The publisher does not have any control over and does not assume any
responsibility for author or third-party Web sites or their content.

This book is dedicated with love to my mother,
who is, simply, the best.

And to my husband,
who taught me the meaning of Big Trouble
(with a capital Q).
Grá mo chroi,
Grá mo bheatha.

ACKNOWLEDGMENTS

For their much-appreciated help, support, and information, I would like to thank:

Joanna Novins, Karen Kendall, Jerrilyn Hutson, and Deirdre Martin, for being wonderful writers and even better friends. And a special thanks to Jerri for a brilliant critique.

Richard Smith, Kevin Smith, and Stephen Collins for their unquestioning help and unfailing support during the computer-related crises that seem to plague me, and inevitably do so when I'm on deadline.

Brian Mitchell, Stephen Bates, Mark Doll, John Howie, and their staffs for giving me not only a crash course in corporate digital security but for bringing me inside the industry and providing me with the opportunity to see how things really work and what happens when they don't. Thanks, guys, for sharing your expertise, your war stories, and your time. You're aces.

My sisters, Patricia, Elizabeth, Kathleen, and Margaret; sisters-in-law Kit, Carol, and Lorraine; and girlfriends Nancy, Ger, Laura, Carla, Deb, Amy, and Aimee for being the best unpaid publicists in the world.

The Romance Writers of Southern Connecticut and Lower New York for their unflagging enthusiasm and support, and bottomless well of talent.

Mike Hutson, who continues to provide entertaining insights into the male mind-set. And that's all I'm going to say about him.

My editor, Laura Cifelli, who continues to have fabulous taste and terrific instincts, and her assistant, Rose Hilliard, who is so calm, efficient, and knowledgeable, and a very good hand-holder to crazed new authors.

My agent, Coleen O'Shea, who continues to be candid, supportive, and open to ideas, and tactful at the same time.

And, of course, my husband, who doesn't qualify for sainthood yet but is getting closer, and my children, who want to grow up to be writers. And parents. And, occasionally, trees.

Although the City of Stamford and the other places mentioned are real, all characters and their names are works of fiction. All mistakes are my own.

CHAPTER
1

"Sarah, I know you're in here somewhere. I need to talk to you." Naomi Connor leaned cross-armed in the doorway and stared at the back side of a flat-screen monitor. It was flanked on both sides by high, untidy stacks of file folders, legal pads, books, spiral notebooks, and boxes of software, but Naomi knew that somewhere on the other side of that barrier sat her boss.

"About what? I'm kind of busy, in case the state of my desk has somehow escaped your notice."

Naomi bit back a smile as the dry, disembodied voice drifted toward her. "The Brennan Shipping project."

"What about it?"

"I want it," she replied, moving into the office and closing the door behind her.

It took another half minute before Sarah McAllister's strawberry-blond head rose like a periscope above the chaos. "Get in line. Every project manager in this company wants it."

"Not every project manager in this company is willing to help you clean your office in order to get it."

"Not interested. I don't need a cleaning lady. I need an arsonist."

"Could I interest you in a simple bribe?"

"You'd have to get awfully creative. Jenny offered me two go-anywhere passes for the U.S. Open, and Richard told me he'd get me a date with Colin Farrell. His sister is the man's publicist's hairdresser," Sarah replied, her gaze flicking back to her screen momentarily. "And all for a standard network security audit with penetration testing. Maybe a disaster recovery exercise. Go figure."

"It's hardly that," Naomi said, settling herself in one of the chic, armless, and thoroughly uncomfortable chairs opposite Sarah's desk. "Brennan is one of the oldest and biggest defense contractors in the country and has its fingers in building everything from cruise ships to cruise missiles. And now it's getting into designing radar systems and satellites." She looked her boss directly in the eyes. "You made it clear that everyone on the team has to have top secret clearance or above, which means at least one of the networks we'll be trying to penetrate is black. Deep black. *Midnight black.* And the entire project has to be conducted behind the scenes and at top speed."

"There is that," Sarah conceded with a grin.

Naomi raised an eyebrow. "You know full well it sounds less like a standard 'pen' testing operation and more like real, old-fashioned, down-and-dirty hacking. Who among us in this company has hacked—*really* hacked—since college? And which of us wouldn't give up our right arm to have a chance to do it again? Hell, darlin', half the people in this company would consider doing this project for free, just for the thrill."

Sarah laughed and leaned back in her chair. "You've almost persuaded me. Keep going."

"My last project went down smoother than my granddaddy's Alabama moonshine, Sarah. You know how good I am. How fast I am. I want it." Naomi paused and smiled. "I also want to make partner before the end of the year."

"Now we're cutting through muscle to the bone."

Naomi said nothing in reply, just watched her boss's expression slip into executive neutrality.

"Partner," Sarah repeated eventually.

Naomi nodded.

"That's a lot to ask for, Naomi. You've been here less than a year."

"I know that, Sarah, and I know it's a crime and a sin to even think about asking for it before two years, but this industry thrives on rules being broken, doesn't it? Just like you, I've been paying my industry dues since I was a 'script kiddie' with an attitude, an Atari, and a push-button telephone." Naomi paused for just a second and watched Sarah fight a smile. "In the eleven months I've been here, every project I've managed has come in on time and under budget, and the clients were pleased. Three of them offered me jobs—good ones—that I've politely refused because I like working for you and this company." *And because Brennan Shipping is our client.*

Sarah narrowed her eyes and took in a slow, deliberate breath.

"Is there any reason I *can't* be made partner so soon after joining the firm?" Naomi asked after a moment.

Sarah shrugged. "Tradition. It's not that you're not good enough, Naomi. You're better than good enough. I just didn't expect you to ask so soon." Sarah sighed thoughtfully, then shrugged again. "All right. Why not? You get Brennan. I'll e-mail you the paperwork and background information. Start assembling your team. Take anyone who's available." She paused and gave Naomi an uncharacteristically stern look. "You'll need to get in touch with Joe Casey right away. He's Brennan's acting chief technology officer and you'll be reporting to him. For your information, he's a personal friend of mine *and* he's a Brennan. I want this one to be flawless, Naomi." She paused. "If it comes in on time and on budget, I'll see that you're offered a partnership."

That was fast. Naomi stood up, casually straightening her suit jacket to provide a disguise for her shaking hands. "I won't disappoint you."

Sarah gave her a half smile. "I don't expect that you will."

The short walk to her office seemed interminably long. Once inside, Naomi leaned against the closed door and just let herself tremble for a minute. Her elation at winning the project and negotiating a partnership so painlessly was overshadowed by deep, churning dread.

She continued slowly across the room, ignoring the chair behind her desk to press her head to the cold and dizzying horizon of glass that spanned one wall. Six stories beneath her, Washington, D.C., sparkled like a jeweled gown in the steamy July darkness, the streetlights striping and circling the night-cloaked city like sequined bands. Part of her felt as though she were free-falling toward those streets through an empty sky, parachute just out of reach.

I've spent twenty years of my life earning this project, this fear, this chance for redemption.

It didn't matter that having it handed to her so suddenly was the next best thing to terrifying.

Straightening her shoulders, she took a half step back and met her own reflected eyes. "Just like last time, there's no going back, R@ptorGurl. I'm going to hack Brennan with everything I have," she said, her voice firm and quiet. "But this time, I'm not hiding behind your name. I'll be out in the open, shoulders back, chin up. When I'm done, the past will finally be the past."

"Are you up for a beer?"

Joe Casey looked up from the set of monitors on his desk in the Stamford, Connecticut, headquarters of Brennan Shipping Industries. His brother, Chas, who was the company's brand-new chief executive officer, stood in the office doorway, hands on his jeans-clad hips.

"Yeah, but what the hell are you still doing here? You've got a wife and a baby. Go home."

"I've been home. Kissed the wife, cuddled the baby, and ate dinner. I just got back."

"What for? Work from home. That's why we set up full remote access for you."

Chas leaned a shoulder against the doorjamb. "Miranda's on deadline. As soon as the baby fell asleep, she kicked me out and told me to stay lost for two hours."

Joe sat back in his chair, grinning. "Let me guess. She's writing love scenes again."

His brother nodded. "She's got a container the size of a Dumpster full of whipped cream sitting on the countertop, and the fridge is filled with bowls of different colored Jell-O—"

"Stop. That's already more than I want to know."

"—and she tells me to *leave* until she finishes her research." Chas shook his head with a grin. "I think I'm losing my touch. There was a time when I *was* her research."

"Yeah, well, you're married now. She's been there and done you. But cheer up. Maybe you'll get to play with the leftovers."

"Now, there's a thought." Chas lowered himself into a wing chair opposite Joe's desk.

"Glad I could help." Joe paused. "Actually, there's something I want to discuss with you."

He motioned for Chas to shut the door and waited for the soft click that ensured privacy before continuing in a low voice. "I just got off the phone with Sarah McAllister. We're nearly set. She'll have a team in place to begin the security audit in a week or so, and the penetration testing team will be here around the same time."

"You're sure we're ready for this?"

"We're ready," Joe said flatly. "There's nothing we can do to be more ready. Our networks have gone live,

Chas. If we wait much longer without testing them and every other security measure we've put in place over the last eighteen months, we'll have wasted a lot of time and money. The longer we go without challenging ourselves, the more vulnerable we become. We've always been a high-profile target for terrorists and corporate spies." He leaned forward, folded his hands on the desk, and looked his brother straight in the eye. "There are hacking attempts made against us all the time, Chas. And every time we enter a new field or embrace a new technology, the potential for getting hit goes up exponentially. That's why we put in all the security features before we announced the microsatellite contract. But now the information is out there and we're going to get slammed. The last big hit cost us millions in terms of down time and bad press, and we nearly lost some contracts over it. And those bastards didn't even get around to stealing anything or fucking anything up. They just got *in*."

"Isn't that a good enough test? We quarantined them—"

"Chas." Joe paused to let silence add weight to his words. "Don't play the devil's advocate with me. Just because they got into our network doesn't mean they were the brightest bulbs in the box. They could have just been lucky. It's just a matter of time before we get hit hard again, and the next crew might be some assholes who actually know what they're doing. I want to be ready for them. I want the smartest, toughest hackers money can buy to attack us and try to penetrate our network defenses. If *they* can't get in, we're probably safe for a while."

"Okay." Chas stretched his legs out and yawned. "Sorry. Web's teething again. He had me up half the night last night. So you're convinced that Sarah's team is the—"

"Yes," Joe interrupted. "Sarah assured me that the project manager she's assigned can kick ass and take names, and if she says that, I believe her. If it's one thing Sarah knows how to do, it's spot a fake." He leaned back in his chair. "I should have the résumés for the project team by tomorrow afternoon. We'll have the clearances squared away in a few days."

Chas raised an eyebrow. "Did she tell you anything else about the project manager?"

Oh, for Christ's sake. Joe gave him a wry look. "You mean like the fact that she's a woman?"

Chas narrowed his eyes and Joe shook his head in mild disgust. "Hey, give me some credit. She's a software geek and digital-security expert. She probably has no personality, and twenty bucks says she wears men's shoes."

"I don't give a rat's ass if she doesn't wear any shoes. I'm not worried about her. I'm worried about you," Chas replied bluntly.

"Well, don't be."

"You're about due, aren't you? It's been, what, a month since you dumped your last girlfriend?"

"She wasn't my girlfriend; it was casual, and it's none of your business, anyway. Even on the off chance that this project manager is decent looking, I'd like to remind you that I'm thirty-eight, not eighteen. I'm not about to cause myself or this company any complications."

Chas didn't look convinced.

"Hooking up with the project manager would be not only incredibly stupid, but counterproductive. I want to finish this project and get back to Washington, back to my real life, and back to my real job as a lawyer who keeps this company out of trouble. That means I want her and her team in and out of here as fast as possible. Does that satisfy you, or would you like it in writing?"

"I'm just saying that I know you, and it's been a month since you've had a girlfriend."

God damn it. "I haven't had a girlfriend in a *year*. What I haven't had in a month is a *date,*" Joe said pointedly, "because I've been too damned busy saving your ass to go out and find one. I'm not getting desperate, if that's what you're worried about, and even if I was, I doubt she fits my profile, Chas." He paused. "For one thing, I don't date women I work with. For another, I don't date women who take life too seriously and, considering that she works for Sarah, work is probably all she thinks about." He grinned. "I like women who bounce when you break up with them, and who are only out for good times and good sex, both of which I'm happy to provide."

"Well, I'd appreciate it if you grow up, at least for the duration of this job."

"I am grown up. I'm just single." Joe glanced back at his monitor as a low bell-like tone announced the arrival of a new e-mail. "I have to read this. I'll meet you at the elevator in five."

Nodding, Chas left the room, leaving the door open behind him. Joe opened the message.

Joe, as I just told you on the phone, I've assigned my best project manager to your situation. You and I have known each other too long for me to feed you any standard lines, so I'm going to cut to the chase. If you try to hire her away from me, I'll have to kill you. And, sweetheart, as you well know, I'm capable of following through on that threat. . . .

Joe laughed out loud.

Her name is Naomi Connor, and she's an old, reformed hacker like me. She's as smart and tough as they come, and, let me repeat: You are to keep your corporate hands off her. Let me know if there is anything else I can do for you before I unleash Naomi on your networks.
  Sarah

Naomi Connor's plane had been sitting on the tarmac for twenty minutes while the ground agents for the outbound flight dealt with some diamond-draped woman making a fuss about her seat assignment. And until they resolved that and got the woman satisfied and ready to be strapped in, the other aircraft's passengers couldn't deplane. Which meant Joe had plenty of time to be bored out of his head at the miniscule airport in White Plains, New York, waiting to pick up Sarah's "security diva." He didn't really care what Sarah called her as long as she lived up to her reputation and didn't act like some overeducated, overpaid prima donna.

His eyes wandered around the waiting room populated with the usual suspects on a Saturday morning on the border of northern Westchester County, New York, and Greenwich, Connecticut. Distinguished, buffed-up older men wearing Polo shorts and Tommy shirts roamed in tandem with young, thin, tanned trophy wives wearing as little as possible. They were followed by squads of toddlers wearing on everyone's nerves.

"Hey, Casey, what's up?"

Joe turned to see a uniformed cop at his side. "Hi, Todd. I'm just picking someone up. What's up with you?"

"Same old shit," the cop replied under his breath from behind an easy smile. "I was cruising the lot and saw Chas's truck up top. You picking him up? How's he handling civilian life?"

"No, he's in town. I just borrowed his truck. They had a baby a few months ago. I think he got more sleep when he was working nights," Joe replied with a grin as he watched the fussy woman finally head down the Jetway and the door close behind her. "Other than that, I'd say he likes it fine."

They stood in an easy silence for a moment, watching the small crowd.

"It's about time," Joe muttered after a tinny female voice announced that the flight from Washington, D.C., was arriving through gate 2.

"So who are you picking up? New girlfriend? This

stage never lasts. Trust me. In a month from now, you'll be telling her to take her own damned car."

Joe gave him a sidelong glance. "If you're having woman troubles, Todd, I don't want to know about it. I never could figure out what Vicky saw in you in the first place. And not that it's any of your business, but I'm picking up a consultant we hired. We changed the location of the meeting and I couldn't get in touch with her on her cell phone, so I thought I'd pick her up to save the hassle."

"What's she look like?"

"Don't know. She's a computer consultant, so I'm not holding my breath," he said with a shrug.

"That one?" The cop tipped his head slightly at the tall, thin, earnest-looking jeans-clad woman with the backpack who was the first to emerge from the Jetway doors.

"Probably." Joe held up the small sign he'd made with Naomi's name on it.

The woman glanced at it, then at him, and smiled. And kept walking.

"You look like a goddamned chauffeur," the cop cracked.

"Could be because I feel like one," Joe replied under his breath.

"See you later. Good luck with the geek." The cop walked toward the small desk near the security area where a few of his colleagues were gathered.

Keeping the sign in plain view, Joe watched a grandmother, a few college kids, and two businessmen come through the doors. In unison, both men stopped to hold open the doors for the woman behind them.

Soft was the best word he could come up with to describe her. Not that it did her justice, but it was accurate. There wasn't a hard edge in sight. Not in her clothes, not in her smile, not in the way she held herself. Her body, her movements were relaxed and self-assured and radiated something more than the confidence of a woman who's beautiful and knows it; something elusive and sexy as hell.

A cloud of loose blond curls framed her face as she turned to make a low, laughing comment to the men. Judging by their dazed expressions, it was more than they'd expected to get. She, on the other hand, looked like a woman who always got everything she wanted.

Before she had to ask.

Damned if it didn't just figure that he'd lay eyes on the most beautiful woman he'd ever seen while he was waiting to pick up some nerdy digital-security wizard. Given Sarah's warped sense of humor, she'd be high-end Mensa material but your basic absentminded academic type. *She's probably still on board now, so absorbed by her Blackberry that she doesn't realize she's on the ground.*

Just as well. The wait would allow him a few more uninterrupted minutes to contemplate the Botticelli blonde with her movie star stroll and in-on-the-secret smile, who was walking toward—*him*?

The Jetway was a blessedly cool change from the heat of the tarmac she'd had to cross moments earlier. The small plane had parked far enough away from the building that the walk to the terminal had changed Naomi from a smooth, polished professional into a soggy, shiny professional. It hadn't been this muggy in Washington all week, and if she'd had a clue it would be this humid or this hot up here, she wouldn't have worn a suit, or at least not a silk suit. A pale silk suit that was now wrinkled beyond all reason. *Some good first impression I'll make. Smart enough to hack a secure network, but not smart enough to turn on the Weather Channel.*

The wrinkles and the weather were two complications she just didn't need. They were two chinks in her business armor, which might already be too thin for what she was about to face. In one of their e-mail exchanges earlier in the week, Joe Casey had indicated he'd be at today's meeting. Her stomach had been in knots ever since. With any luck, though, he'd breeze in for a quick meet-and-greet like every other CTO she'd ever worked with, and then leave her team alone to do their job. Get in and get out as fast as possible; that was her goal. She wanted Brennan Shipping Industries on her résumé instead of on her conscience.

Stepping over the threshold of the terminal, she thanked the men who'd stopped to hold open the doors for her and flashed them a grateful smile. It faded slightly as she turned away to see a large man holding up a small sign.

Anyone would have noticed him.

Make that *everyone*.

The man had *serious reproductive potential* written all over him, from the top of his windblown, sun-streaked blond hair, to those smoky blue eyes that were focused on her, to the embroidered yellow Brennan Shipping Industries logo on the dark blue golf shirt that covered a broad chest. She couldn't deny that the sight of him had her ovaries vibrating in a two-part harmony, but there was something else that drew Naomi to him more strongly than any pheromone could.

The sign he was holding had her name on it.

Not only was she walking into her personal ground zero, but she'd also just lost her getaway car. *Like I don't have enough on my mind.*

She squared her shoulders and, quelling the natural—make that *primitive*—flutter in her stomach, she approached the man with the sign.

"Hi. That's me," she said with a smile, tapping one long, hot-pink fingernail against the sign he held. "You've caught me by surprise. Nobody said anything about being met. I have a rental car reserved."

He blinked at her, and it took him a few seconds to respond. "*You're* Naomi?"

"I was last time I checked," she drawled. She should have been used to it by this stage of her career, hearing that shade of disbelief in a man's voice when confronted with the notion that a woman who had blond hair and big breasts, who wore makeup and high heels, could actually also have a functioning brain. She should have been able to ignore it, but the truth was that it never failed to sting.

Then he smiled. "I'm Joe."

She took the opportunity to blink back at him and managed to keep her mouth from falling open as the full meaning of those two words sunk in. "You're Joe? Joe *Casey*?"

He nodded, turning his smile into a short, silent laugh. "I guess we're equally surprised. You don't fit the stereotype I was expecting to see, either."

The voice was the same but this was *not* the man she'd pictured during the few brief phone calls they'd had this week. That guy was the standard-model chief technology officer: middle-aged, gone to paunch, and balding. Appropriately dull and moderately boring. And shorter. Definitely shorter. The man with whom she'd been communicating all week was definitely *not* a Nordic sun god with a smile that could blind a girl.

But, of course, he was indeed exactly that. Mother Nature obviously had it in for her today.

Almost fully recovered, she smiled again and offered her hand for shaking, which he promptly did. He had warm hands and a good grip. Very warm hands. Very good grip.

Okay, pull your hand away, break the eye contact, and start talking. "It's nice to meet you, Joe. Sarah speaks so highly of you," she said, hoping it didn't sound as blurted to him as it did to her. "Do you always double as the company chauffeur?"

"Not usually," he replied, switching on that smile again. "But we decided to change the location of the meeting at the last minute. I tried to call you but you were probably already en route. I didn't want to take the chance that instead of having your phone turned off, you didn't have it with you. We're meeting at my mother's house instead of at the Marriott. It's more secure, more convenient, and the food's better."

"What a great idea," she said, keeping the smile on her face as her heart headed south. *They recognized my name. It's going to be an ambush.*

He half turned that linebacker body toward the exit. "Shall we?"

"Just let me get my bag."

A blond eyebrow rose slightly. "You have a bag?" A quick glance at the computer bag in her hand indicated that he really meant "another bag?" When his gaze returned to her face, he was giving her The Look, and she managed not to sigh or deflate.

She hated getting The Look and took pains to avoid doing anything that might trigger it, such as letting clients know she always brought a suitcase along, even for a three-hour meeting. What she considered to be a necessary precaution, clients tended to view as an attempt to turn a business trip into a junket.

Feeling another chink form in her armor, Naomi sent him a false, easy smile. "It's my standard operating procedure. I've been in too many situations in which a two-hour meeting lasts for ten and I miss my plane, so I always have a suitcase with me. I usually just leave it in the car, but since I don't have a car, I guess my secret's out."

"It never hurts to be prepared," he replied, not convinced.

"I look on it as the business equivalent of mad money. You know how you never go on a date without cab fare in your pocket, but you don't necessarily tell your date it's there." She added a little laugh that belied her inner churn.

He stifled a grin. "That must be a Southern thing; women up here aren't shy about demanding cab fare for a solo trip home if a man fails to meet their expectations. The baggage carousel is behind you."

A CTO who's good-looking and *has a sense of humor. Imagine that.* "Thank you. I'll be right back," she replied, executing a graceful turn and hoping to have a minute to herself.

It was an idle hope. He remained at her side as she crossed the small open area and stopped near the moving conveyor belt. "So, Joe, is your mother's house far from here?"

"About fifteen minutes away."

"That *is* convenient." Her bag, a small one that would have been a carry-on had she not flown up here in a toy plane, emerged from behind the flaps and she leaned forward.

Instantly, he reached out a longer arm and grabbed the handle. "This one?"

"Yes, thank you."

He hefted the suitcase from the belt, sparing her a surprised glance as he encountered its full weight.

A laugh escaped her. "That's definitely a Southern thing."

His gaze skimmed her from hair spray to high heels and, when he finished his assessment, he smiled. "I'll have to take your word for it."

As she looked away from his smile, she realized that it had been entirely too long since she'd needed sunglasses indoors.

CHAPTER
2

An early morning rain had washed the sky to a bright blue, and the puddles that had been left behind were beginning to steam in the hot sun as Naomi and Joe crossed the top level of the parking structure.

"It's that blue truck," Joe said, pointing to the only pickup in the sea of sports cars and high-end SUVs.

"I didn't think y'all drove those up here," Naomi replied, hoping that it didn't *sound* like it was an effort for her to keep up with his stride. But at five-foot-two, wearing three-inch heels and a short skirt she had never before considered tight, it wasn't easy to walk next to a man who was easily a foot taller than she. "Of course, I didn't think it got this hot up here, either. Today is just full of surprises."

He glanced down at her, amusement tugging at that beautiful mouth, and more than likely lurking in the eyes he'd hidden behind a pair of Oakleys. "You've never been to Connecticut before?"

"I've never been north of Washington before. Well, one trip to New York City, but it was in the wintertime. So, tell me about the situation at Brennan Shipping."

They reached the truck and he opened the passenger's door, then looked down at her.

"Can you make it on your own?" he asked, biting back a laugh.

The seat rested at somewhere near chest height.

Great. Now I get to lose my dignity, too. She glanced at him, feeling less foolish than flustered. "I don't suppose you have a stepladder handy, do you?"

He shook his head. "Given that it's Saturday, I didn't think you'd be in a suit." He paused. "Actually, that's not the whole truth. Having spent some time around network-security guys, I figured you'd be in jeans and Tevas and have a laptop thrown into a backpack with your private stash of green tea."

"I'm saving that look for next week," she said absently, still eyeing the front seat. "Well, I suppose I'm going to have to ask you for a hand up, Joe."

Neither moved. Or spoke. Or looked at each other.

"That skirt isn't going to make it if you try to climb in," he stated a moment later.

"I know." She could feel heat rise to her face, and it wasn't just because she, like everything else in the parking lot, was baking in the morning sun. Eventually, she looked up. To her intense relief, he wasn't laughing at her. "I suppose we'd just better get it over with."

She set her computer bag on the ground and turned to face him, keeping her gaze centered on the Brennan logo on his shirt. Her hands came to rest lightly near his shoulders as his hands slid around her waist, lifted her up, and deposited her gently on the seat. He didn't let go right away, and she didn't dare look up. Or take a breath.

A second later, he jerked his hands away as if his fingertips were on fire.

"Thank you," she said in a voice that sounded more forced than polite.

"You're welcome," he replied tightly as he closed her door. He picked up her computer bag and suitcase and walked around to his side of the truck.

Though her mind was trying to deny that the last

twenty seconds had really happened, her body refused
to forget the warm pressure of his hands at her waist,
the clean scent of him as she'd tipped forward when he
lifted her, the feeling of his chest beneath her hands as
she'd braced herself. It was all a bit too much for nine
o'clock on a Saturday morning when all she had in her
was one cup of airline coffee. Not that she needed any
more stimulants at the moment.

She brushed a stray, damp curl from her forehead with
a hand that was slightly less than steady. *At least he's a
gentleman.* When presented with the same opportunity,
some men would have let their hands slide north and
then claim it was an accident. Joe had kept a firm grip
on her waist, as if to let her know that copping a feel
was the very *last* thing he wanted to do.

He slid her bags behind the driver's seat, then climbed
in.

"Well, that was awkward," he said pleasantly as he
started the engine. A vintage Van Morrison wail came
to life at the same time, but Joe caught it and lowered
its volume.

"There's nothing like getting cozy with a client right
away, is there? We survived, that's the important thing,"
she said, glad that the microburst of adrenaline in her
bloodstream was beginning to dissipate.

"When we get to the house, you'll notice that there
are about six other vehicles I could have taken. For the
record, this is my brother's truck and it was blocking the
driveway. That's why I took it."

She smiled. "I understand. So, I take it your brother
will be at the meeting."

"My mother, brother, and I *are* the meeting."

It's definitely an ambush. She swallowed hard and
turned toward the window, waiting for the strike of the
lightning bolt that was surely aiming itself at her. She'd
had twenty years to wonder what facing her past would
feel like and a week to brace herself for it. The time
was at hand. She was ready. Maybe.

"How much do you already know about the company?"

More than I should. "Why don't you just tell me what you need for me to know?" she replied easily.

"Well, the quick history is that my great-great-great-grandfather started a steamship company and it happened to become successful because of a unique hull design that the navy was particularly interested in. That was one hundred years ago. Since then, we've branched into designing fast-attack submarines, deep-water manned and unmanned submersibles, underwater missile platforms—anyway, research and development have always been our strong points. Our reputation for innovation is one that we're proud of and are determined to maintain. In the last forty years, we've moved into the high-tech end of the defense industry, and right now we are to the maritime industry what Lockheed and Boeing are to aviation." He glanced at her. "It makes us a natural target for everything from corporate espionage to out-and-out terrorism. That's where you come into the picture. When will your team be ready to come on-site?"

Lord have mercy. This is the real thing. She pretended to smooth her skirt over her thighs, making sure to dry her palms, which had become damp during his recitation. "We'll be ready by the end of next week. When will your team be ready for us?"

They left the airport grounds for a leafy, sun-dappled road.

"There is no team. Unless you count me as the team." His voice had cooled slightly.

Okay, I get it. This is karma. Suck it up and take like a woman. She looked at him. "But—" She stopped and took a short breath. "No one on your side will be working with us?"

"No. This operation is completely below the radar." He paused minutely, and the hand that was on the steering wheel stopped tapping in sync with a soft "Brown-Eyed Girl." "I thought I made that clear in my e-mails."

Great. In all of ten minutes, I've managed to convince him that I'm both helpless and incompetent. "Let me backtrack just a minute, Joe," she said with a smile, trying very hard to keep any note of defensiveness or dread out of her voice. "Your e-mails were very clear. I just didn't realize that *no one* else at the company was aware of it. We frequently work with very small internal teams, but I can't recall a project when I had *no* internal counterpart. Just so I have it completely straight, *no one* at the company is involved with this operation and *no one* in the company knows we're here?"

"My mother does. She's chairman of the board, but she's based in Palm Beach most of the time these days, and my brother does. He's the CEO and his office is at the headquarters here in Stamford. No one else at the company knows anything about it and won't until the project is finished. My assistant knows your name but has been told that you're a management consultant. By the way, I've told her that you're to have unfettered access to everything, including me. She won't ask any questions. She's been with the company for years and doesn't think too far out of the box."

I wonder what she thinks of you, big boy. She stifled the thought. "What about the IT department?"

"They have no knowledge that we're going to be audited," he stated flatly.

A blast of pure adrenaline shot through her and she wasn't quite sure whether it was the words or the attitude—or maybe just the man—that triggered it. "And your regular security team? The guards and so forth?"

"They've been told there will be a team of ergonomic experts coming through the offices. All the paperwork and badges have been arranged."

"Ergonomics experts?" she repeated with a smile.

He shrugged. "I couldn't think of anything else that was a good cover to get a team of people into the offices during the day and at night without raising too many questions. If you came in as cleaners, not only would the real cleaning crew get pissed off, but you'd have to clean. But as ergonomics experts, you can poke around in the offices and cubicles, sit in chairs and open desks, and no one is going to think twice about it."

Clever man. Usually her security audit teams did go in as cleaners. Or in the middle of the night with flashlights.

He looked at her. "I mean, that's part of what you're going to do, right? Walk around and see which people are leaving their computers alive all night, or not locking their desks?"

She nodded. "Standard ops. But you are aware of how unusual this is, right? This level of secrecy, I mean?"

"Yes, I do. But it's the only way that I can think of to pull it off." He glanced at her. "Even if I only inform the management level that we're going to be audited at some unannounced time in the future, it will get out. They'll tell their assistants, and instruct them to leak it so their units will be on best behavior until it happens. It's natural. Managers want their departments to look good. You know the drill." He shrugged. "That's worthless, in my opinion. I want to know *for real* what people are doing to safeguard the company. I want them to be on top of things all the time, to be conscious of security all the time." He shifted in his seat and rested his arm along the edge of the door. "Over the past eighteen months, we've spent a fortune, and not a small one, retooling the company. We've had all the security policies and procedures rewritten, and every person in the company, from my mother to the guys who sort the mail and unload the trucks, has gone through security training. We've restructured all the networks." He paused. "If your team members get into our secure networks, and I truly hope they can't, I want you to come in and slam us with everything you've got. I want my IT department to think we're under a real attack. I want to see how they respond."

The challenge roared through her for a heady, dizzying few seconds, until it smacked headlong into her fear. She had no doubt that they'd get in. She'd never yet encountered a system she couldn't hack eventually. And when she did, just like every client whose defenses she battered, Joe would want to know how she did it, how she knew where to look for vulnerabilities, and where she learned how to do it. As sure as night followed day, the questions would come. The answers would be more difficult to give this time.

She sat there, watching the trees and occasional houses flash past the window, and finally looked over at him. His fingers were tapping again, and he was watching her with the shadow of a grin playing around his lips.

The man was truly beautiful to look at. The task he'd described was a geek's dream.

This is more than penance. This, surely, is hell.

"My plan doesn't sound good to you?" he asked.

She gave a silent laugh. "Good? It sounds great, Joe. And it sounds like a challenge. One that we can meet." *If circumstances don't catch up with me first.* "So, how do you know Sarah? Were y'all in the FBI together?"

He turned back to the road. "No. I'm just a lawyer. We met in Washington on a case. What makes you ask?"

She shook her head with a quiet laugh. "Nice try, Joe."

"What do you mean?"

"If you're 'just a lawyer,' then I 'just dabble' in software."

The sound of his answering laughter was warm and slow and it went deep. She reached out casually and aimed one of the air-conditioning vents straight at her face.

"Sarah and I worked together a few years ago when we were hacked pretty badly. They got into one of our most heavily secured, classified networks. I was assistant general counsel at the time, and handled a lot of the legal oversight of the classified projects. I was the liaison between the Feds and the company.''

"And now you're chief technology officer."

"*Acting* chief technology officer. They needed someone in a hurry and I was within reach. I'm heading back to Legal as soon as this project is done."

"It's an unusual career path, if you don't mind me saying. Even for someone whose great-great-great-grandfather was one of the less notorious nineteenth-century industrialists," she said lightly.

"My undergraduate degree is in computer science," he offered, almost grudgingly.

Still smiling, she shook her head. "Come on, Joe, I don't know you from Adam, but I've worked with enough CTOs to know what they do, and being named one because you have a fifteen-year-old degree in a field you never worked in just doesn't fly in this business. I'm not going to ask you anything more on that subject, but let me just say this: From what you just told me, I'd guess this whole security exercise is *not* about establishing a secure perimeter. You're on the hunt. I want to know for whom and why."

He slid his sunglasses down an inch and spared her a quick glance over the top of them, letting her know he was both impressed with her perceptions and unimpressed with her persistence. "After law school, I became a prosecutor for the Justice Department. I was assigned to work with the Naval Criminal Investigative Service Computer Crimes Unit. When I'd gotten what I needed there, I came to work for the company."

A driven man. Goal oriented. Probably a son of a gun to work for. She fought off a shiver of deliberately unidentified origin. "So law school and a few years with the Feds were just diversions?"

"I had to cut my teeth somewhere."

"Cut your teeth on what?"

"Human nature and the criminal mind."

"The criminal mind?" she repeated.

"Hackers," he said flatly.

Her body stiffened involuntarily and she smoothed her skirt over her thighs again just to give her hands something to do. "That's what you've always wanted to do? Chase hackers?"

"Not just chase. Catch. Curtail. Incarcerate."

Lord have mercy. She forced herself to relax. "Not all hackers are criminals, Joe. I mean, you know as well as I do that there are hackers and then there are crackers. *Hackers* are curious pests. *Crackers* are criminal infiltrators with malicious intent. Surely those are the—"

"They all get in where they're not allowed and not wanted," he interrupted, then looked at her. "Which were you?"

This guy could be trouble. She swallowed and met his gaze calmly. "What makes you think I've ever been either?"

"In my experience, most people display some sort of affinity for their chosen field when they're young. For instance, I would guess that girls who play with dolls all through childhood more often end up as fashion designers than digital-security experts," he said pointedly. "You have a résumé that's pretty impressive. Are you going to tell me you played with dolls instead of DOS when you were a kid?"

"Well, I've hacked some," she admitted.

"Right."

"You don't believe me?"

"I don't believe the *some*. I'd say you probably had a long and successful career at it. For one thing, you work for Sarah, and I know that when she was at the Bureau and now that she's in the private sector, she only recruits the best. For another thing, you sound defensive," he said with a casual shrug.

She returned to watching the houses flash past her window. All of them were well kept, but as he kept driving they were set farther and farther from the street, and farther and farther apart from each other. And they were getting progressively bigger. Much, much bigger. As was her sense of doom, or at least guilt.

It was time to regroup.

"Well, of course I've hacked, Joe. I'll bet you have, too. Or did when you were younger. But what made you want to go after them so determinedly as an adult?"

"Our company was hacked—seriously, I mean—when I was in high school."

Uh-oh. "Only once?" she said lightly. "Y'all should consider yourselves lucky."

"Not once. Once *badly*," he said, sparing her an acidic glance. "An Eastern Bloc crime syndicate had an Internet site that masqueraded as a benign place for hacker wannabees to practice their skills. Kids mostly. These thugs monitored their abilities, then picked a few likely prodigies and groomed them. When they were ready, these gangsters set up a 'game' for the junior geniuses, a competition to see who could get into a network that they described as a dummy network of their own making."

Naomi's stomach plummeted as he told his story. *Her* story.

"Trouble was, it wasn't a dummy network. Somehow they'd found the portal for one of our highly classified networks but couldn't crack their way in. One of the kids did, though. A girl."

His recitation pricked her like a sharp pin, but she overlooked it in favor of the larger issue facing her: She'd never heard the facts from someone else; she'd never had to. Now, perversely, she needed to.

"What happened?" she asked, carefully measuring each breath to slow the blood thundering through her veins.

Joe shrugged. "She got in. Luckily, that was about it. Smart kid, obviously, but also smart enough to realize pretty quickly that it wasn't a game. She came forward and told her parents, who alerted the Feds before our people even realized we'd been hacked. Of course, the lowlifes who put her up to it were right on her tail and sailed in and started downloading everything in sight after setting a few logic bombs to hide their trail. They caused a lot of damage in addition to the loss of the information they stole." The loathing in his words sent a cold trickle of dread down the center of her spine.

"Well, the fact that the little girl went to her parents shows she had some good values," Naomi blurted before she could stop herself.

He glanced at her again. "Just in case you're unclear about this, ignorance isn't a defense."

She ignored the comment and forced a smile onto her face. "How old was she?"

"I don't know. A kid. Twelve? Fourteen? She called herself R@ptorGurl," he added derisively.

Two heartbeats collided at the way his voice wrapped around the name. His tone was cold. Poisonous. She shivered involuntarily, and he immediately reached out to adjust the air-conditioning.

He was way too observant.

"I know kids are smart and all, Joe, but she could hardly have known what she was doing. I mean, kids back then were a lot less sophisticated than they are now. And she did come forward, as you said."

"There you go defending criminals again. Are you sure you're out of the business?" he asked with a reluctant grin.

Guilty heat rose to her cheeks. "I didn't say that I was ever *in* the business."

"So you hacked but you never broke the law?"

The man certainly knew how to question a witness. But she knew how to handle men. She gave him her brightest smile, overlaid with lots of Southern spun sugar to defuse her words. "Well, Joe, everyone jaywalks occasionally."

He looked at her for a moment, saying nothing, then turned his eyes back toward the road.

"So," he said a good minute later, "tell me about your team."

She tried not to sound too relieved. "I'll put it this way, Joe. You could try, but you won't come up with a better one. Two of them are former FBI and one is former NSA. The other one we hired away from a Fortune 100 company because we promised him that his company car could be an orange Beetle and that he could take the airport helicopter shuttle from BWI to Dulles when necessary. If he'd asked for a weekly pony ride across the South Lawn of the White House, we'd have arranged it for him."

"Sounds like a nutcase."

"Actually, he sounds like an overgrown child, which is exactly what he is. But he's also a genius, and I'll bet good money that you won't be able to pick him out on my team."

He paused and very deliberately *didn't* look at her. "So you still get a thrill from hacking and you like to gamble. I'm not getting a very good impression of you, you know."

Grateful that he was letting her off the hook so gently, she smiled and settled deeper into the leather seat. "I'm not worried. Just wait 'til you see me in action."

Obviously, Naomi Connor, digital-security diva and all-purpose goddess, had some up-close-and-personal experience with the criminal side of hacking. She spent a little too much energy arguing with him about the subject. Of course, it didn't matter at this point, Joe told himself, keeping his eyes on the road. She was an expert in a field that was the electronic equivalent of vigilante justice in the Wild West. And in the Wild West, some of the best sheriffs had spent time on the other side of the law. The ability to think like a criminal was part of what made both old-time sheriffs and modern-day sneakers—"legal" hackers—good at their jobs.

He narrowed his eyes as the Connecticut countryside flashed past him in all its summer decadence. All he needed to know about Naomi was that she could get the job done the way he needed it done, which was fast and meticulously. Her methods and where and how she learned them were *not* any of his business.

But the thought of her having a criminal past was bugging the shit out of him.

Realizing he was clenching his teeth and gripping the wheel a bit too hard, Joe forced himself to relax. As Naomi had pointed out, there was a difference between hacking and cracking. She was on the bright side of the law now, wherever she might have been before. Her background had obviously served her well. Sarah had called her tough and smart. By turns she was also soft and feminine, cynical and edgy, and, what intrigued him the most, defensive and guilty. She had a smile that could bring a nation to its knees, and spoke in an accent so soft and slow it inspired some pretty entertaining thoughts involving the fluid dynamics of warm honey on soft skin.

Damn it.

He frowned at the road and reminded himself that what really mattered was the security audit, not the auditor. This was not only an expensive project for the company; it was a critically important one and it was in its final phase. Naomi and her team were coming in to conduct a detailed review of the company's everyday security practices and launch a full-scale attack-and-penetrate test against the networks, and do it all without anyone other than people with Brennan blood in them knowing about it. That was it. And as soon as she was finished, he would go back to D.C., back to being a lawyer, back to his own way of life.

It's a critical project, he repeated silently, as if to convince his baser nature. *Too serious to let any—*

He glanced at her, taking in the soft tousle of blond hair, her big blue eyes, painted fingernails, and that magnificent chest, and completely forgot what he'd been thinking about.

Damn it.

Suppressing the urge to shake his head, he turned his eyes back to the road and slowly made the left into his mother's driveway.

CHAPTER
3

"You aren't afraid of dogs, are you?" Joe asked as the truck was surrounded by a swarm of golden retrievers that had come thundering around the side of the house, with tongues lolling and tails beating the air as well as anything else in their way. There had to be a dozen of them.

Naomi looked at him skeptically. "Not usually, but then I've never been in the middle of a pack before." She paused and looked out the window at the dogs, who were beginning to yip with impatience. "They look friendly enough. Are they jumpers?"

"They're goldens," he replied dryly, as if that answered the question. "And they're definitely friendly. Let me get out first. I'll do what I can, but they follow instructions about as well as the average cat does."

After enduring a giddy and tumultuous greeting that included lots of muddy paws and flying saliva, Joe finally shooed the dogs away from the truck and managed to get them to sit before he opened the door.

"Um, Naomi, take this in the spirit it's offered." He paused, the width of his shoulders blocking her exit by default. "You might want to take off your shoes. If we

have to make a run for it, you'll never make it alive
in those."

She met his eyes for a silent moment, punctuating her
look with a slow blink before speaking. "Okay. But first
I have to ask you something. Don't take this question
as a value judgment, Joe, but tell me straight: Is this just
a sort of surreal beginning to this project and things are
going to get better, or are things going to get weirder?"

"Christ. Do you really think they could?"

She fought a smile. "I mean, you really *are* Joe Casey
and there really *are* other people in that house, right?
You're not a slasher or foot fetishist, and I haven't just
taken a time-warp detour into the Twilight Zone?"

He looked at her with genuine amusement and took
a minute before answering, a minute he spent studying
her face from behind those disconcertingly dark glasses.
"Naomi, I'm really Joe Casey and there are other people
in the house. As far as being a slasher goes, I'm not very
good with blades of any description, including the
hockey and roller varieties, and I'm not about to discuss
fetishes of any kind with you, now or ever. However, I
will neither confirm nor deny the whole Twilight Zone
thing, because I'm having a few doubts about that myself." He paused. "Now, have you decided whether it's
your life or your panty hose that you're willing to risk
getting to the house?"

"Well, if that's not the most original question I've been
asked in a long time," she said under her breath as she
slipped off her pale pink leather slingbacks and, holding
one in each hand, reached out to brace herself against a
broad chest that was vibrating with silent laughter.

He wiped his hands on the backside of his jeans before
settling them lightly but securely around her waist. She
slid to the ground in front of him, still protected by the
opened door on one side and him on the other.

Looking up—way up—she saw him watching her with
that same smile. "What?"

"How tall are you?"

"Five-two. Five feet of it is brains, though, so don't try anything funny," she murmured, peering around him to see the still-seated dogs twitching with energy barely held in check. "That line's not gonna hold, Joe. I say we get moving. Which door?"

"The front one. The red one," he replied, shutting the door of the truck.

Naomi kept a wary eye on the beasts as she and Joe started to cross the short stone walkway to the house. Two of them started to get to their feet, and Joe snapped a command in a voice so sharp it made her jump.

"Sorry," he said. "That only works once. We better hustle."

He took her elbow to steady her as she hiked her skirt and doubled her stride, but it didn't work. The dogs couldn't tolerate their confinement any longer and burst toward them in an explosion of fur and feet, and Naomi found herself practically pinned to the doorjamb by five hundred pounds of wet doggy smiles.

The door opened behind her and a calm, disappointed female voice said, "Girls."

The tumult ceased. The dogs sat down with ears pricked forward and tails wagging, as docile as if they'd never misbehaved a day in their lives.

Catching her breath, Naomi turned around to see an attractive silver-haired woman in the doorway. Her heart stopped for a second as she took in the woman's warm smile and the bright blue eyes that matched Joe's. She knew she must be staring at Joe's mother as if she were seeing a ghost. Or a guardian angel.

"I'm Mary Casey. Please come in. I'm so sorry for the dogs. I thought I had them penned up. Sometimes I could swear that they know how to open their gate."

Out of sheer habit, Naomi took the hand that was offered and shook it, but she was still unable to find her voice. She'd read and reread all the legal filings that had to do with her case. She knew it was at Mary Casey's request that her name had been removed from the indictment, that the charges against her had been dropped, that her record had been expunged. If it weren't for Mary Casey, Naomi knew she wouldn't be here today—in more ways than one.

Naomi blinked and forced a smile. Or thought she did. *Why the hell did I volunteer for this?*

Mary's eyes flicked to Joe. "You're losing your touch. This poor woman is in shock. What have you done to her?"

"Mom, don't even ask." He glanced at Naomi and frowned. "Are you okay?"

She swallowed once, cleared her throat, and smiled first at him, then at his mother. "Of course I am. I'm just a little out of breath. It's been an unorthodox welcome so far, but certainly one of the most enthusiastic I've ever encountered on a project. Mrs. Casey, I'm pleased to meet you. I'm Naomi Connor."

She waited for her name to register, for surprise or coldness or fury—some sign of recognition—to appear in Mary Casey's expression, but none did. Her elegant, high-cheekboned face retained its good humor as her amused blue eyes swept over Naomi's thoroughly disheveled self.

"Please call me Mary. And come in. Did you have a purse? The dogs didn't get it, did they?" she asked, opening the door wider and gesturing for Naomi to enter.

Gathering the presence of mind to slip on her shoes first, Naomi stepped into the house, stiffly and a little unsteadily. The foyer's cool air was a welcome respite from the sweltering heat outside, and the cozy, familial warmth of the house would have calmed her if it weren't for the rising fear of imminent discovery that was threatening to choke her.

Recognize me, damn it. I can't do this alone. Acknowledge my name, my crime. Let me apologize.

"Her stuff is in the truck. I'll get it and be right back."

Abandoning her with a casual smile, Joe turned toward the driveway. The dogs instantly rose to their feet in anticipation of another adventure with a human.

A buzz of panic rushed through her as she watched him retreat, the dogs in tow. She was alone with his mother. Surely now—

"Oh, Naomi, look what the dogs have done to your suit. I'm mortified."

At Mary's words, which sounded both sincere and contrite, Naomi looked down at herself and felt something altogether too close to humiliation replace the deeply entrenched dread. Her armor was more than merely chinked. It was destroyed.

You win. I'll die unforgiven. Just please take me now.

The suit she had on was the Perfect Suit. Shell-pink silk. Jones New York. It was her good-luck, meet-and-greet-the-difficult/important-customer suit.

But that was all in the past. At the moment, the Perfect Suit was perfectly filthy. There were dirty, damp swipes from tails and faces all over her skirt. The lower half of her jacket was striped in all directions with what was clearly dog slobber, and two muddy paw prints stood out in high relief dead center on her chest. She swallowed hard, determined not to lose any more of her composure. There wasn't much left to hang on to, but she was going to try.

"It's all right, ma'am. It's my fault, really. I should have just worn jeans and a T-shirt. Then they wouldn't have come near me," she murmured, then looked up at her hostess.

Beyond Mary's shoulder, a tall, dark-eyed, really good-looking man entered the foyer. His smile was like Joe's but easier to look at. It didn't burn her with its intensity as he introduced himself. It just warmed her.

"I'm pleased to meet you, Chas. I'm the formerly tidy Naomi Connor." She extended her hand, then immediately withdrew it before he could touch it, realizing that it was contaminated with substances that were wet, or-

ganic, and canine. "On second thought, you may not
want to touch that." She glanced at Mary, whose hand
she had just shaken. "Ma'am, I'm sorry. My hands—"

Mary started laughing. It was a rich, genuine, soothing
sound that made Naomi feel good rather than stupid,
and made her feel very, very welcome. It was a strange
sensation, given the setting.

"I refuse to allow you to think any of this is your
fault, Naomi. The dogs displayed dreadful manners. To
think that you flew up here on a Saturday to meet with
us, and that you have to fly home in a few hours in that
condition—I'm more than mortified. Is there anything
that I can do for you?"

Joe walked in then and set her suitcase and computer
bag on the floor. "You could delay the meeting and let
her change her clothes."

Naomi swung her head to face him head-on, all of
her manic, shifting emotions bubbling up into one big,
horrified frown aimed straight at him.

She knew her reaction was irrational but she couldn't
help it. Her suitcase was at his feet, in public view. The
fact that she knew she looked like a wreck and should
be glad for its presence didn't change her assessment of
the situation.

He'd just eliminated her options.

She had no choice now; she *had* to change her clothes,
had to remove what remained of her business armor and
spend the meeting looking like Naomi the woman instead of Naomi the professional. That always made it
that much more difficult for her to showcase her brains
and abilities.

But distressing as that was, it wasn't the worst thing.
A second realization weighted her situation with cold,
thick dread. *Any minute now, Mary's going to realize
who I am, and I won't even be able to hold my head high
and* look *like someone who should be taken seriously.*

Joe finally met her gaze and his eyebrows shot up in
surprise. "What? You brought other clothes, right? You

said that you were prepared to stay over in case the
meeting lasted too long."

Naomi swallowed hard and forced a smile both onto
her face and into her voice. "I sure did. And it seems
that was rather prescient, doesn't it?" She glanced at
Mary, who met her eyes with a clear, uncomplicated,
utterly female empathy.

"Joe," Mary said with an easy smile, not taking her
eyes off Naomi's face. "Why don't you take Naomi's
bags up to the yellow guest room? Naomi, you follow
Joe and take your time freshening up after your trip.
We'll be in the library, which is at that end of this hall,
whenever you're ready. Please don't rush on our
account."

Mary turned then and made her way with Chas down
the long Oriental runner that covered the glossy, dark
wood floor of the wide hallway. Clinging to her manners
by a mere fraying thread, Naomi somehow refrained
from glaring outright at Joe, whose expression was torn
between confused and sheepish.

"What did I do wrong?"

He's the client. "Why, nothing at all, Joe," she lied,
keeping her smile in place through sheer force of will.
"Which way to the yellow guest room?"

He motioned for her to go up the stairs. Reluctantly,
she led and he followed, and while she was glad he
couldn't see her face, she would have been happier if
he also couldn't see her behind. It was probably at his
eye level.

She swallowed hard and kept her back rigid and her
face forward. At some point, this torture had to end.

"It's the fourth door on the right."

The instant she stepped into the room, her smile relaxed into a more genuine version of itself. The room
was large, airy, and done all in soft yellows and laven-
ders. A large bed covered with a respectable number of
tasseled throw pillows in coordinating fabrics dominated
the room. Beyond the bed, a small sofa, two chairs, and

the window treatments, also done in similarly coordinating fabrics, helped create an ambience that refused to allow tension to flourish. Or, indeed, exist at all.

Naomi turned as she heard Joe set her bags on the floor just inside the doorway. Before she could say a thing, he folded his muscular arms across that chest, which, despite their short acquaintance, she'd gotten to know a bit too well. It was a nice chest. An inspiring chest. And considering what it was inspiring, she decided it would be more prudent to look into his eyes.

"Okay, I know I did something wrong down there and I apologize for it. But could you just tell me what it was? Was I not supposed to bring in the suitcase?" His look was a really endearing combination of defiance and bewilderment that made her want to groan out loud— then shake him. "You told me you took one along for every project meeting. You never said it was a state secret, and I didn't think it would do you much good sitting out in the truck."

She forced another smile, knowing it probably looked painful. "You're absolutely right, Joe. I did tell you that. I've overreacted and I'm sorry. It's just that I prefer to conduct business appropriately dressed for it, and the other clothes I brought aren't business clothes."

"We're all casual, Naomi. It's Saturday. Even on weekdays, we're business casual at the office up here unless some navy brass is visiting." He shrugged. "Besides, for what it's worth, you don't seem like the type of woman who would prefer to sit around covered in paw prints when there's another option available."

She felt a cold ball of concrete lodge in her stomach. Paw prints. It was a reference to her chest, and not a subtle one, either. Her cover was completely blown. He was seeing her as a woman first and a professional second—if at all.

Knowing she might never regain the ground she'd already lost, she upped the wattage of that painful smile and tried to hang on to whatever credibility she had left.

"You're right, of course, and thanks for the reassurance. I won't feel so awkward about changing my outfit now," she replied, lying to him for the second time in less than a minute. "And thank you for carrying my bag for me." She gave a small shrug. "I'll be down directly."

As the door clicked shut behind him, Naomi sank down on the bed. "I asked for this. I can do it. I will do it," she murmured to herself, then looked down at her skirt. *I just won't do it in this outfit.*

Focus on the project. That's the most important thing. She stood up, crossed the room, and retrieved her small suitcase. "Get in and get out. Do it fast, do it perfect," she said in a stronger voice. "Resolution equals absolution."

She took a deep breath and let it out slowly as she glanced down again at the ruins of her suit. There really was no choice in the matter. She had to wear her "oops" outfit.

Snapping open the suitcase, she lifted out the slim khaki skirt and loose pink shirt with an embroidered neckline. The outfit was nice. Tasteful. That wasn't the problem. The problem was that it was also *cute.* And the kitten-heel sandals that went with it didn't exactly redeem the outfit. She needed something functional; this outfit stopped short at fun.

Of course, he was a guy. Maybe he wouldn't notice.

Rationality regained its foothold in her brain. *He's a guy, and I'm a 36 DD. He's already noticed.*

Naomi shook out the outfit and began to undress. There was no way around it. Her figure wouldn't be concealed the way it was in a well-tailored business suit. She just had to accept the inevitability of walking into a business meeting with her behind defined and some cleavage showing. Not much, of course. She never showed very much. It was too distracting. Men couldn't take their eyes off it, and women judged her by it.

She let out a heavy breath and closed her eyes. "Shoulders back, chin up, honey. This is war."

As she folded the ruined suit and placed it back in her suitcase, Mary Casey's gracious words drifted through her head.

I refuse to allow you to think any of this is your fault.

Seconds later, the insight hit Naomi like a well-served tennis ball to the forehead, making her stand up straight and shake her head to clear it.

Of course this rough start was her own fault. *It's a test.*

The reality of the situation began crowding into her head almost faster than she could process it, and she sank to the bed without even realizing it. Sarah had warned her that Joe was a tough guy to work for, a hard-nosed businessman with high standards and a low tolerance for failure. And Joe himself had indicated that much in the truck when he was talking about hackers.

Good Lord, the meeting hasn't even started yet and he's already forced my hand.

The awkwardness at the airport and the business with the dogs were just parts of a staged power play, and she'd lost. She'd displayed weakness first, right there in the airport when she'd explained about the suitcase. The son of a gun hadn't wasted any time using that weakness against her.

Though not liking one bit that she was the unwitting target of such gamesmanship, she was impressed. After all, what better way could he have devised to see how well she responded under pressure, how flexible she was with regard to changing course, and how fast she could devise new tactics than to throw her totally off balance by using the ammunition *she* had supplied?

How could I have missed it? It was a classic sink-or-swim scenario, and she nearly blew it by thinking it was all about clothes.

Clothes. She rolled her eyes at the thought.

It had nothing to do with clothes; it had *everything* to do with brains.

With a growing smile, she stood up and slipped her feet into the flirty little sandals. "You want to see how well I can run with the big dogs, Joe Casey? Well, honey, I have a surprise for you. Grace is my middle name. You just sit back and watch how lil' ol' Naomi Grace operates under pressure."

CHAPTER
4

Insult the Brains-in-a-Box. Absolutely fucking brilliant way to start the most important project of my career.

Joe turned right at the bottom of the stairs rather than left, and headed for the kitchen. His mother had given the household staff the day off because of the meeting, so he was assured of at least thirty seconds of peace. Not real peace, of course, just some peace and quiet. Real peace, the inner kind that yoga-mongers were always moaning about, would elude him for exactly however long it took him to unravel the mystery named Naomi.

He grabbed a glass out of the cabinet above the sink and filled it with cold water. Sarah had vouched for Naomi's brains and background, and the level of her security clearances pretty much eliminated the possibility of a criminal history. But there was something there, well hidden. And Joe knew that, despite his best intentions, his interest in it wasn't going to disappear until he'd discovered what *it* was. Sarah might have been fooled, but he had prosecuted enough hackers in his years with the NCIS to know better.

It was well established that most hackers viewed their activity as harmless, as an intellectual exercise, or even as a hobby. Rarely did they think what they did was wrong. He lifted the glass of water to his mouth and downed it in one long swallow.

Naomi had completely given herself away on that score when she equated hacking to jaywalking. She hadn't equated hacking to criminal trespass, or breaking and entering, or felony theft.

She'd equated it to *jaywalking*. A misdemeanor. A forty-dollar traffic ticket. *Fucking hell.*

He put the glass in the dishwasher and headed back toward the library.

Jaywalking. As if hacking were a harmless pastime, or some petty offense that could be overlooked as long as no one got hurt.

What utter bullshit. She'd obviously never seen the other side of hacking; the damage that could be done by a so-called hobbyist. *She* hadn't walked into the house one day twenty years ago and seen the look on his mother's and grandparents' faces after they'd learned about the secrets that had been stolen. *She* hadn't sat opposite them through a grim and silent dinner after they'd learned that the plans for a state-of-the-art, stealth submarine hull had been lifted from their most secure network thanks to a fucking "recreational" hacker—a kid—and sold on the open market, setting the Pentagon's program back several years and making Brennan's stock price plunge, not to mention rewarding America's enemies with a four hundred million-dollar gift that was four years in the making.

He stopped outside the library doors and took a deep breath, reminding himself again that none of that mattered in terms of this project. All he needed Naomi to be was ethical *now*. Clever *now*. The past was the past and he had more important things on his mind at the moment, like the future security of Brennan Shipping Industries—and getting his own ass back to his real job in Washington D.C.

He wasn't two steps into the room before Chas and his mother turned looks on him that were exasperated and disappointed, respectively.

"What?" he demanded without any real heat in his voice.

"Did you apologize?" Chas asked.

Oh, for Christ's sake. Not this lecture again. "Yes. Three times. Not that I knew what I was apologizing for." Joe looked at his mother, who was shaking her head and fighting a smile at the same time. "Don't give me that look, Mom. Just tell me what I did. It was the suitcase, wasn't it? I wasn't supposed to mention it."

"Joe, I asked you to put the dogs in the pen before you left."

"I did. I think Zelda can open the latch."

"Wonderful. Meanwhile, that poor girl's suit is ruined. Thank heaven she thinks ahead. And, since you asked, no, you weren't supposed to mention the suitcase. For women in her position, it's plan B, Joe. It's something you don't draw attention to or even admit to having, but it's there if you need it." Her voice was mild, but her eyebrows were raised in a pointed admonishment. "I do it all the time."

"I don't see what the big deal is. If I have to stay over, I stay over. That's what credit cards are for," he muttered, settling himself in a chair that faced the door.

"She'll get over it," Chas said to both of them, pouring himself a cup of coffee from the silver service on the low table in front of the couch. "So, what's your impression so far?"

"Smart. Very smart. No fear. She thinks outside the box." Joe shrugged. "You already saw her résumé and you know what Sarah thinks. Besides, she's been doing this a long time. A lot longer than that résumé of hers indicates, if I'm any judge."

The brothers' eyes met, and the former prosecutor in Joe knew the ex-cop in Chas was extracting every piece

of information from that provocative comment that Joe
wanted him to extract. Then Chas, cop face in place,
settled back into the sofa and took a sip of his coffee.

"And?" his mother asked, pouring a cup. She added
some milk, then handed it to Joe. After that she poured
one for herself and relaxed into her chair.

"I know it's premature, but I'd be willing to bet that
if she can't get in, no one else will be able to, either."

"You mean her team," his mother said after a moment, concentrating on stirring her coffee. "If her team
can't get in, no one else will be able to."

Joe met Chas's eyes again. It was too early to tell
anyone of his suspicions. Anyone but Chas, anyway. The
two of them thought the same way, reacted the same
way. Felt the same way about hackers—

In the space it took to blink, Joe decided to play this
hand close to his chest. He'd analyze the decision
later. Maybe.

"Yes, that's what I meant. If her team gets in," he
agreed, and took a sip of his coffee.

"And if her team does get in?" she asked.

"Then we hire her away from them regardless of the
fight Sarah puts up, and we make her chief technology
officer so I can go back to D.C. and do what I do best,"
he said flatly, and watched his brother and mother exchange a look.

No one had a chance to add or argue anything before
they heard the telltale squeak from the bottom stair.
They all turned toward the sound.

"We're in here, Naomi," his mother called as she
stood and walked to the doorway.

A moment later, computer bag in hand, Naomi entered the room and Joe's already good impression of her
rose a little higher. Mad money, plan B—whatever she
wanted to call it, it worked. The borderline frazzled
woman in the paw-printed, dog-slobbered suit had disappeared. In her place was the easygoing woman he'd met

in the airport, but dressed now in a shirt and a skirt that stopped just above her knees.

She was right about the outfit not being businesslike, but it wasn't sexy, if that's what put her undies in a bundle. It was definitely feminine, though, and it sure as hell left less to the imagination than that schoolmarm suit had.

He blinked and immediately brought his gaze to Naomi's face, which was smiling and aimed at Chas at the moment. Chas, who was doing a hell of a job of not looking at anything he shouldn't be looking at and making it seem not only effortless, but completely natural. Joe knew damned well it had nothing to do with his brother being disciplined, businesslike, or having a cute, sexy, and once-again pregnant wife at home, either. It had everything to do with keeping Naomi's attention on himself and not on Joe until Joe could pull himself together. Which he did. Fast.

Putting on his bland courtroom face, he stood up in one fluid motion, as had Chas, and casually remained standing until Naomi and his mother had seated themselves.

"Well, if you'll allow me to say it, Naomi, you look a lot more comfortable now. Would you like any coffee? I'm sure you must have had a very early start this morning, for which, by the way, I want to thank you," his mother said easily, pouring a cup of coffee and handing it to her. "It was terribly overbearing and unfair of us to ask you to come up here on a Saturday, so let me apologize for that."

"Please don't apologize, ma'am. I'm well used to it. This isn't a nine-to-five line of work," Naomi replied with a smile as she accepted the china cup and saucer.

"Well, before you start thinking we're paranoid or worse, I have to explain that we've fallen victim to that old 'once bitten, twice shy' mentality, I'm afraid. Except that we've been bitten quite badly, and more than once.

We're feeling our way a bit delicately along this path, not being quite sure who we can or should trust—even inside the company. That's why Joe has insisted on such extreme security measures surrounding the audit. It's even why we decided to move the meeting here instead of having it at a public place. Electronic eavesdropping and whatnot."

"He was explaining some of that to me on the drive from the airport. And I have to applaud your decision, Mrs. Casey. Snooping is a lot easier to do and a lot more frequently done than most people care to think about," she said, and something in her voice made Joe turn to look at her.

He was wrong. She wasn't the same woman he met at the airport. She looked the same, but she was actually wound much tighter than she had been in the car. He eased back in his chair and lifted his coffee to his lips, but instead of listening to her, he just watched her.

On the drive over, she'd been fairly relaxed, except when the subject turned to hackers. She had developed a tense edginess then but had remained physically poised. But sitting here, getting the preliminary small talk out of the way, she was fidgeting—playing with the handle of the coffee cup, fiddling with her watch, twisting the pearl ring she wore on her left hand—and probably didn't even realize it.

Joe knew his mother and brother were as aware as he was that she was as nervous as the clichéd cat on a hot tin roof. Accordingly, they were making a discreet but concerted effort to put her at ease. This wasn't a social occasion, though, and Joe had a feeling she wouldn't relax until the subject turned to her area of expertise and the reason she was here.

"—I wouldn't say that security is any tighter in Washington D.C. now than it is anywhere else, Chas. Security measures in parts of New York City are probably more intense than they are in most of Washington," she was saying in response to a question.

"But the security methods being implemented are becoming more refined everywhere, don't you think?" Joe asked, inserting himself into the conversation as smoothly as he could. He knew from the looks Chas and his mother flashed him that they had surrendered the floor.

Naomi met his eyes and gave a tight shrug. "Well, sure. There are a lot more security cameras in use, both hidden and overt, all over the place. Digital fingerprinting is standard in international airports in the U.S. now, and many corporations are employing that and other biometric methods of authenticating identities for even routine, nonsecure functions. If I remember correctly, part of what you want us to do is come up with a set of recommendations for the best methods to use in your company."

"Just at the headquarters. The rest of the offices will be upgraded on a schedule that I'd like your team to devise."

"Well, I understand the cost factors, Joe, but—hold on, let me just boot up here and find a spreadsheet—" She reached for her computer bag and slid out a sleek silver laptop, which she flipped open and turned on without so much as a break in her conversation. "As I was saying, if security is your real goal, as you've said it is, then you have to consider implementing your changes on a fast-track schedule and let cost be secondary to the speed of deployment—"

Joe kept a mildly cynical expression on his face as he watched her. She'd stopped fidgeting and was back to form, relaxed and easy, with a cool fire burning in her eyes. Within minutes, she was making notes on the computer she'd balanced, appropriately enough, on her lap, having politely waved off the offer to use his mother's desk near the windows.

Finally, several hours later, she lowered the top of the computer and set the unit on the table. Joe was more than a little impressed. He'd never seen anyone type so

fast, much less type at all while being an active participant in a four-way conversation.

"If you don't mind, I need to plug that in for a while
and let it recharge, and let my fingers relax," she said
with a smile, flexing her hands in a way that Joe found
mildly distracting.

"Good heavens, look at the time," his mother said,
getting to her feet. "It's after twelve. You must be starving, Naomi. I've given the housekeeper the day off,
again in the name of security, so we're on our own as
far as lunch is concerned. Why don't we adjourn for a
while and I'll go fix lunch?"

"I'm happy to help. What would you like me to do,
ma'am?" Naomi asked, standing up even faster than
Chas, who was always first on his feet.

His mother smiled at her, which made Joe frown. The
smile was her friendly smile, the genuine one, not the
restrained, polite one she usually displayed during business meetings.

"Absolutely nothing, but thank you for asking. I'll
only be a minute. I asked Anna to leave us some chicken
salad and things, so really, all I have to do is set it out.
You stay here and relax. Actually, why don't we eat on
the terrace? It's a beautiful day and here we are inside."

"Mom, it's ninety degrees outside," Joe pointed out.
And humid enough to make stone sweat.

"Good point. Why don't you go out there and make
sure the umbrella over the table is open?" She left the
room still wearing that smile. Chas, biting the inside of
his lip, picked up the coffee service and excused himself
to help her in the kitchen. Which left Joe standing there
watching Naomi, who was giving him a look that was
back to being slightly wary but mostly expectant. He
preferred her relaxed.

God damn it. "That was a great presentation."

"Thank you."

He wanted to roll his eyes. "Would you like to come

outside while I check on that umbrella?" he asked, moving toward the French doors leading from the library out to one end of the terrace that ran along the entire back of the house.

"That would be nice."

He tried to keep his gaze trained on the back of her head as she preceded him to the terrace, but they wandered of their own volition. She was so well curved and . . . compact.

She walked to the railing and took a long, slow, panoramic look at the back lawn, which sloped down, then up to shallow woods on three sides. It took only a minute to secure the umbrella, then he joined her at the railing, stopping a few feet away. Getting closer wouldn't be smart. The air surrounding them was hot and steamy, and lush with the mingled perfume of the flower beds.

It might have been smarter to meet in a hotel conference room that smelled of furniture polish and stale coffee. At least she'd still be in that suit and he wouldn't be noticing the sun casting shapely shadows on the flagstone. After all, she was just a business associate.

"This is a lovely house. Did y'all grow up here?" she asked.

"Mostly. We moved here when I was about four."

"What a great place for little kids. There's so much room to run around."

"It was pretty good," he admitted with a smile. "Where did you grow up? And don't say the South. I've got that much figured out."

She turned her face to smile at him for a moment, then turned away and tilted her face toward the sun, fluttering her eyes shut against the brightness. "It is some sort of beautiful day, isn't it? My daddy was in the air force, well, still is, actually, but he had a bad track record of getting stationed in places my mother didn't want to go to. So she and I mostly stayed in the town where she grew up. We lived with my grandparents."

"Where was that?"

"Starlit, Alabama." She said it with a straight face, her eyes still shut.

"Starlit?"

She nodded, face still aimed toward the sun. "I never have been able to decide if it's a silly name or a sweet one. It doesn't matter, I suppose. There aren't too many people who have ever heard of it." She shrugged. "I don't think it's on any maps, maybe not even the map of Baldwin County."

"Your accent just got stronger."

She laughed and opened her eyes. Shading them with her hand, she tilted her head to look at him again, and as he met her clear blue gaze and hovering smile, he watched the tightly wound professional from the library soften slightly to become a beautiful, sexy woman lit by the sun. Joe folded his arms across his chest in defense against—anything. Everything. *Her.*

"That happens sometimes. Must be nostalgia. Could be senility, too. Anyway, we moved away from there when Daddy was assigned to the Pentagon. Washington was one place my mother *wanted* to live."

"How old were you when you moved there?"

She hesitated, and her voice faltered a little. "Almost thirteen. I've lived in the District ever since, except when I was at college."

"Where do you live now?"

"Foggy Bottom. Do you know it?"

He nodded. "I live in Georgetown. Are your parents still there?"

"No. They're back in Alabama. Daddy's been at Marshall Space Center in Huntsville for the past few years."

"Doing what?"

"Running part of it." She turned around and leaned her back against the railing. "Sarah said you've been the acting CTO for over a year. Why haven't you moved up here?"

Interesting question. He shrugged one shoulder. "It's not permanent. I'm just helping out."

"For how long?"

"Until you hack us or prove that you can't."

Naomi assessed him with a cool blue gaze that held more than just a challenge; it held determination. "I know what happens if we can't hack you. You thank us kindly, wipe the sweat from your brow, and pay the bill. But what if I *do* hack you? What then, Joe?" she asked.

What if I hack you? He smiled. It wasn't exactly the question that a good team leader would ask—but it was exactly the question he'd expect from a veteran hacker. They were lone wolves and rarely played well with others.

"I mean, do you stay here and keep on trying to fortify your defenses?" she continued. "Or do you move back to D.C. and let someone else take over?"

I double your salary, triple your vacation time, give you access to the company jet, and move you up here to babysit. Then *I head back to D.C.*

He watched her eyes for a minute. The spark of challenge in them didn't fade or flicker under his blatant scrutiny; it became more intense. As did his awareness of her.

The heady, sweet scent of the flower beds below the railing stole around him, and combined with the sight of her to form an image in his mind that was a little too pleasurable and a little too potent and had absolutely nothing to do with the subject at hand.

"I'll figure that out if I have to." He looked across the lawn to the woods, where his eyes wouldn't see anything that made him think of undressing a brilliant Alabaman from a town called Starlit.

CHAPTER
5

Naomi kept watching Joe even after he turned away. He stood there silently, blinking in the sun as he gazed toward the woods. The change in him was abrupt, and she wondered if he were suddenly bored with their small talk. She couldn't have said anything to offend him: They'd been talking about her.

She decided to put it down to his personality. He seemed a little moody, and he definitely wasn't the chattiest guy in the world, or the easiest to talk to. He wasn't like his brother, that was for sure. Chas was the type who could get anyone to talk to him.

Still, Joe was the one standing in front of her, he was the one she had to establish a good working relationship with, he was the one she had to impress, and he was the one who had just blown her off. *Challenging* seemed to be the best word to describe the situation.

She turned her face into the light breeze to counteract the sting. "Is there a farm nearby?"

"I'm sorry?"

She sent him a lazy smile intended to charm and disarm. "Pardon my saying so, but either your mother's just had these roses attended to or there's a stable somewhere close."

Amusement tugging at the corners of that too-pretty mouth, he tipped his head toward the far end of the house. "The stables are on the other side of the garage."

"Do you ride?"

He nodded. "Since I was about six. Do you?"

"No, I don't." *There's no foundation garment strong enough to control that sort of motion, Cowboy Joe.* She cleared her throat. "What other kinds of things did y'all do, growing up in a place like this?" She paused. "Hockey's big up here, isn't it?"

He let out a silent laugh and, once again, looked away casually. "That's an understatement. Parents take their six-year-olds to the rinks for practice at four or five in the morning, just to get ice time."

"And y'all think Southerners are crazy," she said lightly. She didn't like this silent Joe; she wanted him to turn back into the more or less pleasant man he'd been this morning instead of remaining this guy who was barely able to hold up his end of the conversation. With a smile, she aimed her gaze at the side of his head, willing him to turn back to her. "Did you play hockey?"

"Nope. Like I said before, I'm not great with blades." *Look at me.* "Football?"

He shook his head again, keeping his eyes trained on the stretch of trees at the edge of the lawn. "Golf, swimming, and water polo."

Jackpot. She widened her eyes and tilted her head just a little, in preparation. "That's not really a sport, is it?"

His eyes were wide and wary as they met her own. "I'm sorry?"

"I thought water polo was sort of like snipe hunting, or fishing for bottle-bass," she said with a shrug. "You know, something people pretend is a real sport but it isn't."

His cold, assessing stare lasted for a full minute. "Of course it's a real sport. I thought you went to Stanford."

"I did. Undergrad and master's."

A short pause ensued, during which he squinted at her as if trying to ascertain her IQ by looks alone. Out of sheer devilment, she ran a hand through her hair, fluffing it, drawing attention to its blondness.

"And you weren't aware that water polo *is a sport*?" The way he said it, it was almost a snort.

Imagine that. The Ice Man has a hot core. She lifted an eyebrow. "I don't understand your point, Joe."

He blinked. "My point is that for a few decades now, Stanford's men *and women* water polo players have been on U.S. teams that have won medals in the Olympics. How could you have gone to school there for five or six years and not known that?"

"I was there for five," she replied with another shrug and a straight face. "And it was easy. For one thing, when I was there, I was a geek. If it wasn't digital, it didn't matter. For another, I grew up in Alabama, and that means I grew up on football. So if it didn't require pads, a helmet, and cheerleaders, it wasn't a sport. That's how." She paused. "So, it's a team sport?"

He was about to reply when Mary and Chas came through a set of doors farther down the terrace, bearing trays that held place settings and food, respectively. Naomi left his side to meet them halfway, but her mind was back at the railing, pondering a big, blue-eyed blond bear.

Joe Casey, you are some kind of adorable.

Joe walked back to the table after setting the umbrella in its stand in the corner. It was four thirty and the sun had shifted to the far side of the house, leaving the terrace shaded and almost comfortable. Their meeting had continued through lunch and beyond, and they remained outside for all of it.

Though the setting was casual and relaxed, the conversation had been detailed and intense, and more than once, Naomi had flat-out challenged him. Protocols, timing, schedules—the subject hadn't made a difference. If she held an opinion different than theirs, they'd heard about it. While she was pleasant and professional about it, she was persistent. She'd gotten her way most of the time, too.

"So what time is your flight?" Chas asked as Joe resumed his seat across from Naomi.

"It departs in ten minutes," she replied easily and took another sip of her iced tea. "The next one leaves at seven thirty. I'm sure I can get on it."

"There's not another one until seven thirty?" Mary repeated. "That doesn't seem right."

"It's a weekend, don't forget. And there actually are other flights, but one goes through Minneapolis and the other goes through Detroit—"

*Dee*troit, Joe noted with a smothered grin.

"—and taking either one would be just plain stupid when the nonstop is less than an hour's flying time. I'd rather just leave at seven thirty and go straight home."

Joe could tell by the look on Chas's face what was coming next, and he braced himself for round three of Entertaining Naomi. Being around her wasn't exactly a hardship, but he couldn't call it relaxing, either. Frankly, he could use some downtime that included a solitary beer and a cold shower.

"Joe will have to do the honors and drop you back to White Plains. I'd stick around to continue the conversation, but I have to drive Mom down to LaGuardia. We're pushing it as it is."

"Please don't delay anything on account of me," Naomi said quickly. "I can catch a cab to the airport, and we can tie up any loose ends over the phone or—"

"Getting you to the airport isn't a problem, and I'm going to be down in D.C. at the end of the week. We can finalize things then," Joe interrupted. "You two had better get going. The Mets had a home game this afternoon and traffic could be a nightmare."

Chas looked at his mother. "Mom, are you ready?"

"Yes." Mary stood up, and the three of them followed suit. She extended a hand to Naomi. "I enjoyed meeting you, Naomi, and I'm glad you're handling the project. I have complete confidence that you'll give it your all. I'll see you when I'm back up here in a few weeks. In the meantime, if there's anything you need or if there's anything I can do for you or your team, please let me know. I have an open-door policy."

"Thank you, ma'am. It's been a privilege to meet you. Have a safe trip."

Naomi's voice had gone soft and almost husky, and looking at her was the last thing Joe was going to do. Those eyes and that smile had wreaked enough collateral damage on his brain before lunch. Her getting all misty-eyed over his mother—not that most people didn't; everyone loved her—would be more than he could handle.

He leaned forward on cue to receive his mother's kiss, and a moment later he and Naomi were alone on the terrace again. The house suddenly seemed too big and too empty and too quiet, and he looked across the table at her. She was concentrating a bit too hard on arranging her laptop in its case.

Okay, so I'm not imagining it. Something is going on here.

He paused for a moment, letting the immediate, instinctive, and pleasurable reaction in his brain settle down. Then he took a deep breath and reminded himself that not only would getting too comfortable with her distract him from the task at hand, but it would mean that Chas was right about Joe's ability to maintain a clear head around her. And there was no way in hell he was going to prove Chas right on that count. "Would you like to see the office?"

She looked up at him. "Yes, I would. If it's no trouble."

"Not at all. It's only about fifteen minutes away. We've taken over some space on one of the lower floors and have everything set up there. For your team, I mean."

"That would be great, Joe. I wouldn't mind getting an idea of what we're walking into."

"Okay. Are you ready to go?"

"Just give me a minute to freshen up."

They walked back into the house, and she went up to the guest room while he checked to make sure the doors were locked. She was just coming down the stairs as he walked into the foyer.

Over the course of his lifetime, he'd known a lot of women who disappeared to freshen up. So far, Naomi was the only woman who'd reach her stated goal. Instead of being merely re-lipsticked, she actually looked fresh and kind of glowing. Her hair caught the late-afternoon sun coming through the half-moon window above the front door. Her lips glistened softly, without the high-gloss mirror finish that some women preferred, and her eyes held a bright shine that wasn't quite a sparkle. She just looked . . . fresh. Decorative. *Not* like his idea of a digital-security expert.

It was definitely a good news–bad news scenario.

"Are the dogs out there? 'Cause I'm plumb out of clean outfits," she said with a smile.

He took the suitcase from her. "Still in the kennel."

He held open the front door and set the alarm after she crossed the threshold.

"Okay," he said as they walked down the stone path. "You have to make a decision."

She looked at him with a half smile. "About what?"

"You have to pick one."

"Pick one what?" The question died on her lips as they turned at the corner of the house and headed toward the parking area. The big blue truck she'd arrived in was gone.

"A car that you can get into and out of," he replied, walking to the garage and punching in a security code on the small keypad between the doors.

She put one hand on her hip and tried unsuccessfully to hold back a grin.

"Is this some sort of revenge?" she asked with the first flash of humor he'd seen in a while, and Joe knew—all of his own rules and Chas's warnings be damned—without any doubt that *not* flirting with her was going to be the biggest challenge he'd face for the duration of the project.

"No. I'm trying to be considerate. The truck was obviously the wrong vehicle, so you get to pick a better one. These are the options," he replied as the three double garage doors completed their upward journey.

She gave him a look that mingled amusement and exasperation, then swept her gaze over the cars. Not the Jeep, not the Yukon—thank God. It was always full of fur and stank of dog. Not the Mercedes-Benz two-door.

He knew before she pointed at it that his Aston Martin had beaten out the big Beemer and his grandfather's vintage Jag.

"That one." She looked at him. "It's all right, isn't it?"

"It's fine," he said. "You're sure it won't be too low?"

"Low?"

"For climbing in and out of."

"Oh, that. I'm built kind of low to the ground, too, so it should be fine," she said. "But are *you* going to fit inside?"

He laughed. "I'll fit." He walked over to the small box on the wall and removed the set of keys.

"So which one of these is yours?" she asked, as he unlocked the door and opened it for her.

"This one and the Jeep."

"Interesting combination."

He waited until he'd slid behind the wheel, then he glanced at her as he brought the engine to life. "Not really. Just work and play. I believe in keeping them separate, but only to a point."

"Which one is this?"

"Play."

"In between work?" she asked lightly.

"Exactly. There's no point to working hard unless you occasionally get some instant gratification as a reward. Like coming out of the office after a long day and getting into a nice car for the drive home," he said with a grin as he slipped the car into reverse.

"I suppose you're right." She smiled, then glanced out the window and didn't say anything as they backed slowly out of the garage and moved down the long driveway.

"Do you like to drive fast?" she asked as they reached the Merritt Parkway and he eased into traffic.

"I like to, but I don't do it very often. Chas was the one who always had the Get Out of Jail Free card. I have to be more careful."

"What do you mean?

"Chas was a cop in Stamford for about fifteen years. He just retired two years ago."

She went quiet again for a few minutes, then turned to look at him with that hint of rebellion back in her eyes. "I know this is none of my business and may seem like a rude question, but I'm going to ask it, anyway. How did he go from being a police officer to being CEO in two years? I mean, he's obviously a smart guy and all, but y'all have some unique career paths in this family, nepotism notwithstanding."

He didn't let his surprise show. Or his desire to laugh. "You don't pull your punches, do you?"

She smiled. "I apologized in advance. You don't have to answer it."

"You asked, I'll answer. Our career paths do have a lot to do with nepotism," he admitted. "But not everything to do with it. Chas has an MBA. My sister, Julie, and I went to law school. She has an LLM in securities and finance, and I have one in maritime law and a master's in computer science. As you pointed out earlier, though"—he kept his eyes on the road on purpose— "degrees don't mean much on their own. All of us have grown up in the company. During high school and college, each of us spent every summer working at the company or in the industry. On the loading dock, as stevedores on the waterfront docks, as interns in the marketing, finance, IT, legal, and a bunch of other departments. All unpaid, by the way. And since our twelfth birthdays, we've had to attend every stockholder meeting and read every quarterly and annual report. Our grandfather would quiz us on them." Now he glanced at her. She looked slightly uncomfortable, as though she'd been put in her place. *Good.* But she also looked more than a little impressed, which was also good. "So we're not exactly new to the business. We heard about it every day of our lives, and the assumption that we would be running it someday was always there."

"That's some collective résumé. Is your sister involved in the company, too?"

"Not officially. I think she will be once her kids are a bit older."

"What's her background?"

"She was a prosecutor for the Securities and Exchange Commission until she started having kids."

She was quiet for a minute. "A cop and two prosecutors. You're a real law-and-order family, aren't you?" she murmured, looking out the window again.

"Our father was a cop."

"What does he do at the company? You mentioned at some point this afternoon that your mother recently stepped down as CEO but has remained chairman of the board."

"My father's dead." Even after more than three decades, the words still never felt right.

She swung her head to face him, her eyes wide with embarrassed surprise. "Oh, man. Joe, I'm sorry. I—"

Oh, hell. "Relax. It was a long time ago. He died

when I was four. But, yes, we're a real law-and-order family," he replied with a smile he hoped would reassure her that he wasn't offended. He angled the car into a parking space in front of the Brennan building. "Here we are."

CHAPTER
6

Downtown Stamford's business district was quiet and almost desolate, as befitted it on a hot summer late afternoon. The street where he parked was dominated by steel and glass superstructures. A building in the middle of the block was the sole anachronism.

Its cornerstone proudly bearing the legend 1902, the Brennan building had that staid, steady, and somewhat formidable look of a turn-of-the-last-century bank. Its pale gray limestone facade sported an ornate laurel-wreath lintel over tall, heavy brass and glass doors, one of which Joe held open for her. The lobby was inviting and comfortable in the way a private courtyard in a Italian villa might be. The atmosphere breathed calm, restrained luxury.

It wasn't particularly large and its mural-covered ceiling hung a mere two stories overhead, but a three-tiered fountain stood in the center of its gleaming marble floor. The fountain—a wild-eyed Neptune and several demurely smiling mermaids with long and modestly arranged hair—was ringed by low stone benches and brightly colored plantings punctuated by the occasional soaring palm. At first glance, the inlaid, multicolored points of marble appeared to be a sunburst, but after a second look, Naomi realized the floor's design was a compass rose. True North led to the elevator bank.

Joe led her to the tall marble semicircle that served as the reception and security desk.

"Hi, Howard. How are you doing?" Joe asked with a smile, which was returned by the granite-jawed guard sporting a white crewcut and coolly assessing eyes.

"Just fine, Mr. Casey. What are you doing here today? I figured you'd be out on your boat," the security guard replied, handing Joe a pen to sign the visitor's log.

"Not today, unfortunately. I've been working." After signing in, Joe handed the pen to Naomi. "Howard, this is Naomi Connor, a consultant we've hired. She's going to be around for the next few weeks. You should have a contractor's badge back there for her."

"Hello, ma'am. I sure do. I saw it just a little while ago."

"Hello, Howard. I'm pleased to meet you."

"The pleasure is mine, ma'am." He looked down at something behind the tall front of the desk, and Naomi could hear the quiet clicks of laminated badges being flipped against each other. "Here we are. I just need to see an ID and then we'll get you set up. Would you like a clip or lanyard?"

"A clip, thank you," she replied, handing him her driver's license.

A moment later, properly tagged, Joe and Naomi stepped into the elevator, old and elegant with ornate brass doors.

The doors remained open for several seconds longer than they should have, and eventually Naomi found herself looking for the CLOSE DOORS button. But other than a small emergency button, a small slit for swiping a smart card, and a small flat-screen panel, the walls of the car were smooth; just acres of rich, dark wood with subtle brass accents. Rather than ask the obvious questions, she lifted an eyebrow and met Joe's eyes.

He lifted one of his own. "What do you think so far?"

She just knew it was another test. *Well, honey, this time, I'm ready.*

"Your lobby is beautiful," she said politely.

He grinned. "You know that's not what I meant."

She smiled. "Physical security isn't my area of expertise, Joe, but at first glance, I'd have to say the lobby isn't very secure. Despite those pretty planters out front, the main entrance provides virtually unobstructed access from the street, and there's just one guard on duty. And while I can't see any, I'm assuming you have cameras trained on the door, the guard desk, and the elevator doors." She paused. "I have to say, though, that given the last-century elegance of the lobby, I wasn't expecting biometric elevators. And I'm impressed that the guard didn't let you vouch for me."

"The lobby is plenty secure," he said with an amused glint in his eyes. "Those pretty planters in front of the building have solid steel cores. They weigh more than a ton each and are anchored with cables that are secured twelve feet underground. They could stop a dump truck moving at forty miles an hour. The glass in the front doors is explosion proof, as are all the windows on the building. A metal detector and radio-frequency sensor are built into every external door frame to alert the guards, but not set off any public alarms, if someone were to walk in with a gun or a bomb or something, and there are three-inch-thick lead plates above the ceiling to contain and diffuse a possible detonation. There are also six fixed cameras with overlapping footprints monitoring the lobby. There's not one square inch of that lobby that's out of camera range." He paused, and smiled.

She acknowledged his litany with a silent laugh. "I stand corrected. Now, tell me about this elevator."

"The elevators aren't biometric, but they're the next best thing." He slid his ID badge into the small slit, and a second later, a keypad appeared on the screen. He touched 18 and pressed ENTER.

Nothing happened.

She met his eyes again. "What now?"

"It's waiting for you to identify yourself."

She blinked at him. "It knows how many people are in the elevator?"

He nodded and pointed to a small strip of decorative glassy dots on either side of the door. "Sensors. It knows how many people cross the threshold and won't move until that many entries have been made with the appropriate number of unique ID cards."

This job may be even more challenging than I thought. She slid her badge into the slot in the wall, then glanced at him. "Eighteen?"

He nodded. "It's the executive floor. You might as well get the full tour."

She leaned back against the wall as the doors silently slid shut and the car began to rise. "So everyone's movement is tracked floor to floor?"

He nodded again. "Before visitors are issued a badge, security has to know which floors they'll be going to, and only certain people can authorize visits to certain floors. Some floors are off-limits without special permission. And on some of the floors, there are sensors that divide areas with different security levels. You have to pass them to go from one area to another, and if you're not cleared for that area, a voice will tell you to turn back. If you don't do it within fifteen seconds, security is alerted by silent alarm."

She actually felt a tingle go through her, right down to her bare toes, leaving undue warmth pooling inside her. It was a silent alarm of an entirely different sort; one that was flashing *Warning: brain sex ahead,* and she knew better than to ignore it.

She reached up to push a few stray hairs off her moistening forehead. A cool breeze would have been nice. Being kissed senseless would be nicer, if a bit inappropriate. "What's the response time?" she asked.

"Human? Short. We have a security presence on every

other floor. But when the alarm is triggered, an instant alert goes to everyone in the area and instructs them to initiate lockdown procedures. If the situation isn't secured within two minutes after that, all systems are overridden and the area is automatically locked down."

She tried not to look impressed. Or overheated. "What does that entail?"

"Office doors shut automatically and lock from the inside, and all computer activity is frozen. Screens go black and you need a special code to bring them back online."

"Have you ever had to institute it?"

"Only in tests. We installed it two months ago." He smiled. "It works."

"And your employees are okay with it?"

"They don't have a choice," he replied bluntly, then shrugged. "It's not like we're tracking how long they stay in the break rooms or copy rooms, although I suppose we could if we wanted to. We've made it clear that the system is for security purposes. Security tags for laptops, PDAs, and all mass-storage devices—hard drives, lipstick drives, you name it—are configured the same way. If a classified device is removed from an area without prior authorization or an untagged one is brought into a secure area, the same security sequence occurs: The voice comes on, security is alerted, a lockdown is initiated. Actually, security is alerted immediately in every case, but they're instructed not to act until the second stage is reached. Most of the employees don't know that." He paused and met her eyes. "You're a tough audience, Naomi Connor. You're the first person that hasn't been even a little impressed."

Oh, honey, I'm weak at the knees. I feel like you've been whispering naughties to me in church. She pushed out a smile. "I'm trying hard not to be, Joe, but I'm failing miserably. Whose idea was all of this?"

"Mine."

"Are we being recorded now?"

An eyebrow rose appreciatively as a warm smile crossed his face. "Video, yes. Audio, no."

"Why not audio?"

"My tag disables it."

Somehow, she didn't break a sweat. "Now *that's* clever. Who else gets to enjoy the silent treatment?"

"The top three tiers of executives: C-Suite officers, vice presidents, and directors. Your team has it, too."

"You're giving free reins to a bunch of ergonomics experts? How did you explain that one to your IT security guys?"

He looked at her with a small frown. "I didn't explain it. I just told them to do it."

Another tingle shot through her. The man was like Machiavelli with morals, or Bill Gates with fashion sense: smart, tough, and convinced he was right.

Honey, you just shot way past adorable. And I'm in big trouble. She took a deep breath as subtly as she could. "What about downloading?"

"Tracked."

"Everything?"

He nodded. "Any transaction involving copying data from a network to a hard drive is tracked, as is anything copied from a hard drive to transportable media, whether it's a floppy, CD, lipstick drive, or PDA. Infra-red transfers are recorded, too."

If she didn't know she was in a climate-controlled elevator, she would have sworn that was a trickle of sweat she just felt between her breasts. But of course, she *was* in a climate-controlled elevator. Standing next to her client. All six-foot-four inches of him. Surrounded by that clean, soapy, mannish scent that was his and his alone. Being studied by those Caribbean, or maybe Adriatic, blue eyes. And getting altogether too turned on by the geek version of talking dirty.

She cleared her throat. "It sounds like you've thought of everything and then some. Who audits all the monitoring data?"

"A few guys from IT," he said as the elevator doors opened onto an open area tastefully decorated in rich colors and dark woods.

Naomi stepped out of the car, reassured by the sheer expanse of space before her, and followed his gesture to the left.

"My office is down here."

Taking a cue from his silence, Naomi said nothing as they walked through the wide corridor, stopping at a closed doorway two-thirds of the way down. He slid his badge into the slot and pressed his thumb onto the small screen above it. A soft click indicated success. He opened the door and ushered Naomi into an office decorated in keeping with the rest of what she'd seen. Dark blue carpeting set off the solid, elegant mahogany furniture. The upholstered chairs opposite his desk were tasteful without being boring.

"What a great view," she said, setting her computer bag on one of the chairs before walking to one of the tall windows. Braving the late-afternoon sun that threatened to blind her, Naomi peered through the half-shut slats to look over a few blocks of low-slung office buildings to a marina and the open water beyond it. The window's deep ledge held a few worn but polished brass objects that she didn't recognize. They seemed vaguely mechanical or at least useful, though very old.

"Do you know what those are?" He was leaning in the doorway, arms folded across his chest. His expression was more bemused than amused.

She glanced at him over her shoulder. "I don't have a clue. Some sort of early telescope or microscope?"

"They're sort of like telescopes. They're called sextants. Sailors used them for navigating in the many centuries before GPS."

An image of him—rakish, defiant, and steady on the deck of a surging eighteenth-century privateer's ship—flashed through her brain. She managed not to smile. "They look complicated."

"I know, but they're not difficult to use if you know what you're doing," he said with a grin.

"I'll take your word for it." Her gaze swept the room as she turned to face him.

His desk was perpendicular to the door, presumably so he could both watch the door and look out of the tall casement windows opposite it. A cabinet flanked by bookshelves was built in behind his desk, and a few understated prints and paintings broke up the pale expanse of walls, but he had no "brag" wall covered with framed degrees or photographs of him with celebrities and politicians. She wasn't sure if she should be surprised or not.

"No corner office? You're chief technology officer, Joe. There can't be that many people ahead of you on the corporate food chain," she said lightly.

"I'm the *acting* CTO. And I don't usually work up here. I'm based in D.C., remember?" He pushed away from the doorway and gestured for her to sit down before he seated himself behind his desk. "Anyway, no one gets a corner office. On each floor, two of the corners are copy rooms and the other two are break rooms. And every administrative assistant has an office with a window and a door that shuts, just like every manager and executive does."

She looked at him in surprise. "That's unusual. Who gets the interior offices?"

"Most of the interior space is reserved for file storage and secure closed work spaces. And you're right, it is unusual to use the prime floor space for communal areas, but my great-great-great-grandfather founded the company in the era when companies were led, not managed, and he believed in leading by example. His office was no bigger or more luxurious than that of any of his executives. It's become a tradition no one is willing to tamper with because it works." His laser blue eyes were trained on her. "In the eighties when so many companies were getting rid of secretaries and converting private offices into cubicles, my grandfather refused to follow suit.

He considers that whole Intel mind-set, in which even the CEO works in a cubicle, to be a drain on creativity and productivity."

"But it saves a lot of money. What about profitability?" she asked.

"Short-term or long-term?" he asked in a deceptively mild voice, which made her laugh.

"I withdraw the question. So everyone gets an office?"

He smiled. "Pretty much. Who can work without privacy or silence?"

"Depends on who you talk to. *Real* management consultants would think y'all are nuts." She paused and shifted into a more comfortable position in the chair. "I just might be tempted to join them in that determination. All that privacy and silence can do more than breed gratitude, Joe. It provides opportunities, and that's a security nightmare."

He leaned back in his chair. "I know. That's why you're here."

We're going to get along just fine, darlin'. She smiled. "Have there been problems other than the hacking incidents you told me about this morning?"

"Not many. The last troublemaker was one of the few guys who worked in a communal space. He was a draftsman in a secure area." Joe's tone held a challenge.

She refused to rise to the bait. "Did that have something to do with why he caused trouble? He wanted an office?"

"He never mentioned that specifically, but it might have played a part in his actions. Paul worked for us for about three years, and for much of that time, he apparently didn't like the music one of the other guys played. And he was annoyed that his manager didn't do anything about it."

Naomi frowned. "That seems kind of petty. Why didn't the manager do something?"

"I'd say the biggest reason was that Paul never actually *said* anything to anyone, including the guy who played the music, and the manager."

"What kind of music was it?"

Joe paused and met her eyes. "Mostly Chopin and Rachmaninoff. The occasional Liszt thrown in for good measure."

Naomi blinked. "He objected to classical music?"

Joe shook his head. "He objected to foreign composers, at least while working on a top secret project for the U.S. military. He thought it was unpatriotic."

"So John Philip Sousa—"

"Would have been fine," Joe finished.

"So what did our little patriot do to remedy the situation?"

"Tried to sell some satellite plans to a group of thugs in the Ukraine."

A familiar finger of unease traced a cold path down Naomi's spine at his words. She tried to hide the involuntary shiver by leaning against the cushioned back of her chair, and crossed her legs, smoothing the fabric of her skirt. "Interesting response for a so-called flag waver," she said coolly. "What happened to him?"

"In cooperation with the federal government, we sent him on an extended vacation to Allenwood, Pennsylvania, where he'll spend the rest of his life making license plates with a few others of his kind." Joe's contempt was undisguised.

Trying to make the gesture seem casual rather than contrite, Naomi looked away from the blue intensity of his eyes. Her gaze came to rest on her hands, tightly folded in her lap. She relaxed them. "How was he caught?"

"A new hire in the IT department actually started reviewing some monitoring data instead of just archiving it, and saw some irregularities in the outbound traffic. He took his laptop and flew down to my grandfather's house in Palm Beach on his lunch hour."

Naomi's head snapped up at his last words and she couldn't help it. She burst out laughing. "On his *lunch hour*?" she repeated.

Joe grinned and nodded. "I know. It sounds crazy, doesn't it? But Tom knew what he was looking at and knew there wasn't any time to waste. And he was smart enough to realize that he didn't know who else might be in on it. Of course, he also walked out of the building with two classified hard drives in his computer bag and no one stopped him, so he helped us see a few other security problems in addition to the spying."

"Where is he now?"

"He's head of IT."

Naomi smiled, then hitched an eyebrow. "But he doesn't know anything about our audit."

"That's correct."

The challenge flared bright and hot inside her again and she shook her head slowly, meeting his eyes. "You're going to be a son of a gun to work for, Joe."

He smiled back as if he understood, and then rose to his feet. "I certainly hope so. Come on. I'll show you the rest of the layout."

CHAPTER
7

"Don't you have a home?"

Naomi looked up from the screen of her monitor to see a tired and slightly rumpled Sarah McAllister leaning in the doorway of her office. "I know I do somewhere, but at this point, I couldn't tell you where it is." She leaned back in her chair and stretched, enjoying the hot rush of blood through sluggish muscles. A quick glance at the clock told her it had been two hours since her dinner break, which had involved not much more than opening a fresh bottle of water and a new pack of cinnamon Altoids.

Sarah moved into the office and curled up on the big, squishy wing chair Naomi had brought in to replace the two small, uncomfortable ones the company had provided. Those feng shui felonies had been moved to the farthest corner where, now disguised with a colorful chenille throw, they were stacked high with the overflow from her bookcase.

"You've been here late every night this week," Sarah said through a yawn.

"A fact you're aware of only because you've been here yourself. Besides, it's only Thursday," Naomi said, trying unsuccessfully to ward off a reply yawn. "Tomorrow, I intend to leave for home before sundown."

"Plans?"

"Big ones. First, I intend to watch the sun set over my neighbor's house, not"—she tipped her head toward the window—"that office building. Then I thought I'd maybe go to one of those funky restaurants near my house, which are part of what sold me on my new neighborhood in the first place. Then I'm going to play with my new kitty, wash some clothes, read more than one page of a book—you know, all that girly fun stuff," Naomi finished dryly.

Sarah smiled. "Sounds divine, actually. How are the plans for Brennan coming along?"

"Pretty well. Joe has done an impressive job of establishing a secure perimeter, so the physical side of the audit will be interesting. The digital side will be a flat-out challenge."

"It's what you wanted."

"It's exactly what I wanted," Naomi agreed with a smile, leaning forward and bracing herself on her forearms.

"You're okay working with Joe?"

Interesting question. Naomi gave a one-shoulder shrug. "I think he's going to be tough, but he's awfully smart. It's a nice change to work with a client who has such a clear idea of what he wants the results to be, especially when those results are realistic."

"He's tough, all right. But he's a nice guy behind the businesslike exterior. If you play straight with him, he'll play straight with you." Sarah paused. "He's pretty good-looking."

Naomi met her boss's eyes and didn't bother to hide a laugh. "You have a very broad definition of good-looking, honey, if that's the nicest thing you can think of to say about him. I'd say he's a gift from the gods to good little Earth girls. The man is gorgeous."

Sarah grinned. "I know him too well to call him a gift

to women, but I do know that he's really good at getting even the most tightly wrapped women all unwound—if he wants to. I've known three different women who would have rolled over and died for him, and I don't think he ever took any of them out more than two or three times. That man is as single as a man can be."

And fully intends to stay that way was left unspoken.

Unsure whether to laugh or frown, Naomi cocked her head and looked at her boss, who had been her friend since graduate school. "You're warning me against falling for a client?"

"I'm not warning you about falling for the client, I'm warning you about falling for the man," Sarah replied pointedly. "I can safely say you probably won't even like Joe during office hours. He can be a tyrant; think Genghis Khan dressed by Armani. But when he leaves the office, he switches it off more completely than anyone I've ever known, and *that's* when you need to be on your toes. He likes pretty women, although I have to say that none of the women I've ever seen him with are in your class. He goes for the plain-pretty up to really pretty, but I've never seen him with anyone that I'd call beautiful."

"Maybe he can't stand the competition," Naomi said cattily under her breath to divert the conversation before it became too personal. "Anyway, don't you worry your little head about me. I'm not about to fall for anyone I'm working for or with. All I want to do is crack his defenses—make that his *corporate* defenses—and get back here so I can start exploiting the many privileges of partnerhood."

Sarah smiled. "Excellent. I'll leave you to it." She unfolded her legs from beneath her and stood up. "See you tomorrow."

It was the low hum of a vacuum cleaner that made Naomi look up from her screen a while later. If the cleaners were on her floor and working their way toward her office, it was late. Very late. They started at nine o'clock—two floors down.

It was definitely time to go home.

Because of her Saturday trip to Connecticut, last week had never really ended, and this week had started on Sunday. Today was Thursday. So far, she'd logged more than sixty hours, setting up the scope of the work and top-level strategy for the Brennan project. It was exhausting but exhilarating at the same time.

The architect of the system—she suspected Joe's handiwork—had been meticulous. It was built like a fortress, yet easy to maneuver through if you knew where to go and how to get there. Users were screened, authenticated, and tracked. Portals were disguised with simplicity and mathematical elegance, and protected with the cyber equivalent of snarling dogs and razor wire. And it was all done seamlessly.

Hacking into his system would require creativity, tenacity, and the right tools. Even though her team had all three, that didn't mean it would be easy.

Joe had admitted unashamedly that he'd assembled a big-talent team to build the system and had worked them like pack mules for eighteen months. Then, a month ago, after they'd finished their last round of internal testing and had gone live with no major hassles, he'd sent the whole team *and* their significant others to the south of France for two weeks, all expenses paid, with five thousand dollars of spending money in each team member's pocket. He'd told her, with a genuinely nonchalant shrug, that they'd earned it.

Sweet.

She sighed and stretched her arms over her head, letting a smile drift across her face. If her team did as well, she wouldn't be sending them anywhere but home; they'd get a few days off for good behavior—otherwise known as comp time—and she'd get her partnership. She'd take that over two weeks in the south of France any day.

After saving the spreadsheet she was working on, she

logged off her computer, then began gathering the classified files scattered across the top of her desk. She was
just turning to the last number on her office safe's lock
when the sharp chirp of her desk phone made her jump.
Out of sheer habit, she left the safe locked and spinned
the dial, then carried the stack of files back to her desk
and glanced at the phone unit's small screen.

BRENNAN SHIPPING INDUSTRIES glowed greenly, followed by the number of their Washington, D.C., office.

The man really must be a taskmaster. It had to be
one of his assistants. She knew it wasn't Joe. He was in
Connecticut. They'd spoken twice today.

The knowledge made the tiny anticipatory zing in her
bloodstream dissolve, and she frowned at the delayed
realization that the zing had happened in the first place.

Do not analyze it.

"Naomi Connor," she said crisply, picking up the
handset before the phone could ring a third time.

There was a pause on the other end of the call, then
she heard a short laugh. "What are you doing in your
office at this time of night? I was only calling to leave a
voice mail."

The smile burst onto her face and into her voice before she could stop it. "Same thing you're doing in your
office at this time of night, I guess." She sat down behind
her desk, feeling her tiredness fade in the presence of a
tingly, sparkly light storm in her brain. "But if you really
want to leave a voice mail, I'll hang up and you can
call back."

"No, that's okay."

"What are you doing in D.C.?" She leaned back in
her chair and rested one shoeless foot against the rim of
her wastebasket. The other was already tucked beneath her.
Her office began to feel cozy and snug rather than
merely small and cluttered.

"I've been here all day."

"But when you called me this morning—" She
stopped.

He'd called her from his cell phone. Obviously, it was registered in Connecticut.

She rolled her eyes. *Duh.* "Never mind. What can I do for you, Joe?"

"Well, I was going to ask for one favor. Since I've got you on the phone, I'll ask for two."

She felt her smile widen. "Why stop there? You're the client; you can ask for a dozen. Just remember that I'll be billing for all of them and my hourly rate is somewhere between merely painful and downright sinful."

He laughed. "Given your reputation, I'd expect no less. The first favor is that I'd like to meet with you tomorrow afternoon if you have some time."

"I just shut down my machine. If you'll give me a minute, I'll reboot," she said, keying in her passwords as she spoke.

"That's not necessary—"

"It's already under way. My calendar will be up in a minute." Less than a minute passed before her calendar application opened to show tomorrow's schedule. "I have about forty-five minutes free at two and I'm completely open after three thirty." *So much for going home early and remembering what it is to read a real book instead of software code.*

"I need about a half hour. I want to go over a few things I forgot to tell you, and I think it will be easier to do in person."

"Why don't you come over at three thirty, then? That way we can talk and when we're done, I can show you the playroom."

He didn't respond immediately, which made her cringe. *Okay, it sounded like a come-on.*

"That's what we call our attack-and-penetration center," she explained smoothly, being careful not to sound flustered. "You know how software developers have their 'sandboxes'? Well, we have a 'playroom' full of all the latest, greatest technology. It's just two floors below my office in the same building, but if you don't have time, that's fine. I just thought you might like—"

"No, that sounds great. I'd love to see it. So, tomorrow at three thirty?"

"Sounds good." She paused. "Now, what's your other favor?"

"Well, I'm about to leave the office, and since it sounds like you are, too, would you like to meet for a drink? Your office is only a few blocks from mine."

"Oh," she said, hearing the surprise in her voice. *Quick. Yes or no? It's business. It's okay. Isn't it?* "Sure, that would be nice."

"Great. I'll stop by your building. Is Red Sage okay?"

"Sounds fine. I'll be in the lobby in fifteen minutes."

"I'll see you there."

Naomi hung up the phone and quickly stored the files and her briefcase in the corner safe after fumbling the combination three times.

Grabbing her purse from her bottom desk drawer, she sailed out of her office toward the ladies room to do what she could to freshen up, all the while wishing the buzz in her bloodstream would fade, even just a little.

He's a business associate. A client. It shouldn't matter a bit that he's good-looking, too. Or even that he's a gift on a short-term loan to this not-so-good little Earth girl.

She pulled her hairbrush from her purse and glanced into the mirror. Her eyes were much too bright and much too blue. "Oh, Lordy. This is going to be some project."

Joe was leaning casually against the semicircular security desk, chatting with the guard on duty, when Naomi stepped off the elevator. As soon as he saw her, he ended his conversation and straightened up. He was in a dark suit with a white shirt that had lost some of its starch. A colorful but tasteful tie was loosened enough to allow the top button of that shirt to be open. The shimmer of a golden shadow accentuated his jaw. His hair had been raked by artless fingers. His eyes never left her.

He looked good. Too good for this time of night. She kept her smile casual and her thoughts under tight rein as she approached him.

"Thanks for joining me," he said as she drew near, and then he conducted a quick and subtle head-to-toe inventory of his own. The look on his face told her she'd been assessed and found acceptable. Maybe even slightly more than acceptable, despite her wrinkled linen suit.

A goodie bomb detonated inside her and it was a battle not to look away from the blue intensity of his eyes. "Thanks for asking. I was a few minutes from walking out the door when you called."

"Great timing, then." He turned to the security guard and said good-bye to her by name, then turned back to Naomi. "What's making you burn the midnight oil?"

"Just a small, inconsequential project that starts on Sunday," she replied lightly.

He laughed and held open the heavy plate-glass door. "Well, I'm sure your efforts won't go unnoticed."

"I don't know. The client is well-known as a taskmaster. And you?"

The still, sultry night air held the sharp, smoky odor of the streets, a combination of the heat, the ginkgo trees, and the Potomac. She never minded it; it was unique to the District and a welcome antidote to the chilled and ionized sterility of the air inside the building. It was pungent, but at least the city smelled alive.

"I flew down this morning for some meetings on the Hill with a rather recalcitrant member of the House Defense Appropriations Committee."

"That explains the business-not-so-casual attire. Were they successful?"

"Business in the District always means suits and ties. As you well know," he said with a shrug, not needing to give her outfit another glance. But he might as well have for all the extra carbonation fizzing in her veins. "And I won't know if the meetings were successful until the vote happens. It's hard to come up with a good argument for a representative from a land-locked state to support something that will benefit the ship-building industry," he added with a smile. "But that's it for shop talk. I'm off the clock as of ten minutes ago. How are you doing?"

"Just fine. Making sure all the ends are tied up before I leave town." She looked away from the warmth of his eyes and watched instead the flashing orange hand on the opposite side of the crosswalk. She deliberately ignored its symbolism. *There's nothing to stop.*

"Where will you be staying?" he asked.

"The Marriott. Seems like it's the hotel closest to the office."

"It is."

They stood together in an almost companionable silence at the surprisingly busy intersection until the light turned and the green figure beckoned them to cross the street.

"The company has a condo that's closer, if you're interested," Joe said, sounding almost unrehearsed. "I mean, since you're going to be there for a few weeks. I'm pretty sure it's available."

It could be a proposition or a genuine offer. Or another damned test.

Naomi counted to five before answering. "Why, thank you, Joe. That's awfully nice. But I—my whole team is staying at the Marriott."

He made eye contact and there was nothing sly about it. "They're not going to be here as long as you are, are they?"

"No," she replied slowly. The physical audit would only take about three days, and then that part of the team would depart. Half the digital team was staying here in Washington, operating from the attack-and-pen center at the office; the other members were coming with her to Connecticut to work from inside Brennan. That side of the effort would take about ten days, but she'd be staying around longer than that to do the analysis, write the reports, and deliver them.

"Well, it's an option," he said dismissively when she didn't continue. "After a few days in a hotel, I start to feel penned in. I just thought it would be more comfortable for you to stay there than in a hotel room for a few weeks. It's yours if you want it."

Okay, fine. I'm going to trust you. Don't disappoint me. "Thank you, Joe. It would be more comfortable," she agreed. "I'd love to stay there if it's available."

"Great. I'll have one of my assistants look into it tomorrow." He stopped in front of the ornate double doors that led into Red Sage and held one open for her.

The air was cool but lush with wood smoke and spices. The background music was just low enough to cover the sound of individual conversations; the muted light and earthy Southwestern decor imbued the space with a warm sophistication. They wove through the maze of small tables, heading toward the bar and the carved stand attended by an elegant, model-thin young woman. She gave them an easy smile.

"Good evening, Joe. It's been a while."

Naomi extinguished her surprise and an unwanted twinge of something uncomfortably close to possessiveness. *Not my business.*

"Hi, Tanya. It has been a while. Business looks as good as ever. Think you can find us a table?" Joe asked, glancing at the almost-crowded room, then returning his attention to the hostess. A lazy, sexy smile spread across his face just as she began to reply in an apologetic tone.

Naomi watched, amused, as the young woman's cool polish slipped to reveal some good old-fashioned fluster.

No Southern woman would ever crumble like that. She smiled serenely at the Yankee.

"We have a table available downstairs," Tanya said breathlessly. "It's kind of out of the way."

"Sounds perfect," Joe replied, increasing the intensity of his smile by one click.

With slightly clumsy fingers, the hostess picked up two menus and a wine list and led them down the sweeping, cavelike staircase to the lower dining room.

Their table was a snug nook lit by a dimmed minispotlight overhead and a tabletop candle flickering in a pierced tin holder. Everything about the setting whispered *romance*, but Joe didn't seem to notice.

"I didn't realize until we walked in that I haven't had anything to eat since before noon. I'm starving. Have you had dinner?" he said, waiting for her to be seated before sliding into the other side of the small booth.

"Not unless Altoids are a food group," she replied smoothly, hoping this wasn't about to turn into a date or something even more awkward.

"Not last time I checked," he replied with a grin. "Why don't we get something to eat?"

CHAPTER
8

Joe still wasn't sure if meeting up with Naomi was a mistake or not. It might not be the smartest thing he'd ever done, but it had started out innocent enough. Contacting her had been the next best thing to an afterthought. If he'd remembered in time, he would have sent her an e-mail, but having already logged off his computer, he decided a voice mail would suffice.

Hearing her voice on the other end of the phone had thrown him. He hadn't expected her to be at the office at nearly eleven o'clock at night—that was excessive even by his standards, and people thought he was a slave driver. But there she was and there he was, and their offices were only two blocks from each other. Going home to a big, empty house wasn't what he was in the mood to do, not after the day he'd had. Spending an hour unwinding with easy conversation over a cold beer was a much better option; having that conversation with a beautiful woman who spoke computers was damned close to his idea of perfection. Asking her to join him for a drink had seemed the natural thing to do. The friendly thing to do. Second-guessing himself, as he was doing now, would never have occurred to him if she were a man.

But, of course, Naomi Connor wasn't a man. Nor was she a buddy or a pal or one of the guys, or ever likely to be. She was, frankly, the most feminine woman he'd ever met. She was a soft, curvy, beautiful—*and smart*—woman, he thought, forcing his logic to override his natural inclinations. He wasn't about to let his mind wander down that road no matter how curvy *or* smart she was.

He'd been around long enough to know that business relationships with women could be easygoing, like the one he had with Sarah, or a fucking minefield. What he had with Naomi was strictly a business relationship, and so far, she'd given no indication that she was going to let it become anything else. The few awkward situations surrounding their first meeting had been handled by her with professional coolness mixed with some unavoidable self-consciousness but, thankfully, not a hint of flirtation.

His invitation tonight had been issued in the same professional vein. He'd given her no reason to believe this was anything other than a spontaneous, agenda-free, semisocial meeting between business associates. Which is exactly what it was. Of course, he acknowledged, his impulsive offer of the use of the company's condo could have set the conversation back a step or two, but she'd accepted it casually and at face value without any coyness or, what would have been worse, a big smile.

Any complication, especially *that* sort of complication, was the last thing he needed. If something were to develop—which it wouldn't—Chas would be mightily pissed off. But that wasn't the worst possible outcome. The worst possible outcome would be a "misunderstanding."

Naomi was not only a friend of Sarah's, but she lived in the District, not far from his house, where he'd be returning in a few weeks' time when the project was done. If something extracurricular developed between them, there would be no possibility of ending it gracefully.

And it *would* have to end. A long-term relationship

wasn't part of his long-term plans. And a relationship of any sort wasn't part of his short-term plans.

So, he assured himself, if he needed reasons beyond mere common sense as to why everything had to stay totally aboveboard and professional, he'd just given himself three really good ones: job security, sanity, and Sarah.

He glanced at Naomi over the top of his menu, glad to see that she was busy studying her own. She looked great. Kind of fresh, and definitely not like she'd put in a fourteen- or fifteen-hour day. Frankly, if she looked a bit more tired, as tired as he was, he'd feel better. Right now, next to her, he just felt grubby. He needed a shave, a shower, and a toothbrush.

She looked up at him then and caught him watching her. He smiled a little too quickly and knew it didn't go unnoticed. *Damn.*

"Have you decided what you'd like?" He folded his menu and set it on the table.

She nodded and he signaled to the waiter, who approached immediately. After ordering a bottle of wine and their food, he relaxed into the leather-covered squish of the banquette and loosened his tie a little more, giving her a lazy smile intended to get her to smile back. All it did was make one golden eyebrow twitch upward minutely, and he knew she was analyzing him. Or more precisely, his motives.

Great. "So, are you flying up?"

She shook her head. "I'm driving up on Saturday."

"Why? I mean, it's not a bad drive. About five hours. But why not fly?"

"I haven't driven up there before and I thought it would be pretty," she said with a half smile.

It was a reason only a woman could give, but somehow, coming from her, it didn't sound ridiculous. It sounded kind of sweet.

He blinked. *Hell. Did I really just think that?*

"You go through Baltimore and Wilmington, and then

all the way up the New Jersey Turnpike. It's shipping ports, chemical plants, and oil refineries almost the whole way. And it reeks in the summertime," he replied with an edge to his voice that was meant more for himself than for her. As punishment for even thinking the word *sweet*. *Christ.*

She laughed, sliding her fingers around her water glass and lifting it to her lips. She didn't grip the glass; she held it with the pads of her fingers, gently. He didn't remember ever before noticing the way a woman held a glass.

When she set it on the table, he glanced back to her eyes, which were trained on him. Her lips had a polite curve to them that stopped just short of being a true smile. Her expression held a not particularly flattering sort of tolerance.

His surprise was dulled by the lateness of the hour; nevertheless, the realization that she might be patronizing him fueled a weary annoyance. He was her client, but he wasn't a moron. He was also done working for the day, and not in the humor to persuade her to do anything, even listen. *I should have just gone home.*

"I don't mind driving," she said evenly, filling in a silence that had lasted a moment too long. "The Baltimore-Washington Parkway is beautiful and almost peaceful on the weekends. The stretch from Baltimore up to Wilmington is very pretty, from what I've been told, and so is the bottom half of the turnpike. And Sarah said to take either the Garden State Parkway or the Palisades Parkway and cross over the Tappan Zee Bridge, because those routes are more scenic and less hectic than going through New York City. I'm inclined to like that idea, since I've never driven there and I've heard bad things about Yankee drivers." She lifted the glass and took another sip, arching that finely shaped brow again as she did so.

Okay, so you're no pushover. Keeping his eyes focused on hers, Joe couldn't help but give a silent laugh in return. "All the more reason you should just fly up. Take a commuter plane. You'll still see all the trees and the water but you won't have to deal with the drivers. Or take the train."

She cocked her head slightly and let her smile turn friendly. "Are you sure you're not a lobbyist for the travel industry in your spare time?"

"What spare time?"

She laughed. "How are you getting back?"

"I'm flying up on Saturday. I'm just in town for a few meetings tomorrow and then a thing tomorrow night."

"If you're flying, why not stay the weekend? You have a house here, don't you? Or an apartment?"

He nodded. "I'd like to, but I can't stay. One of my sister's girls is turning eight on Saturday. The party is at Chas's house and I'll be kicked out of the family if I don't turn up for it, bearing a sickening quantity of gifts."

She kept smiling but didn't reply as the waiter arrived at the table and made a show of presenting Joe with first the bottle, then the cork, then a half teaspoon of wine swirled in the bottom of an enormous goblet. After murmuring something obsequious when Joe tasted the wine and nodded his approval, the waiter ceremoniously poured two glasses, nestled the bottle with a flourish into a chilled terra-cotta cylinder, and disappeared. Joe shook his head and met Naomi's eyes with a grin.

"Don't be fooled by the dog-and-pony show. I guarantee you won't be transported to a higher plane of existence by this," he said dryly, picking up his wineglass and tilting toward her. "It's nice, but it's the same stuff you can buy in the shop down the street for half the price."

Something in her relaxed just a little as she laughed and lifted her goblet by the stem, inclining it toward his until the rims touched. "Here's to simple pleasures."

After his first, very welcome sip, Joe set his goblet on

the table and leaned back again. "That's a good toast. I like simple things."

"What kind of simple things?" she asked, her eyes flicking to his as she tasted the wine.

He shrugged. "All kinds. Any kind. Most good things in life are simple. It's people that complicate them."

She failed miserably at hiding a smile. "How so?"

"We just do. It's in our nature." He paused, liking the way her lips were twitching with amusement. "Name one simple thing and I'll tell you how people have complicated it."

Their eyes met and held through a momentary pause. The merest spark of challenge had come alive in hers. He'd seen that spark before, on the terrace at his mother's house. It was good. Uncomplicated.

He answered her smile with one of his own.

"Okay. Water."

"It's bottled and sold," he replied without hesitation. "And it's being marketed, which is a joke. About ten years ago, people stopped being thirsty and started to need rehydration. And then there are the companies that bring in the water for your swimming pool on the back of a truck. Across state lines."

She looked kind of—*oh, God, not that word again*—sweet as she sat there biting the inside of her cheek and searching his eyes, as if trying to see into him. Her eyes were less challenged than amused now.

And he was wrong. She wasn't sweet.

She was stunning.

Only heavy sarcasm was going to keep him from making a complete horse's ass of himself.

"Air," she said after a moment.

"We pollute it, then purify it, ionize it, heat it, cool it, condition it, compress it, and can it. Surely you've seen those cans of compressed air that you're supposed to use to clean out the dust between the keys on your keyboard? The ones with the thin tube for a nozzle?"

She nodded. "Fire?"

"Gas grills. Enough said."

She took a sip of wine and set the goblet carefully on the table, her fingers playing absently with its stem. "Earth?"

"Visit any garden center. You can buy it by the bag or by the truckload. A woman who lives down the road from my mother was persuaded by her landscaper to import all the dirt in her rose garden from some famous garden in England. Can you imagine what it must have cost to ship four containers of dirt across the Atlantic, not to mention get it through customs?"

"How are her roses doing?" she asked, a laugh entering her voice.

"They're pretty," he conceded, then picked up his goblet and took a sip to hide his own smile.

"Okay. What about charity? Helping others is not a complicated thing, even today."

He shook his head. "Nope. You're wrong. Charity is no longer one of the Graces. It's become a business and a tax deduction and, in my experience, usually involves wearing a tuxedo and dancing with women who wear too much perfume." He shrugged. "Even helping a little old lady across the street could be a punishable offense under the right circumstances. Third-degree assault, attempted battery, attempted kidnapping."

Smiling, she sat back against her seat and shook her head in lighthearted exasperation. "You are truly the man with all the answers, Joe. I thought lawyers viewed everything in shades of gray, but you're Mr. Black-and-White. In fact, maybe just Mr. Black. There isn't much sunshine in your point of view, is there?"

He looked back at her with a grin, enjoying the way her eyes had taken on a sparkle. A clear blue sparkle like sunlight on tropical waters. "Well, you've got me there. It's true. I don't do sunshine very well. I told you I used to be a prosecutor." He shrugged again. "In a criminal case, there are three basic results: incarceration, probation, or freedom. A court finds someone guilty or not guilty; they're never found to be innocent. It's all the other guys, the defense attorneys, who think in shades of gray. Their client is a little guilty, or guilty of a lapse in judgment but not the crime that followed that lapse. Or their client is responsible for his action but not quite responsible for the harm wrought by that action." He shrugged again. "The truth is probably the easiest thing to complicate."

She was silent for a moment, and watched the wine swirl in the goblet she hadn't stopped playing with. Eventually, her mouth pursed into a thoughtful frown. "That's exactly the way it should be. Truth is complicated. It isn't an absolute. It's relative."

This could get interesting. He leaned into the back of the cushioned bench. "Since when?"

"You're a corporate lawyer now, Joe, not a prosecutor. Haven't you learned to see the gray? Or to look for it?" she said in a voice that was softer and held a hesitancy he hadn't heard before.

When several minutes passed and she still didn't meet his eyes, Joe was intrigued. She wasn't merely on the other side of the issue and she wasn't playing devil's advocate. She was defending something. And asking for leniency.

"I can see it," he replied, "but that doesn't mean it's become my favorite color. I still prefer things to be simple and uncomplicated. Even the truth."

"But life is complicated," she protested. "People are complicated."

"Are you?"

"Not particularly." Then she laughed a little bit nervously and reached forward to take a sip of her wine.

Curious about the cause of the change in her manner, Joe ignored the warning that had begun buzzing at the back of his brain. He waited until she'd set her goblet back on the table and had swallowed her wine, then he lifted his own. "I beg to differ."

Her eyes flicked to his. "What do you mean?"

"I think you're pretty complicated."

"That's only because you don't know me very well." She tried to cover up her wariness with a smile, and failed.

"What about your criminal past?" he asked softly over the rim. "I'd call that a complication."

Her pupils dilated wildly and her lips parted, then snapped shut. Both of her hands went into her lap, clutching each other. Color rose to her face and she looked away.

When she looked back at him a long moment later, her eyes were snapping with irritation overlaid with more than a little fear. And that's when he realized that whatever she'd done had struck her deeply.

It wasn't a joke to be shared or a mystery to be solved.

It was what defined her, and he had damned well better leave it undisturbed.

CHAPTER
9

Naomi shut the front door behind her and leaned against it, finally letting her legs turn from rigid steel to soft rubber. She'd been hoping that her reaction to him in Connecticut had been a fluke, but now she knew it wasn't. Joe Casey truly *was* the most nerve-wracking man she'd ever met, client or not.

She looked around her cozy, softly lit living room, but for the first time, the sight didn't soothe her. Nothing would tonight. Nothing could. Trying to maintain a professional distance while being half-spellbound by his lips, which seemed always on the verge of curving into that don't-tempt-me smile, had been nothing less than exhausting. But every time she managed to drag her gaze away from his mouth, she ran straight from the devil there into the deep blue sea of his eyes. Eyes so intense that she had no doubt they could burn right through a titanium wall if he wanted to see what was on the other side.

Seeing through a bad liar with a big secret would be child's play for him.

And he knew it.

She closed her eyes and let out a heavy breath she didn't realize she'd been holding. Damned if that lighthearted question about her "criminal past" hadn't put her into the heart-attack zone. She'd been rendered speechless for a least a solid minute, and by then it was much too late to laugh off the question *or* her response. For a split second after he'd asked it, Joe looked like he'd swallowed something nasty. Then he politely, smoothly ignored her reaction and changed the subject with an easy smile and a smart comment.

It hadn't helped much. She'd been dancing on a tight-rope with no net for the rest of the evening. It was all she could do to smile back at him and pray for the waiter to arrive and make a fuss over the food like he had over the wine—of which she had proceeded to drink more than she should have.

She slid to the floor in anguish. *I deserve this. Every minute of it. Penance isn't supposed to be easy and redemption will only feel good after I've earned it.*

A soft, sudden thump in her lap made her open her eyes. She looked into the muted green eyes of her kitten, which were mere inches away from her own, and was rewarded by a gentle, clawless swat on the nose. *I deserve that, too, for leaving you alone for sixteen hours.*

"Oh, Smoke, your mama is in big trouble," Naomi said, her voice barely above a whisper as she stroked the kitten's downy head. "And it's part man trouble, which is always the worst kind."

Unimpressed, Smoke blinked once, rearranged herself on her haunches, and settled in for a good long stare.

Naomi stared back for a minute, then had to laugh. "That's what you're here for, baby. To help me keep a sense of perspective."

She gathered the fragile fluffball into her hand, stroking an idle finger behind one miniature ear. The kitten began to purr; it was the only thing about her that was big. Then she gave a big, kitten-breathy yawn and followed it up with a tiny, sandpapery lick to Naomi's nose. No longer concerned about being ignored, Smoke curled

into an elegant ball of fur and fell asleep in the cradle
of Naomi's hand.

Naomi looked down at her and felt tears build up
behind her eyes. "Oh, darlin', if only life were that easy
for everyone," she murmured against the kitten's head.
"I've made such a fool of myself."

After one strong sniff and several determined blinks,
Naomi realized there was only one thing left to do, and
that was to go to sleep. Balancing the kitten against her
chest, she got to her feet and walked through the apartment to her bedroom, shutting off lights as she went.

After that not-very-entertaining time with Naomi last
night, sleep had been an elusive goal for Joe, and it
showed. He woke up late, too late for a swim, which
would have taken care of those Bill Clinton–sized bags
under his eyes Then he proceeded to cut himself three
times while shaving. The milk he'd put in his coffee at
six thirty had been sour. Watching the curdled particles
float to the top of his mug, he told himself that the day
could only get better.

He was wrong.

Stopping at Starbucks on his way into the office, he'd
held open the door for a woman with a toddler in tow.
He followed her to the counter and listened in disbelief
as she ordered six iced Caramel Macchiatos—made with
skim milk—and then realized by the time she reached
the cashier that she'd left her purse in her car.

Not only was he late for his first meeting, but the
coffee had been too damned hot to drink until he was
in his office. At that point, the caterers had come and
gone, and he knew fresh coffee was waiting for him in
the conference room, in a heavy, sterling silver pot
parked next to a china cup.

Annoyed and concerned that, because of it, he would
end up being even more blunt than his reputation allowed, he called one of his staff attorneys out of the

conference room and told her to handle the meeting with Congressman Biedersdorf's staff. Together they re-entered the conference room, which had a wall of windows that provided a stunning frame for the Capitol. With his suit coat on and his tie snug, he parked himself at one end of the large conference table and greeted the group, flicking his eyes from participant to participant, all of whom had their jackets off, their ties loosened, their sleeves rolled up, and their jelly doughnuts half-eaten.

He'd even made Biedersdorf's unflappable chief of staff nervous, but what the hell? Unnerving them with silence was better than destroying four months of delicate negotiations by doing what actually needed to be done, which was to inform the chief of staff that the honorable gentleman he worked for could shove it sideways. Biedersdorf's state wasn't the only one that liked pork.

Joe closed his sore, sleep-deprived eyes and rubbed them. That meeting had ended—successfully—by mid-morning, so just sitting there for three hours with his mouth shut, his face grim, and his mind elsewhere hadn't been a total cop-out. His staff knew the issue as well as he did—which was inside out and upside down—and they knew what the goal was. After all, the ability to delegate was one of the hallmarks of a good executive.

So was being able to concentrate.

God damn it.

He blinked hard and refocused on the small print again. He'd been staring at the same brief for the last ten minutes, but damned if he could remember what the topic was.

"Mr. Casey?"

He glanced up to see his summer intern looking at him from around his cracked-open office door.

"Yes?"

It wasn't said rudely, but she recoiled, anyway. *Great.*

One more thing to feel shitty about. Scaring a twenty-two-year-old law student.

"You put a note on my desk last night to remind you about a meeting at three thirty. It's three ten. Would you like me to call a cab for you?" Her voice was barely a whisper.

"Thank you, Sasha. It's nearby. I'll walk."

"It's raining."

He paused, looking at her and wondering if she thought he might dissolve. *She could only hope.*

"See if you can find me an umbrella," he murmured, returning his eyes to the papers on his desk.

"Yes, sir." Her response was followed immediately by the soft click of his door closing.

A walk in the rain might be what he needed to snap out of this foul mood. He had better snap out of it, because he was going to be facing the cause of it in twenty minutes.

No, that's not quite right. She's not the cause of it; I am. Me and my damned ignorant idea that I have a right to know what she did ten or twenty years ago. She's just the—

He closed the folder with a snap and stood up. He wasn't about to spend time trying to define what she was. She was a business associate, period. And he'd offended her. Or at least embarrassed her.

Last night, in the immediate aftermath of his raging stupidity, dropping the subject had seemed the smartest thing to do. Now that he'd had approximately fifteen hours—he shook his head in disgust—to think about it, he needed to apologize to her if for no other reason than to make himself feel better. And that in itself was pretty pathetic.

A soft, almost inaudible tap at the door was followed by the painfully slow widening of a gap in the doorway. The intern stuck her head in again and thrust a large navy blue umbrella bearing the corporate logo into the room. "Here you go, Mr. Casey," she whispered. Leaning it against the wall, she quickly withdrew and shut the door.

"Fucking great," he muttered.

Seconds later, his Blackberry started chirping at him. He picked it up, glanced at the screen, and let out a heavy breath as he answered the call. "Hi, Mom."

"Hi, honey. How did the meeting with Biedersdorf's people go?"

"Better than expected. I sent you an e-mail." He glanced at his watch. *Three fifteen.*

"I got it." She paused. "I also got a call from Betty Sullivan. She said you were on a rampage."

Joe closed his eyes and drew in a slow breath. It was either that or indulge in some primal-scream therapy. Betty Sullivan was the General Counsel's executive assistant—for the company's last three General Counsels, which translated to roughly forty years of service. Within the company, she ranked somewhere just below his grandfather and God: she was omniscient and damned near omnipotent. Despite the lack of a law degree, she probably knew more about corporate and maritime law than the rest of the legal staff combined. And the best parking space in the building had *her* name on it. Her boss had the next one over. As Assistant General Counsel for Government Affairs, Joe's space was several slots down the ramp.

Although Betty hadn't been at the meeting, it came as no surprise to Joe that she knew what had gone on.

"I wasn't on a rampage," he said calmly. "I just let Karen handle the meeting. I sat next to her and kept my mouth shut."

"Is anything wrong, Joe?"

Is anything right? "No, Mom," he said with deliberate patience. "Everything is fine. Biedersdorf's team is happy. We're happy. Everybody's happy."

"Then why did you put Karen through it?"

He let out a hard breath. "Put her through what?

She's worked her tail off on this deal and I thought she deserved to bring it home. To get some of the glory. It was hardly a punishment."

"I think she might see it differently. Next time you want to reward someone, try flowers or an extra day off, or even just a pat on the back."

Flowers? "What are you talking about? I just gave her experience. That's what she's here for: to do a job and get experience."

He knew by the short silence that his mother was shaking her head in resigned disbelief. "Joe, Betty found her throwing up in the bathroom after the meeting. The poor girl was in bits. You didn't give her any warning. She thought you were setting her up. Betty sent her home in a limo."

Christ. "She's the best negotiator we've got on the staff. Why would I try to sabotage her?" He paused. "In fact, I'm thinking about giving her a raise," he lied. "She did a great job." *Okay, that part was true.*

His mother let out a mildly exasperated sigh. "Honestly, sweetheart, we ought to hire someone to follow you around and sprinkle rose petals in your wake. You terrify people."

"Mom, I barely said a word," he protested, and glanced at his watch again. If he didn't leave in forty-five seconds, he was going to be late.

"Well, let me give you a tip. Send Karen and her boyfriend on a weekend to The Inn at Little Washington. Dinner, massages, the works. And *then* give her a raise."

"Fine."

"Have Betty take care of it."

"I will." *Thirty seconds and counting.*

"Today."

"Okay."

"Good. Now, that's not the reason I called."

Shit.

"I'm not going to make it up there tonight."

The meeting with Naomi was momentarily forgotten as the realization hit home that he was going to have to entertain Biedersdorf, his wife, and two other members of congress and their spouses alone. Tonight. At the Kennedy Center.

It was too much to ask after the last twenty-four hours.

"You can't. Bag out on me. *Now,*" he said in a low voice, somehow refraining from clenching his teeth.

"You know I wouldn't stand you up if it weren't serious."

"What could be more serious than this?"

"I dropped a planter on my foot this morning and broke three toes."

His heart skipped a beat and he clutched the unit in his hand tighter. "Jesus, Mom, are you okay?" he demanded in a hushed, harsh voice. It would be just like her to downplay an injury.

"I'm fine," she replied in a voice determined to soothe. "It was just three toes. They're taped up and the front half of my foot is a perfectly awful shade of purple, but nothing else was broken, fractured, sprained, or chipped. Or even bruised," she added. "But the doctor doesn't want me flying today and wants me off my feet at least until tomorrow. So high heels are out of the question for tonight. I'll be back in Greenwich for Corey's birthday on Saturday, though." She stopped and gave a short laugh. "I'm sorry it's not enough of an emergency to keep you from having to entertain the delegation, honey. I wish I could have at least provided you with a reasonable topic of conversation."

"Don't even joke about that." He raked a hand through his hair, his concern converting itself to annoyance. "Do what the doctor tells you for a change, and stay off your feet."

"I will, I will. Try to have fun tonight, Joe. And don't glower at them. Congressman Standish's wife thinks you're quite charming."

Congressman Standish's wife is sixty-three years old and propositioned me last time I saw her. "Good-bye, Mom. Take care of yourself."

After ending the call, he grabbed his suit coat and the umbrella and stormed out of his office. Halfway to the elevator, his conscience lassoed him, bringing him up short. He stopped, turned around, and walked calmly back to the intern's desk.

She was on the phone. He forced himself to wait patiently until she turned and caught sight of him, at which point she dropped the phone in alarm. "I—it was—"

He smiled at her, putting as much warmth into it as he could manage. "I just wanted to thank you for getting the umbrella for me, Sasha. I'm sure they're in short supply today, and I appreciate the effort. Have a good weekend."

Leaving her wide-eyed and speechless, he turned and walked back to the elevator. Smiling.

Naomi glanced at the small crystal carriage clock on her desk, then checked her watch. Maybe they both needed new batteries.

Joe Casey just didn't seem the type to be twenty-five minutes late for an appointment without extending her the courtesy of a phone call. The man had four assistants, for heaven's sake, and he was only in the Washington office a few days a month.

She stood up and turned to look out her window. Her team had been assembled in the conference room for half an hour, waiting for her to come in and introduce them to Joe. If they spent any more time in there, the cookies and coffee she'd ordered for the meeting would be gone, they'd be totally wired, and the maturity level would dip dangerously low. It wasn't a statement about them; it was just a fact. She'd watched it happen before—on other people's projects. Not hers. *Oh, please. Not on this one.*

Her intercom buzzed and Naomi jumped. She sent off

a quick prayer that Heidi, the receptionist, had been listening when she'd stressed to her the importance of not being "cute" when Joe arrived. She was absolutely *not* to engage in any of the "Hoochee mama!" "Are you married, honey?" or "Hellloooo cupcake!" sort of banter that she typically did with the men who came through the door, client or not. Joe was a *big* client, Naomi had warned, and one who had *absolutely no* sense of humor. Heidi, whose thirteenth grandchild had been born last week, had nodded solemnly.

"Naomi?"

Okay. Sound calm and relaxed, not like you've been making a meal of pencil erasers for the last half hour. "Yes, Heidi?"

"Joe Casey is here to see you."

"Thank you. I'll be there directly."

She took three slow, deep breaths, smoothed her skirt, fluffed her hair, reapplied her lipstick, checked her nail polish, and opened her office door. And nearly walked straight into Joe Casey's chest.

Her head snapped back as she looked up at him. "What are you doing here?"

His too-blue eyes met hers. They were alive with humor. "We have an appointment, for which I'm really, really late. I didn't see the point in making you walk all the way out there. Heidi told me where to find your office." Then he smiled, which only added to the tumult in her head. And launched that internal harmonic vibration. She fought a shiver.

"I'm sorry to have kept you waiting," he continued, keeping the smile on his face and his eyes boring into hers. They were warm and made her warm. Too warm. "A call that I had to take came in right as I was leaving the office, and then I had to go a few blocks out of the way because Fourteenth Street was blocked off to all traffic. Cops, Secret Service, the full-court press. I think the First Child was having a snack at a hot dog stand.

And the battery in my Blackberry died en route." He held it up for her inspection.

"That's fine. No apology necessary," she said a little breathlessly. "The team is in the conference room, waiting—"

"Could I talk to you privately for a minute?" He glanced past her into her office.

"Oh." She paused for a split second and blinked, trying to remember the state of the top of her desk. Entertaining him in her office hadn't been part of her plan. "Certainly. Come in."

She stepped back and let him enter the room, then sneaked a peek at her desk. Only three piles of papers. Not bad. That half hour of waiting had obviously been well spent. Not that she could remember any of it.

He stepped into the center of the room and she shut the door, stepping around him to stand behind her desk. It was only a few feet, but putting some distance between them helped her nerves. "Have a seat."

"No, thanks. I just need a minute."

His eyes were so blue. Bright blue like early morning on a clear day. And they were watching her very carefully. *Scratch that thought about the distance helping.* "Okay."

"I want to apologize for the comment I made last night. It made you uncomfortable, and that wasn't my intention."

Her heart was already beating faster than was called for. The soft contrition in his eyes didn't do anything to slow it. She swallowed and forced a small laugh. "Thank you. It was—"

He shook his head slightly. "Don't explain. It's none of my business."

Oh, heavens. Maybe it would be better to confess than to be discovered. And maybe this is the right moment for it. "Joe, please. Ask me anything," she said much too quickly.

She watched one golden eyebrow hitch and a moment later, a neutral, lawyerish expression took up residence as the apology faded from his eyes.

Or the utterly wrong one. "I mean, I'd rather not have any awkwardness between us at the start of the project. Let's wait for that to happen when we're butting heads on something that really matters, like my methodology. Or the invoice," she said with a weak smile. "But I mean it. Ask me anything."

He looked at her in silence for a moment, then he folded his arms across that chest.

The stance made him seem a lot bigger for some reason. Or maybe it just made her feel smaller. Either way, she was glad the desk was between them because it was *definitely* the wrong moment for soul baring. That look in his eye was meant for a perpetrator, an unrepentant felon.

And she was repentant. Very.

"Okay. With your permission." He gave her time to rescind her offer, which she would never do. Verbally, anyway.

"Your background check came up clean, so we must be talking about sealed juvie records. What did you do and how did you get caught?"

She covered her gasp with a laugh. "Well, that's about as direct a question as I've ever been asked." *And there is absolutely no way I can look you in the eye and answer it. Not now, anyway.* It was childish, she knew, but she clasped her hands behind her back and crossed her fingers. "You're barking up the wrong tree, Joe. I told you that I hacked, but I never said anything about getting caught." *I turned myself in.*

He waited a moment before responding. "You just stopped on your own?"

She met his eyes calmly. "As a matter of fact, I did."

"For no reason." It wasn't a question.

She smiled, hoping it looked natural. "Well, of course

I had a reason. I realized what I was doing was wrong. And I stopped."

"But you didn't know what you were doing was wrong before you got caught? Or when you started?"

Damn, he's tricky. "I told you that I never got caught."

"But you hacked." Another question that wasn't a question. The expression in his eyes was still neutral. Not quite cool, but neutral. It chilled her, anyway.

It was time for a dignified retreat. Unclasping her hands, she leaned forward slightly and splayed her fingertips lightly on her desktop just to keep from fidgeting. "I told you in the truck on the way to your mother's that I hacked, and I'll say it again, Joe. A long time ago, for a very brief period in my life, I was a hacker. Now, before I say anything else, I'd like to ask you something."

"What's that?"

"Do I need a lawyer?" she asked softly.

That slow, dangerous amusement crept into his eyes. The one that tickled the backs of her knees and made her breathing go funny.

"Of course not, Naomi. Besides, I'm a lawyer, remember?" He paused. "You can trust me."

Please don't be playing with me.

The intensity of the thought shook her. Needing a moment to pull herself together, she cocked her head and let her gaze roam over his face before meeting his eyes again. They were no longer amused, but were studying her intently.

"Of course I trust you, Joe," she said quietly. "Maybe even a little more than you trust me."

The silence lasted only a heartbeat. "If I didn't trust you, you wouldn't be working for me, Naomi."

I would love to believe that. "Thank you."

His eyes held hers for a moment, but when she didn't offer any other response, he glanced at his watch and motioned to the door. "I don't want to keep your team waiting any longer than I have already. I know they have a lot of things to get organized before Monday."

"Right. The conference room is this way." She straightened and picked up a short stack of file folders she didn't need, just to busy her shaking hands, then walked to the door and opened it. Turning left into the corridor, she let out a slow breath when she was sure he couldn't see her face.

Situation defused. Temporarily.

CHAPTER
10

Naomi wandered around her apartment, unable to sit still. She still couldn't believe she was actually going out with him again. To a formal event at the Kennedy Center, no less.

The invitation had come out of the blue, as they'd been sitting in the conference room going over the last of the system architecture. Her team had left them an hour earlier, and the conversation since then had been easy and project related, with no reappearance of the awkwardness that had transpired earlier in her office. He'd glanced at his watch, run a hand through his hair, and made a comment under his breath that had sounded more frustrated than coherent.

She'd asked him if he needed to get going, and he'd told her, in a voice laced with barely disguised annoyance, that he had to babysit a bunch of congressmen and their wives at tonight's gala performance of the Washington Opera's *Samson and Delilah.*

"We can finish going over this on Sunday," she said, trying to keep the envy out of her voice as she tidied her stack of notes and slipped them into a waiting manila folder. "It's going to be a wonderful performance. The

President and First Lady and the King and Queen of Norway will be attending."

"So I've been told," he muttered, his voice revealing just how unimpressed he was. He stood up and stretched.

"You're not looking forward to it?" she asked, trying not to watch. It wasn't easy to ignore the soft, rumpled cotton of his white shirt stretching taut, however momentarily, across those shoulders. That chest.

"Personally, I'd rather sit by myself on my patio with a cold beer in my hand and some hot blues on the stereo," he replied, reaching for his suit coat, which he'd draped across the back of his chair earlier. "My mother was supposed to be in town and I was going to accompany her. But she hurt her foot this morning and can't make it. Now I'm the host."

Naomi stopped what she was doing and met his eyes. "Is she okay?"

"She's fine. It wasn't anything too serious—" He'd just finished shrugging on his suit coat when he stopped and stared at her. She knew immediately what he was going to say. And just as quickly she knew what her answer would be.

"Would you like to go?"

Yes! "To the opera?" she asked instead, feeling her eyes widen and her heart start to thud. It had been at least a year since she'd been. And she'd gone alone.

He nodded. She realized her fingers were gripping the folder too tightly and she tried to relax them.

"Tonight?" *Quit asking stupid questions. Just say yes!*

He grinned. "Well, it's the only night I have tickets for."

The heat in her face couldn't be just adding a glow to her cheeks. It felt as if her entire head was on fire.

"I was planning on meeting my mother for a drink beforehand and there's a reception afterward," he continued. "But we can probably skip that—"

"No."

He stopped and looked at her. "You don't want to go?"

"No. I mean, yes, I do want to go. A lot. This is just—" She took a deep breath and exhaled carefully to regain some of her poise, then met his laughing eyes. "Thank you, Joe. I would love to go. And whatever you have planned is fine." She stopped again. "This is just really a happy surprise. I love the opera."

"Great. Then you can explain it to me," he said, still grinning as he looked down to gather his paperwork. "Just keep in mind that it's a business thing."

Though lighthearted, the comment was unexpected and it stung. "I won't embarrass you," she said, lifting her chin, however involuntarily, against the assumption that she would.

His hands stilled and he looked up at her slowly. "That never crossed my mind, Naomi."

She felt that annoying heat steal back to her face and she glanced down again.

"I meant that I can't vouch for the company," he continued. "My mother knows these people better than I do, and they're in her age group. Other than the performance, it could be an excruciatingly dull evening. Unfortunately, we're stuck with them 'til the bitter end."

Relief warmed her and, with a smile, she reached for the last of her notes. "Maybe I can save you this time," she said lightly. "My mother was a Washington hostess for nearly a decade, Joe, and has been a Southern lady her whole life. Her crowning achievement was when the first lady attended one of her luncheons. Believe me, I had no choice but to learn the social butterfly routine at a young age. I presume this is black-tie?"

"Because the president will be there, I think it's white tie and tails. But if you're not comfortable with that—"

"That's fine, Joe," she said softly, glancing up at him. "I have evening clothes."

He looked mildly embarrassed and looked back at the table to make sure he had everything. "Great. Then why don't I drop you off at your place now, and I'll come back and get you at seven thirty?"

And that's how it had happened. That's why she was storming around her apartment like a caged and hungry tiger scenting fresh blood on the air.

This performance sold out in an hour, eighteen months ago, and at extortionate prices. I'd have been a fool to say no and let the ticket go unused. She stopped and caught sight of herself in the mirror above the table in her small foyer. *Given that the ticket was for the seat next to Joe, it wouldn't have gone unused.*

That doesn't matter. I'm going because I love the opera. No other reason.

"No other reason at all. And all of those other reasons that I don't have for going with him are exactly why I can't wear this dress," she muttered, and charged back into her bedroom and yanked open the closet door.

The last time she'd worn this gown had been to one of the presidential inaugural balls she'd attended two years ago with her parents. It was midnight blue and had large, graceful swaths of dark blue sequins that swirled across the flowing silk skirt and up the demure bodice to curl around the jewel neckline. It would be perfect for the event. It was elegant. Beautiful. Tasteful.

It just didn't have a back.

She looked over her shoulder to catch a rear-view glimpse of herself in the mirror on the back of the closet door. The designer not only had a talent with fabric but an understanding of how to harness forces of nature and combat gravity. That meant the gown was not only a work of art, it was a mechanical miracle.

But that didn't matter at the moment. Naomi had to get out of it. Immediately. Her basic black standby would be adequate, she assured herself. She had the neck unhooked and the hidden side zipper halfway down when the door buzzer sounded.

She closed her eyes and swallowed hard, then closed

the zipper, refastened the hooks, and scurried back into her living room to press the intercom button. "Hello?"

"Hi, Naomi. It's Joe."

"Hey, Joe. Come on up," she said, forcing a smile into her voice as she pressed the button that unlocked the downstairs door. Then she opened her front door just a crack and dashed back into her bedroom to check one last time that everything was securely in place—hair, jewelry, breasts.

Mildly panicked blue eyes stared back at her as she heard him walk in the front door. She returned his called greeting with false gaiety, then took one last, deep breath, picked up her evening bag, and walked slowly into the living room.

He was standing near her balcony doors, his head tilted down and toward the glass as if he were watching something in the garden below. His hands were casually shoved in the pockets of his trousers. His dark, cutaway jacket was open to reveal a plain, elegant white vest. Small, tasteful black studs punctuated the front of his white pleated shirt. His white tie was impeccably tied.

The evening sun streamed through the window, back-lighting his golden head, and burnishing hair that bore signs—again—of fingers having been raked through it hastily. A pair of sunglasses hung outside his breast pocket with careless charm.

He looked better than the bridegroom on top of a cake.

He looked better than the dinner-jacketed guy from the Mystery Date game she'd played as a child.

He looked—

He turned his head and looked straight at her, and they both caught their breath.

How the hell did she have time to get better looking? He'd only left her two hours ago, and she'd looked damned fine then. And that was after a full day's work in another one of those business suits that was sexy without intending to be.

But here she was, with her hair pushed up into a tou- sled explosion of curls, leaving exposed a long neck that he hadn't really noticed before. Dangly earrings com- peted for his attention, but there was no contest. They only led his eyes right down the sleek lines of her neck to the front of a dark blue dress that covered her from neck to toes. Only her shoulders were bare. Lush and bare and glowing like old gold against the midnight darkness of the fabric.

Once again, not a hint of cleavage was showing. Once again, she was about the sexiest woman he'd ever laid eyes on. He'd met movie stars and models that hadn't looked as good. Probably because they hadn't stood there looking at him with a hesitant half smile below dark blue eyes that matched the sequins on her dress sparkle for sparkle.

"You're beautiful." It was an understatement, but the only thing he could think of.

Her smile widened, easing whatever tension had been in the room. "Thank you. So are you. My nana would say that you clean up well." She paused and gave a small laugh but didn't look away. "Actually, she'd say you clean up better than Granddaddy's old Buick on a Sun- day morning."

He laughed, not because he thought the comment was funny but because he was just so glad that she was real, and not some dream girl who would fade to ordinary when he blinked.

With a quiet, rustling glide, she approached him. The faintest scent of flowers surrounded her.

"Would you like a drink?"

"Thank you, but no. We can have one when we get there." And without meaning to, he glanced at his watch.

"That's fine." She lifted one glossy, lightly tanned shoulder, extended one slim arm to reach for a nearly transparent golden shawl draped over the back of the couch. "I'm ready."

Then she turned her body one way and her head another, and met his eyes over her shoulder. If he'd been a cartoon character instead of a human, his eyeballs would have popped out on springs and bounced across the floor at the sight of the uninterrupted curves and seductive hollows of her very naked back.

It took him a minute to remember how to speak. Blink. Breathe.

When he met her eyes again that hesitancy was back, but stronger than before.

"It's too much, isn't it? The gown, I mean."

"No." He cleared his throat and shook his head. "No. Definitely not too much."

A wry smile crossed her lips then, and she turned to face him, hiding that satiny expanse of no-man's-land and leaning a hip against the couch. Graceful fingers draped over the edge of it.

"Too little, then? Maybe that's what I should have said to begin with."

He crossed the room, coming to a stop as close to her as he dared. The urge to touch her was overwhelming, so he kept his hands at his sides and just let his senses feast on the sight of her, the light scent of her perfume, her sheer proximity.

"It's perfect. You're perfect. I'm just unarmed."

She studied him for a minute, head cocked, Bali blue eyes caught between laughter and confusion. "I give up," she said finally. "What does that mean?"

"Damned if I know," he murmured, eventually tearing his gaze away from her and picking up his keys from the table where he'd laid them. "But I thought it needed saying. Shall we?"

"You should have told me you knew Congressman Standish," Joe murmured through a smile as he turned to accept his drink from the waiter.

The motion caused his arm to brush lightly against hers. It was a welcome sweep of soft warmth in the chilled, aristocratic air of the Kennedy Center's Bird Room; a warmth that crept into every cell in her body and lingered in some.

Flatly refusing to admit to herself how much she enjoyed that touch, or to let anyone in the room know how much she was enjoying herself at his expense, Naomi kept a polite smile firmly in place.

"You should have told me that's who you were entertaining." She nodded her thanks to the same waiter as she lifted a flute of Champagne from the tray. "Missy Standish and my mother were Kappas together at the University of Texas, and bridesmaids for each other's wedding."

"She patted my ass the last time we met." He sent the dry remark over the Scotch-wet rim of his glass.

You're lucky that's all she did. "She has two sons who are only a few years younger than you. Their family is as solid as Alabama limestone," she replied blithely.

"I thought limestone was porous."

She was torn between giving him a hard poke in the ribs and laughing out loud. Instead, she merely smiled and glanced serenely around the room. "I wouldn't worry about it. She won't try anything. Seeing as you're with me," she added, because she couldn't resist it. "And now, in case you might be interested, Congressman Reilly—he's over there in the corner; still Minority Whip, I believe—he was the ranking Democrat on the House Armed Services Committee the first year Daddy was at the Pentagon. They still play golf a few times a year." She paused and took a sip. "Anybody else you want to know about, Joe? I'm happy to help."

"I'll let you know."

She swallowed a laugh and looked away. The crowd in the elegant room glittered with jewels and fame. Movie stars were rubbing elbows with cabinet members; rock stars were chatting with lobbyists. At least two former presidents were working the crowd from within their phalanxes of tuxedoed Secret Service agents. And Naomi Connor, a nobody, was smack in the center of the room with the sexiest man she was ever likely to meet, client or not. It was time for another deep breath and a reality check—

"Someone's perfume is threatening to asphyxiate me," Joe said, a little too close to her ear. His breath set fluttering a few strands of misbehaving hair, among other things.

"Let's set a course for the box. I'll steer. You navigate. Let me know if I'm about to step on toes I shouldn't." His palm cupped the apex of her elbow; his fingers lightly but firmly circled the rest of it.

A single hot pulse shot up her arm, initiating a high-voltage circuit she wasn't inclined to break, though she straightened her already erect posture in an involuntary response. A second later his words registered and she glanced at him. "Did you say 'box'?"

He nodded, moving them steadily forward through the peacock-hued throng of glitterati.

"We're sitting in a box?" she repeated in a whisper.

He glanced at her this time, a smile lurking in his eyes. "That's what my mother said and she's the one who arranged this gig. That's okay, isn't it?"

She nodded, slightly awed by his casual disregard for the evening's extravagance, and moved with him without further comment. This was as close to living a dream as she'd ever get.

The crowd thinned appreciably as they wove their way through the labyrinth of corridors that led to the exclusive seating areas. As they entered the intimacy of the box, Naomi saw the Standishes standing near the front of it. They were chatting with another couple, and all four of the formally attired guests turned toward her in unison.

Congressman Standish's eyes were friendly and avuncular. He was a big, bluff man, with a gentle smile and

easy Southern ways about him. Naomi had always liked
him. The other man's famously dark, famously doelike
eyes moved over her figure furtively, like a snake slith-
ering off a sun-warmed rock. She fought a shiver as
those eyes met hers and that deliberately shy, photogenic
smile spread across his handsome, weathered face. Joe's
hand tightened minutely on her arm before he let go and
reached forward to clasp the man's outstretched hand.

"Senator Birk, Mrs. Birk, it's a pleasure to see you
again. May I introduce Naomi Connor?" he said evenly.

Naomi extended her hand on cue, wishing like anything she could avoid touching the hand of a man whose
inside-the-beltway reputation belied the clean-cut, Great
Plains farm-stock image he cultivated everywhere else
the media reached. Senator Thompson "Tommy" Birk
was ambitious and good-looking; he was also a flirt and
a lech, and well-known for standing too close to young,
pretty women. Not to mention sleeping with them every
chance he got.

"Senator Birk, it's always a pleasure," she lied, then
turned to his wife, who was looking at her with eyes
considerably cooler but no less appraising than her husband's. "Mrs. Birk."

"Naomi. Lovely to see you again, my dear. How are
your parents?"

"They're just fine, ma'am. Thank you for asking.
How's Betsy? I haven't seen her since I don't know
when. Probably our ten-year high school reunion. I think
she'd just gotten married."

"Oh yes. Her husband was just elected to the State
House at that time. She's pregnant with her fourth
child," Mrs. Birk replied, casting a quick, deliberate look
at Naomi's left hand. "And you're still living in the
District?"

"When I'm allowed to. My work takes me a little bit
of everywhere these days," Naomi replied with a slow,
easy smile, keeping her gaze firmly focused on the wom-

an's chilly gray eyes while she could feel the senator's gaze burning a hole through the bodice of her dress.

The conversation limped to a quick death when the last members of the group joined them. It was another congressman and his wife, someone who's name Joe had mentioned in the car as having been in negotiations with earlier in the day.

After fifteen minutes spent in the safe haven of Missy Standish's presence, Naomi was relieved when the house lights dimmed and the stage lights came up. She wouldn't have to endure Senator Birk's hypocritically indulgent smiles for at least forty-five minutes.

The performance was pretty good, considering he didn't like opera. Of course, Joe knew he'd spent more time watching Naomi than watching the stage. Not openly, of course. But it had been much more educational, not to mention more scenic. She'd been enthralled, leaning forward during the high points, and very subtly wiping away a few tears in the final moments of the last act. It surprised him to realize how good *he* felt just seeing how much pleasure the performance had given *her*.

That little buzz—glow—whatever—had ended rather abruptly and too soon after the house lights came up. The group had made their way to the private reception room that opened onto the rooftop terrace, and he'd spent the rest of the evening—the last hour, anyway—running interference as that asshole Senator "Call Me Tommy" Birk kept finding excuses to leer at Naomi.

Now—finally—the crowd was beginning to break up and he was ready to hit the road. Six hours was more than enough time to spend rubbing shoulders he didn't want to rub.

He glanced at Naomi, who was standing nearby chatting with two well-preserved women he'd met earlier, but damned if he could remember their names. This was one of the reasons he left this sort of socializing to his mother and Chas. They remembered names and didn't mind making small talk, two things he'd never developed a talent or an affinity for. His eyes wandered back to Naomi and he revised his earlier assessment.

Now, there were some shoulders he wouldn't mind rubbing.

He saw a slight shiver run through her and a second later she glanced up at him, a small question in her eyes, and he wondered if he'd said it out loud. She excused herself with a smile and moved to stand next to him.

"You have a look in your eyes that means it's time to leave," she said, amused. "I don't suppose I can persuade you to indulge me with one little old dance. Can I?"

It sounded flirtatious. He skimmed a skeptical eye over her face, taking in the laughter in her eyes, the color in her cheeks, the bottom lip caught between straight white teeth. "I surely don't know, Miz Scarlett," he said in a parody intended to encourage a touch of acid to dispel the sweetness of her smile.

In the dimmed light of the gold-draped room, her skin held the subtle glow of sunlight seen through honey. A dance would spoil everything, including, maybe especially, his composure. "Sorry to disappoint you. I'll give you a rain check."

Her shoulders went back and her chin went up, but her eyelashes fluttered downward. Only for a second, though; then she met his eyes again, wearing a smile that didn't look entirely genuine, and curled her hand around his elbow. "Lead the way, boss."

CHAPTER
11

It was nearly midnight and the city was fairly quiet. At some point in the evening, it had rained, but that had merely redistributed the humidity. Combined with the unrelieved heat, the sheer intensity of the damp air was enough to wilt the most stalwart resident. Naomi could feel the lining of her dress begin to stick to her skin. Getting out of it would be a pleasure. At the thought of it, her eyes wandered to the left and the profile of Joe's face.

They'd been waiting in silence since the valet parking attendant disappeared to fetch the car, and Joe showed no signs of wanting to break that silence even as the car was brought to a smooth stop in front of them. He had just glanced at his watch for the third time in as many minutes, a slight wrinkle of annoyance tightening his forehead.

She looked away before he could catch her looking at him. *He can't be annoyed at me. I haven't done anything other than ask him to dance with me. Then again, it* was *sort of a date-ish thing to do.*

If he hadn't been beside her, she'd have pounded something in frustration. Imagining that something was wrong and that she was the culprit was the innately female thing to do. She knew it, and hated it, but that didn't stop her from doing it.

Well, hell, she thought a minute later, *we were at a gala and there was an orchestra. We were probably the only couple there that didn't dance. I'm not going to worry about it. Let him.*

Breathing in a lungful of the heavy, steamy air, she straightened her back, pushed the thought away, and took a step toward the car.

As if he'd encountered an impenetrable force, the valet stopped midreach, his arm extended toward the handle of the passenger's-side door. Naomi glanced up in time to see the young man's gaze riveted on Joe. The valet dropped his hand and stepped back with a respectful, mildly abashed air. A second later, a stony-faced Joe opened the door for her.

Well, this is just dandy. His annoyance was spreading like a puddle on the sidewalk, engulfing everyone in its path.

What did I do to annoy him? He'd liked the dress, he'd been amiable at the opera, even joking with her about the fact that she knew more people there than he did. If it was the hot-and-bothered variety of annoyance that had more to do with her dress than anything else, she could deal with it. After all, it was about time, she thought with a little annoyance of her own. Her dress wasn't designed to be ignored, and ignoring it was precisely what he'd been doing since he'd recovered from his first glimpse of its back—or lack thereof. But his mood seemed to be about something else, and she didn't have a clue as to what it was.

The car door closed with a solid thump.

Maintaining a silence that seemed to be getting thicker by the minute, Joe pulled away from the curb and began the distinctly Washington weave through the city's innumerable roundabouts, one-way streets, and construction zones.

They were stopped at a red light at the edge of Georgetown when he finally let out a muffled curse laced with irritation. "I have to ask you a question and I don't want you to take it the wrong way."

"Okay," she replied, slightly startled by the harsh edge to his voice.

"We're two blocks from my house. How much would it bother you if we stop there so I can change out of this monkey suit? I know you don't live very far away, but I've got to get out of this thing *now*. I feel like I'm wearing a straitjacket in a steam room."

A cool wave of relieved amusement washed over her. She blinked at the mutiny in his eyes, then started to laugh. "*That's* what's been bothering you? I thought it was me. By all means, let's stop. I don't want you suffering a heat stroke."

The tightness went out of his face then and he smiled. "Why would you think you'd done anything wrong? You were great tonight." The light turned green and he swung the car into the left lane and onto the side street. "I don't like these get-ups in the dead of winter, but at least I can tolerate them then. In the summer they're deadly. Thanks for being a sport."

A sport?

No man with romantic intentions, or even aspirations, called a woman a sport. Especially a woman wearing an evening gown like hers.

One lovely compliment and an endearing protective streak should have been more than enough to keep her mood buoyant over the course of a long and fabulous evening. *I should be glad he's not interested. It would only cause trouble. For lots of reasons and in lots of ways.* Refusing to let herself frown, Naomi glanced out the side window of his little sports car.

They crossed through another intersection and Joe brought the car to a stop in front of a traditional, narrow-fronted red-brick Georgian house with a handkerchief-sized front garden and a bright yellow door.

"This is really sweet, Joe," she said as he shut off the engine.

"I know. So is the little old lady who lives there. When I shovel her walk in the winter, she makes me hot chocolate." He paused for just a second. "My house is across the street."

His voice now held more than a hint of laughter, and Naomi swung her head to look at him. And then past him, to the imposing pale stone exterior that rose above the street's small, old two-story Georgians like a haughty dowager. Tall windows hemmed with elegant wrought iron window boxes flanked the double front door, which was painted a rich dark blue that glowed under the light from a brass lantern. Two more tiers of windows appeared above the door, and there were twin dormers set into the steep, artful slant of the slate roof.

A four-story townhouse in Georgetown. With an English flat beneath it. She brought her eyes back to his face and hoped she wasn't gaping. "That's yours? The one with the blue door?"

He nodded and got out of the car. She still hadn't fully recovered when she heard her door open and felt the rush of hot air against her feet. She took his hand to ease out of the low-slung car; he held on to it as they crossed the street and mounted the five ivy-draped steps.

There's no reason I should be surprised, really. He's a Brennan.

"It's beautiful," she said, as she walked past him into the cool, elegant foyer. He closed the door behind her and locked it, pressed some buttons on the alarm keypad, then tossed his car keys in a Chinese-type bowl on a low chest.

"Thank you. You're not the first person to be surprised by it. I'm not sure what it is about me that makes people think I live in a roach-infested frat house," he said, already pulling off his tie and opening the top stud of his shirt. "Let me get you something to drink before I abandon you for a few minutes. What would you like?"

He motioned for her to precede him down the center hall, which led into a sleek, modern kitchen resplendent with dark wood cabinets topped with slabs of sleek, dark granite, a glass-fronted, double-door refrigerator, six-burner industrial-strength stove, and wine chiller that looked like it held two hundred bottles. The center island was clearly designed with a serious cook in mind. Part of its surface was marble, part well-used butcher block, and part stainless steel. A deep sink under the windows was mirrored by a smaller vegetable sink on the island.

With a curious combination of mild disbelief and sheer delight, as if she'd uncovered a secret, she turned slowly to look at him. "I never pictured you in a roach-infested anything, but I also didn't imagine you lived in a house like this. Now, I know this is going to be a rude question, Joe, and I apologize. But what in the Sam Hill possessed you to buy this house?"

He had shed his jacket and was removing his vest, which, she noted, was the real thing and not a fake front that had no back. *No wonder he'd been uncomfortable.*

"Well, it's direct, anyway," he said, his grin never diminishing. He walked to one of the cabinets and removed two delicate crystal flutes. Then he walked to the wine chiller and pulled out a bottle of Champagne. And a bottle of Harp.

"Is this okay? I'm not much of a Champagne drinker, but this is supposed to be good." He glanced at the bottle in his hand. "Nice bottle, anyway."

Perrier-Jouet. In the hand-painted bottle. Good Lord. "Don't open it just for me," she protested.

"You're as good a reason as any." He eliminated her argument with a wink and a warm smile, and a moment later was handing her a thin-stemmed but surprisingly heavy crystal flute filled with sparkling golden bubbles. "Here's to you, for saving me. You turned what would have been a painful night into a pretty entertaining time." He touched the rim of his flute against hers and the delicate ping drifted through the room.

She demurred with a minute shake of her head. "No,

Joe. Thank you for inviting me. It was—is—was magical," she stammered, feeling oddly out of her depth, and wanting to wade back into the warm, familiar shallows she didn't remember leaving.

"So a good time was had by all," he said easily, taking a sip and then setting the wine on the counter. "I'll be back in a minute. Make yourself at home. The living room is in there, the library is in there." He pointed in two different directions. "And there's a sunroom off the back of the kitchen, where most people think the pantry should be."

He picked up his beer and headed toward the foyer, grabbing his jacket and vest on the way. She watched him leave the room, and only after he was out of sight did she realize she'd been studying the way his broad shoulders tapered to a narrow waist and hips that were camouflaged behind the shirt he'd loosened slightly after he took off his vest. She also realized that she'd been watching his behind. Mostly.

She spun on a heel and closed her eyes tight. *Don't even think about it. He's obviously well able to keep himself under control. Take a lesson from him.*

"He's made it clear he's not interested," she scolded herself in a harsh whisper. "And with good reason: He's my client, not my date. I'm here because he asked for my help, not for my . . . anything else. A man like him has to have a girlfriend stashed somewhere, if not a dozen of them. Just get that brain of yours back on track, Naomi Connor, and shut down your body."

She took another small sip of the Champagne, which was truly divine, and headed toward where he said the sunroom was.

She stopped in front of the glass-paneled door. *Sunroom* was an understatement. What lay before her was an indoor jungle of the sort found only in coffee-table garden books. It wasn't feminine, though. There wasn't a hint of white wicker here. No fussy knickknacks or country garden flowers; just thick, twisting ropes of vines and dark, large-leafed plants that cast ominous shadows on the moonlit walls. The chairs and tables were a smooth, rich wood, like teak or maybe mahogany, and ornately carved. The fabric gathered into loose folds along the top of the bank of windows was bold with dark, smoky blues and reds slashed randomly with gold. Rough, primitive carvings hung on the walls.

The man is just full of surprises. She stepped into the room and closed the glass door behind her, feeling as though she'd stepped across a few continents to find herself in subtropical Africa. The dense, gravid scent of green, growing things and wet earth hung in the air, but against a backdrop of something exotic and spicy. She breathed it in, tried to define it. Cloves and sandalwood. Maybe cinnamon, but so faint she couldn't make it out. It teased her senses around the edges and she moved farther into the room to find its source.

She lost interest in it, though, as a glance behind her revealed a pair of doors offset in the corner. The double, floor-to-ceiling glass doors led to a shallow set of stone steps. Beyond the steps lay a lush and dark outdoor garden, splashed almost randomly with small pools of silvery light from well-hidden lamps. There was just enough illumination to pick out a meandering wood-bark path. At the very back of the garden, subtle up-lighting turned a large, spreading, blooming Southern magnolia into a living sculpture against a screen of fluttering bamboo.

She couldn't resist a closer look. She set down her wine and walked to the door, easily slipping the small lock on the ornate brass lever and pulling open the door. Half a heartbeat later, a shrill alarm pierced the air as a deep, aggressive voice echoed through the house, warning her that she had violated a protected zone and the police would be called.

Heart thudding in triple time, hands shaking, she slammed the door shut and spun around, half expecting to see uniformed officers with guns drawn, advancing toward her. Perhaps only a few seconds passed before

the alarm abruptly quieted. She sank into one of the
chairs and closed her eyes as she tried to calm her
breathing and steady her hands.

"Are you okay?" Joe's shout reached her from somewhere else.

"I'm fine, thank you," she replied weakly and made
herself stand up.

A moment later, a damp-haired and barefoot Joe
came jogging into the room, wearing pressed khaki
shorts and a soft yellow golf shirt, the collar of which
he was still arranging. "God, I'm sorry. I should have
said something or just turned the damned thing off." He
paused. "You don't look okay."

"I'm fine. Just a bit startled, is all."

"Why don't you sit down for a minute until you get
some color back in your face." He glanced around and
spotted her wineglass on the small table near the door.
A moment later it was in her hand and she was sitting
down again. "Here. Take a sip."

Squatting down in front of her, balancing easily on the
balls of his feet, he gently took her hand and raised the
flute to her lips. His eyes held an appealing mixture of
amusement and concern.

She took a sip and managed a weak smile. "That is
one loud alarm. I should have realized that—"

He shook his head, cutting off her apology. "I have
the alarm zoned. The front door used to drive me nuts,
beeping every time I came through it, so I fixed it. Now
it doesn't start making any noise for two minutes. Pretty
much everything else is instant." He smiled and gave
her other hand, limp and draped over the arm of the
chair, a little squeeze. She felt its echo everywhere. "I
set it off every time I go into the basement, because I
forget to turn off the motion detectors. And it never
fails to scare the hell out of me." He fell silent for a
moment and just watched her, then seemed to shake
himself and stand up. "Let me get my beer."

Naomi had pulled herself together, or at least somewhat, by the time he returned. She stood up as he came through the doorway from the kitchen.

"I got upstairs and decided to jump across the shower. Guess I took too long. So, I take it you want to see the garden?"

She nodded. "If you don't mind," she said, and then stopped as the strains of a guitar softly wailing reached her ears.

"Do you like the blues?" he asked. "I can put on something else."

"No, it's fine. It sounds familiar."

"Gina Leigh. The woman's got a voice that could make the Washington Monument break into a sweat in January." He pulled open the garden door and stood back to let her pass.

The music filtered around her gently as she walked down the steps, and the night's soft heat wrapped itself around her once again. It helped diffuse the last traces of adrenaline in her blood.

"This is beautiful, Joe."

"Thanks. It's a little more tolerable out here without five layers on," he said with a grin, and took a drink from his bottle of beer as he crossed the stone patio. He set it down on a small table and turned to her. "Come here."

She closed the gap between them, expecting to be shown something in that corner of the space. Stopping near him expectantly, she felt a delicious warmth rush through her as their eyes met.

"I believe I owe you a dance."

Joe wasn't surprised when everything about her went as still as the heavy night air that surrounded them. Then she tilted her head just enough to the right and widened her eyes. She was studying him.

"No, you don't."

"Sure I do. You mentioned it before we left the reception."

"I wasn't—".

"Serious? Yes, you were. I didn't want to explain myself there, but it wasn't my intention *not* to dance with you tonight." He held out his hand. "This song is a long one, but it doesn't last forever, Naomi. One dance, then I'll take you home."

"Because you turn into a pumpkin?" she said with a smile.

"No. Because I told you I would."

He wasn't surprised at the heartbeat of hesitation she displayed. She began moving toward him not just slowly, but cautiously—he could see that in her eyes—but that didn't mean her movements lacked sensuality or grace. She looked like she was floating.

Her soft palm met his and her other hand curled lightly around his shoulder. Only then did he let his other hand come up and around to rest lightly on her back. She was so small, he wouldn't be able to rest his chin on her head if he'd wanted to, and she was altogether too soft, too lush and female. It was going to be difficult to remain focused on—

Start moving.

After only a few steps, she looked up at him in surprise. "You can dance. I mean, really dance. Properly," she said with delighted laughter in her voice. And her eyes.

He wasn't a religious man, but he'd be willing to bet that angels looked like her.

"Of course I can dance." He shook his head in mock exasperation. "See, that falls into the same category as the frat house assumption. Do I come across as some sort of Cro-Magnon Lite?" he asked as he initiated a slow spin and brought her back into his arms. "I could try to crush a beer can against my head if that would soothe your sensibilities."

"No," she said, breathless from the twirl, her eyes lit with sparkle he hadn't seen before. Then she laughed out loud, and the moonlight shimmered off her upturned face and the smooth, pale column of her neck. "No. It has nothing to do with—you never struck me as a fraternity boy, Joe. It's just so rare to find a man under sixty who knows how to dance. How to lead properly, I mean. Especially barefoot."

"Well, the barefoot thing is just to show off," he said with a grin. She had a way of putting thoughts together that was not quite unpredictable but that definitely intrigued him. "My mother made Chas and me take lessons in high school, but I took them again before my sister got married, which was about ten years ago or so. It was a big, black-tie affair and I didn't want to make a fool of myself."

"Your conceit paid off, and I, for one, appreciate your efforts." She scaled back her smile then and dimmed the sparkle in her eyes. Almost as if she were reminding herself that this was still a business date, just as he had been doing all night. Despite the repetition, remembering that wasn't getting easier; if anything, it was getting more difficult.

I could ask Sarah to take her off the project—and then make it up to her.

"So, Joe, if you're such a good dancer, why didn't we dance at the reception?" she asked, dropping her gaze to his mouth and, seconds later, to the top button of his shirt. "Based on what you said last night about charity events, I figured that maybe I was wearing too much perfume."

"Nope. Just enough." That light, flowery scent that had teased him all night from a slightly greater distance had begun to cloud his senses the moment she stepped into the circle of his arms. He breathed it in again, let himself savor it as he watched her mouth move, watched her lips form words, her even white teeth flash in another smile. Her words drifted past him unheard. Only their slow, sultry cadence penetrated the heady fog in his brain. That and the realization that her small, beautiful, laughing face was that much closer to his.

You're not going to pull her off the project and you're not going to sleep with her.

As rationality reclaimed its grip on his mind, Joe sent her into another unexpected twirl. When he brought her back into his arms, he made sure they were separated once again by an appropriate distance.

"I had a reason for not dancing with you there," he said, pretending to glance idly around the garden and hoping his comment was still on topic. He wasn't sure how much time had passed since he'd last paid attention to what she was saying.

"So you could dance with me here?" The question held more laughter than flirtation, and he met her eyes again.

"No. I didn't know we'd be here. This really was a last-minute decision, because all those layers were killing me in this heat. I *intended* to dance with you at the reception, but I changed my mind once we got there," he admitted.

"Because . . . ?" she prompted.

He hesitated. "Because of the look on your face when you saw Tommy Birk."

As he knew it would, the smile faded from her face. It gave him one more reason to dislike Birk.

She looked away, taking in a slow, thoughtful breath. "Good old Tommy."

"Excuse my language, but he's an asshole."

"He's the ranking member of the Senate Intelligence Committee," she replied lightly.

"Is it just me, or has that always struck you as slightly oxymoronic, too?"

She laughed then and looked up at him again. "You're not really fooled by him and that aw-shucks nonsense he spouts, are you? That man is as dumb as a fox." Her gaze dropped to the middle of his chest. Her voice dropped, too. "I went to school with one of his daughters. She was a sweet girl, kind of sheltered. She never could understand why nobody ever wanted to sleep over at her house."

Joe felt his jaw clench at the layers of meaning behind her words. "Why didn't anyone?"

"We weren't allowed. She had one sleepover when we were all about thirteen. Her mother came into the room to say good night while he was taking the babysitter home, then he came in later. It was about midnight. He hung around to chat." She shook her head, the tightness around her mouth displaying remembered disgust. "All six of us had to kiss him good night on the cheek before he'd leave."

Joe's blood started to simmer, and it had nothing to do with the warm smoothness of Naomi's skin beneath his hand.

"That was it?" The question came out sharper than he'd intended.

She glanced up at him. Her eyes were cool and impenetrable. "The prosecutor in you is showing, Joe," she said mildly. "Yes, that was all. But it was enough to give me the whim-whams. I mentioned it to my mother the next day, and by the end of the weekend all the mothers had been alerted. That was the end of sleepovers at Betsy Birk's house."

"That was, what, about twenty years ago?"

"Just about that. I think he was still in his first term in Congress."

The son of a bitch. Joe shook his head, choosing to refrain from making a comment.

"Well, it's not like he was doing anything but looking. Now, I know that sounds bad enough, considering how old we were. But don't forget, Joe, some thirteen-year-olds look like thirteen-year-olds. Some look like they're twenty-two. A few of us fell into that category," she added, looking away again as her voice trailed off to silence.

That explains the high-necked blouses and conservative suits. He took in a slow, deep breath. *The son of a bitch.*

"That doesn't matter. If you see an attractive woman on the street or in a restaurant, or whatever, that's one thing. If you know that 'woman' is thirteen years old and your daughter's friend, it's not okay, period. It's not okay to look, it's not okay to imagine. Any man who can't figure that out is literally one touch away from committing a felony that will get him hard time."

She let a small silence build, then looked up at him again. "So how did Tommy Birk make you decide not to dance with me?"

He looked away from the blue depths of her eyes. They were having an unnerving softening effect on some parts of him, namely his resolve, and a pretty dramatic stiffening effect on another part. He was trying to ignore both consequences.

"He spent most of the evening watching you like you were a deer in his sights. I knew he wouldn't ask you to dance with him before you danced with me. Not with his wife there. But once I danced with you, he'd be free to ask. I didn't want to put you in the position of having to say no to him, and frankly, I don't think I'd be able to tolerate the sight of you having to dance with him." He shrugged and looked down at her again, mentally preparing a defense for what he assumed she would term his arrogance, if not worse. "Call it overbearing, arrogant, chauvinistic, whatever. Say anything you like about it, Naomi, but I'm not about to apologize for it. I think I did the right thing. And I'd do it again."

She said nothing for a minute, just studied his face as they moved to the last few steps of the music. They stopped as the last note faded into the night. He dropped his hands and stepped back before things got awkward. *More* awkward.

She swallowed hard and started to say something, then hesitated.

"I can say anything about what you did and you won't get annoyed?" she asked eventually.

He nodded and tried not to make it look like he was bracing himself.

She took a breath and met his eyes. "It's the most considerate thing any man other than my daddy has ever done for me, Joe. Thank you."

She took a step toward him, stood on her tiptoes, and kissed him lightly on the cheek. Before he could respond, she had walked toward the little table at the edge of the patio and picked up her flute of Champagne.

CHAPTER
12

Well, it had been a kiss, but it hadn't been a cannonball over the yardarm. It had been a peck on the cheek. Literally a peck. Over before it started.

The quick, casual, and decidedly *friendly*—as opposed to *romantic* or *inviting*—nature of it hadn't been lost on his brain, but his body had sure as hell missed the point. While his head understood it was only a gesture, from the neck down, he'd been aware only of her nearness. And her gender. And that perfume. As if he hadn't been aware of all of those for the last—he glanced at the clock on the dashboard—six and a half hours.

He turned the corner onto her street and slid into a parking space two doors down from her apartment. "Here we are."

She took his offered hand as she was getting out of the car but let it drop as they walked toward her house. She had her house key out of her small purse before her shoe hit the first step.

"You can just leave me here, Joe. You don't have to make the climb up those stairs," she said, glancing up at him with a polite smile.

No. A *friendly* smile.

That word again. There should be a law against applying it to male-female interaction.

"I appreciate your concern, but I'll see that you make it into your apartment," he replied, keeping at least a foot away from her. "This is the third time I've been here, and it still looks like no one else lives in the building."

She smiled as she slipped the key into the ornate lock and opened the door. "Well, the woman downstairs is an environmental lobbyist, and she's on some sort of research mission in the Australian outback," she confessed, lifting the front of her gown daintily as she crossed the threshold.

He noticed her shoes for the first time. How she could maintain such good posture all night in heels that skinny and high was nothing short of amazing.

"And the guy upstairs is a lobbyist for a cattleman's association, and he's gone, too."

"You've got to be kidding. That combination must make for interesting tenant meetings."

She glanced at him and laughed. "He just changed jobs. She's not too happy about it, but there's not much she can do. When he signed the lease, he worked for one of the big religious lobbies."

"He went from selling God to selling beef? Not what I'd call a natural career path."

"I just smile and nod," she said as she began walking up the inside stairs.

He couldn't help watching her. The smooth sway of her hips was hypnotizing, and made him want to see her naked, but letting his eyes trail up the pale, creamy gold of her back wasn't going to get him thinking about anything involving clothes, unless it also involved taking them off. Closing his eyes was an option, but he'd probably lose his balance. Of course, he'd been in danger of that for the last few hours, with his eyes wide open.

Finally, she reached the small landing and turned to face him. Her sparkle-clad stomach came into view and, by the next stair, he was on eye level with a well-anchored but very well-curved chest. Two more steps and they were on equal footing again, and thankfully separated by fourteen vertical inches and almost as many horizontally. He found it much easier to breathe at this altitude.

"Would you like to come in for some coffee? Or a drink?" she asked, not looking at him as she pressed in a code on the keypad outside her door.

There was more color in her cheeks than there had been earlier, and he doubted it had much to do with the climb up the staircase. Not her climb, anyway. She knew her ass had been at his eye level the whole way up. It wasn't like she had anything to be embarrassed about, though; she had a great ass. Introduced by the most tempting and edible dimple he'd ever seen, just to the right of her spine an inch below her waist.

"No, thanks. I'll just make sure you get in all right and that there are no surprises waiting for you."

When the door opened, she crossed the threshold and turned to him. "Thanks so much, Joe. It was really a wonderful, wonderful evening."

"It was my pleasure. Thanks for coming with me. Especially on such short notice."

She smiled and he smiled back, and their good-nights came out at the same time.

Not waiting for an awkward moment to begin, Joe turned and jogged down the stairs. When he was halfway down, he heard the soft click of her door locking.

Wonderful? She shook her head with a dazed smile as she walked toward her bedroom. Tonight had been ten times more than wonderful. A gala, star-studded performance. A star-studded party. A slow dance under a star-studded sky with one of the few true bone-deep gentlemen she'd encountered in—ever? And who had a playful streak of seven-year-old in him that revealed itself every so often when he wasn't being a tough guy.

As she slipped out of her inherently cruel shoes, she

let out a sigh that she knew was both totally corny and totally appropriate.

Obviously, chivalry wasn't dead. Joe Casey might not be the smoothest man in the District, but he had to be one of the most genuine. He'd been fending off Tommy Birk all night—the same Tommy Birk who was his guest, and who controlled so much of the money and so many of the projects Brennan Shipping relied on—and Joe had done it so subtly that she hadn't even noticed.

She couldn't remember the last time she'd danced with a man who not only knew how to dance, but who put considerable effort into *not* copping a feel. Or the last time she'd kissed a man who let her walk away without making a move to prolong the moment or turn up the heat.

She unhooked the halter neck of her gown and peeled the fabric contraption away from her chest, then shimmied out of the rest of it, enjoying the rush of cool air over her nearly naked body.

Ten minutes later, she had her makeup off and had taken a quick shower, and was on the couch in her bathrobe, flipping through the channels with the sound off. Smoke was curled up on her lap, asleep again, leaving Naomi in peace to relive the evening.

That is, until her cell phone chirped, shattering the apartment's stillness. She knew without looking at the screen that it was Joe. "Hello?"

"You weren't asleep yet, were you? It's Joe, by the way."

She grinned and pushed deeper into the corner of the sofa to get comfortable. "Hey, Joe. No, I wasn't asleep. How can I help you?"

"I was wondering if your invitation had expired. Can I still come up for coffee? Feel free to tell me to get lost."

The easy question held just a hint of hesitancy, which made a welcome warmth blossom inside her and flourish.

"Of course you can. What's the matter? Can't find your way home?"

"Oh, I found it." She could hear the smile in his voice. "I just didn't feel like going inside. But I knew if I sat in my car while I was deciding what I wanted to do, the sweet little old lady across the street would call 911. And I wasn't in the mood to go to a bar, because at this time of night, they're not the best place for thinking. So . . ." He let out a sigh that sounded more resigned than designed to induce guilt. "It was a great night, Naomi. It should have ended more slowly."

The statement landed at her feet like a short-fused firecracker, and she was up walking off an adrenaline buzz before she realized it.

"That's—" She paused. "That's a really nice thing to say, Joe." *Was it?* "Why don't you come on up for a little while? I'll put on some coffee. How long will it take you to get here?"

The downstairs intercom buzzed and she jumped, scaring herself and the kitten, who was cupped in her hand and curled against her chest.

"Shouldn't take more than thirty seconds," he said with a laugh.

She swallowed against the flurry of panic that had shot through her. "I'll leave the door open."

She switched off the phone, propped open the door, and ran to her bedroom to get decent.

Setting the kitten on the bed less gently than she normally would, Naomi grabbed for her lingerie drawer with one hand while yanking open her closet with the other. The pale blue satin bra and panties were on and she'd just pushed her head through the top of a bright pink oversized T-shirt when she heard him call a greeting from the living room.

"I'll be there in a second, Joe," she replied, trying to hop quietly as she tried for the third time to push her remaining foot through the leg of her shorts.

A moment later, confident that she was properly

hooked and zipped, appropriately untucked and barefoot, she caught sight of her hair in the mirror.

"Oh, hell," she whispered in annoyance. The upswept
confection she'd created for the first part of the evening
was still in place. She hadn't intended to brush it out
until just before she went to bed.

*Lord knows what it might look like once I start fussing
with it.* She took a steadying breath that didn't do a
damned thing to calm the herd of heavy-winged, jack-
booted butterflies skirmishing in her stomach. After a
quick inspection to make sure it was tidy—just in case—
she left the security of her bedroom and walked into the
living room at a deliberately easy pace.

"Hey, there. Welcome back."

He gave her a slow, only mildly sheepish grin. "Hi.
Thanks for letting me come back."

"Well, we Southerners are known for our hospitality.
I wouldn't have felt right about it if I'd said no. Might
have been struck dead by a ghost of generations past or
something." Feeling only a little light-headed from the
effects of his presence, she breezed past him with a smile
and a moment later opened the ceiling-to-countertop
blinds that closed off her kitchen from her living room,
then set about making coffee.

He remained in the living room, leaning against the
back of the couch with his arms folded across his chest
and one foot propped across the other. Watching her.
She could feel it.

She managed to get the water in the reservoir and the
coffee in the basket and to press the correct buttons
before she looked up. And it was a good thing she did.
There he was, burnished and broad, with warm, amused
eyes and a dare-me half smile—she could swear she
could feel her toenail polish start to melt.

He looked casual and comfortable, as if he'd dropped
in at one thirty in the afternoon instead of one thirty in
the morning. And what was even worse—much worse—
than all that was that he looked right at home. In her

apartment. At one thirty in the morning. *Saints preserve me.*

"At the risk of making this seem planned, which it wasn't, I didn't come in empty-handed." He lifted a brown paper bag from where he'd set it on the couch, out of sight, and held it up for inspection.

Oh, *hell*. On top of everything else, he didn't even forget his manners in the middle of the night. *Go home, Joe. You're just going to get corrupted if you hang around me.*

"Chinese food?" she asked.

His face fell just a little. "No. Are you hungry?"

"Mercy, no. I stuffed myself earlier. I can't believe you didn't notice. So what's that?"

He smiled again and opened the bag, tilting it toward her for inspection.

Five cartons of ice cream stared back at her.

She raised her eyes to his. *I don't care what flavors they are. You are my kind of man.*

"I noticed you didn't go near the dessert table tonight, but you don't seem like the diet-obsessed type. And I mean that in a good way," he added hastily, crossing the room.

"Thank you. I'm not. And the only reason I didn't go near it was that there wasn't any available room in that dress. This outfit's more roomy." She held her hands across the counter. "Come to mama, honey."

Obviously delighted that he'd made the right call, he handed over the bag and she began to pull out the small tubs one by one. "Chunky Monkey. Cherry Garcia. Mocha Latte. Natural Vanilla. Lowfat Mango Sorbet." She lifted her eyes to him. "One of these things just doesn't belong here, Joe."

The smile that framed his laugh made her appetite evaporate. One of them, anyway.

"I was hedging my bet. I'm sure you've heard that lawyers hate to be wrong. I grabbed the sorbet just in case you *were* diet obsessed and hid it well. Of course, if you were, you probably would have thrown me out by now for being a boor. I figured I couldn't go wrong with the others. There's something for every taste."

She felt the urge to flirt coming on like a bad flu, and was just as helpless to arrest it. "And which type do you figure me for?"

"Plain vanilla," he said without hesitation.

She raised an affronted eyebrow. "And just what about me strikes you as plain vanilla?"

"Plain vanilla isn't a bad thing. It's a classic. It's uncomplicated but satisfying. No frills, but you still don't get tired of it. And you can always dress it up if you want to." He shrugged and didn't *look* like he was speaking in some sort of sexually charged code. "I like plain vanilla and I like you. We get along and there's no pretense. For the most part, you're uncomplicated and straightforward. Except for that little matter I said I wasn't going to bring up anymore," he finished with a really sly twitch to the left corner of his smile.

The only possible comeback she could think of that didn't involve a defensive stance was to roll her eyes and reach for the supersized bowls she usually used for pasta. Lots of cold, creamy calories would have to suffice as the best remedy for soothing the sheer lust simmering within her.

"Hey."

She opened one eye when the point of his elbow made gentle contact with her forearm. "Yes?"

"You snore."

"I do not."

"You do, too. I just heard you. It was very ladylike, but it was definitely a snore. Stand up and see me to the door."

"What time is it?"

"Two forty-five."

"For pity's sake, what are you still doing here?" she demanded behind a yawn. "I've got to drive to Connecticut tomorrow morning to start a project for a really hard-nosed client. You're going to make me lose my job."

She could feel his weight pitch forward on the couch and when he stood up, the motion sucked all the warmth from her airspace. Frowning at the chill, she felt her eyes flutter open.

"You also drool," he said, grasping her hands and pulling her to her feet. "Come on. Up you get."

Her eyes snapped open. "I don't snore and I most certainly don't drool."

His ocean-blue eyes were tired but highly amused. "You're calling me a liar? I'll be sure to mention it to that hard-nosed client."

"Go right ahead. Meanwhile, I'll figure in a secret multiplier for the nonsense I'm obviously going to have to put up with from you," she said, stifling another yawn as they walked to the door.

He brought her to a halt next to her front door, and the atmosphere changed within the space of a breath. He let go of her hand and his gaze slid from her eyes to her lips, making her pulse jump.

"Good night, Naomi."

"Good night, Joe," she replied in a voice that was a lot softer and a lot less sleepy than it had been a minute ago.

Then he opened her front door and stepped out of her apartment, closing the door behind him. She stared at it, feeling like she'd awakened too fast from a fairy tale dream.

That's why the knock didn't surprise her. She hadn't completed the transition to reality yet.

She opened the door. Joe was leaning his shoulder against the doorjamb, his hands in the pockets of his shorts.

"I forgot something."

I want you— "Your phone?"

He shook his head slowly, his gaze never leaving hers.

—*To kiss me.* "Your car keys?"

"No." He stepped into her apartment, leaving the door open behind him. The look in his eyes was neutral but observant. And what he was observing was *her*.

"Your wallet?" Her voice had dropped to a whisper. The urgency was building within her in slow motion, setting every cell into harmonic convergence. If he didn't touch her soon—

"No."

"Then what did you forget, Joe?" *Kiss me, damn it, before I melt.*

"My manners."

He slid his hands around her hips as her palms came to rest against the broad, warm wall of his chest.

Joe's heat, his scent, were heady and rich, and they enveloped her, pushing reality back into the shadows where it belonged. His lips were . . . perfect. Soft and exploratory; sweet, warm, and expert.

Her hands roamed upward, smoothing along his shoulders and the back of his neck until her fingers met amid the cool tangle of his hair. Opening her eyes for a moment, she saw only the crescents of dark gold lashes resting on the high curve of his cheek. It was a picture too appealing to be endured, and she closed her eyes again, only to feel the warning burn of approaching tears behind her lids.

His mouth left hers to trail along her jawline, then dipped to caress her throat and returned to tease her ear before he placed a final kiss in a spot that left her tingling, and whispered another "Good night."

Deep and dark, his midnight eyes held banked fires, and a finality that made her unclasp her hands and drop them to her sides. His hands lingered at her waist for only a moment more, then they were gone, leaving behind only their heat, which dissipated slowly.

She felt her mouth curve into a smile, felt her pulse slow. "That was awfully mannerly of you, Joe. Your mother raised you right," she said softly.

A twitch teased his lips. Those wonderful, talented lips.

"My mother had nothing to do with that." He paused and his amusement faded. "Good night, Naomi."

"Good night, Joe."

His gaze skimmed her face one more time, absorbing her, then he turned to the doorway and went through it, pulling the door firmly behind him.

Fuck an elf. Joe scrubbed a hand over his face as he let himself out the street-level door of Naomi's building.

Tonight, Naomi had been arm candy plus. Dazzling to look at and entertaining to be around, she'd had all the old farts from Capitol Hill eating out of her hand. She'd been completely comfortable with the understanding that it was a business thing and not some sort of an ersatz date, and had been a good sport about letting him get out of that monkey suit. Unarguably, the night had been a success—until five minutes ago. He should never have come back in the first place, but no way in hell should he have walked out and then gone back for—

Shutting down his brain, he walked to his car, got into it, and drove home, accompanied by the wailing brass and sobbing guitars of whatever CD was queued in the stereo. The music didn't matter right now. What mattered was the project, he told himself, and what that kiss might have done to it.

Pulling up in front of his house, he sat behind the wheel for a moment, the engine still running.

Nope.

Sleep alone wasn't going to do it. He put the car back into gear and pulled away, heading for the marina. Only a night spent out on the water would clear his head.

CHAPTER
13

Spending five hours in her car driving to Connecticut was the last thing Naomi wanted to do this morning. Doing it on a few hours of sleep was even less appealing. She stretched and rolled over to look at the clock with one slitted eye. Eight thirty. Too early for a Saturday, especially considering she hadn't gone to bed until nearly three. And hadn't fallen asleep until nearly five.

Closing her eyes again, she rolled fully onto her stomach and buried her face in the pillow. She might have felt better if she'd just had too much to drink, if she'd overdosed on Champagne and moonlight instead of ice cream and hormones. She would have been just fine this morning if she hadn't let him kiss her. Hadn't kissed him back.

No, those things could be taken in stride, she told herself. It was lying in bed for those two hours reliving that kiss that had done her in. But, damn, it was one big hot granddaddy of a kiss and it deserved to be relived.

She'd never experienced one like it before in her life. It was the classic 1940s Hollywood kiss. The one that had allowed wives to send their husbands off to the Second World War with a wave and a brave smile, the one that had assured audiences that love would never die, people would never grow old, and that "for worse" would never happen. The kind that Heathcliff gave Catherine, that Scarlett gave Ashley and Rhett gave Scarlett, that Jimmy Stewart gave Donna Reed—

She smiled and hugged the pillow. It had been chaste. There wasn't another word for it. It hadn't been innocent. There had been passion, just not hunger. Desire but no demands. His mouth hadn't opened. There had been no tongue involved, not even a hint of one. Not even a reconnaissance lick or a teasing flick.

And she knew something about kissing. Boys had been trying to suck her tonsils since a few hours after she'd put on her first training bra, which made Joe's kiss more than just a refreshing change. It was more like a miracle, and it ranked up there as the undisputed number one most intensely sexy, most intensely intimate kiss she'd ever experienced. She'd felt it down to her toes, out to the tips of her fingers, up to the roots of her hair. It hadn't been teasing and it hadn't been tentative. The man knew what he was doing and did it well.

Just what she was supposed to make of it was another thing entirely, and thinking about *that* would surely ruin her day.

The phone beside her bed rang, and Naomi closed her eyes. Only Sarah would call her this early. Sarah, the self-appointed mother hen, calling to make sure that Naomi was ready to get on the road in time to get to Stamford by four, with plenty of time built in for any possible asphalt-related calamity, including beach-bound traffic jams, jackknifed semis, police dragnets, broken tollbooths, emerging sinkholes, and collapsing bridges.

Not yet ready to face the sunshine that she knew was trying to pierce her bedroom draperies, Naomi kept her eyes shut as she reached out and grabbed the phone before it could screech a third time. "Yes, Sarah, I'm awake, but I'm not out of bed or dressed, and the car is not packed. What other questions do you have for me?"

"I guess that about covers it."

She sat up so fast she gave herself a head rush and leaned gingerly against the headboard until the dizziness faded. "Joe?"

His laughter initiated a burst of pleasure inside her before she could stop it.

"Yes. I'm sorry to call you so early, but I wasn't sure what time you were intending to leave. Sounds like I could have waited a few hours."

"Not really. I'll probably be out the door in about an hour." Other than a few last-minute items, everything she could possibly need had been packed two days ago. Her three suitcases stood like sentries next to her dresser, flanked by her laptop case on one side and her purse and the small carrier for Smoke on the other.

"Why so early?"

She shrugged with a secret smile and slid down into her pillows, then immediately sat up again. *Don't get cozy. He's your client. And you're his nemesis.*

"To beat the traffic, I suppose. And to make sure I get up there with enough time to get organized before the team gets there."

"When are they arriving?"

"Tomorrow. Anyway, what can I do for you?"

"Fly up with me."

A laugh bubbled out of her, taking her by surprise. "What? I can't."

"Sure you can. I'm leaving at about eleven thirty."

She blinked and looked at the clock again. "Thanks for thinking of me, Joe, but I haven't booked a ticket or a car. And I have way too much stuff to get on an airplane. Besides—" She stopped. *Why am I making excuses?* She shook herself and smiled. "Have a good flight."

The silence on the other end of the phone didn't last very long, but it lasted long enough for her to wonder if she'd offended him. To wonder if that kiss last night had changed things and now dealing with him was going to be—

"Naomi." His voice was calm, and slightly amused rather than offended.

She let out a silent breath of relief. "Yes?"

"You don't need a ticket. I'm flying up on the company jet."

Her eyebrows pushed upward. "What?"

"The company jet," he repeated. "It's a small plane. Pretty fast. Takes off when I say it should."

Her mouth opened and shut twice before sound came out on the third try. "I can't fly up there on that. What would it look like? People already saw us together last night—"

"Nobody's going to see you. We take off from a private airport in Maryland and land at a private hangar in New York."

"The pilot will. We've gone to such pains to keep this project—" She stopped talking as he started laughing.

"You're worried about gossip? The pilot won't say anything. Neither will the steward."

"How do you know?"

"They like their jobs too much. Besides, who would they tell? Look, we both know the real reason that you're balking at this. Just forget about last night."

She closed her eyes and lay back against the pillows. "I can't, Joe. Look, I had a really nice time, but—"

"But I kissed you."

"Yes, you did, but that's not the worst thing."

"I'm glad for that, anyway. What is the worst thing?"

"I kissed you back."

"I know. And I'm grateful."

She stifled a smile. "It can't ever happen again, Joe."

"Not ever?" he asked, his voice softening on the last word.

Her eyes popped open at the blatant invitation in those two small words. Actually, at the cardiac arrhythmia inspired by that invitation.

She swallowed hard. Swallowed that flicker of hope, that lick of desire, that slither of panic that sprang up at the easy confidence in his voice. "Not until the project is over," she replied slowly. *Not until I come clean. Not until you know who it is you're kissing.*

"Much better idea."

"I'm serious, Joe. I don't get involved with clients. It's my cardinal rule and I just broke it." *Oh, brother.* "Not that we're involved," she said hastily. "I didn't mean to imply—"

"I know what you meant. I have a similar rule and I just broke it for both of us. Will it make you feel any better if I say that I feel terrible?"

She didn't have time to squelch her grin. "No, because I think you'd be lying."

"Not entirely," he said, not making any effort to conceal his amusement or his insincerity. "Let me make it up to you by giving you a no-strings trip up to Connecticut. If you want a rationale, think about how fiscally responsible the decision is. Your client will be impressed that you're going to save the project thirty-six cents a mile times just under three hundred miles each way. Including tolls, that's probably at least three hundred dollars, round trip. Which, considering your final bill will be somewhere around one hundred thousand dollars, is, you know, almost significant. And think about the time you'll save. Our little jet will get us there in well under an hour. That's time we can spend discussing the project in absolute security, and you'll have a few extra hours to get organized. Time is money, Naomi."

Rolling her eyes, she tried to turn her smile into a frown.

"Okay," he continued when she didn't respond. "All banter aside, we both know I shouldn't have kissed you. But I did. We're both adults, we're both professionals, and you're going to be working for me in a few hours."

"I'm already working for you."

"True, but once you're in Connecticut, Mr. Nice Guy disappears. I'm a total bastard at the office. Everyone says so."

"I know. Sarah told me."

"You're very direct," he said after a split-second pause.

She sighed. "It's one of my flaws."

"I like it. So, have I persuaded you, or do I have to keep arguing my case? Keep in mind that it's one of the things I've been trained to do. And I usually win."

She smiled and leaned back against her pillows. "Okay, Joe. Against my better judgment, I surrender. By the way, I have a cat."

Joe stared down at the cage Naomi was holding. "That's not a cat. That's an overgrown cotton ball. It looks like a Tribble."

Naomi smiled and lifted the small cage higher so he could see into it. Tiny green eyes stared back at him without blinking. "She's a miniature Persian. The mother of a woman at the office raises them and is trying to get them recognized as a breed."

"How old is she?"

"A little over three months. I've only had her for about two weeks, but so far she hasn't been any trouble."

"Is she supposed to be?"

"I don't really know. I've never had a cat before. We were dog people. And everyone I've spoken to says that kittens generally look cute and behave like devil spawn." She glanced up at him. "I wouldn't call her angelic, but she's sweet."

So are you. He forced a smile and turned away, ostensibly to pick up one of her suitcases but really to roll his eyes and give himself a mental kick in the ass. *Not sweet. Not again.* "I'll take these two down and come back up for the other one."

This could be a mistake. He wasn't really sure why he'd been so intent on having her fly up with him. He'd actually called just to make sure she was okay with how last night had ended, to make sure she wasn't entertaining any notions of—any notions of *anything*. But from the minute she answered the phone she'd been self-assured and so adamant about pretending it hadn't happened, or at least that it hadn't been great, that he was hell-bent on proving the same to her. Proving that he could avoid temptation, too. And that's why he'd put temptation right into each of their paths. By the time she'd showed him her cat, he could tell she'd gotten over her reluctance to join him, but the easy banter they'd enjoyed the night before was long gone.

So was the relaxed attitude and everything that went with it. Last night, she'd gone from being as glamorous as any movie star to being about as unvarnished as a woman could get. No makeup, no shoes; just a T-shirt and shorts. He wasn't sure which look he preferred—she was beautiful both ways—but he'd take either one over what she'd done to herself this morning.

She was back to all business in a pair of nondescript khakis with a pressed shirt and navy blazer that effectively neutralized her figure and toned down her looks. He may not ever have realized what she was hiding if she hadn't worn that dress last night.

Jesus H. Christ. How it had stayed up was something that he still couldn't figure out. But what kept chewing at his brain was how and, more importantly why, she hid her figure at this age. She wasn't an awkward teenager now; she was a stunning and self-assured woman, yet she routinely and effectively hid her attributes. Most really built women he knew flaunted it; after all, the majority of them had paid for the privilege. Hell, half the sixty-year-old women at the opera last night had been sporting well-exposed breasts that were smoother, perkier, and less mature than the Champagne they'd been drinking.

He walked back into her living room, picked up the remaining suitcase and her laptop case, then met her eyes with a pointed look. "You go do whatever last-minute checking you have to do. I have a rule about turning around after six blocks to make sure the iron is off."

Her eyebrows rose slightly and, if he wasn't mistaken, so did her chin. "What's the rule?"

"I don't stop."

"What if it's been left on?"

"That's what fire departments and home owner's insurance are for."

She bit the inside of her lip, not quite hiding a smile. "The iron is off, Joe. Don't forget who you're talking to and how much you're paying me not to forget things." She paused. "Or are you saying that I seem like the forgetful type?"

"That's a loaded question and I'm not answering it. I just thought it was fair to warn you. Are you ready?"

"For almost anything," she replied, and motioned for him to go out the front door ahead of her.

Naomi stood in the living room of the condo, letting the silence enfold her and absorbing the slightly unreal aspect of the day so far. The project so far.

She was inside the company, inside the very secure perimeter of Brennan Shipping Industries. Legally. And poised to hack it.

If she didn't sit down soon, her knees were going to give out.

She walked over to the couch and sank onto it, ignoring, for the moment, Smoke's plaintive mewling. Leaning back, she closed her eyes and took a deep breath that she released slowly.

The flight up to Stamford had been thankfully uneventful. After making sure she had everything she needed, Joe had booted up his laptop and spent the whole flight working. Naomi had eventually relaxed and done the same, glad that their interaction was limited to the occasional under-the-breath murmuring endemic among computer users. When they'd landed at the private-plane area of the airport in Westchester, he'd driven her directly to the high-rise condo in downtown Stamford.

He'd taken a few minutes to point out some things on the skyline, like the Brennan Building in one direction, and the Long Island Sound and Long Island beyond it in the other. In an attempt to conclude their time spent together, he informed her that a car would be dropped off tomorrow morning and the keys would be left with the concierge; one of his assistants had arranged it. They were saved from any awkward silences by a phone call that he had to take, and he left her.

It's time for a reality check.

If Joe knew, or even suspected, that she was the one who had brought his company to its knees twenty years ago, he'd have let her know—immediately, and the experience wouldn't have been pleasant. No matter how talented an actor he might be, nonchalance like his couldn't be faked. He was too black-and-white; his world had too many absolutes in it. Deception—no, make that anything other than the whole truth—would not be tolerated. His reaction to Senator Birk was enough to assure her of that. There's no way she'd ever want him looking at her with that same icy anger in his eyes, she thought with a shudder. And if he knew what she'd done, who she was, that would only be the beginning.

But she couldn't quite accept the probability that he, and the rest of his family, for that matter, might *not* know that she was the one. It was entirely too naïve. He had to have researched the case; as one of the corporation's lawyers, he'd have full access to the records. And despite what she'd been told, she had never really believed that her name had been removed from the court documents. No system was that thorough.

She opened her eyes. Her decision not to confess to him in her office yesterday afternoon was the right one. Of course, trying to anticipate when a possible ambush might occur would be stressful, but being prepared was better than being surprised. And at the moment, preparing was all she could do. She pushed herself off the couch.

Bringing one of her suitcases into the large master bedroom, Naomi decided that her home-away-from-home had to be at least three times the size of her apartment in the District. There were spectacular views from the kitchen, living room, dining room, and all three bedrooms. The roomy interior study was decorated in such a way that the lack of windows went virtually unnoticed.

All of the rooms were homey and cozy and luxurious at the same time. Everything about the space and its furnishings, from the art on the walls, which was obviously original, to the glassware in the cabinets, which was obviously crystal, was understated. She wasn't as surprised by it as she might have been had she not had the chance to meet Mary Casey and see her home. *This must be how the Brennan family operates. They wield their power and wealth subtly, but they don't pretend it isn't there.*

Joe wielded his sex appeal the same way.

It was all there for anyone to see, but he didn't flaunt it. Not much, anyway, she thought, shaking out her clothes and distributing them in the walk-in closet. He was a guy, after all, and she was under no illusions. He knew exactly how potent his looks were. Anyone as handsome as he had to be aware of it. He was big, broad, and blond: three things that would make nearly any woman with a pulse sit up and take notice. And then there was the matter of his pedigree.

But he had even more than that going for him. He was smart and funny and had a smile that could melt the strongest resolve. She knew about that firsthand.

But.

She opened the second suitcase and brought the kitten-related supplies into the all-marble bathroom. *But,* she repeated to herself sternly, although she'd obviously noticed Joe's looks and succumbed once to his somewhat sporadic charm, she couldn't let this dangerous game continue. It was a mark of professionalism—of simple maturity, really—to assert self-control and maintain a reasonable degree of self-discipline. And that word *reasonable* was the key.

She wouldn't be able to focus on the project, run her team, and hack her way into his systems if she let her hormones rule her head. Nor would she be able to reveal her identity to him with any shred of credibility unless she behaved like the professional she was. She had to be relaxed, cool, and unflappable, especially when it came to situations that were less than businesslike.

Basically, she had to be more like him: controlled and compartmentalized. He could obviously resist her; he made it clear that it had been his *choice* not to resist her last night. And, granted, she told herself, it had been her choice to respond to him, to let him kiss her. Not that she could even imagine passing up the opportunity, but still, she'd had a choice.

She stored the two empty suitcases in the closet and opened the third and last one, which contained the personal stash she always brought with her on extended trips: the Chanel No. 19 bath salts and Rigaud candles; the heating pad and the massaging foot bath; and the care package her mother had just sent: Duke's Mayonnaise, MoonPies, GooGoo Clusters, Luzianne tea bags, and homemade cheese straws. Sometimes, they were the only things that made life on the road bearable.

Not that she would have trouble with being away from home on this trip, she thought as she carried her goodies into the kitchen. This was the kind of place she could get used to. The kitchen looked like it belonged in the pages of *Veranda* and the rest of the condo looked like it was straight out of a furniture showroom's catalog. Nope, staying here wasn't going to be a hardship.

Getting me to leave—now, that might be a problem.

CHAPTER

14

"You put her up in the condo? I thought they were all going to be staying at the Marriott."

Joe watched Chas hang onto his squirming eight-month-old son as the child fought determinedly, and loudly, to be let down. "You want a straitjacket for him?"

"He'll settle down in a minute. How did the condo enter the situation?"

Shrugging, Joe took a long swig from his can of Diet Coke and leaned against the counter in his mother's kitchen. "I offered it to her. She's going to be here for a few weeks, and after the first week, the rest of her team will be gone. I thought she'd be more comfortable there. No one else is going to be using it."

"And you flew her up here?"

Joe nodded, not even tempted to get defensive, because he knew there was nothing to get defensive about. He'd extended the same professional courtesies to Naomi that the company extended to VIPs all the time. It was no big deal. At all.

"Do you not see the beginning of a trend here?" Chas asked, shifting the towheaded dynamo to his other arm.

"There's no trend," Joe replied flatly.

"Perhaps you didn't see this morning's *Washington Post,* but the rest of the world did. There was an article in the arts section about the opera last night. It was accompanied by a few pictures. One was a shot of Cooper Townsend talking with the president. You and Naomi provided a nice backdrop. That was some dress she had on."

Okay. Maybe there's something to get a little defensive about. But he still wasn't going to give Chas the satisfaction of seeing it happen. "It certainly was. I doubt the picture did it justice."

Chas finally caved in and set Web on the floor, where he promptly wobbled to a four-point, arse-up stance, then rose to his feet. After a minute of standing there weaving like a drunken sailor, he crashed headfirst into the legs of the kitchen table. Chas picked him up again, and over the heartbreaking, ear-shattering wails, nuzzled his downy head with comforting murmurs about boo-boos.

When the screaming subsided into slurpy, shuddering breaths and a renewed battle for liberty, Chas looked at Joe. "Tell me again why she was at the opera with you?"

Not bothering to hide his annoyance, Joe crossed the room to toss his soda can into the recycling bin. "I asked her to join me. For business purposes. You know how I feel about that sort of stuff. I didn't want to go alone and it turns out that she loves opera. Besides, she's very well connected—"

"She's also very well built," Chas pointed out.

The comment rankled, and Joe shot his brother a cold look that needed no explanation. Chas silently raised an eyebrow in response.

"She went to high school with one of Tommy Birk's daughters, and Missy Standish was her mother's bridesmaid. Her father used to manage procurement for a satellite research and development group at the Pentagon, and now he's running an entire division down at Marshall. He still plays golf with half of the Senate Appropriations Committee." He folded his arms across his chest and leaned against the counter again. "She's more than just a pretty face, Chas. She's a political gold mine, and she's a hell of a sharp security guru. When she was outlining her attack strategy, it damned near blew me out of the water. Not that I told her that, but if we can withstand the attack, I'll be surprised."

"Her credentials aren't in question—"

"Good."

"It's your motives that I don't trust. There's no way any man with a pulse could be near a woman like her, who's wearing a dress like that one, and not get a little"—Chas paused to choose his word—"forgetful."

No shit. "Well, I hate to break it to you, but there is one and you're looking at him," he lied in a convincingly droll tone. "It was a business event."

"Whatever you say. The rest of her team is arriving tomorrow?"

Joe nodded. "Today and tomorrow. The software guys are going to get their command center set up on the fourth floor, and the security team will get going on the standard security audit stuff Sunday night."

Chas frowned. "Standard? As opposed to what?"

"She wants to sweep for bugs on Monday night."

"What? That wasn't part of the—"

"I know it wasn't," Joe interrupted, glad the topic had finally shifted. "But in the course of that last meeting, she mentioned that she wants to do an electronic sweep."

"She thinks we're being bugged? Does she realize this is only a war game and not the real thing?"

Joe shot his brother a grin and shook his head. "Chas, this is what I keep trying to tell you. It's both. I was a little surprised, too, when she suggested it, but it makes sense. We've been hacked really badly twice; once from the outside and once from the inside. We don't know where the next attack will come from, we just know there *will be* a next one. I know you had a meeting with the finance guys yesterday, and I can just imagine what they were whining about. 'Big capital outlay with no measurable return on investment.' Yada yada yada. I'm half-tempted to tell her to attack the accounting system first, just to make them shut the fuck up." He let out an annoyed breath. "I get the same shit from the R and D guys, except they're moaning about security measures interfering with collaboration software. And the IT guys are bitching about safeguards slowing down the system. I understand the money end, Chas, and I understand that if security is too heavy it can impede business as much as it protects it. It's a fine line and I'm trying my damnedest to stay on it. Having the offices swept for eavesdropping equipment is the least of my worries. I've given her the go-ahead for that."

Chas met his eyes and shrugged. "Okay. How long will that take?"

"I'm not sure. She can tell you at the kickoff meeting on Monday. You're going to be there, right?"

Chas nodded and turned to grab the diaper bag off the counter while maintaining his grip on his squirming, roaring son. "Look, I've got to get this guy home. He needs food and I'm not equipped. Is she renting a car, or are you loaning her one of yours?"

Get over it. "Trudy arranged to have one dropped off tomorrow."

Chas swiveled to look at him. "She's in the condo and doesn't have a car? Joe, do you realize that there isn't a grocery store within ten blocks of her? There's a Starbucks and a 7-Eleven. Is she supposed to live on biscotti and Mountain Dew until tomorrow afternoon?"

Joe blinked at him. "Never occurred to me."

"Christ. Bring her over for dinner tonight. We're throwing some steaks on the grill. Miranda will be thrilled to meet someone else who talks funny," he said over his shoulder as he walked out the door.

Naomi hurriedly swallowed the mouthful of Moon Pie— *dinner*—before pressing the TALK button on her cell phone. Southerners never spoke with their mouths full. Especially to clients. "Hello?"

"Hi. It's Joe. Have you settled in?"

She kept her voice friendly, but didn't let herself smile. Not in front of an audience. "Hi. Yes, I have. It's just wonderful. Thank you again."

"Good." He paused for a second. "I realized that I left you there with no food and no idea where to find any," Joe began. "It was a pretty drastic oversight on my part, so I thought I'd make it up to you by taking you to dinner."

She winced and deliberately didn't make eye contact with any of the four people gathered in the living room, who were openly watching her. "Thank you, but I've already taken care of it. Half the team is here, actually, and we're just hashing over the possibility of getting things underway tonight instead of waiting until tomorrow."

The surprised silence lasted for only a few seconds. "Okay."

"Can we get into the building?"

"Everything's ready for you. There shouldn't be any reason why you can't. If there's any hassle, have security give me a call."

The tightness in his voice made her pause. *Now* she smiled. "Would you like to join us?"

Another small silence confirmed her suspicions.

He's jealous. Okay, maybe *envious* was the better word. It wasn't the first time she'd encountered this reaction. In fact, it was common among executives who'd risen out of the ranks of the techies: She was in the field leading a chase he wasn't allowed to join. By default, he was a bystander now, despite how much he might want to join in and get his hands dirty.

"No. You guys are the pros," he said eventually, and she knew they weren't easy words for him to utter. "If I'm there it will only raise questions in the minds of the security guards."

"That's a good point," she said, hoping she didn't

sound soothing or insincere, but knowing she could be accused of both. "I think we're going to head over there now and just see the lay of the land. So I'll see you at the kickoff meeting tomorrow morning."

"Right."

"Good night."

She ended the call and looked at the four faces that were alight with prospect of a challenge. The blood in her own veins wasn't exactly flowing calmly.

"Let the games begin," she said with a grin.

The executive-floor offices of Brennan Shipping Industries were cast in a strange blue-gray half-light articulated with stark angularities of deep shadow. The eeriness of the scene was underscored by the almost deafening white-noise hum of the building's air-conditioning system. Naomi had left Jason, the lone network guru, in their command center on the fourth floor while she took the physical security team up to the top floor. Silently, they had fanned out to the first three offices they came across and began their investigation—checking the contents of wastebaskets, opening desk drawers, and checking computers and desktops for anything that shouldn't be there.

Leaving them to their task, Naomi was heading back to the elevators to work with Jason when she decided a slight detour was in order. She continued down the corridor toward Joe's office.

The shift from the planning stage of a project to full deployment rarely went as smoothly as she intended. In a typical security audit, her teams had to hit the ground running and move fast to get an accurate snapshot of the company's security culture before anyone inside the company caught on to what they were doing. Changes to the project plan had to be made and executed at top speed; lengthy discussions and debate were never an option. That's why her research phase always included casual interviews with her client's employees in addition to top-level discussions with the executives.

Executives inevitably told her what *they* wanted her to know; employees generally told her what *she* wanted to know. Not that she relied too heavily on what anyone said; she knew better than that. People brought their biases and egos into discussions without realizing it and, frankly, people lied too easily. It wasn't always deliberate, usually just a small stretch of the truth here and there to make themselves look good. But it was enough misinformation to distort the real picture.

Despite it all, there were always nuggets to be gained from any conversation if you knew what you were looking for, which Naomi did. But she put one step in her preparation that she'd never heard the other project managers mention.

She liked to wander through the offices when no one else was around.

It was a personal quirk more than a sanctioned task, and one she kept to herself. If clients knew about it in advance, they became nervous. But her midnight strolls provided depth and coherence to the sometimes deliberately misleading picture executives presented, and revealed significant details that were so buried in mundane, everyday behaviors that they simply eluded people. Like the senior executive who kept a comprehensive travel schedule on the whiteboard in her office, and the administrative assistant who was meticulous about taking detailed telephone messages for his boss— but kept all of those messages on a spindle on his desk.

She smiled as she moved silently through the half-lit space. The average person rarely realized that such simple things could provide missing pieces of a puzzle to someone who was adept at mining information. On this project, though, her reconnaissance mission wasn't just a quirk; it was critical. In addition to all of the other unusual circumstances surrounding the Brennan Shipping project, Naomi didn't have the opportunity to get different opinions on the situation. The only people she could talk to were Mary, Joe, and Chas, and all of them had given her variations of the company line. It was all she had to work with, and it wasn't much.

She came to a stop in the open doorway of Joe's office and leaned against the doorjamb with her arms folded as she looked around. The air held the faintest trace of his presence. It was indefinable, but there.

The top of his desk was clear, the wastebasket had been emptied, and the carpet displayed the alternating nap of a recent vacuuming. The computer was silent; the monitor's screen was dark and the glowing yellow light on the front of it indicated it was in hibernation mode.

Things felt right. Safe. Secure. The room held no surprises. Not that she expected any. She hadn't *expected* anything in particular. She wasn't here for that. At the moment, she was just here to observe.

Okay, if I'm going to be completely honest, there's a bit more to it than that.

She wanted to see the space that surrounded the man, the place that he filled, his natural habitat. It was silly, she knew. Maybe even stupid, and undoubtedly the decision of a schoolgirl with a crush, or a woman with a taste for some forbidden fruit, but she didn't have to admit that to anyone. It wasn't like she was going to leave him a note written in lipstick or leave a kiss print on his monitor screen. She wasn't going to sit in his chair or look out his window or touch his stuff. She just wanted to absorb the atmosphere. To absorb him.

After a few minutes, she silently moved to the office next door, where Joe's senior assistant worked. Trudy Barker had been with the company for nearly three decades, and had worked for every top executive in the company at one time or another. She was trusted and valued, according to Joe. But he'd also described Trudy as an employee who didn't think too far outside the box. Which could mean that they didn't get along, Naomi thought with a smile, or that Joe was just being his unvarnished self.

She stopped in Trudy's doorway as she had in Joe's,

but the feeling she got was different. It struck her right away, stopped her like the palm of a prohibitive hand thumping against her chest wall. Something wasn't right. She let her gaze sweep the room.

Trudy's office wasn't any larger than Joe's, but it was configured differently. His desk was perpendicular to the door. When she asked him about it on her first visit to the offices, Joe had said that arrangement kept him from being distracted by every person who walked past. Trudy's desk, on the other hand, faced the door, although it was offset from it and centered in the middle of the room. Its placement brought a frown to Naomi's face. Trudy had the same huge windows in her office that Joe had in his. It didn't seem right that someone would keep her back to such a great view.

Maybe passersby are less of a distraction than a bird's-eye view of downtown Stamford.

It didn't feel like the right answer. Joe had described Trudy as friendly but someone who maintained her distance; she did her work well but lived her life solidly outside the office.

Naomi remained in the doorway, chewing on the inside of her cheek, bothered by something she couldn't discern.

Maybe she's afraid of heights.

No, that doesn't work, either. If she were afraid of heights, she'd be in an interior office.

She continued scanning the nondescript room. A vase of fresh flowers was centered behind the desk chair, set on a low credenza that ran the length of the room. A large mirror hung between the windows, above the flowers. It reflected the wooden, floor-to-ceiling bookcases opposite the desk and was wide enough that Naomi could see herself in it as she leaned in the doorway.

"Okay, let's take a different approach," she said softly. "Why would someone prefer to face the door and her bookcases? It enables her to see what's going on beyond her office. No one can sneak up on her or walk in without being seen."

Was she paranoid? Naomi narrowed her eyes. Okay, so nobody could get in without being seen—but there was no reason anyone would want to enter the office, anyway. Trudy couldn't hold a meeting in there, even a small one. She didn't have any chairs, despite having plenty of room for them. It was completely at odds with every other office she'd glanced into on her way to Joe's.

Maybe she just doesn't like people.

It was the closest fit, especially given Joe's comments. Her office was so orderly and clean that it was completely uninviting. The flowers provided the only warmth and color. Just a few personal knickknacks stood on the credenza—nothing that would inspire a question or a conversation. The desk held a flat-screen monitor and two framed photographs. Nothing else. Not even a speck of dust. Its surface shone like a mirror.

It could easily be the office of an antisocial, unimaginative control freak, Naomi decided. Who else would polish her desk before she left on Friday night? Joe's desk had been clean, with a few streaky wipe marks as evidence that the cleaners hadn't been slacking off. Those same cleaners hadn't touched Trudy's desk, though, or if they had, they'd paid a lot more attention to what they were doing.

She stood there for another moment, bothered by something she couldn't name and couldn't see, and then moved to the next office, which was full of personal items to the point of being cluttered. It fairly shouted "soccer mom." A small table and two chairs stood in the far corner. Stuffed animals and school pictures of young, redheaded children lined the credenza. The walls were a warm peach, accented with framed watercolor florals. Company awards scaled the narrow strip between the windows, which were covered by the same narrow-slatted blinds that were standard in every office.

Nothing going on here. She smiled and kept walking.

When she'd finished her perusal of all the executive floor offices, Naomi found herself back in Trudy's doorway.

The space was just so bland. It was as dull and uninspiring as any office she'd ever seen, which was even more remarkable when compared to all of the other offices on the floor.

Clearly, there was a standard policy that allowed personal decorating. Some offices held rich furnishings that were as nice as what stood in Joe's office. Other occupants had gone in more contemporary directions, or had just indulged themselves in random clutter like Trudy's neighbor. Someone at the far end of the hall had gone so far as to paint two walls hot pink and the opposing walls acid green. How she—or he—could get any work done in such a space was open to speculation, but in Naomi's mind, it only served to underscore the unusual drabness of Trudy Barker's office.

She took a deep, thoughtful breath. The woman had been with the company for nearly thirty years. She'd been on the executive floor for the last twenty. Surely in that time anyone would have tired of the institutional dun-colored walls and windows that were unadorned except for thin, off-white aluminum blinds. Anyone, apparently, except Trudy.

Exhaling, Naomi shook her head. It would have to go on her list of questions to be raised later. Right now, she was overdue to meet with Jason to discuss some network issues, and then maybe she'd get a chance to hit the keyboard and have a little fun.

As she turned to leave Trudy's office, the blinking lights of a distant airplane appeared within the dark frame of the right-hand window, and the sight of it made her snap to attention.

It's not practical. She stood frozen in the doorway, looking around at the same furnishings she'd just been studying, but seeing them as if for the first time. The placement of Trudy's desk made no sense. Her windows faced west. Keeping her back to them meant that the afternoon sun would beat through the glass, causing a glare on the computer screen that would be blinding. Closing the blinds, as Joe had done when they were in his office that first afternoon, no doubt kept the office dim and cavelike all afternoon and into the early sunlit summer evenings, but Trudy's blinds were open now. She had to have opened them before she left for the day.

The average person would wait until morning to do that.

Naomi's cell phone chirped, startling her back to the present.

"Hello?"

"Hi, it's Jason. Did you get lost? I thought you were coming back here."

"I'll be there in five minutes," she replied with a grin as she did an about-face and headed for the elevators. Trudy's taste in office design would just have to wait. There were too many other things to think about right now, like hacking her way back into the heart of Brennan Shipping.

CHAPTER
15

Tuesday morning at nine thirty, Naomi poked her head into Trudy's office and gave a small knock on the door frame. "Good morning, Trudy."

"Hello," she replied, looking up with a generic smile on her sweet face, which warmed when she saw who was addressing her. "Oh, Naomi. Good morning. Are you all settled in?"

"Yes, ma'am."

"The condo is okay? And the car?"

"Yes, ma'am. Thank you for setting everything up."

"Oh, you're welcome. What can I do for you?"

Naomi slipped into the room and came to a casual stop next to Trudy's desk. "I really hate to bother you and all, but I was wondering if Joe was available for a few minutes this morning? I don't need much time. His door is shut right now or I'd ask him myself."

Trudy looked back to her monitor and made a few movements and clicks with her mouse, then glanced back at Naomi over the frames of her bright blue reading glasses. "He's on a conference call at the moment, which is scheduled to go until ten. He has a little bit of time right after that. Shall I tell him to call you?"

"No. I'll wander back in a little while. Thanks, Trudy."

"You're welcome. Any time."

Naomi walked away pretty certain that Trudy's eyes were following her down the hall. She kept her back straight and her gait relaxed. The last thing she wanted to do was appear tense in front of the woman. Especially in light of what she'd learned from the electronic sweep last night.

Frankie, the gadget wizard they'd brought in to sweep the offices, had been at it all night, and her quick recap of the high points had been waiting in Naomi's e-mail in-box when she logged on this morning. If Naomi had had the slightest clue what it contained, she would have made sure she was fully awake and not drinking a hot beverage when she opened it. The mess hadn't been pretty.

Joe made a habit of not keeping his e-mail application up while he was on the phone. The very thought that he'd be off-line for the duration of a conference call drove people crazy, but frankly, it bugged the shit out of him when people sat through meetings, typing away on their PDAs or laptops when they were supposed to be paying attention. Not that anyone dared do that during any of his meetings. If they answered a question with a vague answer that indicated they weren't paying attention, he nailed them to the wall and let them squirm. Nearly everyone had done it once. There weren't too many people left who'd done it more than that.

Unfortunately, there was a downside to this hard-ass policy of his. Every time he got off the phone, he had thirty or forty e-mails waiting for him, and this morning was no different.

He opened the one from Chas first. He could count on Chas to be brief.

Lunch? 12:00 at Tiernan's w/ Gruber & Pellegrini

was all it contained.

No, he typed, and then hit SEND. He was heading to his boat for lunch, as he did most days. Ordinarily, it was just his idea of the best spot in town, but lately it had become his sanity check. It was about the only place he could go without someone from the office tracking him down. While he was on dry land, he felt compelled to keep his Blackberry on and within reach; on his boat, the first thing he did was turn the damned thing off.

He skipped over the next ten e-mails, then saw the one from Naomi, which had been sent as a high-priority, high-sensitivity message ten minutes ago.

Please call me when you're free.

He picked up the phone and dialed her extension.

"Naomi Connor," she said crisply.

"I'm free. What's up?"

"I was wondering if you might have time to go out for a quick coffee?"

Coffee? A whole string of completely valid reasons why he couldn't go sprang to mind, but instead of uttering any of them, he just blinked and tried to keep his incredulity out of his voice. "Sure," he said tightly. "Is Starbucks okay? There's one next door."

"Sounds good."

They didn't make any small talk when they met near the elevator. He gave a few curt nods and murmured one or two greetings to the people they encountered; Naomi tried harder, with cheerful hellos and bright smiles.

As if that will convince anyone that what we're doing is standard ops. Speculation of any type was exactly what this project didn't need. He refrained from shaking his head. Had she somehow forgotten that little imperative called discretion? *Christ.*

Word that he had left the building in the middle of the morning with the pretty new face on the executive floor would rifle through the ranks before they hit the sidewalk, and the news was bound to generate undo interest about Naomi and her role. The concern surrounding his social life wasn't anything new; it had been a hot topic on the company grapevines up here and in Washington since he came on board.

He knew the men just monitored the situation, but the women were both more subtle and more active. The married ones were trying to marry him off, and the unmarried ones tended to try to get in line, generally by being a little too accommodating when he needed something. It still hadn't sunk in for a lot of them that that particular queue didn't lead into his social orbit or his bed. Nor would it ever.

He didn't get involved with people from work. Period. It was a rule he'd set for himself very early, while he was in college and working at the company during the summers. In all these years, he'd only bumped up against it once, in Naomi's apartment a few nights ago. It had never been a problem—up 'til now—but he fully admitted that the rule was part of the reason he was such a hard-ass at work: It kept women at a distance. The other part of the reason was that it was just his way of doing things. Chas was the diplomat; he was the general. It had always been that way.

"Okay, what's up?" he asked, holding his unsweetened latte with an extra shot of espresso, as he watched her stir another packet of turbinado sugar into her milky iced coffee.

She reached for a tall straw and smiled up at him. "Let's take a walk."

Knock off the fucking games. I've got sixteen high-priced corporate lawyers sitting with their thumbs up their asses while I watch those painted fingernails of yours twiddle your coffee stirrer. "We just took a walk," he pointed out with deliberate patience. "I'm a little pressed for time this morning, Naomi."

"Then let's take the long way back," she said. Ordinarily, her smile never faltered, but for the first time, that smile didn't make it anywhere near her eyes. *That* got his attention, as did the edge in her voice and the fact that she had just turned on her heel and ventured back into the stifling heat of Stamford in July. He had no choice but to follow her, intrigued, still annoyed, and trying very hard to keep his gaze locked on the back of her head and not the very sexy high-heeled sway of her hips.

She was waiting for him when he came through the doors, and they began walking in the direction opposite the Brennan Building.

"We did the electronic sweep last night. Just a few offices. Yours, your mother's, and Chas's. And all of the relevant assistants," she said quietly after swallowing a small sip taken through her straw.

He frowned. It sounded like she was looking for something instead of just looking. Chas's comment echoed in his head. "Why did you check out the assistants' offices?"

"Sometimes the best way to find something is via an indirect route. Your assistants probably have access to a lot of your information, right? Your network drives, maybe certain e-mail accounts, a few passwords."

"Okay."

She swallowed another sip of her drink and looked up at him, her clear blue eyes bright with excitement held in check. It was an expression he wouldn't mind seeing under other circumstances, but under these, it could only mean one thing. He lifted his drink to his mouth and looked away, hoping his gut was feeding his brain bad information.

"We found something. I need to know if it's authorized surveillance or not. Because if it isn't, these may not be war games after all, Joe. It might be the real thing."

Not again. His heart stopped for a split second and so did his feet. Two steps later she realized he was no longer next to her, and she stopped and turned around. Everything inside him was clenched, his nerves over-wound and nearly vibrating with tension. He trained his eyes on her. "There is no authorized surveillance going on beyond what I told you about. The elevators, the file tracking; that stuff. There's nothing targeted," he replied in a low voice, then stopped to take a slow, deliberate breath. "What did you find?"

She studied his face as she took another sip through her straw, then swallowed daintily. "Trudy has a nanny cam set up in her office."

"What? My Trudy? Trudy *Barker*?" Joe knew his disbelief was obvious. He didn't care. *No way. The woman doesn't have the imagination or the drive to—* "What do you mean, a nanny cam?"

"Yes, Trudy Barker," she said calmly. "I think it's best if we keep walking, Joe." She retraced her steps to his side, then slid her hand around his forearm and gave him a little tug.

He let her set him in motion along Tresser Boulevard, the air thick with bus fumes and summer heat. Somewhere in the back of his mind, he registered the contrast of her cool hand as it displaced the clamminess of his skin.

"By *nanny cam,* I mean a concealed video camera with a fixed footprint."

"I know what they are," he snapped, wishing he could have a solid minute of silence to clear his head and let some of the adrenaline in his blood dissipate. "Tell me what you found in her office."

"I will, but let's keep moving. Once around the block ought to do it." She paused and looked at him. "You don't look so good, Joe. On second thought, maybe we should sit down somewhere."

As she studied him, she let go of his arm. He might have been imagining it, but there seemed to be some reluctance to the gesture.

Stay on point. He rubbed his hand over his face. "No. I'm fine. Just start from the beginning."

"Frankie came in last night to sweep for electronic

surveillance devices. She's former NSA. Very thorough. She runs checks for everything: motion detectors, microwaves, lasers, parabolic eavesdropping equipment, electronic trip wires, spread spectrum, pulsed and burst transmitters—just about every device on every available transmission frequency there is. Basically, if it can transmit or receive through a wall, a window, a doorknob, or from a key chain in someone's pocket across the street, she'll find it." As she spoke, she kept her eyes moving over the people surging around them. "Of the seven offices she swept, Trudy's was the only one that registered anything."

"How did she find it?"

"She picked up its frequency."

"No, I mean, did she see it? Was she caught on the tape?"

"No. She sent in a robot—"

"She what?" he demanded, torn between disbelief and irritation. *Robots?*

"I should have suggested that you get decaf," she said, glancing up at him with a small smile that faded as rapidly as it had appeared. She resumed watching the crowd they were part of. "The robot isn't a big one. It's just a little thing that I devised. It's about the size of a child's toy truck—"

"*You* created a *robot*?" He couldn't help himself; couldn't keep the envy or the disbelief out of his voice, or the incredulity out of his expression.

The annoyed glance she snapped in his direction was gone in an instant, replaced by a brittle and utterly false serenity. "Should I be flattered by that question?" she asked with a little too much whipped cream in her voice.

Great. "I'm sorry. Please go on," he said stiffly and took a too-large sip of his coffee, which scalded the back of his throat. He refused to start choking in front of her, though. It would be too symbolic.

"Yes, I created a robot. It's nothing fancy. I'll show it to you later if you'd like." She cleared her throat.

"Anyway, it moves along the perimeter of a room and scouts for frequencies. When it crossed in front of the bookcase, it picked something up. Frankie got the electronic signature, then went back to Jason—"

"Which one is he again?"

"Jason is one of our network guys. They pulled in a few of the others to define the signature and type it, and they eventually found it." She paused and stepped out of the flow of traffic, coming to a stop close to the granite front of a neighboring building. He followed, standing to the side of her, blocking her view of oncoming pedestrians. Blocking their view of her.

Her gaze locked on his. The excitement was back in her eyes, but tempered now with a gravity he'd not seen before. "This is no rookie effort, Joe," she said in a voice so low it was almost a whisper. "It's not your basic cheap videotape recorder. It's digital. It constantly films an area that covers her desk and the space immediately surrounding it. The footprint is about a sixty-degree arc that covers an area from the floor in front of her desk to about two feet below the ceiling and about three feet on either side of her desk. Nothing can get near the desk without being seen."

"Anything else?"

"It's a cable feed, thank goodness. Wireless would be much harder to track. Of course, it would have been harder to hide, too. Anyway." She brushed away that tangent of the conversation with a quick wave of her hand and took another sip of her drink. "We haven't found out where it's going yet. We put some sniffers in place to see if we can trail it, and I won't tell you how, but we managed to put a data line tap on the actual cable so we could see what it's uploading." She paused and her eyes seemed to get darker and more intense. "Whoever planted it didn't just go to Circuit City and pick up the no-name brand spy cam, Joe. They bought the best. The camera and peripherals alone set someone back at least a thousand dollars."

"Peripherals? Do you mean audio?" *What next?*

"No. There's no audio feed. I meant the cable and the connection. The images are very high resolution, and they're traversing a very high-speed conduit either to a computer inside the company or to an outside line; we're not sure which. Yet." She gave a small shrug. "I have to say that I'm impressed. It's an elegant little setup."

"Okay, let's stop for a minute so I make sure I've got this straight." He braced his legs as if he were expecting a body check, folding his arms across his chest. "She blew a thousand dollars on a camera that's just recording footage of her desk?"

"And the windows behind it."

"That makes no sense. For sixteen hours a day she's filming an empty office, and for the other eight she's filming herself working?"

"Or someone else is filming her."

Her calm words chilled him to the bone. *Keep moving.* Looping one hand around her elbow, he propelled them both forward again. With the other hand, he lifted his cup to his mouth. After sucking down the last of his coffee, he threw the cup in the trash can outside the convenience store they were passing.

"I told you there's no authorized surveillance underway," he said tightly.

"Joe, if you don't mind, could we slow down? I'm in high heels and my legs are only half as long as yours."

"I'm sorry," he said, slowing down immediately and managing to give her a smile that was mostly contrition and very little mirth. She was flushed from the heat, and their pace had left her slightly out of breath. And more than a little gorgeous. It took a lot not to let his eyes slide south, gravity of the situation notwithstanding.

"Thank you. I know you said nothing has been authorized. That leaves us with the ugly truth that whatever is going on in her office is unauthorized."

"It could be harmless."

She glanced at him with raised eyebrows, her surprise edged with doubt. "It could be," she agreed carefully, but her tone indicated she was treating him like a typical client. Translated from consultant-speak, that meant as if he were utterly clueless.

"But harmless or not," she continued, "We have to find out where the information is going. That will give us a clue as to who put the spy cam there."

"What does the unit look like?"

She shook her head as she took another sip. "We won't know until we can actually get in and find it. We only know the technical specs based on the output. I'm going to try to get in and talk to her tomorrow and see if I can do some open snooping. Anything covert is out of the question because we'd end up on the tape and that would tip our hand."

"You're already on tape," he pointed out.

"Just standing in the doorway. It's not like I was snooping through her stuff. The rest of the team never made it that far, so—"

"What about the robot?"

"It's only four inches high, so it was out of range. We stayed well out of the way when we sent it in and we swept the area outside her office before we set foot near it."

He felt himself start to frown and knew it didn't have to do with anything that could be described as professional or mature. He shook it off. "Good thinking. So, what next?"

She glanced up at him. "I'm not exactly sure. I was hoping you could help since you've known her for years. Can you give me any insight? She's not exactly warm and fuzzy, and her office seems deliberately not conducive to hanging out."

"My mother is coming into town tomorrow. Talk to her. She knows Trudy better than I do. Look, I'll go in and look around. It will be less suspicious."

She paused so long that he turned to look at her.

She was looking straight ahead as they walked, her expression carefully blank. "I think that's a bad idea."

Like hell it is. It's my company and she's my assistant. He let his courtroom face fall into place. "Why?"

"Do you ordinarily go into her office?" she asked, still not looking up at him.

"No, but I can. I'm her boss. I don't need a reason to change my operating procedure."

Now she looked at him. She didn't seem impressed. "If she's the one who put the camera there, it will look suspicious, Joe."

"Why?" he asked again.

"Well, first she sees me standing in her doorway, and a few days later you're in there out of the blue, poking around on her bookshelves. You might as well just send her a memo."

"I can go in without making her suspicious. I'm a lawyer. We're trained to be part actor and part liar," he said, putting as much finality in his voice as he could.

He suspected that if he hadn't been her client, the look that appeared on her face would have been partnered with a roll of her eyes. "Well, I appreciate your candor and your willingness to help, but it's not an option," she said with polite firmness. "*I'm* going to do it. I can go in to discuss something like your schedule or whatnot, and be a typical female who's interested in all the stuff on her bookshelves." Before he could even open his mouth to argue, she paused and actually did roll her eyes. "I'm blond and Southern, Joe. If need be, I can go in and act like a fluffy little sugar-covered marshmallow ditz. I've done it before."

He tried not to smile. "I have a hard time believing you'd get away with that."

The corner of her mouth twitched provocatively as she sent him a sidelong glance. "Believe it. Men fall for it all the time. The challenge would be convincing a woman. We see through each other. But I could pull it off. She's a Yankee after all, and y'all think we're a bit crazy, anyway."

I'm not touching that one. "I have to discuss some things with her later today. We could just as easily have the meeting in her office instead of mine."

"You're not listening to me, Joe. Besides, she doesn't have any chairs for visitors."

"I'm listening. I'm just not agreeing with you. And the lack of chairs is a plus. If I have to stand, I'll be able to pace. Tell me what I should look for."

She let out a resigned sigh and shook her head slightly. "Look for a shiny black dot. It might not be any larger than a pinhole, and it could be on anything," she said wryly. "They're almost impossible to detect unless you're looking for them, and an obvious hunt will appear to be exactly that to whoever watches the tape." She shrugged. "I've seen surveillance cameras built into the spines of hardcover books and videotape cases, the eyes of stuffed animals, the stems of fake plants, exit signs, pencil sharpeners, wall clocks, alarm clocks, the base of a lamp, the top of a pen, a picture frame, a necklace—you name it. I've even seen them built into air purifiers."

"Air purifiers?"

"And the air purifier part actually works." She took a slow breath. "Those are only the devices that I've seen, Joe. Whoever had this one installed could have had something custom made. I'm just thanking my lucky stars they didn't opt to go wireless. Then we'd have a real time of it."

Christ. "You're saying that we don't know what to look for except that it has a cable coming out the back of it?"

She nodded. "Chances are the cable will be concealed somehow. I think the only way we'll be able to find it is to wire me when I go into the office. One of my guys will watch the tape and tell me when I'm in front of it and when I make eye contact with it."

He stared at her without speaking for a moment, mostly because he didn't know what to say. *I'm trapped in a fucking spy movie. Or some warped reality TV show.*

She glanced up at him. "Are you okay?"

"I'm fine," he replied curtly. "You didn't find anything anywhere else?"

"In terms of electronic surveillance, this is all we've discovered. The physical security team has finished checking the open areas and found the usual: people turning their monitors off but leaving their computers on, leaving CDs stacked on their desks, not locking their drawers. So far only one person had a list of passwords lying around. She was very clever, though. She taped them to the bottom of her mousepad instead of across the front of her monitor." She finished the litany with a short laugh. Its soft silkiness was too effective at getting him off track.

"I'm glad you find it amusing. I happen not to," he snapped, and couldn't help but feel like an ass—again— when she looked at him with eyes that held the merest shadow of hurt surprise.

"I'm sorry, Joe. I didn't mean to imply that I take this project or our findings lightly. I don't." She paused for a split second. "The physical team is going to start on the closed areas tonight and that shouldn't take too long. They're planning to leave town tomorrow. I should have their report in a few days. The attack-and-pen team has been giving it their all and they haven't gotten into the networks yet, so they'll keep trying. They'll probably be done by the weekend. Based on our findings in Trudy's office, though, I'm going to have Frankie stay in town for a few more days."

"Sounds good. Anything else? I don't want to discuss this inside the building," he said as they approached the main entrance to the building. Naomi shook her head.

Cool air rushed to surround them when he opened the door, and they crossed the nearly empty lobby in silence.

*   *   *

"Well that was fun," Naomi said under her breath as she walked into the office they'd assigned her, on the opposite side of the building from Joe. Sitting down in her chair, she swiveled to face the window, then leaned back and closed her eyes.

The instant bliss afforded by the position felt altogether too good. She'd been operating on about three hours of sleep for the past few days. Friday night had been late due to the opera, and sleepless due to lust. Every night since then had been sleepless due to her workload. And the niggling fear of discovery that was at war with her situation-dependent desire to confess. And lust.

Okay. So Joe was wandering in and out of her dreams as much as he was wandering in and out of her presence during the day. He was a big part of her life right—no, she corrected herself, he was a big part of her *work life* right now. Real life had nothing to do with work. Real life was what you did after work and before work and on weekends and lunch hours.

She opened one eye and glanced at her watch. *Lunch sounds good.* She'd been up since five thirty, reviewing Frankie's notes and incorporating them into the report she was putting together. And she didn't really care that it was only ten forty-five in the morning. At this point lunch sounded absolutely fabulous. These damned Yankees might think that bagels and cream cheese were the Chosen Food that had saved mankind and could, therefore, be consumed at any time of day, but she knew better. It was time for some *real* food. Southern food. She stood up, grabbed her purse, and headed for the door.

She made it as far as the bank of elevators. Then she ran into Joe.

"You're heading out?" he asked, giving her a quick, neutral once-over, as if he hadn't seen her yet today.

"As a matter of fact, I am," she replied, glancing away

with a tight smile. *Take that, Mr. "I Don't Find That Amusing." Mr. "You Created A Robot?"* That one had stung.

She focused on the lit arrow that pointed downward. It suited her mood.

"Where are you going?"

Oh, no. I am so not in the mood to be near you. "I've been up since dawn, so I'm going home for an early lunch."

"Home? So you found the grocery store?"

She looked up at him, lured by the amusement in his voice, knowing she'd see it reflected in his expression. "It found me. There was a brochure for something called Peapod.com in one of the kitchen drawers."

He gave a low laugh that sent a lush tremor through an unguarded part of her brain, and she really couldn't suppress it. There was just something about him that pulled her in tight.

That's why she relented, just a little, and smiled back. "I think I died and went to heaven. I spent ten minutes online Sunday morning, and there was a whole kitchen full of food waiting for me when I got back to the condo last night."

The doors slid open and four people stepped out, mumbling greetings at Joe and sending curious glances in her direction.

Just what this project needs—more gossip, she thought with a mental grimace. *So much for his requirement of discretion at all costs.*

When the elevator was empty, the two of them stepped into it, swiped their ID cards, and directed the car to the lobby. When the doors closed, Joe looked down at her.

"You caught me with my pants down this morning. I'm sorry."

She turned to look at him, feeling her eyes widen. *"I what?"*

He laughed, and the sound of it sent more of those

shivers through her, the ones that made body parts prickle and tense. Parts she didn't particularly want prickly or tense. Not now, anyway.

"Wrong choice of words. I've always wanted to mess around with robotics and have never had the time. Between that and your other news, you took me by surprise. I've recovered, and if you don't have firm plans for lunch, would you join me?"

An immediate *Yes, thank you* was the right answer. He was her client. She was a professional that he was paying to be at his beck and call, and they had things to discuss.

But *Thank you, no* was the honest answer. He was a nice guy, a beautiful man, and she was terribly attracted to him. But at the moment, she was also tired, crabby, and in need of some solitude and down time. And real food.

Upbringing won out over attitude, though. She met his eyes and managed to brighten her smile. "Thank you, Joe. That would be nice."

CHAPTER
16

While she wasn't sure if it actually clashed, Naomi was dead certain that blaze orange didn't really complement her outfit or her coloring.

She glanced down again at the life vest she had strapped around herself. Perhaps merely telling Joe that she wasn't a boat person would have been the wiser thing to do, instead of smiling and going along with his plans. After all, she was a professional; it wasn't in her contract that she had to like boats, and she wasn't particularly interested in being labeled a "sport" again.

Of course, now that she'd put herself in this situation, she was in danger of being labeled a total weenie, which was worse, from a career standpoint, than being a sport.

She looked over at Joe, who by this time had abandoned all propriety and was openly laughing at her. All blond hair, white teeth, and dark glasses, he looked entirely too good while he did it, too.

"I swear to you, Naomi, you really don't have to wear the life jacket. The sound is as still as glass, there isn't more than a breeze in the forecast, and I've been a lifeguard since I was twelve. If an unexpected microsquall capsizes us or sweeps you over the side, I'll save you."

"You'd better," she said with the shadow of a grin,

even if it was forced. "My mother would never forgive me if they found me floating facedown, dressed like this."

She saw him do a quick head-to-toe sweep, then look away with a stifled grin.

It was a first, as far as business luncheons went. For one thing, she'd never before considered how different a business suit looked with bare feet. Now she knew.

Her shoes and nylons were tucked in a tidy stack beneath her purse on the bed in the forward cabin. Her shoes—coral-colored slingbacks with insets of teal lizard, which matched her suit—hadn't lasted thirty seconds after boarding. Or attempting to.

Her slim skirt hadn't allowed her the step it took to go from the dock to the deck, so Joe had to lift her. And then he'd had to hang on to her because the minute she set foot on the polished deck, she started to tilt and flail in all directions.

Walking around flat-footed in nylons hadn't helped her gain any stability or balance; she'd just started to slide and ended up back in his arms. He'd admitted then—they were both laughing at that point—that inviting her for lunch on his boat wasn't one of his better ideas. Of course, that provided him with a natural opening to suggest going back into the yacht club and having lunch on the big awning-covered deck. She, trying to be not quite so girly, had dismissed the idea a little too convincingly; that's when Joe had told her to sit down and hold on.

He'd proceeded to throw off the ropes that kept the sailboat in place against the dock, and fire up the engine. They hadn't gone far. Just a little ways into the marina, away from all the other boats. It was a pretty day and being out on the water was pleasant, but that wasn't uppermost in Naomi's mind. Nor was the situation with Trudy, or the audit team's findings, or the attack team's efforts.

No. What mattered to her at that precise moment, out

on the water, in Joe's boat, was that she had to walk back into the office in approximately one hour.

Lots of people had seen them leave the building together today. Twice. Only this time when she came back her hair would be a tousled disaster, her suit would be wrinkled beyond recognition, and her nose would be sunburned.

Discretion was one thing that wasn't happening on this project.

And Joe, bless his heart, was oblivious. Or setting the stage to force a confession. The sweat trickling between her breasts felt cold all of a sudden, and she shook off the thought.

Stop it. He couldn't know who she was. The law of probability was against it. Besides, no one was that good an actor, despite all his big talk about his lawyer training.

And after this morning's conversation, she told herself firmly, it no longer mattered if he discovered her identity the wrong way, or even if he already knew who she was. She was at least halfway in the clear: She'd found a security breach, a big one. Maybe even a serious one. That would certainly serve to mitigate his anger.

She brought her eyes up to look at him. He wore the same soft, medium blue golf shirt he'd been wearing all morning, but he'd exchanged his khaki trousers for a pair of khaki shorts as soon as he'd cut the engine. He'd returned on deck with two icy cans of Diet Coke, a pair of sandwiches he'd fixed in the small galley, and a large bag of salt-and-vinegar potato chips that they were sharing.

Lazily draped against the railing opposite her, one long, lean, bare foot on the deck, the other propped on the bench he was sitting on, Joe was clearly enjoying his lunch, the weather, and the rhythm of the water that was gently rocking his world.

The light breeze rippled his hair and gently molded

his shirt to his chest. Not that he cared, or even noticed, but from Naomi's vantage point, it was a sight that was hard to ignore. He reached to the deck to pick up his drink, then tilted his head back and took a long pull from it, his throat moving in a way Naomi had seen throats move on other men a million times. But this was Joe's throat, and the smooth motion did things to her.

He was profiled against the sun and she could see from the side that, despite his sunglasses, he had his eyes shut tight against the glare. It was an opportunity too good to squander, so she let her eyes roam.

The sun-bleached gold of his hair nearly sparkled in the brightness, and a few thin slashes of white striped his strong, corded, deeply tanned neck. Two hundred years ago, they might have been mistaken for the scars of a pirate lucky to have escaped with his life, but today they just assured her that he was no sunbather. He got his color on the water, aboard the *Presumed Innocent*.

She wasn't ready when he swung his head to face her.

"So, is it boats you don't like, or ham sandwiches?" Had he not been smiling, the question would have stung.

"I'm sorry, Joe. You must think I'm terribly rude—"

"Hey, I may not be the most tactful guy around, but I'm not that crass. It was a question, not a comment. And you're not being rude." He swung his other foot onto the cushioned bench, then wrapped his arms loosely around his knees. "I didn't give you much of an option to back out of having lunch here and I didn't ask you if you wanted a sandwich before I handed you one. You've gone quiet, so I figured it was one or the other." He paused. "Unless it's the combination. Are you getting seasick?"

A smile slipped onto her face. "No. My stomach is fine. The sandwich is fine, too, Joe."

"So it's the boat." This time it wasn't a question.

The boat was a pretty little thing with a dark, polished wood deck and bright blue pads with white piping, which sat atop the benches along the perimeter. Highly polished brass hardware glistened in the sun. "No, it's not the boat, either."

"That leaves . . . me? Are you still annoyed that I want to search Trudy's office?"

She squelched an inappropriate laugh and tried not to pay attention to how good he looked, how at ease he was, even when cross-examining her. "Of course it's not you, but we do have a few more things to discuss." She paused, took a deep breath, and met his eyes. "It's the water, Joe. I don't really like being on the water. I should have said something."

He looked at her as if she could not have said anything more startling, and she realized right then that she'd been wrong the other night.

This, not the office, was Joe's natural habitat. The office was just where he worked. Out here, on the water, on his boat—this was where his soul lived. And she'd just dismissed it.

"You don't like being on the water?" he repeated incredulously. "You're the first person I've ever heard say that. Why not?"

Torn between feeling sheepish and defensive and not wanting to be either, she finally just shrugged. "For the most part, I grew up in a landlocked area. There were a few shallow creeks and the odd pond nearby. We weren't too far from the gulf, but we didn't get there much. The closest I came to dealing with boats was a little rowboat that my cousins used for fishing."

"You didn't like it?"

"I didn't get much of a chance to form an opinion. For one thing, I was a girl, and they didn't like having me along. Then one time when I was six, I finally pitched a hissy fit, and Nana made them take me."

"Only once?"

She nodded. "They rowed a few feet from shore, then pushed me overboard."

"And?"

"I don't swim."

His forehead creased with incomprehension. "You mean 'didn't.' At that time. You do now, though."

That wasn't a question, either.

She shook her head slowly. "I didn't at that time and I don't now."

He unclasped his arms, swung his legs to the floor, and leaned forward slowly, with his brow furrowed and his head cocked toward her as if he hadn't heard her correctly. "You can't swim?" he repeated.

She nodded and took another bite of her sandwich, hoping that by the time she stopped chewing, he'd have changed the topic.

But the rough-hewn gentleman in him had reappeared, and he pushed his sunglasses into his hair and waited patiently for her to finish. "Why not?"

"I'd rather not get into it."

"Well, okay, but did getting pushed in make you afraid of the water? Or of boats? I mean, is that why you're wearing the vest?" His tone held the rugged softness of well-worn corduroy, and his eyes were full of more concern than curiosity. All in all, Joe Casey was melting her resolve faster than the sun was melting her mascara.

But.

While his interest was kind of sweet, it was still not going to get her to tell him anything personal. They were business associates. And he was a man. There was *no way* she was telling him the swimming story.

She sat up a bit straighter and brushed some stray hairs out of her eyes. "No. I'm not afraid, I just never learned how to swim. I don't mean I'd sink like a stone if I fell in. I can keep myself afloat. I just mean that I don't really swim. I've never been the type to hang out poolside or anything like that. I don't even own a swimsuit." She paused. "It's just not my thing."

"Why didn't you say something? We could have had lunch in the clubhouse."

She met his eyes and couldn't keep a straight face as she debated the wisdom of telling him the truth. "Actually, Joe, I didn't say anything because I didn't want you to think I was a wuss."

After a moment he started to laugh. "A *wuss*? For God's sake, Naomi, you build robots and work with former NSA spies and know more about software than I ever will. I'd love to ask you what you do for fun, except that I'm afraid the answer will be something like disarming nuclear warheads."

Feeling rather smug and pleased at the implied compliments, she smiled and took another bite of her sandwich. "So, what's the story behind the name of this boat?"

Being rendered speechless by a beautiful woman three times in one morning was a new experience for Joe.

The situation with Trudy was just sort of unreal, and he'd prefer to get to the bottom of it. And the robotics thing was—well, it was just genius envy, frankly. He sat behind a desk and dealt with lawyers while she got to build robots and hack computer systems. He wouldn't mind playing with toys all day instead of toying with legalities.

But her latest declaration was nothing short of unbelievable. How could anyone not like being on the water? And how could anyone reach their thirties without learning how to swim? He couldn't comprehend either one.

According to his mother, their father had put each one of them in the pool before they were a year old. Of the three siblings, only Joe hadn't cried. Apparently, he'd laughed. And he'd loved the water ever since, becoming one of the youngest kids on the country club swim team and learning how to sail well before he got his driver's license.

"I'm sorry, Naomi. What did you just ask me?"

With a smile, she pushed those errant curls out of her

eyes again and made another attempt to take a sip of her soda. "I asked you about the name of this boat."

"*Presumed Innocent*? It's just a lawyer joke."

"Does it apply to you and your motives for bringing me here?"

Without a smile, her question would have been obnoxious; if she'd been flirting, it would have been an invitation to trouble. As it was, he didn't quite know what to make of it.

"I come out here almost everyday just for a quick break from the office, the phone, the e-mails, and the bullshit. Just to get some peace and sea air and sunshine. I suppose people might wonder what I'm up to, but I don't think anyone actually knows where I go when I leave the office. Other than Chas and my mother. And I don't have any motives for bringing you out here, innocent or otherwise. You were heading out for lunch and so was I." He put his sunglasses back on and took another sip from his soda.

It was the truth. He'd set out for his usual solitary lunch on his boat, but when he'd seen Naomi standing there in front of the elevator, looking beautiful and downright mutinous, he'd figured that he'd ruined her day, so he'd try to make it up to her. He'd issued the invitation on an impulse. There wasn't any motive for it beyond wanting to show her. . . . He looked away from her and into the sun as the truth hit him between the eyes.

He did have a motive.

He'd brought her out here because he'd wanted her to see his boat.

He'd wanted her to *like* his boat.

But she didn't—which left him a little bit crushed in an uncomfortably adolescent way.

He looked back at her. Her painted toes were curled into the deck as if she was trying to find something to hang on to, and the grip she had on her sandwich plate was turning her knuckles white.

"I didn't mean to offend you, Joe. I was trying to be lighthearted, but the truth is, I'm a little confused. I mean, we're not talking business, and we've got a lot of business to discuss," she pointed out in a voice that had gone a bit softer than it had been a minute ago.

Absolutely fucking great. She was expecting me to hit on her. "That's because we're having lunch and I don't discuss business over meals," he said, trying to keep the coolness out of his voice.

A look of mild embarassment passed over her face. "That's right. You told me about your policy that night we went out for a drink. I forgot about it."

Why did she have to be so decorative? Even in that ridiculous life vest? He glanced back to the horizon. "Don't worry about it. And it's a family policy. My mother refused to have the dinner table conversation dominated by business when we were growing up, and now it's just automatic. It makes sense, though. You need a break from it. At least I do."

"Who would have talked about business at the dinner table?"

"My mother and grandparents," he replied, turning to look at her again.

"Y'all lived together? In the house I was in?"

He shrugged. "It was the sensible thing to do. She had three little kids and they had a big, empty house. She had built-in babysitters, and we grew up with three parents."

Gingerly, she leaned against the railing. She didn't look comfortable, but she wasn't complaining. "Has your mother always worked at the company?"

That's a new one. After a quick glance at his watch, he stood up and took her plate from her, stacked it on his own, and walked down the four short steps to the galley, talking over his shoulder. "When we were little, she didn't formally work. She and my grandmother handled a lot of the social things for the company. The business entertaining, I suppose you'd call it. A few years after Julie started grade school, Mom started work-ing full-time doing different things. Human Resources, some legislative issues. Marketing. About twelve years ago, my grandfather stepped down from being president and CEO, which he'd been for most of my lifetime, and my mother took over. He remained chairman of the board, but he retired from that position a few months ago and my mother took over. I'll be right back."

Talking about his family with outsiders was something he'd never been comfortable doing. And while he wasn't annoyed by her questions, he wondered why she wanted to know. He quickly washed the dishes and wiped things down and then changed back into his office clothes, half hoping she'd be on a different topic when he returned.

She wasn't.

"Is that when Chas took her spot as president and CEO?"

"Yes," he said, walking to the cockpit.

"How do y'all get away with that?"

He looked at her. "Excuse me? Get away with what?"

"I'm sorry. That came out all wrong," she said, a flush rising to her cheeks. "What I meant was that you're a publicly traded company. How do you keep everything so close to the family?"

"Between our family, the board of directors, and the employees, we own most of the stock," he replied.

"Oh," she said, surprised. "That's handy."

He looked straight at her and, for effect, lifted his sunglasses to ensure direct eye contact. "We think so."

He started the engine and pushed forward gently on the throttle, then swung the boat slowly back toward the dock.

They were quiet for the short trip back, but Joe knew the conversation hadn't ended. He maneuvered the boat into its slip, cut the engine, and walked over to grab the ropes. It must have been her cue.

"How did Chas end up marrying a Southerner?"

He smothered a laugh. *If she's this tenacious with her*

testing, we're in good hands. "She's a writer and she was doing some research on cops. She interviewed him."

"Sounds providential."

He glanced at her out of the corner of his eye. "There were some twists and turns."

"What kind of things does she write?"

"Romance novels."

Her eyes lit up and she smiled at him. "No kidding?"

"No kidding," he replied, and held out his hand.

Joe helped her off the boat, steadied her, and even held her purse while she put on her shoes, then proceeded to practically carry her across the docks when her legs refused to acknowledge she was back on stable ground. It was awfully nice of him, considering that she'd inadvertently insulted him at least twice, and then hadn't been able to stop herself from asking a lot of nosy questions about his family.

He'd been a gentleman about it all, though. She'd just blundered on and he'd let her, only showing his irritation by making his answers shorter and shorter, rather than by changing the subject or something more blatant. He seemed to be over it, though, which was good because the day so far had left her exhausted. She didn't want to go another round with Joe Casey.

They were nearly at his car when she felt her heel come down onto a pebble, but didn't have time to prevent the wobble it caused.

"Are you okay?" His arm shot around her shoulders again. Under almost any other circumstances, she would have welcomed it. Right now, she just wanted to move steadily under her own power for a few yards if for no other reason than to maintain Joe's antiwuss perception.

She glanced up at him after a breathy laugh. "Do you realize how many times we've asked each other that since we've met? Anybody overhearing us would have to wonder what we keep doing to each other."

He didn't answer, but she saw one burnished eyebrow quirk upward just a little.

Joe brought the Jeep to a stop in the semicirclular drive-way in front of the condominium's resident entrance and turned to look at her. "Here you go."

She put her hand on the door release, then met his eyes. "Thank you. I'll be working from here for the af-ternoon and will be back at the office at about five. Will I see you, or are you heading out before then?"

"I'll be there. I've got a conference call with some guys out in Long Beach that doesn't start until then, so I should be around for a while."

She paused. "Do you have a minute to come upstairs, Joe? There's something that I was going to bring up on the boat but I sidetracked myself. I'd rather not discuss it here, if you don't mind, and I'd rather not wait until I see you at the office later."

He froze, different organs interpreting her soft request in remarkably different ways. "Okay. For a minute."

They were both quiet in the elevator and when they entered her condo. The cat came streaking around the couch and leaped at her. Naomi caught the little ball of fur to her chest and took a few steps into the living room, then turned to face him.

"We need to talk."

Shit. Those words in that tone of voice could only mean one thing: The conversation was going to get per-sonal.

But not if he could help it. No matter how memorable or inappropriate it had been, he was *not* going to let one kiss that happened several nights ago suck him into ver-bal quicksand. "I have a conference call at one thirty, Naomi. Are you sure it can't wait?" *Forever?*

"I'm pretty sure, Joe. I hate to push things, but we need to face the facts and come to a decision," she said quietly.

Christ almighty. A decision? He turned to face her fully and fought the urge to fold his arms across his chest. That would send the wrong message, and it was critical that this message—*there is no relationship; this is a very mild flirtation at best*—came across loud and clear and unmistakable. So just as he had in front of juries, he let his body language say everything he wouldn't. Face impassive, legs braced, car keys flipping idly around a finger, his posture implied boredom and his gesture indicated mild impatience. The conversation, he knew, would be brief.

"We need to come to a decision about what?" he asked.

"The situation with Trudy."

That's one bullet dodged. He stopped flipping the keys and leaned against the molding that surrounded the doorway between the foyer and the living room. "What about it?"

"Obviously, it has me very concerned, so I want to run something past you. Frankie floated an idea to me last night and I dismissed it at first, but I've changed my mind."

"What's that?"

"I'd like her to sweep your car and, now that I know you have one, your boat. I'd also like you to get a new cell phone."

He frowned. "Do really think that's going to turn up something? I mean, right off the bat it seems sort of extreme, Naomi."

She didn't even blink. "Maybe it is, but I've rubbed up against wiretapping and covert surveillance before, and there's something just not right about this. Why would someone want to watch Trudy other than to get to you? I think you're the target."

The word made the back of his neck prickle. "Target of what?"

"Industrial espionage, for one thing. But it could be something else." She lifted a shoulder. "Blackmail?"

Now he folded his arms across his chest and stared
down at her. "Okay, the first threat you could persuade
me to believe. The second? No way. There's nothing
that anyone can use against me, for any purpose. No
booze, porn, debt, drug, or gambling problems. No pa-
ternity suits or bribes. No secret sex tapes, no oddball
perversions, no criminal behavior."

Two heartbeats later, she went into what he presumed
was battle mode. She folded her own arms across her
chest as the kitten sat comfortably on her shoulder and
swatted at her hair. "Fine. We'll eliminate blackmail as
a motive for the moment and stick with industrial espionage." Her voice didn't sound as tired as it had a minute
ago. "I don't know how much you happen to know
about it, so let me assure you that it happens all the
time. The motives are usually economic, the opportunities are innumerable, the means truly range from the
ridiculous to the sublime."

She continued after a momentary but significant
pause. "Tactics range from having somebody cozy up to
a critical target at a cocktail party or after-hours hang-
out, to bribing people on office cleaning crews to steal
information that's left lying around the office, to hiring
professional Dumpster divers to do exactly what it
sounds like they do, to installing electronic surveillance
equipment. I'm willing to bet we're facing more than
just the last scenario, Joe. Whoever set this up had to
plan it: They had to plan what equipment to buy, how
and where to place it and connect it, when to install it,
and how to monitor it. They made a reasonable investment in hardware, and the configuration demonstrates
some serious know-how." She paused again, her voice
dropping, her eyes turning dark as sapphires and just as
cool. "Tell me what they're looking for, Joe."

He allowed himself a few quick blinks to break the
mesmerizing effect she was having on him. "Naomi, I
realize that you take your job very seriously, and I know
that you're an expert—"

"Don't patronize me," she snapped, and he actually felt himself recoil at the unfamiliar heat in her voice.

"I'm not patronizing you. But aren't you jumping to conclusions? Shouldn't we find out who *they* are first? That's what you suggested this morning."

"I've been thinking." She said it as if that explained everything.

He let out a controlled breath. "When? We were apart for ten minutes before we ran into each other at the elevators. We've been together for over an hour."

She unfolded her arms and stood up a bit straighter.

"I can think and talk at the same time, Joe," she said softly, causing him to wince at her deliberately patronizing words.

I probably deserve it.

"It's called multitasking, and I'm awfully good at it," she continued. "It's why you hired me and why you're paying me so much money, so you just might want to listen up." She paused and took a deliberate breath. "I've been in your offices for three solid nights. Y'all leave your office doors open."

"That's for the cleaning crew. And that's why the physical side of the audit is so impor—"

"I know that," she interrupted again, and he allowed his eyebrows to shoot up this time, just to remind her who was footing the bill for her rudeness.

Either she didn't notice or she didn't care, and either way, Joe was a little impressed.

"That's not why I mentioned it," she continued, and paused to give him a very businesslike, very serious look. "What I want to know is where do y'all—you, your mother, Chas, and your assistants—work on classified material? You rarely close your doors when you're in your offices, and I don't see any safes in your offices, anyway. Is there some special closed area back there that you haven't told me about? Do you have hidden safes in your offices? Behind false panels or something?

Because if you do and you're leaving your doors open,
that's big trouble. On the other hand, I can't really imagine you trooping over to the closed areas that I know
about every time you need to look at—"

Joe slowly held up a hand and Naomi stopped talking
in midsentence, bracing herself to hear the worst.

"Okay. You win." He shrugged in an unconvincing
display of surrender that sent a flame of anger shooting
through her.

*I believe I need a new strategy for dealing with you,
honey. It's time to take off the businesslike gloves and
show a little less restraint.*

Looking him straight in the eye, she took a step closer
to him, then another until she could smell the sunblock
and sea air that clung to him.

"I *win*?" she repeated in disbelief. "Perhaps I've mis-
understood things all along, Joe. Is this a contest? Just
what did I *win*?"

He took a deep breath and clearly wished he were
somewhere else. "Bad choice of words. I apologize. No,
it's not a contest, and what I'm about to tell you wasn't
left out of our discussions on purpose. We don't talk
about it, ever, so it was an unfortunate but critical omis-
sion that I didn't realize until you just brought it up."

She kept her mouth shut and her hands unclenched,
but she was sure he could feel the fury pouring off her.

"There's a room we call the bubble that's only accessi-
ble from our three offices. It's like the secure rooms in
embassies, basically a glass room inside a lead box. The
floor is mounted on springs and there's a constant stream
of white noise generated around it if anyone is inside.
It's off-limits to everyone but the three of us. The assistants don't know about it, and they don't have access
to it."

She felt her lips tighten as his words registered, and
counted to ten before responding. She divided the time

between trying to ignore the almost unbearable irony of her situation and choosing her words carefully in anticipation of the day they would come back to haunt her.

"Why, thank you for letting me in on the secret, Joe," she said in a voice deliberately soft and just as deliberately cold. "It's a little late in the game for surprises, but since we're on the subject, there's something *I* need to tell *you*. And if I'm not being crystal clear, you be sure to let me know." She paused. "Joe, I need to understand the full scope of the situation. I've got security clearances up to my eyeballs, and can get a few more if it will make you more comfortable telling me anything." She paused again. "Make that *everything*. I won't even question your statement about why the information about the bubble was withheld, Joe, but let me just tell you this: I need you to come clean right now. If you're holding back *anything* from me, you've got me operating in the dark. And that means you are wasting a sinful amount of money to watch me run a half-assed project that isn't going to help you one bit."

He remained silent even though she'd stopped talking. Of course, she made it pretty obvious that she wasn't finished.

After a moment's silence, she took a deep breath. "None of the assistants know about the bubble?"

"That's right."

"Not even Trudy?"

"No."

She watched him for another minute, and he watched her back with that lawyer face in place.

"Why not?" she asked finally. "How did it get built? Where does she think you go when you're in there?"

He shrugged and began flipping the keys around his finger again. "We renovated the entire floor about ten years ago and put it in then. We've updated it a little, but didn't make any dramatic changes. And I just close the office door and tell her I'm on a conference call or whatever and don't want to be disturbed. It's never been an issue, as far as I know."

"When can my team get into it?"

"I'll show it to you tonight." He paused, as if he was going to ask her something, then stopped. A few seconds later, he met her eyes again. "Do you think someone is after something specific?"

She let a silence build. "I've been asking myself all kinds of questions, Joe," she said slowly. "And I haven't even made it far enough to ask that one. I don't have any idea if there is a somebody, and if there is, if he wants anything, and if so, what that thing might be. That's a lot of ifs, and I don't generally like ifs. I like cold, hard facts, not speculation or guessing games."

"What do you need from me to get past the questions to some answers?"

She paused again and took another step closer to him, and had to tilt her head back a little farther to maintain eye contact.

"What I really need right now, Joe," she said in a soft and deadly serious voice, "is for you to tell me what you haven't told me. And then I need you to step aside and let me do my job."

Naomi was absolutely beautiful, standing there with windblown hair and sunburned cheeks, a wrinkled suit, and grave, angry eyes. One hand was cupping the kitten against her chest while the other stroked its head. Its purr practically echoed in the silent space. The only other sound was the crackle of the air around her as she stared him down.

"Boats," Joe said.

"How many?"

"The one you were on today is the one I usually keep in Washington. I had someone sail it up here yesterday for some repairs. I have another one I keep up here. I'll bring Frankie out to both of them tonight."

She nodded without smiling and took a step back, then another. She broke eye contact when she set the kitten on the floor, then she straightened up. "Thank you, Joe. I'll have her go through your car while you're on that conference call tonight. When you get back to the office, send me an e-mail and tell me where you've parked it."

"I will." He paused. "Anything else?"

"Not at the moment."

"See you later." He left the condo with a curt nod. It was either that or abandon all pretense of a business relationship and spend the afternoon in bed with her. Spies or no spies.

CHAPTER
17

"Chin up, shoulders back," Naomi whispered to herself as she walked toward Mary Casey's open office door. More than forty-eight hours had passed since they found the spy cam in Trudy's office, but they were no closer to finding out where the information was being sent. They hadn't found any other clues or glaring problems, either. Sweeping Joe's cars and boats had turned up nothing, and the attack-and-pen team had just about finished their assault on the networks. It was approaching a critical time frame.

The rest of the team would be gone soon, even Frankie, and this was nothing Naomi could cope with on her own. If she didn't get a break soon, she would either have to reassemble the team, which wouldn't do much for her chances of getting a partnership, or contact the authorities, which wouldn't do anything to ingratiate her with the Casey family and their stockholders. Not that she was looking for that result, she assured herself a little too hastily.

Before she could even lift her hand to knock on the door frame, Mary looked up and smiled, inviting her in with a warm greeting.

Closing the door behind her, Naomi sat down in a

wing chair opposite her desk. "Thank you for agreeing to see me on such short notice. I won't take much of your time."

"It's yours to take," Mary replied easily, with a smile that was altogether too much like Joe's to be reassuring. "From what I hear, you're working nearly around the clock. How are things going?"

"They're going well, for the most part. Every violation found during the physical audit was on the minor side. A good talking-to should eliminate most of them." Naomi realized she was fiddling with her ring, and pulled her hands apart to drape them casually over the arms of the chair. It wouldn't do to appear tense. Not when she actually was so tense. "In the closed areas, the biggest problem is that the daily documentation for the safes isn't being completed. You know, the time-in, time-out, and lock-up sheets. Again, that's something that can be dealt with in a memo or during a staff meeting. I'll be finishing that report a bit later today, and you should have it in hand tomorrow."

"Sounds good. So what can I do for you today?"

Cleanse my soul, but we'll get to that later. "Ma'am, I need to talk to you about Trudy Barker."

Mary nodded. "Joe mentioned that you found a closed-circuit camera in her office. Have you found out where the information is going?"

"Not yet, which is cause for concern at this point, but not cause for alarm. It's a very strange setup, which is making me more curious by the moment. That we still can't find the end point is not a good thing. But what flummoxes me just as much is why it's in her office at all. I'm hoping you can give me some insight into her."

"Have you seen her personnel file?"

"I've seen everything about her that's stored digitally," she admitted, hoping Mary wouldn't ask her *how* she happened to see it. Of course, since Joe had given her "God rights" to the networks, her tiptoeing through the files wasn't illegal. The question of whether it was ethical just wasn't quite as easy to answer.

"Digitally," Mary repeated, then settled back into her chair with a knowing grin.

Naomi had to fight to keep a similar one off her own face, but she was not going to let herself be drawn into any conspiratorial confidences with the chairwoman of the board, even if she was Joe's mother.

"What would you like to know?"

Naomi settled into her chair and met Mary's eyes. "At the risk of sounding too forward, ma'am, I'd like to know everything there is to know, relevant or not. Let me start by telling you my observations and then, if you wouldn't mind, you can fill in the blanks." Naomi paused. At Mary's nod, she continued. "I know she's been with the company a long time and she's both trusted and highly valued. That also means she has access to a lot of things, and has had for a long time. At one time or another over the last two decades, she's worked for almost every senior executive here at the corporate headquarters."

Mary's mouth tightened just a bit, and she clasped her hands loosely in her lap, elbows on the armrests. The slight movements were enough to let Naomi know that the subject of Trudy was not one that would be entertained for too long. She had to cut to the chase.

"No disrespect intended, but her office decor is dull and impersonal, and her personality is such that she tends to blend into the background somewhat, yet I wouldn't call her shy. Joe seems to think she's not much of a creative thinker, but has told me that she's extremely competent and well organized." Knowing she may have pushed it too far already, she paused again. "I'll stop there."

Mary let a small but pointed silence build, her eyes holding Naomi's gaze with a carefully neutral expression. "Joe's assessment isn't quite accurate, Naomi. At one point, Trudy was extremely energetic and a very creative thinker. In the past few years, she's slowed down a little." Mary lifted a shoulder. "Trudy's a little bit younger than me, and she's had a harder life. She deserves to slow down. There are younger people on staff with more energy to pick up the slack. Trudy has achieved the rank of elder statesman around here, so to speak. It's well deserved." Her voice held a note of finality.

It went against everything she was brought up to do, but Naomi pursued the subject, anyway. "According to her file, she lives in Bridgeport now. Has she always?"

Mary nodded.

"That's quite a commute," Naomi suggested, watching Mary's eyes for signs of . . . anything.

"She doesn't seem to mind it."

"Why didn't she ever move to Stamford? She's been working here for a long time."

"Her parents lived in Bridgeport, and her husband's parents did, too. She wanted to stay there so her daughter could grow up near family." Mary paused as if she were going to continue, but instead just looked down at her hands.

The edge of an icy fingernail traced a thin trail of suspicion up Naomi's neck. Shrugging it off, she looked at Mary's hands and noticed the slim, elegant fingers had begun toying with her wedding ring, twisting it first one way, then the other.

Her expression had become slightly thoughtful, but she raised her eyes and met Naomi's a second later. "Naomi, Trudy is a very strong woman, and loyal. That's not to say I don't think people can change, but it would shock me to my core if Trudy is behind something that could hurt this company."

The question has been raised before. Naomi held her breath to squelch the hot match flare of irritation at the realization. "I noticed that she doesn't wear a ring. Is she married?"

"She used to be."

"Divorced?"

"Widowed."

Something in the way Mary said it told Naomi this was becoming even less of a welcome discussion topic. The certainty that it was, therefore, a critical one began to war with her sense of decency, and she let a silence build as she considered which line of questioning to pursue. As if she had a choice.

"Mrs. Casey," she began quietly, "the last thing I want to do is to cause you any distress. I'm not a trained investigator. Not when it comes to people, anyway. But may I ask you to please tell me what Trudy's history is? You hired me to do a job, and I just can't do it as well as I'd like to if I can't see the whole picture."

Mary's eyes flicked downward and came to rest on a framed picture that sat on her desk. Naomi could only see the back of it, but the frame was good-sized. It was old. It was Tiffany. And it was just a few inches from the very center of the desk. It would be in Mary's line of sight no matter what she was doing.

"Trudy's husband, Dan, was a police officer in New Haven. He was a rookie, and my husband's partner."

Mary's utter stillness and the hollowness of her voice made every muscle in Naomi's body tense. *This isn't going to be a good story.*

Mary met Naomi's eyes. "They had apprehended a suspect and Dan Barker had him pinned on the ground, ready to handcuff. He was putting his gun back in his holster when the man tried to get up. Dan lost his balance, the gun went off, and the bullet hit my husband in the chest, killing him instantly. After giving his statement and blaming himself for it, Dan went home and killed himself." She stopped for a moment, and her eyes dropped to her hands again. "I was twenty-eight years old and four months pregnant with our fourth child. Trudy was twenty and three months' pregnant with their second. We both miscarried."

Her words shredded the air between them, and Naomi closed her eyes over a heavy breath.

"I'm so sorry." An aching, immovable lump in Naomi's throat refused to allow the passage of any words beyond that harsh whisper, but Mary remained dry-eyed, and Naomi knew she couldn't do any less. She became aware that her nails were digging into the fabric on the underside of the arms of her chair, and she slowly relaxed them and brought them into her lap.

"It was an accident. A horrible, tragic accident that shattered a lot of lives in the space of less than a second." Mary paused and took a deep breath. "Trudy came from a very poor background. She was bright but barely more than a child herself. And she was taking on the blame for all of it. I couldn't let her do that." She lifted a shoulder in a gesture that forestalled any other opinion on the matter. "I set up trust funds for her and her daughter, and I put Trudy through college. After she graduated, she came and asked me for a job. She said she wanted to give back. We hired her, and she's always done everything she could for this company, as we have for her."

Mary met Naomi's eyes again. They were grave and held a certain heat that Naomi couldn't identify. It wasn't anger and it wasn't grief, but it was deep and unsettling. "I'm not going to say you're wrong to pursue every lead, Naomi, but I think you're focusing on the wrong person. Trudy has never been anything less than a perfect employee. We're her family."

Naomi nodded once and tried to find her voice amid the dense emotion filling the room. "Thank you for telling me, ma'am. I'm sorry I made you relive it."

"We all have our black moments, Naomi. But it's how we absorb them into our lives and move forward that makes us who we are. Trudy's no villain," Mary replied quietly, then took another deep breath and turned on a tired, businesslike smile. "Unfortunately, I have a scheduled call in about ten minutes and I need to review some notes beforehand. I was wondering, though, if you have no plans, whether you might want to join us for dinner

tomorrow night. Joe and Chas have mentioned the kind
of hours you're working, and I know most of your team
members are gone, so life must be getting dull or at least
quiet. Joe will be there, of course, and Chas and Miranda are coming over with the baby. A few of their
friends are coming over, too. It's casual and I would love
to have you join us."

"Thank you, ma'am. I'd be delighted," she said automatically, feeling a cool surge of admiration for this
woman who wore so many hats and wore them all with
such easy grace.

"Wonderful. I'll have Joe get you the directions."

It was her one and only window of opportunity to find
the spy cam, and Joe's demands notwithstanding, she
wasn't about to squander it. Naomi readjusted the ciga-
rette lighter–sized transmitter she'd tucked into her bra
and gently touched the tiny wireless earpiece that rested
in her ear canal. "Am I coming through?" she asked
quietly.

"Like a charm. Let's do it." Frankie's voice filled her
head and the sensation almost sent Naomi off balance.

"You have to turn down the volume, darlin'. They can
hear you in Tuscaloosa," she replied with a laugh.

"How's this?"

"Much better. Okay, here goes." Naomi pulled open
her office door and walked casually down the hall
toward Trudy's office, stopping in the doorway with a
smile designed to melt Yankee steel. "Hey, Trudy, how
are you doin'?"

The furry gray curls rose above the monitor to reveal
a smiling face and eyes that were warm behind small,
bright blue eyeglass frames. "Hi. What can I do for
you?"

Naomi moved into the room and was instantly rewarded with a low and constant buzz in her left ear. She
ignored the angry blast of adrenaline the noise inspired
and continued her task.

"I was wondering if we could talk about Joe's schedule for next week. He mentioned that he's going to be gone, but I'm going to have to meet with him at least once." She drifted farther into the room, coming to a stop in front of Trudy's desk. She'd studied the downloaded video feed and knew she was probably immediately in front of the unit, although it was probably slightly above her line of sight. Unfortunately, she was flying blind right now, because the unrelenting static was blocking out any information Frankie was trying to transmit. She was going to have to find it on her own. And figure out who had installed the white-noise machine, and when. It hadn't been there the other night.

"Let me just look at his schedule," Trudy replied, and shifted her gaze to her monitor as she began to click her mouse.

"Thank you." After a count of four rapid heartbeats, Naomi turned and wandered to the bookcase. "Oh, my goodness. Look at this. You collect turkey calls?" Naomi let out a delighted laugh. "My daddy collects these, too."

"You're the first person who has known what they are right off the bat."

"Like I said, my daddy collects them. My goodness, you have some pretty ones." Her eyes drifted from the meticulously dusted collection of ornate wooden boxes to the shelf above them. It held a small collection of books, mostly hardback, and judging from the titles, mostly related to the international shipping industry. Some were fairly old and they all looked genuine. A bronze sculpture of Neptune stood between them and the next set of books, which were off-the-shelf manuals for standard office software applications. Next to them, at the right side of the shelf, stood three tall, thick volumes that looked like law books. She slowly shifted her gaze from right to left, across the entire collection of books, making sure she stared at each spine for a count of two heartbeats. Then she turned around, stumbling face-first into Trudy's perplexed and watchful silence.

"Is there something you'd like to borrow, Naomi?" she asked calmly.

"Mercy, no. I'm sorry if I seemed nosy. I was just giving myself something to do while you checked his schedule. I read very slowly," she fibbed. Neither Naomi's stammer nor the hot blush in her cheeks was feigned. She'd never been a good liar or a very good actress, and getting caught red-handed doing anything underhanded was an occurrence she'd deliberately avoided for most of her life. The last twenty years, anyway.

Trudy was watching her, unsmiling and unconvinced, but she didn't seem terribly bothered. Naomi responded with a smile meant to charm, or at least deflect suspicion.

"I'm just always fascinated by what people keep around them in their offices. It can say a lot about them. Like that person at the end of the hall, with the wild pink-and-green walls and all the hippie art. I really want to meet him or her. I haven't seen anyone in there yet, but I'm keeping my eyes open."

Finally, Trudy seemed to buy into her babbling, because she let an answering smile drift across her mouth. It didn't quite reach her eyes. "I suppose a person's office does say a lot about them. As you can see, I like things quiet and orderly. It helps me concentrate. As far as the office at the end of the hall is concerned, don't hold your breath. That person has left the company." She glanced down at her desk console. "Joe's off the phone now, if you'd like to meet with him."

As Joe approached Naomi's office, the door was closed, which was unusual—especially since she'd just called him and asked him to come over. He knocked, only to have the door immediately pulled open by a tall, thin black woman with close-cut hair and large hoop earrings.

"Hey, Joe."

"Hi, Frankie. What's up? Trudy said Naomi was looking for me a minute ago."

"Just a minute." Frankie looked toward an area ob-
scured from Joe's view by the door. "Are you okay?"

The question caused an abrupt spike in his pulse,
which disappeared at Naomi's murmured though unin-
telligible reply. Frankie turned back to him, stepping
aside. "Come on in."

He noticed on the periphery that Frankie shut the
door behind him, but he was too busy looking at Naomi,
who stood facing him in the corner behind her desk.
Her hands were fluttering around the top button of her
silky pink blouse, and her suit jacket hung over the
back of her chair. Her eyes were huge and he had the
feeling she was on the downside of a major adrenaline rush.

"Sit down. You look like you're about to pass out,"
he said much more forcefully than required. Her looks
were alarming, though. "Do you need some water?"

Naomi sank into her chair and shook her head. "No.
I'm fine, Joe. You just caught me at an odd moment—"

"What's wrong?" he asked, folding his arms across his
chest. He wasn't in the mood for any of her delicate
Southern euphemisms. Trouble was trouble, and she
looked like big trouble.

"What's the CFR?"

He frowned at her. "What?"

She took a breath so deep it snugged her blouse across
her chest momentarily; he tried not to be distracted by it.

"Trudy has some books on her shelf that have CFR
written on their spine. What are they? Law books?"

Damn it. Either she was sneaky or she was rash, and
neither was a quality he would tolerate in someone who
worked for him. "The *Code of Federal Regulation*," he
snapped. "You went into her office? I thought we agreed
the other day—"

"Yes, I did, and I didn't agree to anything, Joe. You were just giving orders, which, by the way, I never had any intention of obeying," she interrupted in much the same tone as his. "What does volume thirty-two cover?"

There was that disconcerting fearlessness again. He blinked and decided to regroup. "It's Title 32, and it covers national defense."

"What about Title 46?"

"Shipping. Why do you need to know this?"

"I'll tell you in a minute. What about Title 47?"

I'll tell you in a minute? He glared at her. "Telecommunications."

She held his gaze without saying a word for several heartbeats. "Well, isn't that clever?" she murmured, then looked at Frankie. "It's hiding in plain sight."

"You found it?" The surge of triumph crested within him, but began an instant retreat as she swung her eyes back to meet his.

They held no such elation. Her unsmiling face was backed up by a grim nod. "That's the good news. But whoever put it in there is on to us."

"How do you know?"

"She was broadcasting subaudible white noise, and it scrambled our transmission. I couldn't hear anything but static while I was in her office."

He stared at her in disbelief as his heart came to a stop. "Is that even possible?" He looked at Frankie. "I can use my Blackberry in my office and I'm right next door."

Frankie glanced at Naomi, who gave a miniscule nod, then back at him. "It's possible, but it's not cheap and it's not easy. And that sort of equipment isn't on the shelves at RadioShack."

"It's also a problem we didn't encounter the other night."

Joe returned his eyes to Naomi, who was still behind her desk, leaning against the back of her chair, her eyes wide and blue and intense. She didn't look calm, though, and he knew instinctively that her gut was churning and her blood was running as high as his. "What now?"

She looked at Frankie. "Go. I don't want you to miss your plane. It's Friday afternoon. You'll never get on another one."

"Are you sure?"

"Positive. Thanks for sticking around this long, but I think from here on out, I can handle it. If I need you, you know I'll get in touch with you."

"Okay. You know how to reach me. Joe, it's been a pleasure."

He shook Frankie's hand and managed to say the right things until he heard the office door shut behind him and he was alone with Naomi.

"Have a seat." Her voice was slightly shaky but her hands were steady and still, folded in front of her, elbows on the armrests.

"I think I'll do that." He lowered himself into one of the chairs opposite her and met her eyes. They held a slightly wild mixture of excitement tinged with disbelief. He could understand it; he'd felt it enough times while he was at the NCIS. It was the thrill of the chase. Except that in this case, the chase was on his turf and every outcome would be damaging. How damaging was the only variable.

A thick, heavy layer of dread had coalesced at the bottom of his gut and lay there, weighing him down. It wasn't the first time in his life that he wanted a pause button, one powerful enough to stop real time.

"Does this mean what I think it means?" The words were harsh and flat. It took him a moment to recognize them as his own.

"It means a couple of things, Joe," she said in a voice that was cool and more composed than it had been a moment ago. "One, it means we're busted. Two, it means that we're dealing with someone very smart and very talented, who has a lot of money to work with, and who is very much inside this organization. And three, it means we're going to have to work fast to plug this leak. Very fast."

"You think there's a leak?"

"There has to be a leak. Either that or we're dealing with someone who has a Trudy fetish." It was a weak attempt at humor, and it sank to the bottom without either one of them attempting to save it.

"Who's we? You and me? Your team is gone," he pointed out.

"I want to bring back part of the team. The network guys."

"Why? What do you have to do?"

She gave a one-shouldered shrug. "We need to start reviewing everything. Particularly all the monitoring logs. We need to get sniffers in place on every portal. And we need to find out ASAP where that damned feed is going."

"You still don't know?"

She shook her head. "I had two guys spend two days on it, Joe. Two really, really good guys. The information is packetized according to the same protocols used by the internal system. And we've traced the packets as far as one of the servers, then they get lost in the shuffle."

He took a deep breath and pushed a hand through his hair in exasperation. "Naomi, that's not possible. It's tagged with—"

"Joe." She waited until he met her eyes. They were taking on the light of battle. "I know it's impossible. That's what makes it so frustrating. But the one thing that has become unarguably clear to me is that the people who did this are really, really good. They're pros, Joe. They're not rookies or kids playing a game. They're criminals with criminal intent, and this is war."

He allowed himself the luxury of being stunned and frozen by her words for about ten seconds. Then he leaned back in his chair and fixed his glare on her, not particularly caring if it bored right through her. She might only be the messenger, but she was within target range. "You're a pro, too. So what do we do? What will reassembling the team do? What's your plan?"

She let out a long, slow breath and sat back in her chair, leaning her head against the top edge of it. She seemed almost relaxed, as if she hadn't noticed the look on his face or the tone of his voice. "I only have one theory, and it's so far-fetched that even I can't think of how it might actually work."

"Go on."

"Well, Joe, this is not only outside the box, it's completely off the map. What if code is embedded in the pictures themselves as they're created? I mean, at the bit level, or maybe even at the pixel level. It would be completely buried. No antivirus software, no firewall would be able to detect it."

"It's been done before," he snapped.

"Then when they reach the server," she continued, ignoring his interruption, "another embedded script scans files for the code, and when it encounters a certain string, it changes the file name and redirects it to a different data stream."

He stared at her. It sounded like something out of a B movie.

Or the case study of an expert hacker. Make that *cracker*.

He breathed out slowly. "So the packet literally gets lost in the flow of traffic." It wasn't a question.

She nodded.

"How difficult would that be to do?" he asked.

"Writing it or finding it?"

"Either. Both."

She shifted her position, bringing her feet up underneath her onto the chair. Her toenails were painted a hot pink. And she wasn't wearing nylons.

Do not go there.

He blinked and refocused on what she was saying.

"—so writing it wouldn't be any more difficult than

writing any other code. Getting it in place would be tricky. Finding it could be close to impossible."

"How close?"

She met his eyes, then looked down at her nails, long and painted, and responded in a tone that was almost bored. "Like looking in a large haystack for something that might or might not resemble a needle." She looked up at him and added, "In the middle of a force-five hurricane."

"Do you think you could do it?"

"Yes."

No hesitation; not even a blink. He bit back a smile that felt curiously close to pride. "So, what do we look for first? The script? The code?"

Her shoulders rose as she took a breath. "That's just it, Joe. I don't know. I think the first thing we have to do is review the monitoring data. Start with, say, the last two weeks' worth and see if we can find some traffic pattern."

"I thought your people already did that."

"Not really. We were scanning for anomalies. I'm talking about looking for something that's so close to normal, it wouldn't be worthy of much notice."

It sounded like a nightmare.

"Give me a minute." Joe closed his eyes and rubbed them with one hand as he drummed a rhythm on the arm of the chair with the fingers of his other.

She was right. Her idea was the next best thing to crazy. She'd need a team of people to start immediately reading thousands of pages of transmission data, probably millions of lines of code, in the hope of finding something no one could identify or define until they saw it.

He'd have to be out of his mind to allow her to do it.

Depending on who their enemy was and what they wanted, and how long they had been bugging Trudy's office, this could be a situation beyond the company's—make that *his*—ability to control. Word would get out. It always got out. And when it did, it wouldn't be her team that leaked it. They got paid to keep their mouths shut.

The leak would come from an insider, and it would be inadvertent.

He let out a harsh breath. He'd have to pull in the IT department and confess all in order to get that much data transferred anywhere, and once he did that, someone would allude to it casually at lunch, or in the copy room, or during pillow talk.

That's how it would get out.

And then it would hit a blog site, which meant it would be only minutes, maybe an hour at the most, before the national press and the government would be crawling all over the company, waving microphones and subpoenas, respectively.

Wall Street would sidestep Brennan stock like it was a pile of steaming dog shit on the sidewalk, and his family and his company would end up reliving a twenty-year-old nightmare.

But this one would have happened while he was in charge, instead of on the sidelines.

He raised his head and looked at her, as sure of himself as he could possibly be at a time like this. "No."

Her eyes widened slowly, then her lips parted, but no sound came out. She swallowed once, then again, and blinked at him. "No what?"

"No team. I won't authorize it."

She shot to her feet in what had to be a purely involuntary motion. "You don't want me to do anything about this?" Though it remained at a whisper, her voice was edging toward shrill. Her eyes were spitting cold blue fire, and a dark flush was spreading upward from the opened collar of her blouse.

"Sit down," he replied coolly. "I didn't say that. Of course I want you to do something about it. That's what I'm paying you for."

"I don't want to sit down, thank you. Then what did you mean?"

"Sit down anyway. I meant that I want *you* to do something about it."

She didn't so much sit as fall into her chair as her knees seemed to give out beneath her.

"Me? *Alone*?" She stared at him. "With all due respect, Joe, have you lost your mind? Did you not hear what I just said?"

"Yes, I heard everything you just said, and no, I haven't lost anything yet, including my mind or this company," he said evenly. "And no, not alone. I'll help you."

After another long, disbelieving look, she leaned back in her chair and started to laugh. It wasn't a pretty sound.

"You?" she said when she'd stopped. Her voice was heavy with sarcasm. "When? In the twenty minutes a day that you're not busy doing your real job? Make that *two* real jobs? You work longer hours than I do, Joe."

"I doubt that. Besides, it's not like I don't know my way around software code."

"I know you do, but that's not the point." The last vestige of sardonic mirth faded from her face, leaving only frustration and disbelief. "The point is that this is not a one- or two-person job. We're talking about possibly hundreds of hours of work that have to be completed as quickly as possible. I need a *team*. One that's trained to hit the ground running. I need attack dogs, Joe."

"What am I, a show dog?" He was deliberately keeping his voice calm, but it wasn't easy. Not with that wild fire greeting him from the eyes across her desk.

"For the love of God, you're the CTO. And you're leaving town next week."

"I'll cut my trip short. I'll be gone for forty-eight hours."

She shook her head slowly. "You're just not getting it. I won't agree to this, Joe. I *can't*. If it's not downright illegal, it's certainly unethical. We're covering up a crime."

He wondered if her irony was deliberate. There was one way to find out. "Naomi, *I* am the last person on earth who would break the law, unintentionally or otherwise," he said, watching the coldness in his voice register on her face seconds before his words did. Then she recoiled as though she'd been slapped.

Squelching the guilt that rose within him, he decided he could apologize later. Right now, the insult underscored his point, so he let it stand and kept talking. "We don't know that a crime is being or has been committed. As such, we're not covering up anything. We're investigating an alleged incident."

Her eyebrows shot upward. "Alleged? This is a clear-cut case of industrial espionage, Joe—"

"Which, unfortunately, isn't always a crime, Naomi," he snapped.

She stopped talking but, to her credit, she didn't back down. A long, tense minute passed during which neither of them broke eye contact. He wasn't even sure if either of them breathed.

"Fine," she said, her voice low and aching with restrained anger. "But for the record, I want you to know that I think this is wrong. It's the wrong action and it's the wrong decision, Joe, and I won't pretend that I understand it. If I wasn't fairly certain that I know how you feel about this company, I'd walk off the project right now. But I do know, so I'll go along with it for one week. *One week.* And if we don't find something, either you take the appropriate steps or I'm out of here."

He didn't let his surprise show; he merely acknowledged her words with a brief nod. "Understood. In the meantime, you're gagged. You don't say anything to anyone. Not even Chas or my mother."

She was on her feet again in seconds. "*What? Joe—*"

"My rules. No appeals."

Her lips flattened into a razor-thin slit and her hands were clenched into balls of white-knuckled fury. "Fine."

He let a few seconds tick by, and watched some—not much—of the tension in her ease. He stood up then and walked to the door. "I like your idea of looking at the monitoring data. Start downloading whatever you need onto your laptop. We'll get started right away. I'll pick you up at your condo at four o'clock."

"Why download anything? And why would I go to the condo? Aren't we—?"

"We're going off-site."

"That's crazy. We have the networks right here—"

"Quit arguing with me. We're—"

Her eyes blazed. "When you're making damned-fool decisions I will *not* stop arguing with you. This is not your area of expertise, and quite frankly, Joe—"

"Quite frankly, I'm paying you, Naomi," he said flatly. "And neither one of us knows for sure what we should be doing. I'm willing to go along with your idea even though it is a long shot. So *quit arguing with me.* We're going off-site. If all we're going to be doing at first is reviewing monitoring data, the best place to do it is someplace where we won't be disturbed or distracted."

"Who would disturb us here?" she demanded. "And as for downloading all that network data—"

"Who would disturb us? Pick a name," he said exasperatedly. "This place won't empty out until seven, and an hour later the cleaners arrive. Download whatever you need from the network, and I don't really want to hear about how much data it is, okay? I don't care. I've got a box full of gigabyte lipstick drives that I'll give you if you need more space."

"But—"

"You're not going to change my mind. I've made my decision. We're leaving."

She let out a harsh, frustrated breath. "Where are we going?"

"Out on my boat."

"Oh, that's just great." She threw her hands into the air and plopped into her chair, shaking her head.

"I suggest that you don't wear a skirt." Without giving her any time to argue or refuse, he walked out of her office and shut the door behind him.

CHAPTER
18

Naomi wasn't proud that she'd lost her temper with a client, but she wasn't exactly in a hurry to apologize, either. In fact, she wasn't even sure she was over it yet. It had only been two hours since that rather unpleasant exchange with Joe had ended, and just thinking about it could make yet another adrenaline bomb detonate in her bloodstream.

At best, he was an insensitive, overbearing clod with autocratic and possibly felonious tendencies, whatever high horse he thought he rode. That Brennan legacy be damned; he was out of his ever-lovin' Yankee mind if he expected her to just follow meekly along with his *absolutely ludicrous* plan for finding and plugging the leak. Like the two of them could accomplish anywhere near the quality or quantity of work her team could—

She stopped short, realizing she was on yet another aimless trip through the condo. Once their conversation had ended, she'd downloaded what she needed and had packed up her laptop and come home. There was no point to staying in the office; it would just make people wonder what was going on, since she was fuming and was pretty sure Joe was, too, after that little exchange.

But coming back to her home base hadn't cleared her

mind any. If anything, it had just given her more time to think and therefore add to the clutter in her head. And the moment that refused to stop replaying itself was the moment he'd insisted on secrecy.

Bells and sirens had gone off as all the reasons why that was the wrong thing to do flooded her brain. It was too much work. It might be illegal. It was certainly unwise. It was most definitely unnecessary. But the elephant in the living room that she kept trying to ignore was the very chilling fact that the decision put Joe squarely in a box marked SUSPECT.

I am not going to follow that line of thought. It's ridiculous and paranoid and probably induced by my own guilt.

"He's trying to help. He's just going about it all wrong." Saying it out loud didn't help.

Finding herself in the kitchen once again without a clue as to why, she reached down and scooped up Smoke, and brought her up for a kiss and a conversation. After all, she had to do something to make herself quit thinking about it.

"Darlin', the man is a *lawyer*," she explained, emphasizing the last word the way she would if she were substituting *serial killer*. "Sure, he knows something about system architecture and networks and software, but he doesn't know enough to do what that nasty hacker has done. And that means it can't be him. Besides, he was too surprised at what I found and too willing to go along with my ideas on what to do about it. Nope, he absolutely can't be the mastermind," she said with half-hearted finality. "Now, his ideas for helping out—well, they're another story altogether. Heaven knows he's got his heart in the right place, but this is a job for Superman, which he's not. I'm the best he's got handy, and I'm not Superwoman." She paused, half hoping for a reaction.

Smoke blinked.

"I'm damned close, though," she added with the first

bit of humor she'd felt in several hours, if not days. She was rewarded with a velvety and well-deserved swat to the nose.

She brought the kitten close for another kiss on the head, as she wandered back to the living room, ending up in front of the expanse of windows. The sun was just sending out the early, heavy rays of late-afternoon light, making the sound shimmer and turning the citified white of the Brennan Building's edifice a creamy gold. It would deepen to bronze over the course of the next few hours. She'd watched the transformation before.

She wouldn't see it tonight, though. She'd see the first streaks of pink and lavender appear above the horizon from the deck of Joe's boat. It wasn't the worst place she could think of, but under the circumstances, it was close. She'd much prefer to be working with him while they were both in their offices, the width of the building apart from each other. Or even at opposite ends of a conference table. But on his boat? They wouldn't even be able to sit at that fold-down table in the galley without bumping knees, and bumping anything against Joe Casey was a bad idea.

Being in Joe's company was stretching her thin even before today's display of fireworks and the doubts it inspired. She could handle the fact that she was furious with him for his whacked-out decision: It was work related. It was when their encounters *weren't* work related and he *wasn't* infuriating that had her concerned. Because when Joe Casey wasn't annoying the daylights out of her, he was handsome, funny, charming in his own scattershot way, and smart. Really smart. Their conversations were unlike any she'd ever had with a man. Well, any man she'd ever been interested in.

Which was part of the problem. She was interested in him, but showing it any more than she already had was out of the question. Not only was he her client, and not only had she once been his company's nemesis, but, embarassed though she was to admit to herself that she even cared about it, he wasn't interested in her. And her ego was having a tough time with that, despite every attempt to use logic to counteract the sting of it.

One kiss. They'd shared one kiss, and that was all it had taken to knock the reason out of her, but it hadn't affected him at all. And that's where they stood.

It was probably for the best.

No, it's definitely for the best.

She let out an exasperated breath. Forget life not being fair. Right now life was downright irritating. After all, she was Southern, raised in a glorious tradition that taught women how to know what to want and precisely how to get it. Much as she no longer followed every lesson she'd learned, she could still play the game and play it well.

And despite all those rules of his, Joe Casey was still a man. No matter how much she tried to pretend or occasionally wish it wasn't the case, men found it difficult to ignore her. It wasn't a pretty fact but it was a fact, and Joe Casey was the sole aberration.

"It just figures, doesn't it, darlin'?" she said, glancing down into depths of Smoke's devilish green eyes. "I finally find a man who talks to me like I'm an equal, treats me like a queen, kisses me like nobody's business, and then he just stops there. Talk about leaving me hanging. Until today, of course, when he got my blood pressure high enough to launch a rocket and then ordered me to accompany him someplace romantic for about the most unromantic purpose a man could think of." She shook her head slowly, rubbing her chin against Smoke's downy-soft head. "There ought to be some sort of law against treating a woman that way, baby. The least he could do is have a flaw beyond the occasional lapse in judgment."

"Are you ready?" Joe asked when Naomi answered the intercom.

"I am." Her voice was chilly and her drawl was thick, which meant she was still seriously pissed off.

"Great. I'm in the lobby. I'll be right up," he said as he reached the elevators.

"I'll meet you down there."

Definitely pissed off.

"That's okay. I'll come up to help you with your bags."

She hesitated for a beat. "I only have my computer bag, Joe."

"You're going to need more than that," he said, and ended the call. She could be as pissed off at him as she wanted to be. His demands were unreasonable and might not even be achievable, but it was still the way he wanted to do things and he was the boss. End of story.

At least with other people who worked for him, that would have been the end of the story.

He didn't recall anyone ever arguing with him to the extent she had, and certainly no woman had ever hung in there that long. Naomi had gone way past the stage at which most women would either surrender or quit.

She hadn't done either. She'd gotten furious, though, and hadn't bothered to hide it. And even though he had tried damned hard not to pay attention to it, he couldn't help but be struck by the sheer magnificence of what that anger had done to her. She'd looked like an avenging goddess—all sparking eyes and high color, with tension surrounding her like a white-hot cloud of radiation. The weekly teleconference with his IT managers that had followed their conversation had been incredibly frustrating; his concentration had been shot to hell.

He stepped off the elevator and tapped on her door. She opened it, holding the kitten, which mewled its hello.

It was warmer than Naomi's greeting.

She shut the door behind him as he entered the condo, and gave him what was supposed to pass for a polite smile but missed its mark by a nautical mile. "What other bags should I be bringing?"

"You should probably bring some jeans and a sweater. It can get cold out on the water after the sun goes down."

Her eyes were wary and she must have tensed, because the kitten leaped out of her arms and sped across the floor, stopping a few feet away. It sat down then and stared at them.

"We're going to be out there that late?"

"Probably."

"Wonderful," she said, and walked stiffly toward the bedroom.

"Socks, too."

She didn't answer.

By the time she'd finally walked out of the condo, Naomi was carrying a small overnight bag, because Joe kept adding things to his list. Sunblock, which she had. A hat, which she didn't. Not an appropriate one, anyway. Finally, she'd just tucked some clean lingerie, her toothbrush, and a few condoms into the bottom of her bag. She knew spending the night with him was a long shot, but she believed in being safe rather than frustrated. After all, high temper was just another form of passion, and all that togetherness could possibly generate more than one kind of heat.

They'd driven to the Greenwich Yacht Club, where he kept his other boat, the *Mirabile Dictu,* which, he said, was Latin for "wonderful to behold." Despite its lofty name having been unofficially shortened to the *Mirabelle,* the boat lived up to its original description. Bigger and sleeker than his other sailboat, the *Mirabelle* was just as pretty, especially with the huge sail fully unfurled and heavily pregnant with the soft breeze.

She admitted to herself that it wasn't as bad as she'd thought it would be. Not that she was allowing herself to enjoy anything about the trip. As far as she was concerned it was little more than a reprimand for another power play she'd undertaken and lost. She'd worked alongside enough powerful men to understand that, from his perspective, he'd simply made a business decision. But from her perspective, he'd flatly dismissed her knowledge, her experience, and her expertise for no good reason. She knew, of course, that he had the right to dismiss her recommendations and ignore her skills; he was paying dearly for the privilege. She also knew that she had to be the one to cave in first, and that was another thing fueling her mood.

Sitting on the hard deck, legs stretched in front of her with the laptop balanced on her thighs, she'd begun working her way slowly and painfully through the first batch of monitoring data. Despite her stiff-backed determination, her concentration was sketchy, thanks to the fact that he was sitting less than ten feet away from her reviewing a batch of data she'd handed him the minute he'd dropped the anchor.

Windblown and framed in gold by a sun beginning to slant long rays across the water, he was a magnificent specimen of a man in his element. Ignoring him took a lot of effort.

"So, just how angry are you?"

It wasn't his question that brought her keystroking to a surprised halt; it was the hint of amusement in his voice. She wanted to bare her teeth and hiss. She deserved to wallow in this black mood for at least another hour, even though she wasn't particularly enjoying it. Being so out of sorts was unnatural for her; she hadn't been brought up to be rude. But neither was she used to being overruled so forcefully by a client. A nicked ego resulting from an asinine decision was a tough match for a lifetime of automatic smiles and a soft voice.

"I'm not sure *angry* is the right word," she said with a chill in her voice, keeping her eyes on her screen. "You're the client. You call the shots. I'm only here to make suggestions and see that your decisions are carried out. Anger doesn't enter into it."

"Oh."

The calmly spoken, inflection-free word held more meaning than would a tirade, and Naomi knew she was on the verge of shedding her credibility. *Shoulders back, chin up.* "I think I've made it clear that I'm disappointed at your decision, Joe, and I surely don't understand it, but if this is how you want to handle it, I'll work with you. For a week."

"Thank you."

"You're welcome."

She waited a few heartbeats, and when he didn't pursue the conversation, she resumed her task.

"I bought something for you," he said a few minutes later, and she finally looked up. He was watching her from over the edge of his laptop, looking relaxed, tousled, and utterly gorgeous. His dark sunglasses were aimed at her. She raised an eyebrow.

"An assistant?" she asked sweetly, and was rewarded with a laugh that the breeze swept away, leaving behind his brilliant smile. Her mood lifted slightly at the sight of it. She wasn't sure if she minded.

"In a way. They're in those two bags in the galley. Would you mind getting them? You're closer."

Relenting a little, she stood up and headed belowdeck. A moment later, she returned with the two large, unwieldy bags.

"Open them."

She did as she was told and glanced up at him, not quite sure what she was supposed to make of the contents.

"I could tell you weren't thrilled with the selection I offered you last time," he explained with a grin, "so now you have a choice. The puffy yellow one is for open or rough water, the pink-and-black one is for calm water, and the one that looks like a collection of straps is the inflatable kind competitive sailors wear. It stays flat until you either fall into the water or pull that tag." He paused. "That one is for when you either decide you can trust me or you learn how to swim."

She surveyed the collection of life vests that surrounded her. There had to be six or seven, and every one of them was garishly bright.

Well, damn. It was that sweet, unexpected, no-dancing-around–Tommy-Birk chivalry coming out in him again. Just how was she supposed to remain cool and borderline bitchy in the face of this? The gesture didn't even seem ingratiating.

She looked up at him. "I—thank you for thinking of me, Joe. When did you do all this?"

"The day after we had lunch. I was picking up some other stuff—" He stopped and shrugged. "I thought I'd better be prepared in case you ever agreed to come back on board. Not that I expected it to be this soon, or to be against your will."

She felt herself start to blush at the implication. "It's not against my will—"

"Okay, against your better judgment."

"You didn't exactly have to sling me over your shoulder, kicking and screaming," she pointed out. "Working out here just wouldn't have been my first choice. Why did you get so many?"

If she weren't mistaken, a look that came close to embarrassment crossed his face, but it was immediately replaced by a very slight frown, and he looked away, squinting into the sun. "I wasn't sure what size to get."

She picked one up and checked the tag, glad the visor of the baseball hat he'd loaned her hid her face. And the laughter that was threatening to erupt.

The sizes were based on bust measurements, and he'd gotten sizes ranging from 32 to 44. Ordinarily, such blatant evidence that a man had been considering her chest so analytically would have mortified her. Under the circumstances, though—and she knew it was more than a little crazy—the realization that he hadn't wanted to make a mistake generated a lovely, irrational burst of warmth inside.

She turned to face him and caught him looking at her. "Thank you, Joe."

He gave her a curt nod and turned his face to the sun once again.

They weren't getting as much accomplished as Joe had hoped they would. They'd been out there for three hours, looking at all sorts of different data logs and chasing down false leads. It was boring, brain-numbing work, and concentrating on it was a real challenge. Coming out here might be perfect in terms of not having any phones or e-mails disrupting them, but the weather wasn't cooperating as well as he'd hoped it would. Not that he'd wanted choppy seas, but the clear skies, quickening breeze, and smooth water made it a perfect evening for sailing, and frankly, he'd rather be tacking into the wind at the moment than tracking a hacker.

Finally, he'd put aside the laptop and pointed the boat toward the mouth of the sound and the Foggy Harbor Marina on the eastern tip of Long Island. He'd just finished his term as the club president and knew he could sweet talk the chef out of a few dozen cherrystone clams and a couple of lobsters for an impromptu on-board picnic. After all, they had to eat at some point, and all he had in the galley was the sliced ham and sandwich bread he'd picked up the other day. He hadn't had time to restock anything before they cast off. He'd been too busy thinking about the company.

Of course, he hadn't been too busy to make a special stop at CVS to pick up a box of condoms. Just in case.

Yeah. Just in case I accidentally seduce her. Or just in case she happens to get naked and fall on top of me when I least expect it. He lingered on that scenario for an unguarded moment.

Chas would flay him if he knew what he was thinking. Not that the old Chas wouldn't have done the very same thing under the circumstances. But for Chas, the situation wouldn't have involved any speculation about whether something might happen; it would have been more a matter of choosing his moment.

Hell, it ordinarily would be for me, too. He shook his head with more than a shred of disgust. He hadn't had to play offense with a woman in years. They came on to him. Not in droves like they did to Chas—they never had—but enough that he could afford to be choosy.

But he couldn't read Naomi the way he could other women. Her flirting didn't really seem like flirting. Which meant there was a good chance it wasn't flirting at all; it could just be a Southern thing that he was misunderstanding.

For one thing, Naomi was a hell of a lot smarter than most of the women he dated, and a hell of a lot more opinionated, too, and not shy about vocalizing those opinions. She was also a lot more beautiful and *that,* if he was going to be perfectly honest with himself, was the real issue.

He'd always shied away from truly beautiful women. He'd learned the hard way, starting when he hit puberty, that the combination of outward beauty and inner depth was a rare combination. And he preferred depth. Even if he didn't bother to explore it in most of the women he dated, he just wanted it there. Just in case.

A glance at the horizon brought him back to the moment. "Naomi?"

"Yes?"

"You might want to put away your laptop. We're heading out of the sound and we're going to be on the Atlantic for a little while. The water's a little rougher." When she didn't respond, he glanced at her. She was still sitting on the deck, wearing the Brennan baseball hat he'd given her, just as she had been for most of their trip.

She was wearing big, girly sunglasses that would go flying when they hit the first big swell, but he didn't need to see her eyes to know that what he'd just said had alarmed her. Her still face and her hands frozen above the keyboard told him that.

"How rough?"

"Calm."

"You said it was rough. It can't be rough and calm at the same time."

"I said the Atlantic is a little rougher than the sound. What we're on now is like glass. The ocean is rarely this calm. It's a bigger, deeper body of water, so the swells are bigger."

"How big?"

This wasn't going well. Every answer intended to soothe her made her more anxious. "A light chop. One to two feet," he said with a nonchalant shrug. "Small."

"That's small?" She'd gone pale. "For you, maybe, but that's halfway to my waist."

"Yes, but they're going to be under the hull, Naomi. Not crashing over the bow."

"Don't make fun of me, Joe. I told you I don't like the water."

Damn it. "I'm not making fun of you. If I hadn't told you, you may not have even noticed the difference. If you're nervous, you can go below, but—" He caught the words before they left his mouth. Tasted them. Rolled them around in his head.

Naomi had taken off her sunglasses and was looking at him expectantly. "But what?"

Okay. Why not? "But I'd like it if you stayed up here with me."

Painless. He felt the momentary tightness in his neck dissolve.

"Why?"

"Because I'd like the ocean to meet you." *What the fuck does that mean?*

A surreptitious glance at her eyes made him realize he'd never have to analyze it, because, incoherent or not, the statement had worked some sort of magic on her. The worried look on Naomi's face had changed to one that had *bedtime* written all over it. If he hadn't just announced his intention to sail around the headland, he'd have dropped the sail, dropped the anchor, and dropped every pretense of neutrality.

They'd be on their way to naked.

CHAPTER
19

Joe was right. The Atlantic had been a little rougher than the smooth waters of the sound, but just enough to get her heart rate up without scaring her. And enough to make her grab ahold of him as she laughed into the wind at the sheer exhilaration of riding the waves and reveling in the sound of the wind snapping the sails. It was the best mental break from her work that she could have imagined.

He'd invited her to stand with him at the wheel. "For the view," is what he'd said, but she figured it was probably more so that she didn't start to wig out or get hurt. She was glad to be where she was when the first big wave hit the boat, because she hadn't been ready for the jolt. Joe had been, though, and his arm had fastened itself around her waist and pulled her against him before she'd had time to lose her balance. He'd made sure she was okay before letting her go, but *okay* hadn't been exactly accurate. *Like a kid on Christmas morning,* was more like it.

After a quick glance at her face, he'd coaxed her into actually taking the wheel for a little while as he stood right behind her, telling her what to do. She'd fallen back into him a few times when a wave—or *swell,* as he called them—had taken her by surprise, and had leaned back onto him a few more times when it wasn't entirely necessary. But he was so warm and solid and steady that it was a nice contrast to the tilting deck and wet breeze. It was also a nice contrast to the distance they'd been keeping from each other.

Just when it seemed like they were both getting comfortable being so close, he'd left her there, frozen in place with a white-knuckled grip on the wheel, when he'd gone forward to do something with the sails. He'd taken over as soon as he came back, and neat as you please, he'd brought the boat into the marina and eased it up against the floats along the edge of a dock.

He glanced over his shoulder at her as he secured the last line, and burst out laughing.

"What?" she demanded, pretty certain his answer was going to have something to do with the big, silly grin she knew was plastered to her face. She couldn't help it. It hadn't lasted too long, but the experience had been unlike anything she'd ever dreamed of. Better than a roller coaster, better than skiing. Even better than sex.

"Does that smile mean you're glad you didn't go below deck?" he asked, reaching for her hand to help her onto the pier.

"A little," she replied in a deliberately offhand manner. The slide of her fingers against his roughened palm didn't help get her mind back to business.

He laughed again and didn't drop her hand as they began walking toward land. "I think I know you well enough to say that you, Naomi Connor, are a really bad liar."

"Hmm. Is that another Joe Casey compliment?"

One eyebrow rose above his Vuarnets. "What's that supposed to mean?"

"It means that you have your own brand of charm," she replied, knowing she was flirting with him as if she had a right to.

He pretended to ponder that one for a few seconds. "Are you susceptible to it?"

Oh, mercy. He's flirting back. This can't be good. She shaded her eyes from the sun and turned her face to the horizon. "My goodness, are those dolphins out there?"

He didn't reply, but when she sneaked a peek at him from beneath her borrowed baseball cap, he was smiling.

Once inside the building, he told her he had to talk to someone in the kitchen; she headed to the ladies' room to see what sort of toll the trip had taken on her. Passing through the open space that separated the bar from the dining room, she felt light and buoyant. The tension of their early afternoon meeting was forgotten, and they'd even progressed beyond their usual easy banter to a quasi-romantic plateau that could be a nice place to rest until the project ended. The job, as critical and time sensitive as it was, could wait for an hour while they had dinner. Her laptop battery would need charging soon, anyway, and nothing she could do could hurry that. Besides, she'd had a brain wave half an hour ago and had written a few quick scripts that would sort and prioritize the monitoring data according to what she hoped were correct assumptions. And if she launched those, they might just have time to stop on the way back to Greenwich so she could see what the stars looked like from the water.

She turned at the top of the stairs and began to descend them, following the signs indicating the ladies' room.

"Holy shit. Did you see the tits on that blonde?"

Naomi froze midstep, her newfound good mood shattering into razor-sharp shards at the loudly whispered words.

"Where?"

"The one going down the stairs to the head."

She'd noticed the table of three thirtysomething men as she'd walked past them but had been too intoxicated by the aftereffects of Joe's smile to keep her guard up. And her chest hidden.

"Check her out when she comes back up. I wouldn't mind getting my hands full of those while she was bent over a table."

She hurried down the last few stairs to the small landing. A despairing gasp punctuated the realization that there were only three doors down there: two bathrooms and an alarmed fire door. With too much adrenaline in her and too few options in front of her, she pushed open the bathroom door and shut it behind her. Leaning against the cool tile wall, she let out a heavy breath and tried to scold herself back to calmness.

"It's not the first time it's happened," she told the flushed woman in the mirror. "It's not the last. Some men are just pigs." Closing her eyes, she sagged against the wall, fighting back tears of frustration. She'd been dealing with unwelcome comments and leers since she was ten; she knew she should be used to it by now, but some things never got easier.

For a while there, she'd been free of it all. The looks, the leers, the rude suggestions, the gropes. Or at least she'd imagined she was. On the boat with Joe, she'd felt as if that wicked breeze had blown away all her cares, all her complications. Her hang-ups.

She hadn't even thought about whether the wind had plastered her T-shirt to the front of her, hadn't once looked down to check her appearance. Those few times when the bow was lifted by the crest of another wave and she'd rocked against him as he stood behind her at the wheel, her breast had unavoidably encountered his forearm. And for the first time in a very long time, the instinct to shield herself from unexpected contact hadn't kicked in. It hadn't mattered. She'd been free.

And those jerks, those pigs upstairs, had stolen that freedom and trampled it.

The worst part was that she had no alternative. She'd

have to walk past the men again, on parade like an animal in a zoo. They knew it, too, and were probably lying in wait for her, lurking like buzzards at a fresh kill, hanging around until she came back up the stairs and they could ogle her some more. And here she was in the bathroom, trying to talk herself out of tears that were building a steady pressure behind her eyes.

Damn them. And damn me for still letting it get to me after all these years.

"Naomi? Are you okay?"

She gulped a clumsy breath as Joe's voice followed a tentative knock on the door. She didn't want him to see her like this, didn't want to have to explain.

Forcing a smile, she pulled open the door and stepped into the small corridor. "Sorry, Joe, I didn't realize I'd taken so long."

"Don't worry about it." His blue gaze swept her face, not missing a thing, and she watched his expression change. In seconds, mild concern was overshadowed by anger, which faded just as fast as his lawyer face fell into place. She had to look away from the set of his jaw, the way he'd just stood up a little straighter. As if he were gearing for a battle.

Without saying a word, he shrugged off the light cotton windbreaker he had on and held it out for her. Biting her lip against a fresh urge to cry, she slipped her arms into it and zipped it up. It hung loosely around her body and draped down to the middle of her thighs, effectively hiding her figure.

She couldn't meet his eyes. She couldn't. She knew the naked gratitude in hers would make both of them uncomfortable.

He turned around then, slipped his hand into hers, and they walked up the stairs together.

Going rigid as they approached the bar area was not something she could prevent, but she kept her eyes firmly set forward. A sliver of white-hot panic shot through her as she felt Joe's hand drop hers; it intensified when his arm slid casually around her shoulders and he steered her to the right.

Straight toward the table of the pigs.

She didn't know what the next few minutes would entail, but she knew she was about to see Joe Casey in action.

Shoulders back, chin up. If only her knees would stop knocking.

"Hello, boys," Joe said in a deceptively easy tone as he brought her to a stop at the high-top table. The two men on the ends rose to their feet as if by habit, if not a bit cautiously. The one in the center remained seated, his eyes flicking between Joe's face and hers—and her chest.

As they returned Joe's greeting, she knew exactly who had said what. Her stomach had begun to settle and, standing up a little straighter, she met their eyes more calmly.

"I believe you expressed an interest in meeting my friend Naomi Connor." He paused and looked at Naomi. "Naomi, this is Boyd Heffernan."

He was the one who hadn't seen her.

"Chandler Travis."

He had, but he hadn't said anything rude.

"And this is Arthur Farnsworth Devlin the Fourth," Joe finished more slowly. "But everyone calls him . . . Tuffy." Joe's inflection alone was an insult, and it wasn't lost on the recipient, who flushed a dark, not entirely natural red.

Joe Casey, I think I love you.

"How are y'all?" she blurted, much too shocked at what she'd just thought to make herself stay silent.

They murmured their hellos and one of the men held out his hand, which she pretended not to see. A moment later, she and Joe were walking wordlessly through the maze of docked boats to find the *Mirabelle*. His arm was still slung, reassuringly heavily, across her shoulders, his hand cupped warmly around the curve of her shoulder.

He helped her onto the boat, then stopped short and looked at her. "I left dinner at the hostess stand. I'll be right back," he said, flashing her a smile that held only a trace of its usual brilliance.

The fuckers.

Joe's temper was white-hot by the time he returned to the restaurant.

"Fran, are they still in there?"

The hostess nodded her gray head, a thoroughly disgusted look on her face. "They've been parked at that table since three thirty."

"Have John get their check ready. If they don't have time to sign it, put it on my account. They'll be leaving very shortly," he said grimly, and continued into the bar.

He came to a stop at their table, and noted with satisfaction that Boyd and Chandler, at least, seemed to understand that it wasn't simply a social call.

"Joe, we didn't mean anything—"

"We didn't know she was with—"

He held up a hand. "Yes, you did. And it shouldn't matter, anyway," he replied with blatantly false calm. "I just came back to make a few suggestions, *boys*. The first is that you"—he looked pointedly at Boyd, then Chandler—"review the bylaws of this organization. Pay particular attention to the section addressing acceptable and unacceptable behavior by members while on the club premises. I guarantee you'll find it interesting reading."

Their eyes widened as his words sunk into their vodka-soaked brains.

Satisfied that he'd made his point, Joe shifted his attention to Tuffy. Short, bloated, obnoxious, and in possession of a lot more money than sense, Tuffy Devlin had been a weasel when he was twelve, and age hadn't improved him. He was still short, bloated, and obnoxious, but he'd evolved from being a weasel into an utter asshole.

"I'd like to be the first to tell you about the outcome

of your membership application, *Arthur*. It's been rejected. And not only have you been rejected as a member, you've just been declared persona non grata on these premises, in perpetuity. Don't bother to finish your drink. Just go. Fran will be more than happy to call a cab for you," he said evenly.

"Shut up, Casey. You don't scare me. Who the fuck do you think you are, anyway?" Tuffy demanded loudly, causing a few more heads to turn in their direction.

Joe folded his arms across his chest and smiled as he looked down at the pasty bastard, who, he knew, wouldn't get off his ass and stand up like a man. He was taller sitting on the bar stool than he was standing up.

He made sure his voice was even and calm. "I think I'm the outgoing president of the club and the incoming chairman of the membership committee. I also think you had better stop making a scene and leave under your own power while you still have a choice in the matter. John"—with a tilt of his head, he indicated the bartender, who was paying close attention to their discussion—"is a Montauk firefighter, and Fran"—he tipped his head toward the equally interested hostess—"is a Southampton cop. I know they'd both be more than happy to assist you to other premises, irrespective of your willingness to participate."

Boyd cut off whatever Tuffy was going to say in reply by grabbing his short, fat, pickled friend by the arm to lead him out the front door.

"Just when did I join the police force? Before or after I joined AARP?" Fran asked with a grin as she handed Joe the Styrofoam ice chest he'd left with her when he'd gone in search of Naomi.

He winked at her. "I was admitted to the New York Bar a few years back. I think that means I can deputize you. I could be wrong."

"You're one of a kind, Joe. She's a lucky gal, whoever she is. Say hi to your mom for me."

Naomi was sitting on the deck, plinking away at her

laptop by the time he returned. Her eyes flicked up in greeting and she gave him a small, perfunctory smile, then looked back at her screen.

All the energy, all the exuberance inspired by a few minutes of tacking into the wind had left her. She seemed deflated and shapeless as she sat there with her back against the bench, his windbreaker billowing around her like a whitecap that wouldn't break. Between that and his baseball cap, she looked kind of forlorn and—*nope.*

He cast off and took them around the tip of the island and back into the sound. She stayed put on the deck, eyes glued to her computer, not looking at him and not making conversation. He couldn't tell whether she was embarrassed or just angry at him.

Neither was good; he'd thought he was doing the right thing.

Damn it, I did do the right thing, just like I did with Tommy Birk. And if she doesn't like it, that's too damned bad. It needed to be done.

The clouds had gone from white to pink to lavender by the time he pulled down the sails and dropped anchor. Naomi had continued to work in silence, not questioning where they were going or how long it would take them to get there. Which was good, because they'd been going in circles since they'd reentered the sound. Big, lazy circles while Joe thought less about what to do about the company and more about what he should do about Naomi. He was more than a little tired of doing nothing, especially after seeing her face this afternoon when she'd been handling the wheel. He wanted to see that life, that laughter and passion again. Preferably facing him from a horizontal position.

"Hungry?" he asked as he secured the main sail.

She looked up at him, shielding her eyes against the glare of the setting sun. "Getting there. Can I do anything to help?"

"Maybe in a little while. I have to get a few things started first." *Like this conversation.*

He left her on deck while he went into the galley and set two pots of water to boiling, and pulled out a plate for the appetizers he'd wheedled out of the sous-chef.

Cradling the cold bottle of New Zealand Sauvignon Blanc against his chest, he threaded the stems of the wineglasses through his fingers, balanced the plate and bottle opener in his other hand, then headed up the steps. She had shut down her computer and was standing at the starboard railing. She turned as he approached her.

"Oh, my, Joe. Look at you. What should I take?" she asked, reaching for the wineglasses.

"The plate, actually. That's probably the least secure."

She lifted it from his hands and looked around for somewhere to put it.

"Anywhere is fine." He sat down on the bench and lay the plastic glasses next to him, then proceeded to open the wine.

"These look wonderful," she said, sitting down a little farther away than he expected and putting the plate of shrimp between them.

"They're great. They cook the shrimp in some sort of a sesame marinade, then wrap those Chinese peapods around them," he said, forcing a smile and wondering how long it would take this time before she began to relax.

"You said that almost as if you know how to cook."

He sent her an amused look. "Of course I know how to cook. I live alone, remember? And you saw my kitchen."

A smile crossed her lips, softening her expression.

Progress.

"I figured you bought the house that way."

He just shook his head. "It's happening again, isn't it? No, I didn't buy the house that way. Not that it matters, but I didn't buy the house at all. I did, however, put in the kitchen."

She accepted the glass of wine from him. "What do you mean?"

"My great-grandmother grew up in that house. She let me live in the basement flat while I was in law school, and then she left me the house when she died." He leaned back against the railing and squinted into the sunset, hoping that she'd watch him the way she seemed to do whenever he made it look like he wasn't paying attention. He'd never considered himself especially conceited, but knowing Naomi was looking at him caused a pretty good sensation. And not just in his shorts.

"She's the one who put in the garden," he continued. "And when she became too ill to get down the steps, she had the sunroom expanded. Originally, it was a small greenhouse where she'd mess around with her plants. Some of the plants in there are seventy years old."

"Sounds like she was more than a hobbyist."

He glanced at her and watched her quickly look away. "She was a botanist for the Smithsonian. Her specialty was South African wildflowers."

She twirled her wineglass again and took another small sip. "That explains the art in there. Do you take care of them? The plants, I mean?"

He gave a silent laugh. "No way. A team from her old department comes in once a week to make sure I haven't killed anything. They were mightily annoyed when she didn't leave the plants to the institutions. And they're even more pissed off that I haven't donated them."

"Why haven't you?"

He shrugged. "I like having them there. They remind me of her. I used to sit in there with her if I was around in the evenings. She was a pretty fascinating woman. Traveled all over the world. Didn't get married until she was in her thirties. Stopped traveling when my grandmother was born and didn't start up again until she'd gone off to college, and then she only stopped when she broke her hip. She continued doing research and writing papers until she was in her eighties, and died when she was ninety-four."

"Your family seems populated with fascinating women."

It wasn't a flirtatious comment, but if it had been, he didn't think he'd have been annoyed. He took a sip of his wine and set the goblet on the deck. "Let me go check on what's boiling."

Naomi knew that it was really now or never. If she didn't say something to him, she'd never be able to relax. Being hunched over that computer all afternoon had given her the beginnings of a nasty backache, and the tension from that exchange in the bar had settled in deep just under her right shoulder blade. She knew it would disappear as soon as she said something. The trouble was, she didn't know what to say.

So, figuring it would come to her, she just put her hand out and touched him on the forearm as he got up to check on dinner.

"Joe?"

He stopped and looked at her, the same cautious neutrality in his eyes that had been there since he'd returned from the marina with the ice chest. His smile didn't quite mask it.

"I'm at a little bit of a loss as to how to put this, but—" She took a deep breath. "Thank you for what you did back there. At the marina. I just—" She paused again, hating the emotion she heard gathering strength in her voice. She thought she'd buried it over the last hour. "I shouldn't let things like that bother me. It took me by surprise and it shouldn't. I just—thank you for handling it. It was a really nice thing to do."

The look in his eyes told her nothing, and she wondered how inappropriate it would be to kiss him. If she were standing or he were still sitting, it wouldn't be a decision she'd have to think about, she would have just done it; she would have just leaned over and given him a kiss on the cheek. But he was towering over her, and if she stood up it would look like she was offering more than just a thank-you kiss. Which, of course, she might be, but she wasn't about to humiliate herself any further today by making a pass at a man who, apparently, was being nothing more than gentlemanly.

"I didn't hear what they said, but I know them well enough to figure it out. But why should you not be surprised by something like that happening?"

She blinked at the question and at the annoyed intensity of his eyes. "Well—" She stopped. However she put it, it would sound conceited. Finally, she just shrugged. "Joe, men have been whistling at me and making rude comments since I was ten years old. I should be used to it by now. But sometimes it just—" *I am not going to lose it in front of him.*

She looked away from his face and toward the sunset. The sky was striped and swirled with clouds the colors of a tropical garden, hot oranges and deep purples.

After a long moment, he reached out and ran his hand lightly over her hair, as a parent would to a favorite child, sweeping his hand down her cheek and tilting her face to his. "You're an incredibly beautiful woman, Naomi. It's a damned shame that things like that happen to you," he said softly, and then excused himself to go check on what was happening in the galley. Leaving her a good solid minute or two to get herself under control. She could have used thirty.

She made sure she was standing up when he came back on deck with a smile. The sky had started to darken, and the clouds overhead were becoming deeply purple, edging toward dark gray.

"The stars will be out any minute. And dinner will be ready in about fifteen minutes," he said, picking up the ice chest from where he'd left it near the wheel.

"That sounds just divine, especially now that I know you're a good cook," she said with a cheerfulness that wasn't as forced as she thought it would be. "Can I see what we're having?"

He set the ice chest on the bench and lifted the top with a grin that made it clear that he was delighted with himself. Naomi peered in.

Her heart dropped into her stomach and kept going as she stared at the two large lobsters waving their rubber-banded claws and trying to scale the scattered mountain of seaweed and small clams. She knew Joe was waiting for a happy exclamation of some sort, but her wits were just too frayed. She lifted her eyes to his.

"You can't eat seafood." It wasn't a question, and what was worse, he didn't sound surprised. He sounded resigned.

A sip of wine didn't help. She still didn't know what to say.

She cleared her throat. "Not exactly. I just can't eat those." Flicking her eyes back to the occupants of the box only generated an involuntary shudder.

He must have seen it, because he slid the lid back on. "You mean that of all the kinds of seafood you can eat, I picked the two kinds you can't?"

She swallowed hard and focused on the small spray of golden hairs that were visible against the dark golden skin at the placket of his shirt. "No. Not quite. I—" She met his eyes again, knowing she was killing any possibility of something happening between them. "I just can't eat anything that I have to kill first."

At least a full minute went by. He just stared at her for most of it, then looked to the horizon as if for guidance. His voice, when he spoke, held overt patience. "They're crustaceans. Lower-order species, Naomi. Kind of like rocks with legs, and they really don't scream when you put them in the pot."

She just shook her head, feeling more foolish with every moment that passed. "I know all that, Joe, and if they were filleted and frozen, I'll be champing at the bit. But they're alive. I can't kill them and then eat them."

"I'll cook them and pull them apart for you. You don't have to watch."

She shook her head again. "I've seen them waving their claws."

"You're not about to tell me you've bonded with them, are you?"

She tried not to smile as she shook her head this time.

"What about the clams?" he asked.

"Are they alive?"

He didn't answer. He just blinked at her once. "Okay. Don't move." He shook his head and under his breath muttered, "I can't believe I'm about to do this."

He bent down and slipped the rubber bands off the lobsters' claws, narrowly retaining his own fingers in the process. That accomplished, he picked up the ice chest and flung the contents overboard in one smooth, unhesitating motion. "Have fun, kids. Stay out of trouble."

He set the container on the deck and looked at her, a half smile on his face as he shook his head. "I hope you weren't too hungry, because dinner will be settling on the bottom of the Long Island Sound in about thirty seconds."

As she stared at him—his windblown hair and the smile-crinkled tan lines fanning out from his eyes, the bottomless depths of those same eyes and the subtle depths of his soul—Naomi realized that it hadn't been just a stress-induced cliché that had crossed her mind earlier in the day. He was no god; he was just a man, but what a man. And although she knew it was too soon and entirely inappropriate, it couldn't be helped. She was falling thoroughly, deeply, incurably in love with Joe Casey.

Emboldened by the knowledge, she reached down and turned over the ice chest, stepped onto it, leaned into him, and kissed him full on the mouth.

Southern style.

CHAPTER
20

Joe had barely gotten past the surprise of her kiss when the roar of an outboard motor coming to life sliced through the evening. Its wake, as it took off in a hurry, slapped against the *Mirabelle*'s hull, pitching Naomi against his chest, into his arms, and much more firmly against his mouth.

It was a good fit. A perfect fit. She was soft and warm and lush, and tasted like wine and heaven.

The motion of the deck had startled her, though, and she'd tried for a few seconds, anyway, to push him away or maybe just regain her balance. Leaving him to wonder if she'd meant this to be a quick kiss like the one she'd given him in his garden, or the G-rated one he'd given her in her apartment—instead of the one that he'd been hoping for: Deep. Passionate. Preliminary.

Not wanting to misread her, he set her feet back on the deck and she immediately settled the question in his mind.

Breaking the kiss, she looked up at him for a minute, her eyes unreadable in the moonless dark. "Well, I guess that's enough of that," she said in a voice close enough to a whisper. She went below deck without another word.

Christ. What have I done now?

When ten minutes had passed and she didn't return, he tried to summon a little bit of patience. But it had been too long a day with too damned many unpleasant surprises—mostly at the hands of Naomi Connor—and he had reached his limit. He was hungry, he was horny, and he wanted some answers.

Knocking on the cabin door—*his* cabin door—he waited until he heard a soft "Come in" before opening it. She was sitting on his bed, hands folded in her lap. His jacket lay neatly on the bed next to her. She'd obviously been crying.

Female tears and body language be damned; he leaned in the doorway and crossed his arms. "What's wrong?" he barked.

She looked up at him, relatively calm. "Nothing."

"Don't lie to me."

"I don't know the words."

"I'm a pretty simple guy, Naomi. You don't need to get fancy or be diplomatic. Just tell me what I did."

She recoiled slightly, as if her surprise was genuine. "What *you* did?"

"Yes. Tell me what I did."

She blinked at him. "Well, you didn't do anything, Joe."

"I kissed you."

"I know. You didn't do anything else."

"I know I didn't. So why are you mad at me?"

"I'm not mad."

Famous last words. He took a deep breath to rein in his exasperation. "Well, you're not happy, so there's something not right with this picture."

She looked down at her hands. "Look, Joe, this has been a strange relationship from the start. I mean, not that it's a relationship but it's a . . . an acquaintanceship that just keeps bumping into things it shouldn't, like a bat in the daylight—"

What flavor of bullshit is this? "Wait a minute."

She glanced up to meet his eyes. "What?"

"This is an *acquaintanceship*? Is that even a word?"

"I think it is. But does it matter? What I'm trying to say is—"

He held up his hand and she stopped talking. "Yes, it matters. And for the record, forget the whole workplace thing. This has nothing to do with that. Does it?"

"No." Then she paused and stood up. "What I'm trying to say is that I think we should stop trying to push it, because it's not really happening naturally, is it?"

"Push what?"

"Well . . . us."

This is unbelievable. "You think *I'm* trying to push something?" he demanded. "By that, I take it you mean that I'm trying to make something happen of a romantic nature?"

"You sound like a lawyer."

"That's because I am a lawyer. But I have no idea what the hell you're talking about."

She lifted one shoulder in a shrug. "Well, I mean, there's an attraction there most of the time, or at least I think there is, and then when an opportunity arises, it just falls flat."

I must be delirious. "Hold it. What are you saying?

She turned those big eyes on him again. They were getting a new wet sparkle in them that made his annoyance start to wither.

"I'm saying that, despite the fact that we seem to like each other a whole lot and get along real well, if the romance isn't happening easily, maybe it shouldn't happen at all, Joe."

He stared at her for a full minute, replaying the conversation in his head.

"Let me ask you something, Naomi," he said eventually. "A few minutes ago when I asked you what I did wrong and you said nothing, were you blowing off the question, or was that your answer?"

"What?"

"Is the problem that I *didn't* do something?"

"Don't feel awkward about it, Joe. Sometimes the attraction just isn't there—"

Holy Christ. He wanted to bury his head in his hands and cry. "Not there? *Are you nuts?* I've been driving myself crazy trying to hold back."

Her eyes became impossibly wider, her voice unbearably softer. "Why?"

He went still. There wasn't a graceful way to say it. "Well, to put it bluntly," he began cautiously, "you've got issues. About your body."

The blush started somewhere below the neckline of her T-shirt and spread upward. "What does that mean?"

It was all-or-nothing time. What he gave was going to determine what he got. And he wanted it all.

"It was obvious from the minute we met, Naomi. You have a barrier around yourself most of the time and don't let anyone get within a few feet of you. Except when we were dancing, and again this afternoon when you were steering the boat." When she didn't say anything, he spread his hands in a questioning gesture. "The incident with those assholes today just underscored the issues. I wasn't about to push."

She folded her arms across her stomach and looked at the floor. "So I'm just too much of a mess, is that it?" Her voice had that trying-to-be-strong quality to it, and it was totally out of character for her. He didn't like it.

"A—" he began, then stopped, incredulous. "*A mess?* Where did you get that from?"

"Well, there has to be something keeping us apart. I thought it was you, but maybe it's me," she said, still not making eye contact.

"You're damned right it's you. But not because you're any sort of a mess."

Her head snapped up. "What else is it, then? I just threw myself at you up there on the deck and you just—"

"I just what?" he demanded.

"Oh, never mind."

"No. You're not allowed to say that. I do mind. I just what?"

"Kissed me," she whispered, and he watched her swallow hard as tears gathered in her eyes.

Damn it. "Don't you dare start crying, Naomi. I mean it. You didn't cry in the office this afternoon, and you didn't cry back there in the bar. You can't cry now."

"I'm not crying."

"Good. Now, tell me what was wrong with kissing you?"

"That's all you did."

Okay. This was the most surreal conversation he'd ever had with a woman. The most surreal situation. *Definitely the most frustrating.*

He pushed his hand through his hair. "Naomi, if you want more, I'm there. I've been trying to hold back and let you get comfortable. To let you make the first move, if a move is going to be made. I've never done that before in my life and I'll be damned if I'll ever do it again, because it has damned near killed me. But if I have to spell it out, that's why I ha—"

The look that came onto her face stopped him mid-syllable.

"I didn't know, Joe," she whispered. "How was I supposed to? I've never made the first move. I've only ever fought them off if they happened too quick, which they usually do."

I'm such an ass. He stared at her, unable to think of a suitable response as he saw through new eyes the reason for her boxy suit jackets and fully buttoned blouses, the distance she kept from people during meetings, the way she carried her computer case in her hand rather than over her shoulder. Even the evening gown with the high neckline and plunging back. He'd written all of them off as quirks.

"You deserved better," he replied quietly.

He watched her eyes get wet again, and she bowed her head for a second as she wiped away a tear that escaped. Then she lifted her gaze to meet his once more, and the soft intensity of her eyes was mesmerizing.

She walked toward him, and he stepped into the room so he could stand up straight. Her hands reached up to cup his face, then they slid to his shoulders and to his chest, and came to rest there. "I don't know if I deserve it, but I've got 'better' right here in front of me. Forget about sexy and forget about handsome, both of which you most certainly are." She brought one hand to his cheek. "You, Joe Casey, are the kindest man I've ever met," she said, and kissed him very lightly.

He returned her kiss just as gently, and a moment later felt her lips curl against his in a smile.

She pulled back and looked at him, her eyes warm and amused and bright with desire. "That's not enough to qualify as a first move, is it?"

"No."

Her gaze dropped to his mouth and stayed there for several hard, erotic, irregular heartbeats, then returned to his eyes.

"Make love to me, Joe."

CHAPTER
21

Joe didn't wait for a second invitation. He framed Naomi's face with both hands, lowered his mouth to hers, and settled into the long, deep, slow kiss he'd been waiting much too long to enjoy.

Her mouth was as sweet and soft and warm as the rest of her, and wet and willing and not shy. Desire rolled through him like a summer storm, gathering strength and heat as it headed south. Slow, determined hands smoothed over his biceps and shoulders before curving around the back of his neck and coming to a stop tangled in his hair, pulling him closer. She pressed herself against him, let her breasts share their lush warmth with his chest.

His mouth slid down the side of her neck, tasting her all the way to her collarbone, then settling in for a more leisurely and erotic return trip that had her breath echoing his in soft, irregular puffs. His hands eased down the curves of her back, stopping only when they were cupping cheeks as firm and perfect as he had anticipated, but covered by only one layer of fabric, which he hadn't anticipated.

The realization that she was wearing a thong, or

maybe nothing at all, under her shorts and had been like that all afternoon pulled him one step closer to crazy. He reclaimed her mouth, and by the time he broke contact and came up for air, he was dizzy.

There wasn't a gap to be found between their bodies, and her hands had balled into fists in his hair. More than one small moan that carried his name had erupted from her.

The sheer force of his desire was approaching a critical mass. Getting horizontal was essential.

Sweeping her off her feet wasn't difficult. Setting her down gently in the middle of the bed brought a sweet, sexy smile to her face as she looked up at him from the blue sheets, a shimmering blond goddess resting on a calm, dark sea.

"That was some kiss, Joe," she said in a voice low and rich with laughter, her honeyed accent deepening with promise and expectation. Her eyes were glowing like stars reflected on the water, and her smile did nothing for his composure. "I believe it's finally time to get naked."

She pronounced it *nekkid,* and the way her voice dropped on the word, it sounded like the best, dirtiest suggestion he'd heard in this lifetime. She started to pull her T-shirt out of the waistband of her shorts.

"Don't."

She stopped, eyes wide, wary, and hopeful, and let her hands fall to the bed.

"You made the first move, which was all I was intending to let you do, anyway. You just lay back and close your eyes. Or keep them open. Whatever you want," he replied, and let a heavy, expectant silence build before reaching for her foot and slipping off her sandal.

She laughed softly as he wrapped a hand around that small foot and lifted it, letting his other hand slide down a warm, smooth calf. Holding her gaze, hot and blue and anything but innocent, he brought those Barbie-pink-tipped toes to his mouth. Her smiled dimmed and her eyes widened as his lips closed around her big toe.

"What are you doing?" It was more than halfway to a whisper.

"At the moment, I'm talking with my mouth full."

She watched warily as his tongue played games with her toe, but when he gave that dainty toe a strong, suggestive suck, she pulled it away. "I thought we were going to get—"

"We are. This foot is now naked," he replied, making sure his thumb was doing good and bad things to the sweet spot on her sole. Judging from the way her breathing had just changed, they were good things.

He let his eyes drift over her body, still clothed, still unexplored, and eventually brought his gaze back to her face. He braced her bare foot against his right shoulder and watched her eyes widen again.

"Give me your other foot."

After a flare of startlement, her expression changed again to a soft, seductive half smile that had expectation and deliverance contained within it. With a slow, graceful motion, she straightened her left leg and lifted it, toes pointed. He slipped off her sandal and put that foot against his left shoulder. Then, in a move that was both practical and symbolic, he slowly sank to his knees.

Being made love to by Joe Casey was nothing Naomi could have possibly prepared for. It was the most erotic, slow, sensual experience of her life, beginning with that kiss, which had gone on until she was partially comatose. And that kiss was *a kiss*. Lips, tongue, teeth, and commentary. Not much, but enough, and every single murmur had sent her need exponentially higher. By the time he'd placed her on the bed, she'd nearly been laid waste by desire.

And his hands hadn't yet touched skin.

That he hadn't gone straight for her breasts was the sexiest move a man had ever made. He hadn't even touched them through her clothes. Hadn't even stared at them. He'd begun seducing her with molten blue eyes and a conspirator's smile, then he'd lifted her foot and shocked the daylights out of her. Sucking her toes turned out to be only the first of many erotic games he played.

And games they were. Once he started touching her, he didn't stop. He'd just begun with her toes and moved upward, and now there wasn't a square inch of her that he wasn't fully acquainted with. Whatever he hadn't licked or nibbled or suckled, he'd made sure to stroke and tease. He'd brought her to three slow, tortuously wonderful climaxes. And then he'd slid into her ever so slowly—at first—to bring her to a hot, fast, shattering fourth.

Surely she'd died during that last orgasm and was now in heaven. Either that or she truly was in his arms, her back snug against his chest, the rhythm of his heart in sync with the gentle rocking of the boat.

"Stop it." His voice was a low, sex-roughened growl in her ear.

"Stop what?"

"I can hear you thinking."

With a laugh, she turned around until she could see his face. His beautiful, heavy-lidded, utterly sated face.

"I hate to contradict you, darlin', but this head hasn't had a coherent thought in it for several hours. You completely degaussed my brain the minute you started sucking my toe."

"That could be a problem. I liked your brain the way it was. Wiping it clean of all content was not my intention." He grinned and smoothed a large hand over her stomach, leaving a swath of buzzing nerve endings in its wake. "So you liked the toe job?"

"I liked everything, Joe." She punctuated the statement with a kiss against his soft, adventuresome mouth.

He pulled his arm out from under her and propped

himself up on his elbow, his free hand still resting on her stomach. "Everything? I thought I surprised you a few times," he said, his eyes looking straight into hers.

"Oh, well, you did. But you always have."

He lifted a brow, clearly pleased. "I have? How?"

"Well, when I met you, I didn't expect you to be so good-looking." She trailed a hand along the light golden stubble on his cheek. "And that first kiss surprised me."

"Tonight?"

"At my apartment after the opera. Where did you learn to kiss like that?"

"Good?"

"Good?" she repeated on a light laugh. "It was divine. I mean, there was all that passion and not a tongue to be found. You didn't even open your mouth, but I couldn't fall asleep for hours afterward. I still can't figure out how you managed that."

He laughed, and the sound washed over her with a welcome and familiar warmth. "Practice."

She shook her head. "Maybe I shouldn't have asked. But I'll bet you were something in high school."

His mouth reshaped itself into a sardonic twist. "Yeah, I was something, all right, but it wasn't popular. Pathetic, maybe."

"You can't expect me to believe that. And I don't give out sympathy votes."

"I'm absolutely serious. I was gawky and skinny—"

"But I'll bet you were good-looking and polite—"

The skin near her navel cooled as his hand left it briefly to brush away her compliments. "It had nothing to do with looks or manners. I tried everything to become a babe magnet, but I still ended up with plenty of girl friends and no girlfriends."

"Why?"

He gave a short, silent laugh that held echoes of still-remembered adolescent angst. "Because if a girl went out with me, she lost her eligibility to go out with Chas, and Chas was the big catch in high school. As a sophomore, he was dating seniors, and I mean the most gorgeous ones." He shrugged. "All the girls were as nice as could be to me, but they wouldn't even entertain the notion of a date. Not even homecoming or prom."

"Why?"

He shrugged. "Chas was a charmer from the day he was born, I think."

She stared at him in disbelief, her heart aching a little for him. "So are you, in your own way. And if you could kiss like that back then, those girls were fools who didn't know what they were missing."

He raised an eyebrow. "They weren't missing anything. I didn't kiss like that back then."

"You had to learn it somewhere, and I'm not going to believe you if you say that you had to wait until college to get a date."

His grin returned them, accompanied by a bad-boy twinkle in his eye. "Nope, not quite college. Just my first trigonometry course. Junior year in high school. That class taught me more about microeconomics than mathematics."

She wriggled onto her side and propped herself up on an elbow to look at him warily. "I hope you don't mean that you paid someone—"

He laughed, and gave her a playful push that landed her on her back again. "No, I didn't pay someone. I bartered."

She frowned. "That sounds even worse. I think you'd better explain how that worked before I start looking for my panties."

"You won't find them without my help," he replied, then trailed one finger down the side of her face in an idle, affectionate way that added layers of depth to the warmth in his eyes. "A girl in my trigonometry class decided she had a better chance of flunking that course than she did of ever dating Chas, so we arrived at an understanding. I tutored her in trig and she tutored me in—" He stopped and smiled.

"Kissing?"

He nodded.

"That was all?"

His grin widened. "What are you asking?"

"I just want to get a handle on your morality."

"Yes, just kissing."

"And?"

"She aced trig."

"If we're still talking about the chaste and tongueless kisses, I think she got the better end of that deal."

"Well, not exactly. But that's how it started out. Mere homework wasn't enough to warrant any tongue action, in her opinion. But over time I managed to persuade her to give it a try."

"Oh, mercy. Do I even want to know?" she replied, rolling her eyes. The warmth radiating from him was encompassing and steady. *I could stay here forever.*

"Midterms," he said with entirely too smug a tone in his voice.

"That was hardly fair."

"Anyone who plays fair all the time is generally known by one term: loser. The decision to play fair is best left to the circumstances."

"Spoken like a true lawyer."

"Sometimes it's about the journey and sometimes it's just about the destination." He shrugged. "A man's got to do what a man's got to do."

"So what did all of this teach you, other than to play to win and how to handle frustration?"

"I never thought of it as frustration," Joe replied, lowering his smiling lips to hers. "It taught me how to cut a deal and how to enjoy the anticipation of finding common ground."

"That's all?"

He smoothed her hair away from her face. "That was enough. Well, I suppose she taught me about sex, too."

Naomi frowned. "Just how tough was that trig teacher?"

"By then we were seniors and she was having trouble with advanced calculus," he said with a grin.

"Let me guess. You lost your virginity the week before senior finals," she said dryly, trying to ignore the small but fiery kisses he was trailing down her throat.

"Oh, please," he said, his tone refuting her suggestion as being just shy of ridiculous.

Oh, Lord. If he didn't stop soon she was going to lose the ability to think. "What? Was that too ambitious? It was later than that?"

"That would have been way too late. Remember those nasty things called the SATs?" he murmured, and let his mouth drift below her collarbone.

She tried to swallow her laughter, and brought his face level with hers. His eyes were dark and intense, but his mouth held his own laughter in check.

"So how did you spend the rest of your senior year?"

"Doing *lots* of homework."

"Joe Casey, you're shameless."

"Always have been."

She rolled her eyes again, which made him laugh.

He placed a lovely, lingering kiss on her mouth. "Things balanced out when I went to college. No one there knew Chas, so I was home free."

"No more cutting deals?"

"It morphed into the fine art of delicate negotiation."

She lifted an eyebrow and ran a hand over the lightly furred musculature of his chest. "I've got some news for you. You're a tough negotiator, not a delicate one, and I'll bet you always have been. I doubt there are too many women who would say no to you if you were hell-bent on capitulation."

He reared back in surprise. "What's that supposed to mean?"

"You're a hard man to refuse. If you were giving some woman the full-court press, I doubt she'd have a prayer. I've been on the receiving end of just a little bit of your seducing. Before tonight, that is—"

"When?"

"That night in your garden and a few hours later in my apartment."

He frowned. "I wasn't trying to seduce you either of those times. In fact, I was being incredibly controlled. I amazed myself."

"My point exactly. You had me halfway to yes without even putting the question out there. If you'd been trying, I would have been toast. And as far as being on the other side of a business negotiation, well, I've learned what you're like in the office, and not just from firsthand experience. I know I got off easy yesterday."

"Oh, really?"

"Yes, really."

"You've been discussing me?" he asked with an acidic layer sandwiched between lighthearted words.

She laughed. "Of course not. I overheard some women in the ladies' room after your status meeting with the IT department last week."

He frowned. "What did they say?"

"I can't tell you that. But I will tell you that one of them threw up and another was on the verge of tears. The others just looked all shook up."

He lay back on the bed with his hands under his head and closed his eyes momentarily. "Christ."

"So just how bad was that meeting?"

"In my opinion, it wasn't bad at all."

"Oh. Maybe it's your management style. If scorched earth is your everyday approach, what are you like when you're really on a rampage?" she asked lightly.

He opened one eye. "I'm not that tough. I've just gotten this reputation. Damned if I know why."

Biting back a smile, she cocked her head pretending to give the matter some thought. "Hmmm. You seem to have a problem with people misreading you. It's so odd for such a pussycat like yourself to get a reputation as a fire-breathing dragon. And it's *so* undeserved."

"Get back to me when you find the sincerity you misplaced," he muttered, and closed his eye.

Laughing lightly, she let a silence build as she leaned on her elbow and ran her hand over him again. She enjoyed the play of textures against her palm, memorizing the hard curves of his chest and the whorls of pale hair that was silky in one direction and coarse and wiry when brushed in the opposite. Her hand came to a rest on his stomach. "So, I need to ask you something, Joe."

He opened his eyes. "That's a very odd tone in your voice."

She smiled. "It's just simple curiosity. You should be used to it by now."

"No, the more I get to know you, the more I realize that nothing about you is simple."

"Is that good or bad?"

"Neither. It's just scary. So what's your question?"

"What's with this?" She gently sank her index finger into his stomach.

He frowned at her again. "What's with what?"

"You're so fit and so hard and muscle-y everywhere else that I was kind of expecting six-pack abs. And here you've got a little poochy stomach." Trying very hard to keep the smile off her face, she pushed her finger into him again. "It's the other kind of six-pack abs."

His eyes widened and his mouth opened in genuine surprise. He stared at her for a good solid minute before speaking. "You're complaining about *my body*?" he said in disbelief. "This isn't exactly a beer gut, sweetheart. I swim nearly every day and work out a couple of times a week, which is more than a lot of guys do. I'm not about to apologize for not doing five hundred crunches a day. I have a real job. In fact, I have two real jobs."

"Oh, heavens, don't apologize, Joe."

"I just said I'm not about to," he protested, then his eyes narrowed. "Oh, you little witch."

She burst out laughing and was flat on her back in seconds, a grinning, wicked-eyed Joe looming above her.

"Let's see." He let his eyes wander down her body, coming to a quick stop at her breasts. "Forgive me for pointing out that I didn't make any comments about why these"—he scooped her breasts together, running his thumbs over her nipples in a deliberate bid to get her to gasp, which she did—"why these impressive creatures aren't still standing at full attention."

She could feel her eyes widen. "You were *hoping* they were fake?"

He shook his head slowly. "The only thing I was hoping was that I'd get to see them at some point. And the rest of you."

"And now you're disappointed that they're real?"

He lifted an eyebrow. "Did I say that?"

"It sure seems like you just did."

With a silent laugh, he leaned over to drop a kiss on her mouth. "Payback's a bitch, isn't it?" he murmured. "I knew they were real."

"How did you know?"

"If you paid for them, you'd flaunt them. But you hide them. At least in public," he added against her mouth.

"So I seem prissy?" she asked after a moment.

"No. Definitely not prissy."

"Stop that," she said, ignoring his laughter as she grabbed his wrists and pulled his hands away from the objects under discussion. "What, then? Shy?"

"That's closer to it, but not—"

"Inhibited?" she offered, trying to keep the exasperation out of her voice.

"That might be it."

"Are you busting my chops again, Joe?"

He lifted his eyebrows in surprise as his smile dimmed. "What makes you think that?"

"Well, you're talking about me not meeting your expectations."

"That's not a bad thing. You exceeded them."

"But your expectations were low and *that's* a bad thing. I think I'm a bit offended."

He narrowed his eyes as he watched her face. "You're not serious, are you?"

"I think so."

"Well, hit me with your best shot. Did I meet your expectations?"

Her brain came to a sudden stop. That wasn't the next question he was supposed to ask.

Oh, hell. How am I going to get around this one?

When she didn't answer immediately, that close-to-shocked look reappeared on his face.

"I can't believe this." He paused, as if trying to find the words. "Five minutes ago you said you liked everything, except, apparently, my stomach. Hell, Naomi, how high were your expectations? You came *four times*. I had to be doing something right."

She lifted a hand and eased it over his mouth, gently shushing him. "I know I did, and I did like everything. Don't go making assumptions—"

He pulled her hand away. "It's not an assumption. I just asked you if I met your expectations and you didn't answer. That typically means no."

"I can't help it if my expectations were all wrong," she protested. "I mean, you walk around giving me that bad-boy smile and turning my knees to melted Jell-O most of the time. Well, I just thought you'd be—" She paused. "Wilder. I never equated you with the slow-and-sweet variety of lovemaking."

That familiar, slightly frustrated look replaced his surprised disbelief as he stared down at her. "You wanted it wilder."

It wasn't a question.

"I didn't say that, Joe. I said that I figured—"

"But you wanted it wilder."

She paused before answering, then gave a small, one-shouldered shrug as she met his clearly exasperated eyes. "I wouldn't have stopped you."

He closed those eyes for a minute as he shook his head. "Then you shouldn't have said, and I quote, 'Make love to me, Joe.' "

"What should I have said?"

He opened his eyes and looked straight at her. If she wasn't mistaken, his gaze had deepened and darkened, but not with annoyance. "You should have told me what you wanted, Naomi. You should have said, 'Let's play *spanky spanky,* Joe.' Or 'Let's hang on to the anchor chain and have underwater sex, Joe.' Or 'I'm in the mood for hot, screaming, headboard-banging jungle sex, Joe,' " he said pointedly. "But 'Make love to me' in *that* tone of voice with *that* look on your face, meant long and slow and calm. No sweating. No chase scenes. No handcuffs."

She watched him during a brief and silent pause, desire and a dangerous smile smoldering in his eyes. It was a potent combination and one that was doing good-funny things to certain small body parts that had only just begun to settle down. She licked her suddenly dry lips and blinked. "You have handcuffs?"

He raised an eyebrow, a bad-boy glint changing the blue of his eyes to an even darker blue. "I worked for a federal law enforcement agency, Naomi. Yes, I have handcuffs. Real ones."

She swallowed and knew that quiver in her stomach too well to ignore it. "Well, Joe," she began slowly, "I guess I'll just have to be a bit more clear next time. But for the record, I've never had underwater sex for obvious reasons. And I've never even heard of *spanky spanky.*"

After a brief, expectant moment, a smile began to tease the corner of his mouth. "You left something out."

"Oh, did I?"

He nodded. "What about the hot, screaming, headboard-banging jungle sex?"

She tried and failed to hide a grin. "How's your heart?"

CHAPTER
22

"My heart is fine, thanks, but my knees are completely shot." Joe lay flat on his back on the moonlit deck, one arm upflung and covering his eyes, the other hand holding Naomi's in a light but secure grip. Utter exhaustion had never felt this good. "How are you?"

"I'm going to be walking funny for at least a day."

He laughed out loud, then looked over at her. She was flat on her back, too; sweaty, smiling, flushed, and gloriously nekkid. The sheets they'd dragged up with them were tangled around her but didn't cover any of the parts most women dived to hide the minute the festivities were over.

Not Naomi. She was on full display under a waning crescent moon, and unconcerned about it. Which, in Joe's mind, just served as further proof that there really was a God. He'd finally met a woman who, he suspected, could keep him infinitely entertained in bed, as well as anywhere else. She was the same naked as she was clothed: fearless, energetic, and creative, with a body as limber as her mind. She laughed, she moaned, she shouted, and gave at least as good as she got.

And she was an eyes-wide-open woman.

He smiled at her, feeling lazy and inert. "So, where did you learn that move?"

Her answering smile was sleepy and sweet, as it should be given that the moon had set hours ago and now hung low off starboard. Intriguing silver shadows played along the length of her as the *Mirabelle* rocked in the light breeze.

"Which move?"

"The one with your legs."

"Oh, the—" She made a descriptive motion with her hand, and he nodded. "I didn't learn that. I made it up."

"When?"

"As I was doing it," she said with a laugh. "My sexual experience is probably orders of magnitude less than yours. I don't have a standard repertoire. It's been a while since I've tangoed with anyone and, frankly, it was never like this."

He hadn't needed to know, but it was nice to hear. "So this was good?"

She rolled her eyes and didn't answer. He just laughed. "Why has it been a while? With your looks, you should be going out all the time."

She covered her mouth as she gave a small yawn. "Well, in fairness, I'm asked out a lot. Or at least my breasts are. But I don't accept many dates, and I accept even fewer second dates. I think I've only been out on a handful since I broke my engagement."

Okay, here's a news flash. He propped himself up on one elbow. "You were engaged?"

"A few years ago. It didn't last long."

"What happened?"

"Well, Daddy didn't like him, for one thing."

"Why?"

"They hadn't ever met before Bill asked me to marry him. Daddy's kind of old-fashioned that way."

"He wanted to be asked for permission?"

She smiled. "I don't think he's that old-fashioned. A

game of golf probably would have sufficed, but Bill didn't even do that."

"Is that why you broke up with him?"

"No. I broke up with him because he was a little too economical with the truth, as they say. Daddy called him morally bankrupt, but I wouldn't go quite that far." She yawned again and snuggled against him. "Tell me about the stars, Joe. You must know them all by now."

She felt good, but he wasn't about to let her warm lushness throw him. "I will in a minute. What does he do?"

"For a living, you mean? He was a lobbyist for the software industry."

"Was?"

She sighed. "At the moment, he's finishing up fifteen months in northern Pennsylvania for attempting to bribe a congressman. I think he works in the kitchen, washing pots."

Joe stared at her. "What is it about you and the criminal element?"

"Well, now, that's hardly fair," she said with mild indignance. "His activities came to light *after* I gave back the ring. Do you think I'd have dated him, much less agreed to marry him, if I'd known he was that sort of a man?"

That's a question that deserves to be sidestepped. "So why did you agree?"

She rolled onto her side, facing him. Her breast fell atop its twin in a luxurious cascade, and it took real restraint not to reach out and caress her.

"I was twenty-seven and feeling too old and too smart to be single. Guys who sit next to me at a dinner party or on an airplane or who meet me in a club don't expect me to say I'm a computer security consultant, they expect me to say I'm a stripper. The minute I mention software, their eyes glaze over and suddenly I'm not worth the effort. Bill was interested in what I did."

He watched shadows and memories darken her eyes. "Poor you," he said with soft sarcasm.

"Don't go overboard with your sympathy, darlin'," she replied dryly.

"I never do. But I can empathize. I think women expect me to be things I'm not."

"Like what?"

He shrugged and felt something related to mild embarrassment creep into the back of his mind. It sat there like a pelican, quiet but ungainly, and ready to make a distinctly ungraceful entrance. He chose his words carefully. "Because of my looks, I think they think I'm supposed to be some half-stoned surfer dude, not a type-A businessman. And because of my background and my job, they think I'm looking for a trophy wife."

"What are you looking for? And by the way, I don't think you're a type A. B-plus, maybe, or an A-minus," she said lightly.

He shrugged. "I'm not looking for anything. Or anyone, in fact. I'm just having fun, doing what I love to do."

"Same here, but somehow, that's not allowed, is it?" Her voice was still lighthearted but held a twinge of bitterness. She must have heard it, too, because her mouth curved into that bright smile a second later and her voice took on a teasing lilt. "So, is it time for the stars yet?"

Ignoring her obvious attempt at levity, he reached up to brush some errant, dampened curls from her forehead. "You're a very smart woman, Naomi, but beautiful is what people see first. If we'd met by sitting next to each other on a plane, I'd have been fully reeled in by the end of the flight. But if you'd been one seat over, I wouldn't have approached you."

She looked surprised, maybe a little hurt, which bothered him, and he wondered if he was beginning to scorch some earth.

"Why not?"

"One thing I learned the hard way in middle school and high school was that looks and brains can go together, and brains and depth can go together, but looks and depth are a rare combination. I've known too many beautiful girls who never bothered to develop things like a sense of compassion or a sense of humor or a personality, because people in general and men in particular are only too willing to cut them a break."

"That's one of the most cynical things I've ever heard."

"Probably. But it's true," he replied.

"So, who do you usually date?"

"Women who possess all three traits: brains, depth, and looks, in that order. I've steered clear of drop-dead gorgeous women my entire adult life. You slipped in under the radar."

"Well, thank you for the compliment, but it almost sounds like you're sorry I did." The hurt in her voice, though veiled with an artificial airiness, was impossible to miss.

I just can't win. Tilting her chin so that their eyes met, he looked into the depths of hers and saw starlight and questions reflected back at him.

"That's one thing I will never be sorry for," he murmured, then he lowered his mouth to hers to help her understand just how sorry he wasn't.

It was well after midnight as they sat next to each other on the deck, wrapped in the coverlet from the bed. Naomi was tucked securely under Joe's arm as they leaned against the benches, watching the moonlight scatter and dance on the black water. The breeze had picked up some, putting a chill in the air where warmth had been for the early half of the night. High, wispy clouds had begun obscuring the constellations that were moving slowly across the sky, constellations that Joe had been introducing to her as though they were his old friends, with background and stories about each one.

Naomi shifted the platter with the remaining shrimp appetizers so it was balanced a little more securely on her lap, then reached for a slice of the ham that lay in a deli bag resting on the lump she presumed was Joe's knee. Her laptop crunched information a few inches away, within reach but with the screen half-closed to avoid casting a harsh glow over the deck.

Joe glanced at it with an almost guilty expression. "I never even asked you how you were coming along with the monitoring data. It was making my brain twitch."

"I know. Forgive me if I point out that you also haven't helped me much in the last few hours. That's why I had to relaunch it, as unromantic as that is. As the hired help, I don't really have any time to waste," Naomi replied.

He laughed and took a swallow of beer. "You don't let me get away with anything, do you?"

"I just spent four hours letting you get away with a *lot*," she replied with a raised eyebrow. "Besides, during that simply charming discussion in my office this afternoon, you used the word *we*. Silly me, but I took that to mean you and me. I didn't realize you were using the royal *we*, which meant *me*."

"That's not fair," he protested. "I was working just as hard as you for the first few hours, then somebody had to steer the boat. Then I was cooking dinner, or trying to. Then—" He paused and made deliberate eye contact. "Then I got distracted. I'm still distracted. You, apparently, are better at multitasking than I am."

She rolled her eyes. "Well, if that doesn't beat all. First of all, sugar, you told me that playing fair is for losers and . . . wait a minute. Did you just tell me I have to do *everything*?"

"Of course not. Tell me what you'd like me to do. Feel free to include suggestions that don't involve computers or software." He lifted a shrimp from the platter and took a bite.

She folded her arms and leveled a semidisgusted look

at him. "Lord have mercy. I'm trying to be serious here, Joe. Is sex all you think about?"

"Not usually, but it has been lately. Now, while this has been a great dinner break, I think we really should get back to work. But if something's on your mind—"

She choked back a laugh, and disguised it as indignation. *"Dinner break?"*

He laughed and dropped a light kiss on her head, which had once again taken up residence against his shoulder. "I'm a guy. We have short attention spans. Start talking before I get distracted again."

"Well, I never. Okay, fine. I'm going to take you at your word. After you left my office this afternoon, I gave it at least thirty seconds of thought before I decided that we are never going to be able to do this by ourselves." She ignored his exasperated groan and the thump of the back of his head meeting the wooden bench behind them. "So while you were so busy at the helm, I was writing scripts to ease my pain." She took a leisurely sip of her wine.

"Don't stop there. You've only just begun talking dirty to me."

She elbowed him gently, giving him a sideways glance. "I thought you wanted me to be serious."

"I do," he replied, tilting her chin up for a lingering kiss. "I mean it. Keep going. I'll shut up."

She pushed him away with a laugh. "We'll see how long that lasts. The first script is an attempt to track the data stream coming from the camera in Trudy's office. As I already told you, we can trace the files to the e-mail server, but not beyond. So I'm trying to see if I can find some pattern of file creation at that interface, or to find out how the packets are being dissassembled and reassembled into a different format that comes out the other side. It's a long shot."

"What about the other scripts?"

The tone of his voice had changed, and Naomi knew she'd succeeded in making sex the farthest thing from his mind. His brain was back in the office, which was a bit of a pity, but reclaiming it in the near future likely wouldn't be a problem. Besides, they needed to talk about this. And maybe a few other things, as well, like hacking and personal histories and the law. But she wanted to be a little closer to shore before she ventured into that territory.

But it could be the right night for a confession.

She shook off the thought. "Well, they're all long shots. The first thing I need to find are the anomalies, the odd things that jump out at you. But I figured the only way to find those is to try to find existing patterns. You know, find out what normal is, then try to find when it changes. I thought usage might be the best place to start, so I've started tracking usage by password to see who is on when and how much movement they initiate on the servers."

"Why by password and not by user name?" he interrupted.

She couldn't help the flare of pleasure his question, and his tone of voice, generated in her. He was genuinely impressed. Given the immediate setting, it almost qualified as foreplay. She shrugged nonchalantly. "Well, the way you have your networks set up, everyone needs at least one password per network, and in certain cases they need separate passwords to get into certain files, like drawings and some of those design documents. And your passwords have to be alpha-numeric, they can't spell any English word, and they have to be changed every thirty days with no repetition. With so many passwords to remember, people forget them, then write them down and then they get lost. Or found by someone else. I mean, you have nine passwords, but Chas has fourteen. Not many people can remember that many. If I can interject an opinion here, y'all should go to random-password generators." She stopped for a sip of wine, then glanced back at Joe.

He was staring at her. "How do you know all that? How many passwords I have, I mean?"

She blinked. "I do my homework."

He didn't respond, and her mood flattened. Confessing was definitely off the schedule for tonight. Doing battle wasn't.

"I didn't hack into anything, Joe, if that's what you're thinking. Those days are long behind me."

He didn't flinch. "Naomi, when I said I wouldn't revisit that subject, it didn't mean that I'm not still curious as hell. I suggest that you don't bring it up again unless you want me to pursue it."

Good heavens. She squelched a flair of panic. "I wasn't bringing that up again, Joe," she lied. "I only meant that I could have gone in without permission, and I would have, but I didn't have to. You gave me God rights, remember? I believe the term you used was unfettered access."

"Of course I remember. And I wasn't accusing you of anything. I just didn't think you'd go *everywhere,*" he replied, looking away and taking a thoughtful pull at his bottle of beer.

"That's why I'm the brains-in-a-box and you're the one signing the checks," she said, unable to keep the sarcasm out of her voice.

He glanced down at her with a small grin. "Who told you I called you brains-in-a-box?"

"Everybody calls consultants that. But don't go thinking I'm about to tell you what we call clients behind their backs."

"I'll get it out of you later. Now pull in your claws and tell me what you're looking for by tracking password usage."

"Something out of the ordinary. An intern in Human Resources logging onto the secret server at two a.m., or a rookie design engineer trying to transfer top secret files to an unclassified server, or some such thing. I'm hoping I'll know it when I see it. I'm also compiling lists of e-mail messages sent to the outside world and subdividing those by time and level of encryption, again just to see if there's anything worth noting." She glanced up at him. "Why are you frowning? I told you these were wild, crazy long shots that probably don't make a lick of sense, but if you don't wipe that look off your face, I'm not going to tell you any more."

He blinked as if confused. "Hey, don't get defensive. There's nothing wrong with those ideas. They're—" He shrugged and glanced away. "Hell, Naomi, I'm in awe. And I think I'm jealous. I never would have come up with them, and I'm not sure I want to know how you did."

The explosion of pride his words inspired made her release a breath she wasn't aware she was holding. "Oh. Well. I thought for a minute there you were thinking I was crazy."

He turned to face her, a small, begrudging smile on his face. "Not crazy. Not yet, anyway. Go on. What else are you looking for?"

"Well, this is the crazy part, frankly. I've written a few scripts to find the big patterns, too, just to see if there's a subtle trend waiting to be noticed."

"Like what?"

She shrugged. "Once again, I don't know. Maybe an e-mail gets sent from one internal address to an outside address at a specific time every day, or a certain file or directory is automatically copied to somewhere it shouldn't be. See, if something like that happens all the time, or at least consistently, it might not raise a flag in the data-monitoring software you have running."

"You've looked at that software. It's excellent. We wrote it in-house and scrubbed it until it's as clean as it's going to get," he protested. "In fact, our top IT guy wrote it, and he's damned good."

Wishing she could toss his ego overboard, Naomi squelched the desire to point out who was defensive now and instead kept her voice calm and neutral. "I'm sure he's very good at what he does, but you know as well as I do that nobody's perfect. Besides, we're talking about code here, not people. If he didn't set up the exact parameters, or if the commands are off in any way at all, the very information you're looking for could be slipping past the filters."

Resting a hand on his blanket-covered thigh, she smiled and lowered her voice a notch. "Look, Joe, instead of trying to come up with every permutation of what could possibly be happening all by myself, which an entire fleet of security teams wouldn't be able to do in a lifetime, I'm trying to coax the data into showing me where to look. This grand scheme may not work at all, but I thought I'd give it a try since I really don't know what else to do. I'll know in another few hours whether I need to come up with a different plan of attack."

He was silent for a moment and looked away briefly to the horizon before bringing his eyes back to her face. "You did all of this—came up with the plan, wrote the scripts, executed them—between our meeting this afternoon and when we went below deck to fool around?"

A little warning signal flicked on in her brain. It wasn't necessarily a bad thing. "Yes."

"And they're running now?"

She nodded.

"How are you running the scripts simultaneously on one laptop?" he asked after another moment.

She hesitated for one beat before answering. "It's kind of a high-performance model," she said dismissively.

His eyes narrowed slightly and a gleam that wouldn't be welcome in church appeared in them. He turned his upper body toward her, making her feel just a little hemmed in. The resulting jump in her pulse wasn't unpleasant.

"You just started talking dirty, Naomi. Don't stop now." His voice had dropped to a growl.

"It has dual four-gigahertz processors, eight gigabytes of RAM, and a one-terabyte hard drive."

She could see disbelief flash in his eyes a split second before the glitter of electronics envy settled in them. She dared not smile. Discussing computer specs had never made her this breathless before.

"Where is the data going?" he asked softly, and it almost sounded dirty.

"It's being dropped into an SQL database, where it's being ranked and prioritized," she replied, her voice softer than it should be.

"Is it generating reports?"

"Just a few. They're simple ones."

"Did you build the database this afternoon, too?" he asked, his eyes boring into hers.

"I finished it just before we hit open water," she whispered, about as turned on as she'd ever been.

He held her gaze for a silent, pulsing minute, then tilted his head upward until the back of it was resting on the bench and his eyes were facing starward. Another long moment passed before he turned his head to look at her with a pained expression in his eyes and a faint, rueful smile on his mouth. "You may think I'm one severely twisted bastard, but I've never been harder in my life than I am right now, and I'm beginning to fear for my health."

She burst into laughter, then leaned closer to him, pressed a light kiss to his lips, and let her hand slip under the blanket. "Don't you worry, Joe. I think you'll be pleased to learn that all that thinkin' outside the box I do has an upside. How do you feel about naked coed multitasking?"

CHAPTER
23

As he lay in bed, staring at the ceiling of the cabin, Joe knew that if he weren't sure that Naomi was exquisitely human, he would have been wondering if she was a 'droid. The woman was as close to his idea of perfect as he could imagine; he couldn't have done better if he'd sat down and made a list, which he hadn't done since he was thirteen. Okay, maybe sixteen.

She was beautiful and sweet, possessed a sex drive that kept pace with his own, and she made him laugh. And she had a brain that left him damned near speechless.

Let's not forget that she dabbles in robotics just for fun.

God almighty. He took a deep breath and let it out slowly.

He considered himself a pretty smart guy. A lot of other people considered him smart, too. He'd always been way ahead of Chas academically, and had routinely hit honors lists in high school and college. He'd been third in his class in law school and first in his postlaw coursework. Nevertheless, listening to Naomi tell him what she'd been able to do in three or four hours had left him feeling awestruck. Of course, he'd gotten over it—part of it, anyway—pretty quickly, thanks to her skill and determination.

"Joe?"

He turned to face her. She was curled up on her side with the sheets pulled around her, watching him with a soft smile on her face. Her eyes, though, weren't as serene. There was trouble ahead.

"Yes?"

"I can't cook to save my life, and I can't swim to save anyone else's."

He smiled back at her. "I know. You already told me that."

"I just wanted to remind you." She paused for a heartbeat or two. "I don't make left turns, either."

Uh-oh. True confessions. This isn't going to be good. "Are you talking politics?"

"Driving. I don't make left turns when I'm driving."

He blinked. "Ever?"

She lifted a golden shoulder. "Not if I can help it. And I can't bend over far enough to paint my own toenails, because my boobs get in the way. They're also the reason I don't ride horses. I'd knock myself unconscious the minute it started to trot. And people laugh at me when I try to do sit-ups."

"Why?"

"I'm not really sure."

He fought a grin and rolled onto his side to face her. "Let me watch you some time and I'll tell you. Anything else you'd like to get off your chest, so to speak?"

She reached out a hand and ran it lightly over his shoulder. As exhausted as his nerve endings were, her touch still sent heat in all directions. "Even though my degrees are technically in electronic engineering, I don't like messing with anything powered by more than two volts."

"Anything else?"

"I think that's it."

"Wonderful. Now." He lifted her hand to his mouth and kissed her palm. "You're telling me this why?"

"Because we just had some pretty excellent adventures with body parts and you're laying there staring at the ceiling, grinding your teeth and sighing heavily, while you should be unconscious and snoring." Her fingers twined with his, and her voice had gone soft. It held a hesitancy he'd never heard before. "I thought it might have something to do with me."

Ouch. "That's rather vain of you," he said, putting a teasing note in his voice. To his surprise, he watched her eyes slowly darken with hurt, and then she rolled away.

Shit. He followed her motion and gathered her into his arms and nuzzled her neck. "Hey, what's wrong?" he murmured. "I didn't mean it. I was teasing you. You're not vain."

"Oh, Lord, Joe," she whispered, but didn't elaborate.

Fuck an elf.

Humor wasn't going to get him out of this one. Not that he knew what would. Honesty was out; it was usually the worst ploy in situations like this and only compounded the problem. Silence on his part would only lead to an explosion on her part. Sympathy might work if he knew what the hell the issue was, but coming out and asking her was likely to result in being told, for perhaps the hundredth time in his life, that he was insensitive and unfeeling.

Might as well try humor.

"Since you're enumerating your flaws, Naomi, I think it's time I told you one of mine," he said, peppering small kisses through her hair between words. "You remember that baseball player they called Shoeless Joe Jackson? Well, most women I've dated morphed that and ended up calling me Clueless Joe Casey." He could feel her smile although she was still holding herself rigid. But, hey, progress was progress.

"You see, the downside of all that bartering math lessons for make-out sessions in high school," he continued softly, "was that I never had to go through the basics of all the girlfriend-boyfriend nonsense. Ever since college I've been sort of a short-timer when it comes to relationships. Women dump me after a few dates, and they inevitably work the phrase *You just don't get it* into the final conversation."

He could tell she was preparing a reply and, pretty happy with the way he was handling the situation, he relinquished the floor.

"Would you please"—she stopped for a deep breath, and Joe smiled—"quit patronizing me?"

His smile disappeared and he tried not to sound annoyed as he spoke to the back of her head. "I'm not patronizing you."

"You are, too." She rolled over to face him, the warm lushness of her body causing, once again, an involuntarily but imminently pleasurable reaction. "This isn't about you and other women, Joe. It's about you. And me."

Pushing himself onto one elbow, he looked down at her. Whatever it was, it had to be his fault. It always was where women were concerned. At least that's what they told him, and he usually didn't have a fucking clue otherwise, so it was easier just to accept it and move on. "Okay, we can talk about us—"

She sighed and closed her eyes in exasperation. "No. Not *us*, Joe. *You* and *me*."

He paused. "Okay, maybe it's a guy thing, but you've lost me. When is a you-and-me not an us? I mean, one minute we're having brain-vaporizing sex, the next minute we're laughing, and thirty seconds later you're starring in *Revenge of the Killer Hormones*. What's going on?"

"Well, the sex we just had might have been vaporizing *my* brain, but you weren't that into it," she replied, and started to roll away again.

He stopped her, incredulous. "*I* what? Are we talking

about the same sex? I was totally into it. You came *twice*. For Christ's sake, Naomi."

"I know. I said *I* was into it. You were—how shall I put it?—less than enthusiastic?"

"I was *not* unenthusiastic. Exhausted, maybe. I'm not eighteen anymore, and you're not exactly the 'lie back and think of England' sort of woman, but I thought we were doing okay. For Christ's sake, we've been at it for hours."

"Well, if you were tired, you should have said something. I'm not a nymphomaniac. We could have stopped."

He shook his head, partly to clear his head, partly to make the conversation seem less surreal. And then it struck him. "Wait a minute. Are you talking about the way I was touching you?"

"Yes, Joe. You were—" She paused. "I don't know. Hesitant? It was a pretty dramatic change from the last time. Almost as if you'd lost interest. And if that's the case, that's fine. But—"

God almighty. He took a deep breath and tried not to show his exasperation. "Naomi, stop. It's not the case. You've got it all wrong. I was trying to be a little gentle because of this."

He brought her hand to his cheek. It took her a moment to realize that he wasn't begging affection; he was dragging her palm across the heavy stubble on his cheek. When recognition appeared in her eyes, he let her hand drop and pulled down the sheet, uncovering her.

"Beard burn. You're hot pink from your face to your knees. You look like you've been keelhauled." He brought his hand around to cup her chin. "I was trying to be gentle because I didn't want to hurt you, not because I wasn't into it. Naomi, we've been making love on and off for—what?—five or six hours? How could you possibly think I wasn't into it?"

She stared at him, then blinked a couple of times in rapid succession. Then she closed her eyes and rolled into him. "I'm sorry," she moaned, her words muffled by his chest wall. "I thought you were feeling threatened by me, or intimidated, or something after the talk we had about the project, and I was just hoping so much that that wouldn't happen with you."

Stifling a grin despite a very strong and uncomfortable tugging sensation somewhere near his heart, not to mention what was going on farther south, Joe pushed her away from his chest until he could see her face.

"You're not getting off that easy," he said flatly. "If you thought I was intimidated, you shouldn't have used sex to try to get around it. You should have asked me."

"I know. But would you have answered me honestly?"

An intriguing blend of contrition and defiance in her eyes held him captive.

"Eventually," he admitted. "Because I *am* intimidated as hell. You've got a brain the size of the fucking universe, excuse my language, and the fact that mine isn't as big isn't something I'm proud of. Until an hour ago, I was pretty happy living in my little world where I had the biggest one going." He laid a finger across her lips as she was about to interrupt. "Size *does* matter to guys when it comes to women, but brains aren't usually the organs we're worried about." He let out a heavy breath, then replaced his finger with his mouth for a quick kiss.

"You amaze me, Naomi. I might be clueless, but I'm no idiot. I'm not about to kick you out of bed because you're smarter than me. You keep right on amazing me; I'll deal with it. Now, what was it you were going to say?"

"I can't remember, and it doesn't matter, anyway," she whispered through a smile that was its own source of light.

"You better mean that," he said, and sat up. "Right now, I'm going to go shave, and if you're still awake when I come out of the head, I'll demonstrate how I deal with intimidating women with supersized brains."

She grabbed his arm and pulled him none too gently

onto his back, then flung her leg over his waist to strad-
dle him before he could argue. Which he had no intention of doing, anyway. The view was just too damned
good.

"Don't you dare shave. This is how you should be
right now. Stubbly and sweaty and just been loved. I like
it. Surely you must have some body oil in here? Or some
olive oil in the galley?"

"Good God, woman, where have you been all my
life?" he groaned, and let out a laugh. "I can guarantee
the only oil on board is motor oil. This is a bare-bones
operation, sweetheart, not a love nest. You're the
anomaly."

"Well, aren't you just the sweetest thing," she said,
her voice rich with honey and sarcasm.

He shrugged and ran his hands idly—maybe not so
idly—up her thighs. "The only reason I have any condoms is because I bought them this afternoon in a moment of weakness."

"Well, I had you covered. I did the same thing," she
admitted with an almost guilty smile. "Why isn't this
your love nest? I would have figured it was exactly that."

He shook his head. "This is my escape."

"From women?"

The warning buzzer went off in his sex-suffused brain
a second too late. The woman was as silent and deadly
as a riptide, and had been pulling him into dangerously
deep waters for most of the night and he hadn't even
realized it. It was well past time to head back into the
shallows. "From everything."

"But you brought me aboard. Twice."

He cleared his throat and searched for a new topic.
His gaze fell from those penetrating eyes to, naturally
enough, her breasts, which were swaying happily in his
line of sight. "So, given your general topography, I
would have thought you'd have bigger, um, capital
regions."

She stared at him for a heartbeat, then started laughing, making those capital regions rise and fall like buoys in a storm. "If I didn't think you'd retaliate somehow, I'd consider slapping you for that one. Yes, I realize you were probably expecting something bigger. But see, Joe, I've got the Connor breasts and the Blanchard nipples."

He cleared his throat, feeling like the conversation had entered yet another dimension. "You name your body parts?"

"No, we track them just like we do other family traits. I suppose it must be a Southern thing. I mean, you've got your mother's eyes and smile, so I'd say they're the Brennan features, unless of course they're from your grandmother's side. Then they'd be named after her family."

"And the Connors?"

"Connor women have large breasts. The Blanchard women's are small."

"I think we'll stop this conversation right here. You're starting to scare me."

"Good." She smiled and rolled off him to reach for the bottle of water he'd gotten at some point during a break in the play. Her luscious white backside was presented to him in all its pristine glory, and he couldn't resist. It was payback time.

He bent his head and kissed her dead center on one cheek.

"Joe, what are you doing?" she shrieked through a surprised laugh, and tried to shake him off by sitting up. He grabbed her upper thigh with one hand and placed the other one in the middle of her back, pushing her down with playful firmness.

"Stop it," she insisted, her tone belying her words. "Let me up right now."

"No," he said around a mouthful of her sweet, cool flesh.

"Joe, stop it. You're chewing on me. That's hardly polite." She was shaking with laughter and still trying to dislodge him, but without much determination or, for that matter, success.

"Polite doesn't go with naked," he murmured. "And I'm not chewing. I could start, though, so hold still."

She actually did go still then, and silent. For a moment. "Sweet Mother of God," she said in a hushed tone. "I thought you were making fun of the expression about kissing my backside. But you're not at all, are you? You're giving me a hickey. On my behind."

"Yup." He lifted his head and studied his handiwork. It was nearly a perfect circle, dark red mottled with purple. It would last for days. He flipped her over and grinned at her proudly. "Congratulations. You've just been awarded the red badge of courage."

She rolled her eyes and sighed. "Well, that's just dandy. Another first. What's the damage?"

He pretended to consider the question. "It's bigger than a Blanchard nipple. We'll call it the Casey hickey."

She laughed out loud, then reached up to grab two handfuls of his hair and pull his face close enough to kiss. "What on earth possessed you, Joe? It's my *behind*."

"Obviously the devil. And it's a gorgeous behind." He shrugged. "You rolled over and there it was, shining in the moonlight like two big lumps of vanilla ice cream. I wanted a taste."

"Two. Big. Lumps," she repeated slowly.

"Well, they're big lumps when compared to the average scoop of vanilla ice cream."

"Two big lumps," she said again, and closed her eyes. "What have I done?"

He laughed and pulled her to her feet. "To sum it up, I'd say you've just had the best six hours of your life. Let's go see what else we can find in the galley. I'm starving."

Falling asleep on the boat was divine, wrapped in Joe's arms with the water rocking them gently. They'd awakened too early to a pearly pink sky and the sound of outboard motors and fishermen greeting each other. The decision not to squander the opportunity had been mutual and silent.

One round of easy, unhurried lovemaking had been followed by a nap, and then reality, hot coffee, and a glance at the galley clock had brought them back to their senses. They had a lot of work to do, and not much time to do it. And they had to do it fully clothed, with their hands on the keyboards, not each other.

"My mother said she invited you over for dinner tonight," Joe said against Naomi's lips as he was taking his good-bye in the foyer of the condo.

"That's right," she murmured. He was holding her snug against him, giving no indication that he was in any sort of a hurry to let her go, which was fine with her. He was warm and solid and bore lingering traces of their escapades despite a quick shower and shave. It was earthy and sexy and she was fit to drag him to the floor and hop on him again, sore muscles and scraped-raw skin be damned. She hadn't been this crazy for a guy in her entire life, and spending the next thirty-five years naked and underneath him sounded just fine.

"I'll pick you up a little before six."

"Okay," she said, and deepened their kiss. Again.

He broke the contact after a moment and started laughing against her mouth. "Naomi, you have to let me go or the plans we just made will never work."

"I was waiting for you to make the first move."

"I've created a monster," he said with a small groan, and let go of her.

She unclasped her hands from around his neck and slid them down the front of his shirt, which was woefully wrinkled after having been torn off in haste and spending the night in a heap on the floor. "Don't worry. No one will suspect a thing when we're at your mother's tonight."

He laughed out loud as he turned to the door. "Whatever you say."

She was still smiling by the time the bathtub had filled. She poured in some of her Chanel bath oil, lit her decadent Rigaud candles despite it being only nine in the morning, and then slipped into the tub to soothe long-forgotten muscles and relive the best night of her life.

CHAPTER
24

His mother was in the kitchen when Joe came through the back door, Starbucks cup in hand.

"Good morning. You were up and out early," she said with a smile. She was dressed up and had a set of car keys next to her purse on the counter.

"I stayed on the *Mirabelle* last night. Where are you off to?"

"Jamie Fagan's daughter is getting married at St. Patrick's Cathedral at eleven."

"Again?"

"Her other daughter. How are things? You look tired."

He shrugged and took a long sip of his cooling coffee. "It's been a long week. Between the testing going on up here and trying to knock out those contract details with Lockheed in L.A., I've been pulling some long hours."

"You're flying out there this week, aren't you?"

He tossed the empty cup in the wastebasket and leaned against the countertop. "No. I told them I didn't have time to go all the way out there. I said I'd meet with them in Chicago and give them twenty-four hours. I'm flying out tomorrow. Then I have another meeting on Tuesday, and I'll be back Tuesday night."

She raised her eyebrows. "This is Lockheed-Martin we're talking about, right? The company *we* approached to work with us on a seven-year contract? And you're giving them ultimatums?"

"Nothing is in jeopardy," he said flatly. "The terms are set. It's their legal team that's dragging their feet. You know how lawyers are: If they don't cause trouble and hold things up, it looks like they're not doing their job. Honest, Mom, they're just farting around with some of the language in the contract. I want to get them moving."

"Speaking of language, Joseph," she said, reaching for her keys. "You're thirty-eight and have three advanced degrees, but your vocabulary is stuck in the tenth grade."

"Preschool, actually. I learned that word behind the barn when I was four. And by the way, Chas taught it to me," he said with a grin, and dropped a kiss on her cheek as he walked past her. "Have fun at the wedding."

"Thanks. Oh, I've been meaning to find out, Joe, did you ever send Karen to The Inn at Little Washington like I asked you to?"

Her voice was much too casual, and he froze in his tracks.

Shit. "No. I forgot." He turned to face her. "What makes you ask?"

"You might want to check your e-mail," she said dryly.

Oh, hell. "She didn't resign, did she?"

"Just read your e-mail. And do *not* contact her until we talk. Enjoy the day. I'll see you later. Naomi will be here tonight, won't she?" she said as she walked toward the door leading to the garage.

"She said she would. I told her I'd pick her up at six."

"Excellent. Bye."

"Have a good time." He headed for his bedroom and a hot shower. The shower on the *Mirabelle* was barely adequate. He had to stoop to get completely rinsed, and this morning he'd only been in there long enough to destroy the evidence. Now he needed a serious shower and maybe an hour in the Jacuzzi. Taking a swim was completely out of the question. He was too damned sore.

Naomi glanced idly at the clock and blinked once. The time registered in her brain, setting into motion a cascade of adrenaline. Abandoning her laptop without a backward glance, she jumped up from the dining room table and hightailed it to the bedroom. It was five thirty. She'd gotten out of the tub at ten and had been working ever since, drinking iced tea and poring over the monitoring data that was churning in her database.

The first few hours had been excruciatingly dull and her brain and body were clamoring for a long, cozy nap, which she had to deny them. But in the last hour, the information presented on the screen had begun to get more interesting. While she was a long way from declaring victory, she was beginning to think that her crazy approach might just pay off. A few new scripts were set to run in sequence, arranging the data in different configurations. If the scripts worked as intended, her "night off" would still be productive and she'd have a lot more information to review by tomorrow morning. She might even have some answers.

Strolling into the bedroom, she stepped out of her shorts, then pulled her T-shirt over her head. Leaving them lying around wasn't an option. There was a very good chance she'd have an overnight guest, she thought with a sly smile. The same smile had been coming and going all morning. And all afternoon.

She stepped into a cool shower to rinse off the aloe gel she'd been slathering on herself all day in an effort to tone down her irritated skin. *Life doesn't get much better than this,* she thought with a smile. She had a great job with great prospects, and it had led her straight to a gorgeous man with possible relationship potential. It was a toss-up as to which part of her life, business or pleasure, held the greatest stake for her right now, but she was certain of one thing: The past twenty-four hours and the next would combine to be the biggest turning point in her life.

If she could find the path of Trudy's data, she could find its destination. Once she found that, she could deliver the goods and wrap up the project. Get the partnership. Talk to Joe. Cleanse her soul.

Then she'd step back and let the universe handle the rest. After she talked to Joe and told him who she was and why she'd hidden the truth from him, the rest just wouldn't matter. He'd either understand or he wouldn't. Whatever was supposed to happen would just be allowed to happen.

She felt another smile cross her face as she stepped out of the shower and began to blot herself gently with the towel. It wouldn't do to rub. Not only would it hurt, it would bring up more color. Air-drying would probably be best, she realized, and walked back into the bedroom.

After all that she and Joe had shared in the last twelve hours, she was sure he'd understand, or at least listen and eventually understand what had happened twenty years ago. She wasn't just some consultant he'd hired on a good recommendation; he knew her now, she assured herself. And she knew him. She'd also fallen in love with him somewhere along the way. Smiling to herself, she let her eyes flick to the mirror as she came to a stop in front of her lingerie drawer.

What if it had just been great sex? Or gratitude.

After all, he'd handled the guys in the bar. He'd dumped the lobsters overboard. He'd waited for her to make the first move.

Maybe we were both just horny, and any excuse was a good one.

She closed her eyes tight for a minute, clenched her fists and every other muscle in her body, then breathed out slowly. *I'm not going to do this. It wasn't just sex. And it wasn't an interactive thank-you note.*

They'd told each other stories about their pasts. They'd shared intimacies about what made them who they are and revealed details to each other that they hadn't revealed to others. They'd achieved a level of comfort and trust—

Oh, really? Naomi's eyes snapped open. Rationalizing her behavior was one thing. Lying to herself was another.

"I revealed one or two of my fears. I didn't tell him about my past. I didn't tell him the truth," she whispered to her reflection. "And Joe was just being Joe: funny, romantic, playing with that quirky charm of his. He didn't reveal anything other than that nonsense about getting dumped by women. And bartering for sex."

She blinked at herself. "This is just dandy," she groaned, and sank onto the bed. Call it fantasy versus reality, truth versus fiction, or sex versus love—it was a battle she hadn't fought in a while, but it hadn't changed much since the last time. And she'd lost that one, anyway.

Falling slowly backward onto the luxurious duvet, she spoke calmly to the richly carved details on the crown molding. "It doesn't matter what I call it. He's a warm, sexy, beautiful man and we both had fun. We laughed. We like each other. And now I'm going to save his company. After that, he won't care that I'm the one who nearly broke it twenty years ago."

She stood up and dragged her sore body to the closet, and reached for the sky blue linen sheath. When she'd settled it over herself, she lifted her chin and turned to her reflection with a smile, bravado fueling her expression. The dress was perfect.

So was last night. And it wasn't just sex.

The phone rang, and a glance at the caller ID screen caused hormones to invade her brain. It was automatic now. "Hello, you."

He responded with a laugh. "If that's part of your plan to convince everyone tonight that we're not sleeping together, allow me to make a suggestion."

"No, that's not part of my plan," she replied with a grin. "Where are you?"

"In the lobby."

"I'll buzz you up."

Minutes later he came through the door she held open and, without any preamble other than a brace-yourself smile, scooped her straight into his arms, and fastened his mouth over hers. After pausing only long enough to kick the door shut, he proceeded to walk her backward until she was up against the nearest wall. Once there, his hands slid down to her thighs and then up under her dress to cup her behind.

Breathless and laughing, she broke the kiss and pushed him away. He only moved a half an inch, but it was about all she was willing to forfeit, anyway.

"Is this Yankee manners? I get a hello grope instead of a hello kiss? And you're ruining my dress."

"Unfortunately, I don't really care about your dress, and a hello grope automatically includes the kiss, so it's the better bargain," he murmured and claimed her mouth again. She let him break contact this time, which he eventually did, but only as she was nearing the edges of a wanton delirium.

"Besides," he said as his lips drifted down her neck. "I was trying to be efficient. I had to say hello *and* make sure you weren't wearing a thong again. Don't want an inadvertent breeze or something like that give us away."

"And you figured that simply asking me would be a bad way to handle it?" she asked, already feeling a low and steady interior throb that did nothing good to her composure or her intentions.

His grin set wild butterflies loose inside her. "No, I just figured this way would be more fun," he replied, and slipped a hand inside the front of her panties, making her gasp. "By the way, you're wet," he added, and then did what he could to exacerbate the situation.

Sensation surged through her, spreading in all directions, dizzying her, taking her breath away. "Well, I wasn't a minute ago."

"No? So does that mean you're glad to see me?"

She gasped again, not from surprise this time, and had to lock her knees before they gave out. "Now, stop this."

"I didn't quite catch that, Miss Connor. Could you say it again without all that ladylike panting?"

"You're a bad man, Joe. We're going to be late." Her voice was edging toward a breathless silence as she tried to hold on to sanity for just a few more seconds.

"Damn that heavy southbound weekend traffic," he murmured, laughter simmering on his face as he watched hers. "I could just tell them I was getting a little behind in my schedule."

She couldn't keep herself from crying out at the furious intensity of her body's need for release. Her hands curled, fisting the pressed and pristine front of his shirt as a vortex of heat and color spiraled through her, threatening to consume her. Her focus narrowed to his eyes, so blue, so hot, so full of wicked laughter.

"Are you having fun yet?" he asked, not taking his eyes from her face. Or his hand from her panties.

"No," she lied in a whisper as a thundering wave of pleasure built toward a towering and fast-approaching crest.

"Really?" he said, his grin getting wider as his rhythm turned lethal. "Should I stop?"

Words were no longer an option as every muscle in Naomi's body clenched and strove for the explosion that came a second later, leaving her shattered and shaking but still standing, and about as limp as she'd ever been in her life.

CHAPTER
25

The first half of the drive to Chas's house was silent. Joe was still feeling pretty smug about the effects of his many deliberate strokes of genius on an unsuspecting Naomi, and the woman herself was still in recovery. He glanced at her across the small cockpit of the Aston Martin. She was nearly back on track, though, because she was starting to get tense. He could feel it coming off her in waves, building like a summer storm.

"I'm not convinced this is the smartest thing we could be doing."

He couldn't hold back a laugh. "You mean after just—"

"No. I mean in general."

"I'm not following you."

She hesitated. "We both know that we shouldn't have . . . let things—" She paused. "We both know that we should never have allowed our relationship to become anything other than professional in the first place," she said in a quiet rush. "And I don't think I should be showing up at a social event with you. Particularly a private family one. Not while I'm still working for you."

He glanced over at her. Her toes were tightly curled, as if they were digging into her sandals for a grip, and she was twisting that pearl ring again, just as she had that first day they'd met. He hadn't seen her do that in a while. "Naomi, you were invited by my mother."

"Not to Chas's house, I wasn't."

He let out a slow breath, wondering when or if she was going to tell him what was really bothering her. The woman had more secrets than a sphinx. It was just a matter of time before he learned all of them, but precisely how much time it was going to take was the real issue. In the meantime, humoring her seemed to be the best option.

"It's the same party. Same people, same food, just a different location," he replied with a casual shrug intended to relax her. "Mom didn't want to cancel it just because the cops closed two of the tunnels and she's stuck in traffic in the city. We're just starting without her."

"It's not just that, Joe. I've never been of the mind that mixing business and pleasure is a good thing."

"It's a bit late to worry about that, isn't it? By about twenty-four hours?" He turned his eyes back to the road, trying to hide his smile. "Tell me the truth. Is this just postcoital jitters?"

"No. I'm not just talking about you and me. I'm talking about Brennan Shipping Industries and me," she said stiffly.

Her inflection made him pause. "What does that mean?"

She didn't answer right away and he could practically hear the gears churning in her brain.

"Do you think last night has somehow tainted the project?" he prodded. "Or are you talking about the situation with Trudy's office?"

"Yes, that's it," she said too quickly, and turned her head to the window. Her hands remained wrapped one around the other in her lap, white knuckled.

She's lying. It was obvious as hell, and that annoyed

him all the more. He said nothing, letting the questions stack up in his head.

A few minutes later, he made himself dismiss it. It had to be the intensity of what they'd shared last night that spooked her. In the space of a few hours they'd gone from "just looking" to "seen it all," from business associates to intimate, uninhibited lovers, and now they were about to make an appearance in front of his family—and her clients.

He eased the car off the Merritt Parkway and around the sharply curved exit ramp that would take them into back-country Greenwich. Their few hours of independent solitude today had obviously had different effects. She'd sunk deeper into his brain—maybe too deep—but he obviously hadn't sunk into hers. On the contrary, she was trying to regain some space.

He downshifted into another curve. The shift in the balance of power wasn't quite what he'd been anticipating; playing by her rules might get her to lighten up.

"If it makes you feel any better, no one from the company will be there other than Chas, my mother, and me," he said casually. Taking his hand from the gearshift, he wrapped it around one of hers. Touching her during sex was like playing with a live wire, but even touching her so casually sent an electric buzz up his arm. He idly brushed his thumb over her palm.

"I thought you said your sister was in town."

"Well, okay. She's on the board, but she doesn't know anything about you or why you're here," he conceded. "Tonight is strictly social, and nothing extravagant at that. Just pretty much steaks on the grill and half a dozen or so screaming kids. All play and no work. I promise."

"And that's supposed to make Naomi a not-so-dull girl?" she said with a tense half smile.

It's a start. "I doubt that you're ever dull. And it was just meant to get that look off your face."

"What look?"

"The one that's almost gone," he said and squeezed her hand. "So what are you going to say when one of the women asks you where you got that healthy glow?"

She returned his glance out of the corner of her eye. "I'll say I got it aboard the USS *Joe Casey*. Or would that be a little too bold?"

He laughed and raised her hand to his lips. "Maybe just a little. The condo pool might be more discreet."

"But that would imply I wasn't working."

"So you'd rather say you got it on the job?"

"This isn't going to be a relaxing evening for me, is it?"

Genuine laughter was back in her eyes and her voice; her tension was gone. He couldn't shake the feeling that she was hiding something, but just as he did when he'd been tracking hackers, he'd bide his time. Eventually she'd slip up. Or just confess.

"You'll be analyzed," he conceded.

"Will I be discovered?"

"That depends on our cover story."

"Exactly what is our cover story? You can't just introduce me as what I am."

"My lover?" he supplied with mock innocence.

"Good Lord," she replied, smoothing her dress over her thighs as a light blush rose in her face. "I meant a security professional. How do we know each other?"

"Biblically."

She gave him a look that, despite its intended purpose, had amusement lurking in it.

"As I recall from my days in the NCIS," he said, in a voice intended to let her know he was only humoring her, "people undertaking covert operations try to stick to the truth as much as possible so they don't get tangled up in lies. And the truth is that we met through a mutual friend in Washington. I say we run with it."

She raised a skeptical eyebrow. "It might be the truth,

but it also sounds like we're on a long-distance blind date. I say we stick with the management consultant idea and add the business acquaintance line to that."

"Fine by me. But it doesn't explain why you're with me on a Saturday night, dressed like that." He flicked his eyes over her dress again. It wasn't too short and her high-heeled sandals weren't too high, but it didn't matter what she wore. She was just sexy, plain and simple. Sexy and hot and his.

She swung her face to his, eyes wide. "What's wrong with what I'm wearing? You said it was casual."

"It is casual and there's nothing wrong with what you're wearing. All I meant is that it doesn't seem very business consultant-ish. It seems more met-through-a-mutual-friend-ish," he said.

"Okay. We met through Sarah. But if anyone asks what I do, we say I'm a management consultant. Is that a fair compromise?"

"Perfect. As is your timing. Here we are," he said, pulling into the long, winding driveway that led to Chas and Miranda's new house. "It looks like the gang's all here." He brought the car to a stop next to Paxton Clarke's black Hummer and cut the engine, then turned to her. "Naomi."

She met his eyes. He'd never seen her look so nervous. If he'd been sure that no one was inside possibly looking out at them, he would have leaned over and kissed her into a Zen state.

Instead, he settled for inching his hand across the gear console again and picking up hers. It was cool and clammy. He slipped his around it and gave it a light squeeze. "If you're uncomfortable, for any reason, let me know and we'll leave. No questions asked."

A heartbeat later, a smile spread slowly across her mouth. The urge to kiss her—hell, to do what he'd done when he walked in the condo—was overwhelming.

"Thanks, Joe," she said softly.

That very softness was like a thundercloud on the horizon and he had to steer clear of it. It was entirely too dangerous. "One more thing."

"What's that?"

"Do *not* smile at me like that until we're in the car heading home, or I won't be the one suffering from embarrassment."

Her eyes widened and she sat up straight. "Got it," she replied, turning to open the door.

As she swung her legs out, he couldn't avoid seeing her dress slide a little higher, and word of the sighting made it through his defenses and straight to the command center, which was already on high alert. He took a deep breath and opened his door. He was going to have a hell of a time hiding the evidence.

By the time he arrived at her side of the car, she was already standing. "Hey, no dogs. This is a nice change."

He shook his head with a grin and slipped his hand under her elbow. "Not yet, anyway. Chas and Miranda are still in the child-producing stage. Dogs are the next stage. Come on. We'll go around the side. If we go in through the front door, Miranda will probably kill me. They just moved in a month ago and the living room is still covered in drop cloths."

He led her around the side of the house, along the newly laid flagstone path. She tripped once, and he caught her around the waist before she fell—the result being that when they rounded the corner, four pairs of eyes looked up to see them walking in what seemed to be a cozy embrace.

And that was all it took. The jig was up. Joe could tell by the way Chas grinned and raised his bottle of Heineken in greeting.

Clearly, there would be a brotherly interrogation conducted at the earliest opportunity.

"Glad you could make it," Chas said easily as they approached. "Naomi, it's nice to see you again."

"Thank you, Chas. And thank you for inviting me."

"We have a minute to spare." Joe glanced at her. "Miranda is a stickler for punctuality."

"That doesn't surprise me. It's a Southern thing," she replied with a smile that could dazzle the unsuspecting, and out of the corner of his eye, Joe saw that it did just that to Tony Pellegrini. *I'll save that introduction for last.*

"Naomi, you already know Chas. This is James Clarke and this is Andy Franklin, two friends of ours from high school." Both men extended their hands and said hello, their social smiles firmly in place. "This is my sister, Julie." He reached over to give her a one-armed hug. "And that's Tony Pellegrini, one of Chas's former partners and James's brother-in-law."

Pellegrini was uncharacteristically subdued in his greeting, but he'd at least managed to drag his eyes away from Naomi's chest long enough to make eye contact. Joe kept a smile on his face and buried his annoyance. "I take it the women are inside?"

"The *other* women, yes," Julie replied, tartly but with a smile. Joe rolled his eyes at the comment and saw Naomi grin.

"Come on, we'll take care of the pleasantries," he said, putting his hand lightly on her back as he gestured toward the house with his other. She stiffened immediately and it took him a second to realize what he'd done. He dropped his hand to his side and murmured an apology under his breath as they crossed the large, shady stone patio.

CHAPTER
26

Still not quite over the mini jolt inspired by Joe putting a territorial hand on her back—even though it was only as an antidote to the very male expression on the craggy face of that curly headed, lecherous-eyed Tony Something—Naomi knew she had to shake it off and quickly before she blew her cover entirely. It was obvious that Chas wasn't fooled.

The spacious, airy kitchen contained three slim blond women at the far end of the room. They were clustered near the sink, looking at something in it and talking, their trim, shorts-clad backsides facing her, oblivious to her presence. But not for long, thanks to Joe's theatrical cough.

They turned at the sound of it, and the sight of them made Naomi's eyebrows rocket northward involuntarily. All three women were really attractive in a healthy, suburban way. And all three were visibly, unmistakably pregnant.

"Hey, Joe. It's about time you got here." The woman in the center spoke the words in a soft and very welcome North Alabama accent.

"I'm not late," he protested in a voice that held more than a tinge of exasperation.

"You're always late, bless your heart. If you're here on time, that makes everyone else early, and that just isn't the case," she said in a teasing voice as she smiled and came forward with her hand outstretched. "You must be Naomi. I'm Miranda Casey. I'm so glad you could arrange to come for supper."

"Thank you for having me, Miranda. I'm pleased to meet you."

After shaking Naomi's hand with a firm but feminine grip, Miranda leaned forward and gave Joe a kiss on the cheek. "You, precious, need a another refresher course in manners."

"I'll see what I can do," he replied dryly.

"You do that. Naomi, these are some of my girl-friends, Paxton Clarke"—Miranda pointed to the tall and very elegant woman with a sleek pageboy and absolutely enormous stomach, who nodded with a polite smile—"and her sister, Jane Pellegrini." The shorter woman with a tousled mop of curls, trendy green glasses, and a friendly, slightly crooked smile held out her hand, which Naomi shook.

"I'm pleased to meet you both. I think I just met your husbands outside." Naomi slid her gaze back to Miranda. "I have to say, Miranda, after living in Washington for so long, hearing your accent is a wonderful thing."

"That sentiment is mutual. Oh, thank you. You didn't have to do that," Miranda protested with a smile as she accepted the small package Naomi handed to her.

"It's nothing, really. Is there anything I can help with?"

Miranda let out a small shriek of delight as she opened the hot-pink Chinese food–type gift box to see the matched set of six wrapped GooGoo Clusters inside. "Oh, honey, I like you. You come back anytime." She looked at her two amused friends. "Ladies, y'all are in for a treat like no other, if I don't hightail it somewhere private and take care of these all by myself." She turned back to Naomi, who was laughing at the scene. "There's not a thing left to do. I was just about to shoo these ladies out the door. Joe, why don't you get Naomi something to drink and we can all head back to the patio?"

With a goblet of cold white wine in hand, Naomi followed Joe and the other women out of the kitchen and back to the rest of the party. She tried to hang back and keep quiet, but was included in conversations everywhere she turned. Despite her best efforts to keep her attention on the speakers, her eyes always found their way back to Joe, who was making a concerted effort to be polite and cordial to her, stopping just shy of downright friendly.

At the moment, he was engaged in a conversation with Chas and Tony Pellegrini, giving her a clear opportunity to observe the brothers. They were a study in contrasts; Chas was so dark and smooth and easy, where Joe was so blond, with edges that were a little rougher and manners that seemed to be more instinctive than automatic. He stood next to Chas, bigger and taller, legs apart, arms folded across that solid swimmer's chest, frowning in concentration as they discussed something she was too far away to hear.

Classically handsome and easygoing, Chas would draw the eyes of anyone walking into the gathering. He was just that sort of man, and had a way of making you feel that everything you said mattered. Naomi was willing to bet that good things just sort of came his way, as if he had a magnetism that repelled anything bad and attracted only the best.

Taking a thoughtful sip of her wine, she shifted her gaze back to Joe, who, she knew, would never be the first guy anyone would approach, anywhere. His good looks might be the first thing that registered on a person's brain, but they were neutralized by the impression that he was tough and cool and impervious. Which he was—when he wanted to be. And *that's* what kept people at arm's length; what made men lionize him and

women throw up in the ladies' room when he asked their
opinion on a business deal.

Fools. Any truly astute observer could see that there
was something just below the surface that said his attitude was mostly a lie, or maybe just a show. He was
better-looking than Chas—bigger, blonder, blue-eyed,
with a hard-body bad-boy stance and a smile that could
melt diamonds—and he was an extremely smart man
beyond everything else. Even without the Brennan background, Joe would undoubtedly be a hot property in the
bachelor marketplace if it weren't for his reputation as
short-term material.

Slowly surveying the group in which he stood—
surrounded by his siblings and James—he was laughing
and at ease. But he was also so clearly the second son,
the younger brother. Chas was the natural leader, and
Joe, for all his good looks and solid character, would
never be a Chas, despite how badly some small, adolescent part of him probably wanted to be. And he'd always
known it. The realization made Naomi's heart ache for
him again, and right then, as if he knew what she was
thinking, he looked up and caught her eye. One eyebrow
flicked downward minutely and he returned her smile a
little warily, then dragged his attention back to Chas.

Mary Casey arrived then, crossing the patio with an
apology for Miranda and a warm greeting for Naomi.
She moved through the crowd with ease, leaving smiles
in her wake. It was apparent that she'd known everyone
but Naomi for decades, and equally apparent that her
role over the years had changed, from mother to friend
to, in the case of Joe and Chas, boss. She handled it
well, and Naomi was more than a little in awe of her.

Seeing the family together, watching their genuine and
affectionate interactions with one another and with their
close friends as cocktail hour swirled around her, an unexpected wave of emotion crested and crashed over
Naomi. It wasn't homesickness, exactly, and it wasn't
envy. It was, she realized with no small sense of alarm,

a strong sense of connection. She felt welcome, included. Like she belonged, even though she knew she didn't. Not yet, maybe never.

But I'd like to.

Naomi felt her eyes widen as the thought registered, and she knew she had to get somewhere private. She eased out of a conversation she hadn't been paying much attention to, anyway, and hightailed it to the powder room.

It wasn't just Joe she wanted. She wanted this. All of it. She wanted the Caseys, their warmth and laughter and their strong, steady family bonds, for her own. Her parents were loving and the relationship she had with them was good, but as a family, they had never been like this. They weren't friends, confidants, equals.

It's impossible. Becoming a part of this, having this, deserving this, was a fantasy, not an option. Not until the cloud of history hanging over her head cleared away. Then and only then would there be any possibility of inclusion.

Bracing a hand on the small sink, Naomi lowered herself with suddenly weak legs onto the closed commode, realizing with an implacable sense of dread and destiny that she had to talk to Mary tonight. Right now. Before she lost her nerve.

After a few minutes, she stood up and dampened a corner of one of the colorful linen guest towels, blotting it on her face to help cool down. Two deep breaths later, she met her eyes in the mirror.

"Shoulders back, chin up," she whispered, then turned and opened the door.

Miranda and Joe were standing a few feet away, talking in a concerned whisper. They both straightened up and snapped their heads toward her as they saw her step into the hall.

Giving her a quick once-over, Miranda shot Naomi a half smile and discreetly headed for the kitchen without saying a word. Joe stayed where he was, his eyes searching her face with a mixture of wariness and concern.

"Are you okay?" he asked as she closed the small gap between them.

"I'm fine," she said with a forced smile.

He hesitated. "I know you had reservations about coming here in the first place, so you don't have to lie to me."

Oh, darlin', how I wish that were the case. She didn't trust her voice and just tried to smile instead.

"I saw you bolt off the patio with a strange look on your face. Are you sick? Do you want to leave?"

She winced. "No, thank you. Did anyone else see?"

"Miranda."

She let out a breath that she hadn't realized she was holding. "I'm sorry to have upset you, Joe, but I'm fine. Really. I think it was just the combination of lack of sleep and a glass of wine," she lied. "I got a little dizzy."

The look in his eyes told her that he wasn't buying it, but he didn't argue. "Do you want to sit inside for a little while?"

"No, Joe, we'd be missed. I don't want to make it awkward for you," she protested.

He smiled then, but it was only a shadow of his real smile. "I didn't mean I'd stay with you. My mom's foot is bothering her a little after all that stop-and-go driving, so she just went into the study to put some ice on it and elevate it. You can sit with her for a little while, if you don't mind."

It's a sign. It has to be. She swallowed hard and gripped the stem of her wineglass so hard she thought it might snap in her hand. "I'd like that, Joe. Point me in the right direction."

"Straight down the hall, third doorway on your right." He glanced behind him quickly, then leaned down and pressed a quick kiss on her mouth. "Don't look so scared. I'm the only one in the family who bites," he whispered, and winked at her in an unexpected return to the Joe she preferred. Then he turned and headed for the patio.

She brushed a few damp hairs from her forehead with a hand that wasn't altogether steady and walked down the hall.

Andy was sitting with Mary when Naomi walked into a room dusty from construction and lit only by the smudgy rays of late-afternoon sun streaming through newly installed, heavily fingerprinted windows. The pungent tang of fresh plaster mingled with the warm earthiness of hours-old sawdust.

Even in this state, the room held an invitation, and Naomi knew it had more to do with the occupants than the setting. With a slow smile and an easy grace, Andy stood up and, after a few minutes of casual conversation, made his excuses and returned to the party.

Mary smiled up at her from the worn leather chair that seemed to have been placed there hastily. "That Andy is such a doll. He's like my third son. He practically grew up in our house." She waved a veined hand adorned only by a simple gold wedding band. "Have a seat."

"Thank you." Naomi lowered herself to the tattered wing chair—no doubt another hasty and temporary addition—that sat opposite Mary, and hoped her voice wasn't shaking as much as her knees were. "Joe mentioned that he's just moved back."

Mary nodded with a knowing smile. "He's back for good."

"Oh. Joe didn't mention that."

"Joe may not know yet. But the love of Andy's life just moved back to town, and she's single again."

Naomi smiled. "Lucky woman."

"She is indeed. Would you mind closing the door, Naomi?"

"Not at all."

As soon as Naomi had reseated herself, Mary looked at her expectantly. "So, what do you want to talk to me about?"

CHAPTER
27

Naomi could feel her eyes widen and her mouth go dry at Mary's simple question. She took a small sip of wine to give herself something to do as she tried to come up with an equally simple answer.

"I presume you *do* want to talk to me. After all, why else would you be in here?" Mary continued gently in the void left by Naomi's silence. "I mean, Joe is out there on the patio."

Naomi could feel a blush rising to her cheeks, and she dropped her gaze to her wineglass. "You know."

"I'd say everyone out there knows," she replied with an affectionate laugh. "You're both trying too hard not to look at each other. But the good news is that everyone out there is pretty much in the same state of bliss, and you know that happiness loves company even more than misery does. Besides, I'm his mother. I've known something was happening between the two of you since the day you walked into my house several weeks ago. It was all there in the way he looked at you."

The words warmed and calmed her, and Naomi couldn't hide the small smile they brought to her face. "Does it bother you?" she asked quietly.

"Bother me? I couldn't be happier. He's a wonderful

man and you're a lovely young woman. You're good for each other. You deserve each other."

Lord have mercy. This was it. This was the moment.

Naomi lifted her eyes to Mary's. "I need to tell you something, ma'am. You might want to reserve judgment about me until then." Her voice was a hoarse vestige of itself, and it shook.

Mary sat back with a calm question in her eyes and folded her hands on her lap, elbows on the arms of the chair. "All right, Naomi. I'll do that. What do you need to tell me?"

She closed her eyes for a moment to pool her strength, then sat up straight and opened them and met Mary's. "Ma'am—Mrs. Casey. I—" She stopped and swallowed. "I'm the same Naomi Grace Connor who hacked into your company nineteen years and five months ago. I'm R@ptorGurl," she whispered. And then, like a river in a rainstorm, the words just started to flow out of her in a heavy, chaotic churn. She couldn't have stopped them if she'd tried. "Ma'am, I am so sorry for what I did to you. There's not a day's gone by since then that I haven't thought about it and wished I could do something about it. I know you know it wasn't intentional on my part, but I also know that I caused you and your family and your company a lot of harm."

That she was saying it all without bursting into tears was a minor miracle, and it had a lot to do with her audience. Mary had blinked once, then shifted in her seat minutely, but her expression hadn't changed and she hadn't said a word.

"Ma'am, I knew at the time I caused you a lot of trouble, but as I've gotten older, the magnitude of what I did to you has thunderstruck me again and again. My actions changed a whole lot of lives that day. I've come to understand that. I know it changed yours, and Joe has told me how much it changed his." She paused for a quick breath. "My life changed that day, too, and it could have changed in ways that were much worse. You could have caused me at least as much trouble as I caused you, but you didn't. And you went out of your way to make sure no one else ever could. I want to thank you for that. It's a gift I will never, ever forget. My life wouldn't be anything like what it is today if you hadn't done what you did."

The silence that filled the room throbbed with tension, but Mary remained as still as she'd been all along. Finally, she cocked her head to the side slightly.

"Are you finished?"

The question was asked kindly, but its direct simplicity left Naomi speechless. She sat back in her chair and nodded.

"Good," Mary said gently. "Thank you for that, Naomi. It took a lot of courage for you to come up here to work on this project in the first place, and saying what you just said to me took a lot of strength. We both know you didn't have to do either. You could have gone on with your life and ignored the past. The fact that you didn't says a lot about you, and I'm even more impressed by you for having put yourself through this. It can't have been enjoyable or easy."

Naomi sat there, her stomach churning, her bloodstream chaotic with adrenaline, her mind as chalky and blank as the newly Sheetrocked wall behind Mary's chair as she tried to absorb everything that Mary *hadn't* said. The silence in the room remained absolute, but it held something closer to serenity now, and it was working on Naomi's shattered nerves. Eventually, she remembered how to talk.

"You knew who I was? All along?" she whispered.

Mary smiled. "Of course I did. There are certain names you never forget, and the name of the twelve-year-old who caused us such a setback is one of those names."

"How could you let me into your home?" she asked, still shocked but coming out of it.

Mary laughed silently and there was no malice in it.

In fact, it reminded her so much of Joe's laugh that there was no way Naomi could find a way to fear it.

"Honey, take another sip of wine. You're much too pale beneath your sunburn."

Sunburn. Naomi felt heat rush to her face but followed Mary's suggestion, anyway, and then set the goblet on the small folding table next to her with hands that weren't shaking too much anymore. "Ma'am, I came in here to find absolution, not to pepper you with questions. But I have to admit, I've got a few."

"Ask me anything."

Naomi stared at her, at a momentary loss. "Well, I guess the first is, if you recognized my name right away, why didn't you say anything?"

Mary shrugged; the motion was relaxed and loose. "Approaching me—confessing—was something you needed to do, otherwise you never would have joined the project, Naomi. I couldn't steal your thunder."

Now I know where Joe gets it. Naomi swallowed hard and blinked back tears of sheer thanksgiving.

"Thank you," she said after a moment. "I have to be honest with you, ma'am. I'd never have that sort of restraint."

"Under the same circumstances, of course you would," Mary replied with another smile. "At the time you hacked us, I was a mother of teenagers, Naomi. All children make mistakes, even good kids, and you were not much younger than Julie. I flew down immediately to meet with the federal district attorney, the FBI agent in charge of the case, and your parents. And it was what they told me that determined how we handled the situation. You were intelligent and curious and precocious, and you liked to face down a challenge. Any of those terms could have been applied to my own children. But you weren't a delinquent or a sociopath, or likely to become one. You were the one who came forward and alerted us to what had happened when you could have just tried to run away from it or start a trail of lies.

Either of those responses would have been perfectly normal coming from a twelve-year-old." She took a deep breath. "The local DA wanted to make an example of you, but you didn't deserve that sort of trouble. I wasn't about to let that hothead turn you into a springboard for his career."

Naomi quickly wiped away two tears that spilled over, and straightened her back. "Ma'am, with all due respect, most twelve-year-olds don't cause hundreds of millions of dollars of damage to a Fortune 500 company and compromise national security."

Mary actually laughed, to Naomi's amazement. "Well, when you put it that way, I can't argue with you, but we all survived, didn't we?" She took another breath, leaned back in her chair, and met Naomi's eyes with a rueful smile. "The sad truth is, Naomi, that every single one of us makes mistakes, and you have to make allowances for that. Sometimes huge allowances. Too often, our flaws are what define us. And they certainly help make us who we end up being."

Ask it. You have to. Naomi met Mary's eyes again. "Does Joe know who I am?"

Mary's eyebrows shot up in surprise. "If you're asking whether I've told him, the answer is no. But a moment ago, you made it sound as if you had discussed it with him."

Naomi shook her head slowly. "Only in very general terms. He told me about how that event—my hacking into your company—changed him, or his career choices, anyway. But I couldn't find a way to tell him I was the cause of it." She swallowed hard and felt a lump the size of Alabama begin to grow in her throat. She forced a smile, anyway, and tried to inject some lightness into her voice. "I know I have to tell him and I fully intend to, it's just the *when* that has me in a state." She paused. "What do you suppose he's going to think when I do?"

"He'll be deeply hurt and he'll be angry," Mary replied quietly but without hesitation. "You already know him well enough to know that. But he's a softie underneath all that bluster and he's a lot more sensitive than most people give him credit for. I'm sure you already know that, too."

Bracing herself against the burning ache behind her eyes, Naomi nodded. "Will he forgive me?"

For the first time in the conversation, Mary paused, and Naomi's heart plummeted.

"I can't answer that, Naomi, but I'll be very disappointed in him if he doesn't." She reached down and lifted the ice bag off her bruised foot, then stood up gingerly. "It's time to get back to the party. This will stay between us, of course. Now, just go out there and keep trying to pretend you're not in love with him," she finished with a smile. "Maybe he'll catch on."

They reappeared on the patio a few moments later, and Naomi felt as though half the weight of a lifetime had been lifted from her shoulders. She eased her way back to Joe's side and joined the conversation, and even managed—she hoped—to keep her expression friendly and interested, instead of madly in love. Miranda announced that dinner was mere minutes away from being ready, as Chas joined them with a smile, slipping an arm around his wife's waist and resting a hand on her pregnant stomach. Miranda looked up and leaned into him in a way that seemed to be a comfortable habit.

The sweet intimacy of the gesture pinched Naomi right near the heart and, taking another sip of wine, she looked away to break its piercing grip.

"I believe you told me you don't ever date women you work with."

Here we go. Joe withdrew the bottle of Harp from the refrigerator's top shelf and stood up slowly, glancing over his shoulder at Chas, who was leaning against the counter, arms folded, with *big fun* written all over his face.

"Your memory is impressive." He flipped the cap off the bottle and tossed it in the trash.

Chas laughed. "I suppose I should be pissed off, but I like her. Does she know that the average duration of your relationships is three weeks?" He tilted his bottle to his lips.

Joe sent him a dirty look. "Let me know how long you intend to give me shit. I'll go finish this beer and come back for the finale."

"As long as it takes. I believe it's called payback."

"As long as it takes for what? Maybe I can save you some time." Joe leaned against the counter opposite his brother and took a long, slow swallow of beer.

"As long as it takes for you to make a decision."

"About?"

Chas laughed again. "Don't play lawyer to my cop, Joe. It's obvious as hell that you're a goner, and it's a glorious sight to behold." He pushed away from the counter and headed for the back door. As he pulled it open, Chas glanced over his shoulder. "Third finger, left hand. Call me if you can't remember the combination to the vault."

After dinner, Mary suggested relocating the party to her house, where there was more space and less dust, and, most important, dessert.

Naomi watched in amusement as previously unseen children and nannies began to materialize from all directions, and Joe proudly introduced Naomi to his sister's daughters and to his nephew, Web. He was Chas and Miranda's son, and looked like a blond version of Chas. Paxton just waved a languid hand in the general direction of three towheaded children of varying heights and ages who were being herded into the Hummer by two young, no-nonsense Irish nannies, and said tiredly, "They're mine. Hunter, Bailey, and Charlie. Come back in three months and you can meet the other two."

The children situated and on their way to their various

homes and beds, the adults got in their cars and headed
the short distance to the other Casey household. Joe was
taking his time fiddling with the CD player as the other
cars started down the long driveway.

"I can't believe Paxton is having twins," Naomi said
as James drove past them in a sleek Jaguar convertible
with Paxton, looking very Grace Kelly-ish, next to him.
"She's so calm."

"Nothing gets Paxton ruffled. What I can't believe is
that she's about to have her fourth and fifth kids," Joe
responded, shaking his head. "Somebody needs to talk
to those two and tell them the honeymoon's over."

"Hey, honeymoons should never end, and I think big
families are wonderful."

He glanced at her. "How many kids are in your
family?"

"Just me."

"I figured as much. Only children always think big
families are wonderful," he said as he followed his
brother down the driveway. It wasn't until Chas's car
turned onto the road and was momentarily out of sight
that Naomi realized their placement as the last car in
the queue was deliberate. Because that's when Joe
reached over and lifted her hand to his mouth for a
quick kiss, then held on to it after he pulled onto the
road. The sweet, simple gesture triggered a burst of
warmth inside her.

"I think it's the idea of always having someone around
to play with that only children like. Being an only child
means that you always have to go outside the front door
to play with someone. You and Chas and Julie are all
pretty close in age, and could probably always find something to do together. I would have liked having a sister
close to my age."

"To keep you out of trouble?"

"I didn't get into trouble," she said with a laugh. "I
was always a good girl. Maybe until last night, that is."

He sent her a hot smile and gave her hand a light

squeeze before he let go of it to shift gears. "I like your variety of bad. We'll have to see if you can get any worse. But I was talking about your adventures in hacking," he said lightly. "Do you think a constant playmate would have kept you away from the keyboard?"

The unexpected shift in topic sent Naomi's stomach into a twisting backflip. "It likely would have just doubled the trouble," she said with a forced laugh, and glanced out the window.

"So, what did you talk to my mom about?" he asked after a short pause.

Oh, Lord, he's like a pointer on a scent. She kept her eyes focused out the window and gave a little wave to the two cyclists they passed. Neither of them saw the gesture, but it didn't matter. It kept her from having to look at Joe while she lied to him.

"We just chatted. You know, this and that. Making conversation was the very least I could do, seeing as how she was injured and I slept with her son and all." Her voice held a breeziness she was far from feeling.

"*Are* sleeping with."

"I'm sorry?"

"Don't make it sound like a one-off thing," he said, keeping his eyes firmly on the road.

She lifted an eyebrow. "Hmm. So I get another chance?"

"No fishing allowed. Here we are," he said as he followed Chas's Porsche into his mother's driveway and came to a stop.

CHAPTER
28

Dessert at Mary's was as simple as Naomi expected it to be. Homemade brownies and a peach pie shared space on the table with a bowl of strawberries, and a carton of ice cream was produced at Joe's request. It was plain vanilla, but the richest, creamiest variety Naomi had ever enjoyed. She didn't dare try to find him as members of the group drifted in and out of the dining room to help themselves, because she knew she wouldn't be able to hide a blush.

"Something on your mind?"

His voice was low and naughty and right behind her as she paused in the doorway leading into the living room, where people were gathering into small, conversational clusters.

"Not at all. I'm just enjoying myself," she replied, as calmly as she could given that his words and their delivery enveloped her senses as completely as the dark, warm chocolate smothered the strawberry she held in her fingers.

"How's your ice cream?" He came around to her side and leaned against the doorjamb, casually lifting a coffee mug to his lips. He looked nonchalant and relaxed, and didn't even have a twinkle in his eye to give away the undercurrents in his voice.

She took her time finishing the strawberry, careful not to make eye contact. "It's delicious. It tastes homemade."

"It is. Since I moved back, my mother's housekeeper has been outdoing herself."

"So she's to blame for that squishy tummy of yours?" Naomi asked under her breath, her eyes flicking to Joe for a second before scanning the room casually. She patted her lips with her napkin, more to hide her smile than anything else.

He sent her a big grin, as if she'd told a joke. "You're venturing into deep water, Naomi," he said softly. "And you're no swimmer, remember?"

"That sounds like a threat," she replied, a friendly, answering smile on her face as she met his eyes. There was definitely a twinkle in them now.

"Imagine that. Just keep in mind that I don't write checks I can't cover."

Their sly conversation had to stop there because Paxton was approaching them. They moved apart to allow her to pass through the doorway and as she walked between them, she gave them each a quick look.

"Just to let you know, kids, we all think you're adorable, but you're not fooling any of us," she said dryly, the shadow of a smile gracing her face. "And thank you for behaving so well, but you had probably better start to mingle again or someone is bound to go public."

Naomi's eyes met Joe's as Paxton continued down the hallway.

"Now what?"

"As the lady said, we mingle. You go that way and I'll—"

From across the room, Miranda's soft voice stopped their conversation.

"I hate to sound Victorian and what all, boys, but the girls need some time."

Naomi had to bite back a laugh as Chas, James, and Tony Pellegrini looked at one another and took deep, patient breaths. Andy just started laughing, and Joe turned to Naomi with a pained expression.

"Be strong," he muttered, and made his way into the living room with the men.

The women drifted out of the room, headed toward the kitchen and, based on what Miranda was saying, the GooGoo Clusters.

Forty-five minutes later, they were still in the small sunroom off the kitchen; Naomi had had one glass of wine more than she'd intended to, and the other five women were drunk on chocolate. Mary had left them to their own devices—or maybe just vices—a few minutes earlier.

Jane turned and pinned Naomi to the couch with a determined grin. "Somebody has to take the plunge, so it might as well be me. What's up with you and the stud muffin?"

A brief moment of excruciating silence ensued, during which Naomi caught her breath and blinked. "Just exactly what you think is up, darlin'."

Laughter filled the room and the last vestiges of distance between Naomi and the group of friends fell away.

"So, are you really a management consultant, or is that just your cover story so you didn't get the new-girlfriend grilling?" Julie asked with a grin that resembled her brother's.

"Both," Naomi replied slowly. "I am here on a project that's nearly finished, but in the process of working all those long hours we sort of . . . became close friends."

"If I could play amateur psychologist for a minute, may I ask if the word *boat* means anything to you?" Paxton asked, wiping imagined vestiges of chocolate from immaculate fingertips.

"Actually, Paxton, no, you may not," Naomi replied lightly.

Paxton smiled. "The prosecution rests."

"Well, here's to the undoing of big, bad, indigestible Joe: concrete on the outside, marshmallow on the inside." Julie lifted her wineglass in a toast. "You're to be congratulated, Naomi. You inspired him to break not only company policy but *two* of his own hard-and-fast rules, one being his prohibition against taking women on board his precious boats and the other being his prohibition against dating colleagues."

"Lord have mercy, Julie, don't start in on the Casey Boy Rules," Miranda said, rolling her eyes. "I still keep tripping over them everywhere I go. Sometimes I think those two make them up as they go along, and just *act* like they're the lost set of commandments."

Entirely too sure that the conversation was heading into the Land of Full Disclosure, Naomi cleared her throat. "Okay, so ten minutes ago y'all were telling me about the glories of being pregnant, not that I believe a word of it, bless your hearts, but I need to ask y'all a question. I didn't want to ask it in front of Mary."

Four sets of eyes fell upon her with the eagerness of the initiated educating a virgin.

"How do y'all shave your legs?"

"You don't. You have them waxed," Paxton replied at the exact moment Jane said, "I don't. Tony does it for me when we're in the bathtub."

The sisters looked at each other in horror and surprise, respectively, and the rest of the women choked back laughter.

"You just learn how to stand at the sink and bend funny," Miranda said after a moment, and lumbered to her feet. "Anybody need more ice cream?"

Having covered all the usual topics discussed by actively procreating women—men, food, children, breast-feeding, labor, men, weight gain, weight loss, the state of their pre- and postpregnancy bodies, and men—the women found their way back to the living room and announced that the evening had come to a close.

The good-byes were warm and friendly, and that traitorous desire to be an insider washed over Naomi again,
swamping her ability to compose herself. They'd been
driving for several minutes in silence through the dark,
tree-lined roads when Joe reached over to take her hand
in his, then lifted it to his lips. She felt the light brush
of his mouth echo everywhere.

"Are you okay?" he asked gently. "The guys did their
best to embarrass the hell out of me, in case you didn't
notice, but the women didn't make you crazy or anything, did they? I know they scare the bejesus out of me
when they get together. All they talk about is babies in
some form or another."

She smiled. "No, they were fine. They took it upon
themselves to educate me, but I was expecting that. And
when the guys were harassing you, it just made me feel
included. In fact, I think I'm a little jealous. You have
a great group of friends, Joe, and your family is
wonderful."

"I like them," he said easily, and wove his fingers
through hers more securely as their hands rested on her
thigh. "They liked you, too."

"Thank you. Nobody believed the business-associate
line, though."

"I never thought they would."

She flashed a smile at him and then turned to look
out the window.

*I need a cool shower and a good night's sleep. By
morning, I will have snapped out of it.*

"Are you sure you're okay?" he asked a moment
later. "You're awfully quiet."

"Enjoy it while you can," she said with a light laugh
she thought sounded a bit flat.

He gave her hand a warm squeeze and the sensation
spread to her heart.

*I really can't go on like this. I'm going to explode. I've
got to tell him.*

"You know, Naomi, you're beautiful, sexy, smart as

hell, and a hell of a lot of fun. There's only one problem that I have with you," he said too casually, keeping his eyes on the road.

She froze, her heart flipping over.

I didn't mean here. *Not* now. *Take some pity on me.* She made herself smile at him. "Oh, what's that?"

He swung his head to look at her, amused concern playing on his face. "What's wrong?"

"What do you mean?"

"Your hand jerked a second ago and you look like something just spooked you."

"Do I?" *Oh, mercy. This is it.*

He squeezed her hand again and gave her a smile laced with laughter. "I had no idea you were so jumpy. Must be that guilty conscience."

"What guilty conscience?" she croaked.

"We can come back to that. It's not the problem I was talking about."

She fought the urge to go limp.

He paused for a good, long minute, the laughter never leaving his eyes. "Do you remember when we were in your office and you told me I could ask you anything about your past?"

Another moment I'll never forget. "Yes."

"Do you remember what you said when I asked you what you did and how you were caught?"

"Yes," she said more slowly. "I told you that I never got caught."

"And you had your fingers crossed behind your back when you said it," he added softly, then gave her a look that was sly and triumphant and sexy as bedamned all at the same time. "It was a dark and rainy afternoon, if you'll remember, and that big window behind your desk makes a very effective mirror."

Part of her felt like crying and part just felt like throwing up, but instead she swallowed hard, lifted her chin, and met his eyes with her eyebrows raised. And lied to him again.

"Good heavens, Joe, I know that. I was having some fun with you. Frankly, I'm surprised it took you this long to mention it. I figured you were waiting for a chance to put me over your knee or something."

He laughed out loud and lifted her hand to his mouth for another kiss. "You are the absolute worst liar I've ever met. But that suggestion of putting you over my knee is one you can hold on to. And it brings me back to my original point."

"That's right. Your problem."

He gave her a sidelong glance. "My *problem* is that I can't seem to keep my hands off you."

"And that's a problem why, exactly?" she drawled.

"You are pure trouble, you know that? I'm beginning to think that it's a good thing I'm leaving town for a few days."

"Of course it's a good thing. If you look at me like that while we're at the office, people will start talking."

"Don't be naïve. People are already talking," he replied dryly.

"Do you think?"

"Of course. We were seen leaving the building together twice yesterday. I'm sure that news spread like wildfire."

She bit back a laugh. "No offense, Joe, but the news that spread like wildfire was probably more about the fact that you'd left the building than who accompanied you."

He turned to her, his surprise evident. "What does that mean?"

"That everybody could breathe easier. People are scared of you, sugar."

"What the hell do I do that scares people?" he asked, his question edged in frustration.

"That." She squeezed his hand reassuringly. "Come on, darlin'. Do you realize how rarely you smile when you're at the office? And you tend to speak in one- or two-word sentences whenever you can get away with it. I don't think people see you as a guy because they can't get past you as the boss."

He didn't answer until they'd come to a stop sign and started moving again. "Do they like Chas?"

The question tugged at her, and her voice softened of its own accord. "It's not that they don't like you, Joe. You just keep them nervous."

"But does Chas do that?"

"No. He doesn't intimidate them. The women can flirt with Chas, or they think they can," she replied after a minute.

"Some of them flirt with me."

"No, they don't," she said gently. "They're not flirting with you, Joe. They're trying to be pleasant and innocuous so you won't single them out for destruction."

He paused, clearly not pleased with the conversation. "You're just busting my chops, right?"

"Unfortunately, I'm not."

He sent a glance her way. "Did I intimidate you?"

"No, but the client-consultant relationship is different than the employee—"

"I don't mean that. I meant as a guy. Did I strike you as intimidating when we met?"

"No, but I thought you were the big, gorgeous surfer dude the company hired to chauffeur consultants from airports to offices," she teased. "Just like you thought I was some Barbie doll Stepford wife home from a shopping trip. Don't lie."

"Not a Barbie doll, not a Stepford wife, just the most beautiful woman I'd ever seen." His voice had dropped a little, and his words sparked a bright flare of heat inside her, one that she wasn't sure she should let burn.

When he brought her hand up for another kiss, his mouth lingered.

"While I'd never suggest that you stop doing what you're doing, you really don't have to try to charm me,

Joe," she said lightly. "I'm already under your spell. And if I hadn't been, just seeing how you are around your family would have taken care of it."

"Flattery? Just what are you after, Miz Connor?" The rough-sexy edge to his voice was a guarantee that she wouldn't be getting any work done tonight.

"Is it still called flattery if it's sincere?" she asked with a smile. "You're just a good guy, Joe. I love the way you get along with your mom and Chas and Julie."

He laughed then and dropped her hand as he downshifted to take a corner, then sent her a sidelong glance that was both amused and a little embarrassed. "You just love me—everything about me."

The fumbled words were no sooner out of his mouth than the atmosphere in the small car changed from warm and intimate to silent and dense, as if his words were hanging in the air, crowding them.

"I didn't mean that the way it came out," he began, his voice tight.

"Maybe not, but I think it's about right," Naomi interrupted in a soft rush before her rationality could intrude on the moment.

Another silence ensued, this one not as choking or as tense as the last, and it took a moment before Naomi realized the engine's whine was diminishing. Joe downshifted again and eventually pulled off the road onto a wide, rough shoulder sheltered by towering, gnarled trees.

By the time he brought the car to a stop and pulled on the hand brake, the tumult in her bloodstream was making it hard to breathe.

He turned to her, his face unreadable. "Say that again."

"I said that it sounded about right to me," she repeated an uneven heartbeat later, her voice faint in the shadowy darkness.

"What exactly do you mean by that?"

I'm such a fool. "Am I under cross-examination?" she asked with a forced smile.

His face softened then, and he brought his hand up to brush her cheek. "Seems like it, doesn't it?" he murmured. "Are you going to answer my question?"

"Do I have to?" she whispered, beginning to feel hypnotized by the dense, throbbing silences punctuating their conversation.

He brushed his lips lightly over hers, then drew back. "Yes."

"Well, it means that I actually do love everything about you," she said softly, then paused. *Say it.* "I just love you, Joe." She dropped her eyes to her hands, unable to look into his anymore. The lack of information in them was swamping her defenses. "It's been building. I just didn't expect to be saying it this soon."

He tilted her chin up until their eyes met again. "Are you apologizing?"

"No."

"Good. Because I like the sound of it. And I'm glad you didn't wait to say it." He slid his hand around her neck to cup her head, and brought his mouth to hers. His kiss was soft and slow and deep, exploring her with an unhurried expertise that dizzied her.

She lost herself in the feel of his mouth, the warmth and scent of his body, the strength of his arms, and let every knot inside untie itself and float away. *Surely this is heaven.*

A sharp rap on the driver's-side window snapped them apart, and Joe cursed under his breath as he reached for the button to put down the window. Before he could find it, a blinding light flashed through the car.

"Joe?" said a surprised male voice.

"Who is that?" Joe demanded as the window slid down and the light moved away from his face.

"Frank Gentilli. What are you doing here?"

Naomi shrank into her seat, torn between mortification and laughter, as Joe looked up at the uniformed Greenwich police officer.

"I was kissing my girlfriend, Frank. What the hell did it look like I was doing?" he snapped, and Naomi had to bite her lips to keep from laughing out loud.

"Aren't you a little old for that? I stopped because I figured some kids took your car for a joyride." The cop sheathed his flashlight, then folded his arms across his chest and glared at them. "You know how dangerous it is to stop on a roadway like this? For Christ's sake, Joe, go home and make out on your couch like everyone else does."

Joe pushed hand through his hair and took a deep breath to try to curb his obvious annoyance. "I left my headlights on, and I'm not on the road, I'm on the shoulder. It's also a one hundred-yard straightaway *and, as you know, Frank,* everyone on this street is either at the Vineyard, on the Cape, or in Europe until September. There's not a light on in a house," Joe said between clenched teeth. "I also happen to be staying at my mother's while I'm in town, so I don't really have a couch to call my own. And another thing, Frank. I'd better not hear about this, and you know what I mean."

The cop broke into a grin and hooked his thumbs into his gun belt as he rocked back on his heels. "So you're not only arguing with me, you're threatening me? Didn't you learn anything from Chas?" He shook his head. "Anyway, cupcake, I can't help you. I guess you didn't hear about the new equipment we have in the cars. Video and audio feeds back to the car and the dispatcher. My guess is that right about now, all the guys are getting a giggle." He bent down to peer into the car and met Naomi's eyes with a smile. "Hi. I'm Frank. Joe and I were on the CYO swim team together in high school. No offense intended, ma'am. I'm just busting his chops. I have to take every chance I get. Opportunities like this come along less often than you might imagine."

"Thank you, Frank. I'm pleased to meet you. No offense taken."

"Hey, you're Southern. Are you Miranda's sister or something?"

She widened her smile. "No, it's just a happy coincidence that these Casey boys have the good sense to admire Southern women."

"Amen to that." Then Frank straightened and looked back toward his squad car and started to laugh. "Brace yourself, Casey. I think the rest of the shift just arrived."

Joe just closed his eyes and leaned forward to rest his forehead on the steering wheel.

Naomi loved him.

The knowledge had been rolling around loose in his head since he'd finally gotten away from the next best thing to a hazing he'd had to endure at the hands of the GPD 'tween shift, all of whom he knew at least by sight. And her words were still rolling like loose marbles. He wasn't sure what he was supposed to do with them. What she wanted him to do with them.

It was a nice thing to hear. He'd heard it before from women, but the way she'd said it had been different. Sincere. And she'd had her clothes on.

But fuck an elf. On top of everything else, this was the last thing he needed to happen right now.

"Joe?"

Her soft voice brought him out of his self-absorbed reverie, and he realized that she had unlocked the door to the condo and was standing in the opening with a hesitant smile on her lips and an invitation in her eyes. "Would you like to come in for a minute?"

He took a deep breath. "Of course."

She shut the door behind him and started to walk past him toward the living room. He caught one arm and spun her around gently until she was snug against his chest, looking up at him with deep blue eyes that held desire and warmth—and a distinct case of nerves.

You're not the only one who's nervous. He cleared his throat. "We need to talk."

Her eyes widened. "I don't mean to be flippant, Joe, but that's a sentence I never thought I'd hear you say."

He didn't hide his smile; he only backed her up a few steps. Just until her eyes widened a bit more and her nervousness was replaced by the beginnings of a sexy, sparkly panic.

"Joe," she said, a halfhearted warning in her voice.

"Yes, Naomi?" he said quietly, and backed her up another step. Her eyes were getting hot and dark.

"Where are we going?" She sounded a little breathless.

"Is that question rhetorical, metaphorical, or actual?" he asked, dropping his voice to a growl.

She swallowed and didn't answer. Didn't blink. Most likely decided not to think. She was turned on like a high-intensity lightbulb.

When the back of her legs bumped up against the couch, she fell in a graceful heap on its cushions. And remained there, half sitting, half lying on the couch, watching him. Waiting for his next move.

He stepped to the side and sat down next to her. Picked up her hand. Looked into her eyes.

"Tell me about it."

She blinked once, then again, and sat up. She'd gone from smoldering to flustered in seconds, and not by accident. He needed her to be as off base as he was. Maybe more so.

"Tell you about what?"

"You love me."

Her eyes flicked to their hands, his shirt, the painting on the wall. Everywhere but his face. "Oh. What do you want me to tell you about it?"

"Everything. When did it start?"

She pulled her hand out of his and smoothed her dress over her thighs, then, apparently composed enough, she met his eyes again. "It started on your patio, when you told me why you wouldn't dance with me at the Kennedy Center. And it finally smacked me upside the head last evening on your boat, when you set dinner free. You're the most kind, generous, warm-hearted man I know, for all everybody else thinks you're Attila the Hun. Is that the kind of thing you wanted to know?" she said in a voice that had gone breathy and low, and was the next best thing to a moonlit whisper.

Keeping his hands off her was a penance in itself, but it needed to be done. He wanted answers.

"When were you planning on saying something?" he asked, ignoring her question.

"I wasn't. You're the one who brought it up," she said after a minute. "Don't get all twisted up over it, Joe. I know you're not a long-haul type of guy, and I'm not the pushy type of woman. Except when it comes to work, obviously. And I truly wouldn't have mentioned it except—"

"Who told you I'm not the long-haul type of guy?" he interrupted.

"I just overheard—"

This third-party bullshit is getting old real fast. He had to fight a frown. "I'm going to turn those damned women's bathrooms into one-seaters."

She tried to smother her laughter but failed miserably. "Actually, Joe, it was two guys and they were in the parking structure."

Guys? "Who? What did they say?"

"I don't know who they were. They said that you're good for a week, max, and they can't figure out how you do it."

He leaned against the back of the couch in surprise. *A week?* "Well, they're full of—"

"It doesn't matter, Joe. We've been together one day. I'm not making any long-term plans or lighting the fires of eternal hope. I'm just enjoying you minute to minute," she said softly, with a look in her eyes that he couldn't identify. He'd never seen it before. It wasn't sadness; it wasn't resignation or exasperation. It was just . . . something that he'd rather not see there and it bothered him, because he was sure he was the cause of it.

"You don't look happy."

"Well, I am happy. I just never expected to have to explain myself." She let out a breath that sounded close to a sigh. "Don't make me regret saying anything."

"Do you?"

"No."

"Good."

"Good."

After a short pause he said, "I'm leaving for Chicago tomorrow morning. I'll be back Tuesday night. Are you going to be all right?"

"Am I *what*?"

He fought a grin at the incredulity in her eyes. "I meant with the workload, Naomi. Doing all that work without me. Not doing without *me*."

"I'll be fine, Joe. After all, you haven't helped out much so far."

He winced. "Thanks for reminding me. So, now for the bad news."

The instant the words were out of his mouth, he saw hurt skitter across her face despite her instant smile.

"I know exactly what you're going to say. You can't stay the night. You know, I was actually about to suggest the same thing," she said quickly. "I'm so tired, I could just—"

Yeah, you're tough as nails. The melted kind. "Naomi."

She hesitated. "Yes?"

"I know you need the sleep. I know I need the sleep. I also know that I wouldn't get any sleep here because you are the sexiest, most erotic, appealing woman I have ever known. But none of those things are the reason I'm not staying." He forced himself to stand up, and pulled her gently to her feet. "You have permission to call me a wimp, but I'm not staying over here tonight for the same reason you're not staying with me tonight. I'm staying in my mother's house, and while she's in residence, I won't offend her by being so obvious. I'm a grown man and all the rest, and she would never say a thing to me, but it's just something that I think is the right thing to do." He pressed a kiss to her forehead, then met her eyes. "But for the record, walking out that door and leaving you on this side of it may be the most difficult thing I ever do in this lifetime."

A smile appeared slowly on her face, and she stood on her toes to kiss him on the lips. "There is absolutely nothing I can say to that, Joe, except what I've already said. You are the most wonderful man I've ever met. Now, get gone."

He slid his arms around her and possessed her mouth in a kiss that left him weak in the knees, soft in the head, and hard in between. Finally pulling himself out of the warm delirium she inspired, he tugged her arms gently from his neck and took a step back. "I think you ought to stay right here until I'm out that door."

"It won't be easy."

"You're damned right it won't." After another slow kiss, he turned on his heel and walked straight to the door. It was painful in more ways than one.

"Good night," he said, his hand on the door handle.

"Joe, I think you forgot something."

He turned to see a flushed, bedroom-eyed Naomi lift one languid hand. His car keys dangled from her fingertips.

"How's your arm?" His voice was hoarse and barely recognizable as his own.

"I throw like a girl," she purred, laying on her Southern-ness so thick he could smell the honeysuckle.

"Throw them anyway."

With a laugh, she tossed them and he only had to take one step toward her to catch them. "Thanks."

"Joe?"

If she asked him to stay, all bets were off. "Yes?"

She hesitated, then gave him a tight smile. "Have a productive trip."

"I intend to."

"And a safe one. I'll see you when you get back."

Damned right you will. He smiled. "Count on it."

CHAPTER
29

It was high summer, so the sun was fully up and streaming through Joe's bedroom window by five o'clock. The light didn't bother him; he had too much on his mind to sleep, anyway. The entire foundation of his life had shifted in the last thirty-six hours.

He wasn't sure exactly when, but he knew without a doubt why: He'd fallen in love with Naomi.

Big time.

It had taken her saying the word to make him realize that's what it was, but it had hit him like a sucker punch. Keeping his head on straight while the very thought of it was filtering through his brain had been a challenge.

It didn't feel like he thought it would, though. It wasn't the breathless, silly-grin sort of sensation that chick-flick movies and Miranda's books implied, and it wasn't a rigid iron band slowly crushing his chest, as he'd always assumed it would be. It was just . . . good.

Comfortable.

Easy.

They weren't words he'd ever heard other guys use in connection with loving a woman. Not that he could remember ever having a conversation with another guy about loving a woman. Sleeping with them, maybe, but not loving them.

At least part of it had to be because he just liked Naomi. Deep down *liked* her. He liked talking with her, seeing her eyes lighten and darken with her mood, watching her mouth form words and laughter, watching her think, cataloging her habits and quirks, analyzing them. He found himself actually looking forward to hearing what she had to say.

It was a first.

He could only ascribe it to the way their relationship had started. Going through the usual man-woman flirtation bullshit hadn't been an option; they'd been thrown together as equals—hell, as the next best thing to conspirators.

Joe folded his hands behind his head and stared blankly at the leafy shadows playing on the ceiling. From the minute he'd seen her across the small terminal in the Westchester airport, Naomi Grace Connor of Starlit, Alabama, and Foggy Bottom, Washington, D.C., had turned the tables on him. She hadn't been kidding when she'd told him that she was 90 percent brains. She was easily the most intelligent woman he'd ever met, and because of that, what she thought of him mattered. A lot.

It was definitely a new twist.

Most women, even the ones he'd had to pursue or persuade, had eventually, and deservedly, labeled him shallow and disengaged from whatever relationship they'd shared; Naomi, on the other hand, had somehow managed not only to find his depth but to nurture it. He knew how to pamper women and show them a good time, but he couldn't remember ever actually just wanting to be around one for no reason other than just to be around her. The urge to protect and take care of Naomi had come out of nowhere; odder still was that it felt completely natural.

Becoming lovers had been the next logical step. With

her high necklines and personal-distance issues, he'd been surprised to discover she was playful, uninhibited, and damned creative in bed. Being with her physically was better than he'd ever imagined, but it wasn't enough. He wanted to be in her heart and on her mind.

He took a deep breath and let it out slowly. Naomi Grace Connor was a gift, the kind you're given for unknown reasons, and the only thing you're sure of is that you will never be this lucky again. But he was sure of something else, too.

He wasn't about to fuck this up.

Pushing back the sheet, he got up, crossed the room to his chest of drawers, and pulled on a pair of swimming trunks, then headed downstairs.

"You're up early," his mother said as he entered the kitchen. She was wearing jeans and a sweatshirt, and was just putting the last bit of water in the coffeemaker.

"So are you. Where are you going?" He crossed the room and took a bottle of water from the refrigerator. "How's your foot, by the way?"

"My foot is fine. I'm just heading out to do some gardening before it gets too humid. Enjoy your swim. Are you going indoors or out?"

"Out. The indoor pool is fine for pregnant sisters-in-law and nieces, but too warm for serious swimming," he said with a grin. Stepping from the comfort of the house into the cool morning air sent a chill rippling across his skin, but he didn't stop. He crossed the patio, dropped the bottled water on one of the chairs, adjusted his goggles, and continued to the far end of the pool. When he reached the edge, he executed a shallow dive.

The water was icy and he felt the burning shock of it in every cell. He stayed under until his lungs were tight and bursting, then thrust to the surface for a cold breath, and pushed into a hard, fast, mindless crawl, back and forth the length of the pool until his legs were getting heavy and his arm muscles were screaming for downtime.

Surfacing as he touched the edge, he pulled off his goggles and flung his head to get the streaming hair out of his eyes, sending a shower of droplets onto the flagstone surround.

"I haven't seen you swim like that in years. I swear you're half dolphin, Joe." His mother's voice was amused and affectionate.

He turned to see her sitting in one of the chaise lounges with a thermos pot and two mugs on the table beside her.

"I don't have the time to swim like that anymore," he replied as he floated for a minute to catch his breath. "You're done gardening already?"

She nodded. "I got tired of fighting off the thorns. By the way, I brought you a towel. It's next to your water. What did you do?"

"Thanks." He hoisted himself out of the water and rubbed himself dry with the towel, then downed half the water, carrying the rest of it with him to the chair next to hers. "Seventy laps."

"What is that in real terms?"

"A mile," he said with a shrug.

"What brought it on, the project or the woman?" she asked and took a sip of her coffee.

"The woman," he replied, answering her grin with one of his own.

They sat in a companionable silence, listening to the birds and cicadas, and the early morning stirrings of civilization as the sun rose higher above the horizon.

"What time is your flight?"

"Eleven," he replied, reaching for the pot to fill his mug. "Commercial. Out of Westchester."

"So, what are you going to do?" she asked lightly after another easy pause.

Joe met her eyes without the slightest hesitation or doubt. "Marry her."

He'd never said the words before, never actually thought them, but hearing them come out of his mouth didn't surprise him. They were the right words and Naomi was the right woman. There was no other option.

"Good."

He got to his feet. "I have to take care of a few things before I leave. When are you heading back to Palm Beach?"

"Tuesday morning. When are you back?"

"Tuesday afternoon."

"Have a good trip. Go easy on those boys from Lockheed."

He grinned again and bent down to drop a kiss on her head. "I leave the mothering to you. You leave the lawyering to me."

She smiled up at him. "Do you remember the combination to the vault?"

"Yes."

"Good. Third drawer on the left."

Shaking his head in amusement, he headed toward the house.

Two hours later, he pulled the Jeep into a reserved spot behind the row of shops on Greenwich Avenue and waited for Ted. The street was quiet enough; the alley was like an open-air tomb at eight thirty on a Sunday morning. He drummed a beat on the steering wheel and let his mind wander. Not surprisingly, Naomi's image appeared a second later. Tousled and flushed, laughing, eyes alight with fire and passion. He smiled back at her. He still wasn't nervous. Maybe he never would be. Proposing to her was just the next logical step.

Ted Murdoch's fire-engine red Beemer pulled in next to him, and both men got out of their cars.

"I can't believe you, Casey. You called me at seven o'clock on a Sunday." Ted shook his head in disgust.

"I figured Maggie'd be getting the kids ready for church and you'd be on your way to the golf course," Joe said with a laugh. "Besides, this is important."

"It had damned well better be," Ted grumbled

through a halfhearted grin. "And for the record, it's also going to be expensive. Whatever it is."

"That comes as no surprise," Joe replied dryly.

The first door swung open and they stepped into the small vestibule. Joe looked around the space as Ted punched in a security code on the keypad, paused, then entered another sequence.

They repeated these steps three times before they walked through the final door and into the workroom in the rear of the jewelry shop.

Ted slid into the single chair behind the worktable and reached for a loupe automatically. "Okay, let's see it."

Joe reached into his pants pocket and pulled out a small wad of tissue.

Ted closed his eyes and shook his head. "I can't believe it. You wrapped it in Kleenex?"

"What?"

"Nothing." He put his hand out and Joe put the small packet in it. Ted placed it on the work surface and unwrapped it. "Holy mother."

"Nice?"

"Nice?" Ted repeated, mildly incredulous as he set the loupe into position and lifted the medium-blue, square-cut diamond with tweezers to inspect it closely. "Where did you get this?"

Joe leaned against the wall and folded his arms across his chest, enjoying the burst of pride spreading through his chest. Ted routinely designed *serious* jewelry; it wasn't easy to impress him. "My great-grandmother found a funny-looking rock along a riverbed in South Africa about fifty years ago. That and a pair of earrings were inside it," he said with a grin.

"You want this to be a necklace to match? A solitaire?" The jeweler looked up.

"I want it to be a ring."

Ted paused, then set the stone onto the table's surface again and met Joe's eyes. "No fucking way."

"You mean you can't do it?" he asked with a straight face.

"Of course I can do it," Ted snapped. "I just can't fucking believe someone has finally wrestled you to the mat. Is it the woman you were making out with last night on Sedgwick Road?"

Joe took a deep breath. "We weren't making out. I kissed her. And she hasn't wrestled me to any mat. I'm not even sure what she'll say, but, yes, it's for her."

"Does she get the earrings, too?"

"Not this month."

"Too bad," he replied, picking up the loupe and the diamond again. "This is one beautiful piece of carbon, Joe. Platinum setting?"

"If you think that would look the best. I just want something simple. The colors of the clothes she wears could blind you, but her jewelry is all pretty plain. And she has small hands."

"Enough said."

"Great. By the way, I need it Tuesday."

Ted turned to look at him, still wearing the loupe. *Tuesday?*

Joe nodded.

"That's kind of tight, pal."

"I know. E-mail me a sketch or whatever it is you do. I'll be in Chicago, then down South, but I'll be back Tuesday afternoon. Here's my card. It's got all my contact information."

Ted let out a slow breath and shook his head. "I wouldn't do this for anyone else, so don't tell anyone. And don't make a habit of it."

Joe laughed and stood up straight. "I don't intend to. And if you say anything—"

"Hey, come on. If I told all the secrets I knew, I'd be run out of town. Have a good trip. It will be waiting for you when you get back."

"Thanks, Ted. See you in a few days."

* * *

By daybreak on Tuesday morning, Naomi's stomach was in such knots that she didn't even consider getting dressed to go into the office. Her team was gone; so was Joe. No one would miss her.

She stayed in the condo, took a ridiculously long, ridiculously hot shower, and paced through the rooms. A lot. Every so often, she'd sit down in front of her laptop and try to interpret the data in a different way.

Then she'd get up and pace again because there was no different way to interpret it. The video feed from Trudy's office was strictly a monitoring setup, and the files were being renamed at the server interface, then sent as streaming video to an external IP address. An address registered to someone named Joe Casey.

That shock had come Monday night, and it had been the first of several. Naomi had sat staring at the screen and shaking, feeling sick and used. But that single piece of information made clear a scenario she had never seriously considered, and had put out of her mind days ago: that Joe was the leak.

Straightlaced, law-and-order Joe, who professed such loathing for hackers, who had made her feel so guilty, who had made her feel so good.

Why could he possibly be doing this? She leaned her hot cheeks against the cool glass of the window and fought another wave of nausea.

He had everything: a job he said he loved, a sterling reputation in the industry, a family that adored him. But the evidence was overwhelming. There were late-night log-ons and file transfers that occurred under his user names. Security protocols were skillfully evaded, allowing highly classified files to be renamed or imported into other documents, then downloaded—again under his user names. The series of abnormal actions was subtle. They'd taken place slowly over a reasonably long period of time so that they were buried in a mountain of normal behaviors.

It was a brilliant plan, brilliantly executed. It could

only have been conceived by someone with unfettered access, a clear sense of the outcome, and the ability and drive to achieve that outcome.

It was a description that fit Joe—until the issue of motive was raised. Then it fell apart. But unfortunately, the description didn't fit anyone else in the company.

She closed her eyes, feeling tears burn at the back of her eyes yet again as she called into question—into doubt—every recent exchange they'd had. Could he have really been watching her the whole time like a cat watches a mouse, biding his time, observing her every move, knowing there was no escape?

No, it's not in him to do that. To do this.

She moved away from the window and began to pace a now-familiar path through the condo as hindsight continued to erode every argument that presumed his innocence.

No wonder he looked so stunned when I mentioned the robot.

No wonder he wanted to be the one to go into Trudy's office and had gotten so annoyed when I ignored his demands.

No wonder he'd been so surprised when I told him what I was doing to the monitoring data.

And no wonder he'd kept me in bed for so long.

She came to a stop in front of the windows again. Wrapping her arms around her roiling, clenching stomach, she slid to the floor, tears streaming, wondering if she'd be sick again.

Once she'd told him what she was doing, he had to have known it was only a matter of time before she caught him. And that's where her theory started to unravel. Someone afraid of being caught would have become more circumspect, or would have tried to stop her.

But he didn't try to stop me. He let me keep working—after doing his best to make sure I was exhausted by sex.

Good Lord. She closed her eyes. *He must be so proud of himself.*

But even that thought tore at her as a betrayal.

"I'd know if it was him. He couldn't have hidden it from me. Something would have tipped me off," she moaned to the empty living room.

The silence that greeted her words seemed to whisper back that something *had* tipped her off: Joe himself, and his refusal to let her tell anyone.

Letting out a slow breath, she got to her feet, crossed the room, sat down on the couch, and leaned her head against the back.

Saturday night, I just played into his hands. I told him I loved him. She closed her eyes, loathing herself. *We're both fools. I broke my rules for him without a fight, and because of that, he thinks he's in the clear. After all, I'm the one with the sympathetic streak for felons. Or so he believes.*

She curled into herself and nestled her head against her tucked-up knees. Then a new, chilling thought crept into her mind.

It was a total setup.

She jerked upright, stunned, and stared at the windows, seeing nothing.

He knows who I am.

He'd handpicked her. It had to be that. That's why Sarah had given in so easily, and that's why he kept making jokes about her past but never got around to actually discussing the subject.

Oh, God, what have I done?

The nausea crept ominously up the back of her throat, but she refused to give into another physical display of weakness. *There has to be another way—*

The shrill chirp of her phone snapped her into the present, and grabbing it from the coffee table, she glared at the small screen.

Imagine that. It's the devil himself.

She wiped her face and sniffed, unable to find any tissues within the time allotted by the third strident peal. *Get tough.*

"Hello, you," she said, forcing a pleased, sexy tone into her voice.

"I didn't wake you, did I?" His voice was a sleep-rough growl.

She glanced at the clock. It was six thirty. *Five thirty Chicago time. I guess there really is no rest for the wicked.*

"Mercy, no, darlin'. I've been up most of the night, slaving away to try to find who's out to put your adorable behind in a sling." *Besides me.*

"Well, I appreciate the effort and I'll overlook the bags under your eyes." His laugh ended with a yawn.

"That's mighty generous of you. Maybe I'll get a facial and a massage before you get back. I'll just bury it on the invoice under the heading called recuperation."

"That sounds like a great idea. I'll look forward to interrogating you in intimate detail about all excess charges, Miss Connor."

Stop it. Just confess, damn you. She took a deep breath and forced a smile onto her face again. "So, what are you doing up so early? It's five thirty in Chicago."

"Don't remind me. I'm going to go for a swim, then meet the kids at seven. We were at it until eleven thirty last night."

"You're a bad man, Joe."

"It's all just a game, Naomi. As you well know." His voice dropped suggestively as he finished, and instead of feeling heat rush through her as she might have a few days ago, she felt her core temperature plummet.

Please let that be the case. Tell me I'm wrong. "Well, not everything is a game, Joe."

"You sound serious."

"I am serious," she said softly, and held her breath.

"About me?" he asked after a moment, and there was the trace of true concern behind the lighthearted tone.

"Most definitely about you," she whispered to the ceiling. *Damn you. Damn you.* She felt like screaming it into the phone as tears burned the back of her eyes with the searing flame of such blatant betrayal.

"I think we'll have to continue this conversation this afternoon," he said quietly. "Will you be in the office? I should be there around four."

She swallowed hard and forced words past the lump in her throat. "I'll be there."

"See you then."

She ended the call and tumbled sideways on to the cushions, unable to stop the tears that had already started. She ached everywhere. Brilliant, blinding pain started to rip and shred her inside as if she'd swallowed shards of crystal. She might as well have. She would never be the same after today.

CHAPTER
30

The tears eventually stopped.

Naomi sat cold-faced, coldhearted, at the dining room table and stared at her laptop. Her head was pounding, her throat was raw, her stomach was empty and furious.

It was all just too damned bad.

Now that the emotion was out of the way, she was just not willing to believe that Joe could do this to his family, to his future. *No.* He might be gorgeous and a little conceited in some ways, and more than a little arrogant in others, but to plan and execute something like this, then bring in a high-priced bloodhound who was sure to find him—

If this isn't a sign of utterly narcissistic, sociopathic gamesmanship, then surely it has to be a point in his favor. After all, if he were a sociopath, we would have kept sailing into the Atlantic so he could throw me overboard.

She rubbed her hands up and down her arms as the unstoppable trembling she'd been enduring for the last hour turned into outright shivers.

He could have done it. It would have worked. He knows I can't swim to save myself, and there certainly hadn't been any other boats nearby. She took a deep breath, held it for a count of ten to battle and subdue the pain, then let it out slowly.

"Don't start going crazy," she whispered. "He's not a murderer. Maybe he wants to get caught. Or he's setting me up." She took another deep breath. "Or maybe it's not him."

It was highly improbable.

But it was worth another look, which was exactly why she was there.

Setting her fingers on the keyboard, she logged on and forced the last shreds of emotion from her mind.

He'd be proud of her. She was following his example. Her task was simple; her goal utterly black-and-white without a hint of gray.

She was going to clear his name.

Or find enough hard evidence to convict him.

Joe glanced up from the documents he was looking at, hands casually in his pockets as he stood at the head of the conference table. "Karen, a word, please?"

The last of the lawyers from Lockheed filed out the door of the elegant conference room at the Drake, and his own team was getting ready to follow them.

The tall blond woman at the head of the line froze, her ponytail swaying at the abrupt motion. When she spun around, she had a hunted look on her face. "Sure, Joe. What's up?"

"Have a seat," he said easily.

The rest of the Brennan legal team—comprised mostly of people who worked with Karen every day—departed the room without a backward glance, as if he hadn't spoken, as if she weren't there.

Nice. He refrained from shaking his head in disgust. It was typical. It was also why each of them was expendable. *They had no balls and no loyalty. They would never go the extra mile, or take anything to the wire without blinking.*

He waited until Karen had sat down stiffly in the chair

nearest her, which also happened to be the chair farthest from his. Then he seated himself and leaned back in the chair, resting one forearm on the table. "So, how do you think it went?"

She swallowed hard and flashed him a smile that was too bright and too forced. "It wasn't as good as it could have been. We compromised on more than I thought we should, but since expedience was the point of the meeting, I think we came out even."

He studied her for a moment, taking in her clipped words, her white-knuckled grip on the handle of her laptop case, the dark circles beneath her eyes. They were skillfully but not entirely camouflaged with makeup. "Would you like to know what I think?"

She held her breath, then nodded slowly. "Of course, Joe." Her voice sounded strangled.

"I thought you did a great job. Better than great. You handled them with a lot of skill and diplomacy. We came away with more than I thought we would."

She stared at him without saying a word, then blinked and continued staring for at least another full minute. "I what?"

God almighty. Naomi was right. She's terrified. He felt like frowning but didn't dare, for fear that Karen would lose it. "You did a great job," he repeated. "You always do a great job. I count on you to do it, and you always come through for me."

"Are you serious?" Her voice was shaky now and she was blinking too fast.

Damn it. She can chew up and spit out half of Capitol Hill before breakfast and never get indigestion, and she's going to start crying on me over this. "I'm totally serious. Now, tell me why you submitted your resignation."

"Because I thought you were getting ready to fire me," she whispered. "I thought you were setting me up. I mean, first that thing with Biedersdorf, and now this—"

Joe Casey, Assistant General Counsel for Government

Affairs and Chief Prick. He let out a slow breath. "No, I'm not setting you up. I have never set you up. I *rely* on you, Karen," he said easily, keeping his voice calm and his frustration hidden. "You're the best attorney on my team. I need you to stay on it. I'm not accepting your resignation." He paused. "I'm promoting you to Senior Assistant Counsel for Legislative Affairs and giving you a twenty-thousand-dollar-a-year raise. And I was supposed to send you to The Inn at Little Washington a few weeks ago for doing such a good job on the Biedersdorf negotiation, but I screwed that up, so I'm sending you to the Caribbean. Only for a long weekend, because I can't spare you for more than that, but pick an island and when you get back to the office, make sure you talk to Betty Sullivan. She'll make sure it gets taken care of." He glanced at his watch and stood up. "That's about it. I have to catch a plane. Keep me posted on how things are progressing with the Feiger-Dinsmore bill," he said, zipping his laptop case closed. "You'll be handling that one, too, and if you freak out on me I *will* fire you."

"Okay. Thank you, Joe. I— Thank you," she said, still looking somewhat pale and shell-shocked as she rose from the chair and walked out of the room.

He shook his head, then slung his computer bag over his shoulder, grabbed his carry-on, and headed for the car that was waiting to take him to O'Hare.

God almighty, how do people live down here?

Joe presented his temporary security credentials to the armed guard at the front gate and a moment later was waved through the employees' and contractors' entrance to the Marshall Space Center in Huntsville, Alabama. Just putting the window down for the minute that took had filled the car with air as hot and steamy as what came out of a blast furnace. If he had to park too far away from the building, he'd be a sweaty mess by the time he sat down to meet with General Connor, and that wasn't quite the image he intended to project when he was introducing himself to his future father-in-law.

A brigadier general for a father-in-law. A father-in-law at all.

That alone was enough to inspire a hard sweat.

The air inside the building was blessedly cool. The receptionist was young and attractive, and her lanyard full of ID badges and smart cards nestled between noticeably lush breasts. She watched him with not-so-subtle interest as he crossed the small lobby.

"Hi, I'm Joe Casey to see General Connor," he said, signing the registration book.

One fifty-five. Five minutes early.

"May I see your badge?" she asked in a soft, smiling voice that reminded him of another Southern beauty, who happened to be the reason he was here.

He handed his security badge and driver's license across the tall desk. She made some notes, then handed them back with a smile. "You're a long way from home, Mr. Casey."

Sweetheart, you are way too late. He smiled back. "You'd never know. It's nearly as hot there at the moment."

"Well, isn't that just something? I had no idea y'all had such hot summers. Why don't you just have a seat right over there, Mr. Casey? I'll tell the general you're here directly."

On the stroke of two o'clock, Joe looked up to see a man in air force blue walking purposefully down the hall, and was struck by how much Naomi's eyes resembled her father's. But that's where the resemblance ended. Her father was nearly as tall as he was, though nowhere near as broad. He was dark-haired and thin, built like a long-distance runner, and he didn't have a spare ounce of fat on him. But in his uniform, with a raft of ribbons on his chest and those single stars on his collar, he was nevertheless an imposing figure.

Joe rose to his feet and was surprised at how calm he

felt. Clearly, it was an indication that he was doing the right thing. Not that he had any doubts.

"General Connor, I'm Joe Casey," he said, and held out his hand.

"It's nice to meet you, Joe. Tom Connor. My assistant said you're with Brennan," he said in a deep, easy drawl as he clasped Joe's hand.

The man has a hell of a grip. "That's right."

They began walking in the direction from which the general had come, and in a moment turned into the doorway of a reasonably sized but generic office furnished in a style known as typical government drab. Beige walls met a beige linoleum floor, upon which sat a beige metal desk with a fake wood-grain top. Three-ring binders lined the tall bookshelves that took up two walls, and poster-sized illustrations of spacecraft adorned with insignia badges and an alphabet soup of acronyms covered the walls above the bookcases. The desk was cluttered but not outrageously. Joe could see the surface of at least a third of it.

"I'll be honest with you, Joe. The only dealings I generally have with Brennan are with the space systems division, but I don't recognize your name. Have a seat."

"Thank you, sir. No, I'm not with space systems, I'm with the general counsel's office. At the moment, I'm also acting chief technology officer." Joe remained standing while the older man walked to his chair behind the desk.

"That's a tall order."

"It's a challenge," Joe conceded with a grin. "But frankly, General Connor, I'm not here on company business."

The general stopped his descent halfway to sitting and stood up again, the polite warmth in his eyes fading to a lukewarm neutrality. "You're not?"

"No, sir. Would you mind if I closed the door?"

Her father, now wary, nodded and sat down slowly. "So what can I do for you, Joe?"

Joe sat down and met her father's eyes again. "Well, sir, I'd like to marry your daughter."

The silence in the room was sudden and absolute, and Joe realized with some alarm that the palms of his hands had broken out in a sweat.

Tom Connor stared at him for a few seconds, then leaned back in his chair. "You don't mess around with pleasantries, do you, son?"

"I'm from Connecticut, sir, and I used to be a prosecutor. I have a bad habit of getting to the point."

"Well, that has its merits." He cleared his throat. "What does Naomi think about it?"

"I haven't asked her yet."

He wasn't entirely certain, but Joe thought he detected an amused twitch in the corner of the general's mouth. "I see. Do you think she'll say yes when you do?"

"I'm pretty sure she will. I hope she will."

General Connor let a pause build, then shook his head. "You've really thrown me, Joe. I need to ask you some questions, seeing as how Naomi and I talk fairly often and I've never heard her mention you at all."

Smiling, Joe sat back in his chair. "I apologize for the shock. We haven't known each other very long, so I'm not surprised she hasn't mentioned me. Feel free to ask me anything."

"Is she pregnant?"

Joe snapped upright in his chair, feeling his eyes go wide with the shock of the word more than the question. "Absolutely not."

"Just checking. Now I'd say we're about on par with regard to our pulse rates," her father said with a slow smile. "You're about, what, thirty-six? Have you been married before? Do you have any children?"

"I'm thirty-eight, I've never even been engaged, and no, I don't have any children," Joe replied, trying to keep the annoyance out of his voice.

The general nodded his approval. "So you're a lawyer

with Brennan Shipping Industries and you know something about computers. Is that how you met Naomi?"

"We hired her firm to do a project for us. She's the project manager."

"How long have you known each other?"

Joe kept his face neutral. "About six weeks."

Her father frowned and steepled his fingers as he set his elbows on the armrests of his chair. "Six weeks. That's a mite short of a full courtship, wouldn't you say?"

"We've spent a lot of time together," Joe replied.

"Don't be offended if I say that doesn't ease my mind," the general drawled. "Tell me about yourself, Joe. Where did you go to school?"

Joe let out a slow breath, grateful for the respite. "I spent two years at Harvard, then I transferred to MIT. My bachelor's degree is in electronic engineering. Georgetown Law. I worked for the NCIS for six years as a prosecutor, then went to Tulane for an LLM in maritime law. I started with Brennan Shipping after that. I finished a master's degree in computer science at George Mason last year."

Her father didn't even blink. "Sounds like you like to keep busy."

Joe shrugged with a grin.

The general shifted in his chair. "Where are you going to end up?"

"Chief General Counsel of Brennan Shipping Industries."

"You sound sure of it."

"I am sure of it, sir. It's what I want to do."

"And you always reach your goals?"

"I have so far."

"Is Naomi a goal?"

The edge in the question took Joe by surprise, but he didn't hesitate in answering. "No, sir. Naomi is a gift. Being her husband is my goal."

The general settled into a thoughtful silence. "Tell me

why you want to marry her," he said a few moments later.

Christ. He hadn't anticipated this one. "She makes me laugh," Joe replied slowly.

Tom Connor frowned at him. "That's it?"

Joe paused. "No, but with all due respect, I think it's the most important reason. She's also the smartest woman—make that the smartest *person*—I've ever met. She's warm and sweet and beautiful. I trust her and respect her. General Connor, all I can really tell you is that I know I *could* live without her, but I don't want to. I want to spend the rest of my life with her. Every day of it." He shrugged. "I love her. And she's told me she loves me."

General Connor leaned forward on his desk and spread one hand across his face and rubbed his eyes. It was the gesture of a man deep in thought. Or emotionally affected by having been asked by a stranger for his only daughter's hand in marriage. Joe wasn't entirely sure which reason necessitated the gesture, but he turned to study the framed awards on the far wall, anyway.

"Are you related to the Brennans?"

Joe looked back at him in surprise. "Yes. Mary Casey is my mother and Joe Brennan is my grandfather."

"So I guess you will be chief counsel some day."

"Only if I earn it. Do you know them?"

Naomi's father nodded and leaned back in his chair once again. "I met them quite a few years ago. And I run into them every so often, usually in D.C." He paused. "Your mother is an interesting woman. She makes an impression."

"I'll take that as a compliment."

"It's meant as one. As I recall, your grandfather was a big sailor."

"Still is."

"Yes, I beg your pardon. Is. Are you?"

Joe nodded.

"Naomi doesn't swim, you know."

Joe knew the sweet sound of capitulation when he heard it, and fought the urge to smile. "Yes, sir, I do. She'll learn. I'll teach her."

"And she can't boil water without burning down the kitchen."

"I've got that covered, too."

"She's inherited that damned Blanchard stubborn streak from her mother."

"I've encountered it. Any tips you can give me will be much appreciated."

General Connor leaned forward on his desk with a sigh, wearing a resigned smile, hands folded in front of him. "After thirty-five years of marriage to the woman, I only have two."

"What are they?"

"Choose your battles, son. And get right friendly with the local florist. Welcome to the family." Then General Connor stood up and stretched his hand across the desk.

The clock in the condo's foyer chimed softly three times as Naomi sat at the dining room table, staring at the screen of her laptop. Exhausted after having been working for more than twenty-four hours with no sleep to speak of, she was struggling to accept the fact that the words on the screen in front of her held the keys to her future, her partnership, her life, her love.

She'd found all the evidence she needed to bring in the authorities. It was irrefutable. Clear. Unassailable.

Of course, there was no way she could turn any of it over to them; her methods of finding it and gaining access to it had gotten a little murky at times, and had flirted with the outer edges of strictly legal behavior at least three times. But anticipating that, she'd tracked her movements. She could tell them exactly where to go to find everything they'd need to use as evidence for an arrest for theft, fraud, and espionage—for openers—that would undoubtedly result in a conviction accompanied by a nice, long prison sentence.

Highly classified documents had been copied and sent to dead e-mail drops for at least the last nine months. Which was, according to what Joe had told her in a meeting early in the project, just about the time they had put in place all of their state-of-the-art security features. But no system was foolproof, as she well knew, and all a body had to be to circumvent Joe's security measures was a computer wizard and an insider.

In an average company, that would limit the list of suspects to just a few people, but considering that this was a high-tech defense contractor, there were hundreds, if not thousands, of people on Brennan's payroll who fit that description. However, gaining access to the right networks took either an extremely high level of skill and a complete lack of morals, or simply the right security clearances and the appropriate level of authority. Close to the highest level of authority.

And even within Brennan, there were only a few people who fit that description.

She sat back in her chair, limp with nerves and exhaustion. Her discovery was going to be met with high and very mixed emotions by the family, and its ramifications would ripple through the entire company like a tsunami. After all, it was a classic case of the perpetrator—the traitor—hiding in plain sight.

The apprehension and arrest were going to be painful. And public.

And inevitable.

Pushing herself away from the table, she headed unsteadily to the shower to get cleaned up. Joe would be back in town soon and she'd agreed—*was it really only this morning?*—to meet him at the office. It wouldn't do to meet him there puffy-faced and red-eyed, looking like something the cat dragged in. He had deliberately made this trip a short one so he could come home and spend time with her, so he deserved to see something worth looking at. Putting her best face forward was the very least she could do because as of right now, as far as she was concerned, it was all over but the shoutin'.

It was going to be one hell of a reunion.

CHAPTER
31

After taking more time than usual to pick out an outfit and fix her hair and makeup, Naomi decided to walk from the condo to the office despite the fact that it was a hot and breezy afternoon. She knew the result might be the complete destruction of her carefully chosen facade, but frankly, she didn't really care. Even if she was on the right side of the law this time, bringing the same company to its knees twice in her lifetime was something she was not in a hurry to do. And as she was passing Starbucks, she decided she was in even less of a hurry.

Detouring into the cool shadiness of the coffee bar, she literally bumped into Miranda, who had Web by the hand and was talking to someone over her shoulder when she should have been looking forward.

"Oh, mercy, I'm so sorry—well, hey, Naomi. Isn't this a nice surprise? How are you doing? Seems like you survived the baptism by fire the other night," Miranda said with a friendly grin, giving her a one-armed hug.

"Hey, Miranda, it's good to see you. What baptism was that?" Naomi replied with a warm smile that, she hoped, neutralized her evasive answer.

"Well, from what I can gather, what we girls were doing to poor ol' you was nothing next to what hap-

pened on Sedgwick Road. Don't bother blushing, darlin',
I heard all about it. We *all* heard all about it and I'm
pretty sure only about a third of it is true, if that. You
know how men are," Miranda laughed, and dismissed
the topic with an easy wave of her hand. "Let me introduce you to my stepmother. She's just arrived in town
to stay for a few weeks. Barbara, this is Naomi Connor.
She's doing a bit of work for Joe at the company," Miranda said, stepping aside. "Naomi, this is my stepmother, Barbara Burrows."

Naomi gaped at the chubby, sweet-faced woman with
the stiffly sprayed, washed-and-set blond hair who
stepped forward.

"Miz Burrows?" Naomi blinked, wondering for a moment if she'd fallen asleep and was dreaming or was
wide awake and merely hallucinating. She blinked again
as she was enveloped in pair of cuddly arms and a dense
cloud of Jean Naté cologne.

"Why, Naomi Connor, I can't hardly believe my eyes.
Would you just look at yourself? I haven't seen you in
years. Probably not since your cousin Nancy Beth got
married for the second time, bless her heart. And here
you are in Connecticut. Isn't it just a small world?"

Miranda was looking from one woman to the other in
total confusion. "Y'all know each other?"

Naomi met her eyes. "My mother's from Starlit, and
I spent a lot of time there as a child. A good few years,
when all was said and done." She looked back to Barbara. "Ma'am, may I just say how very sorry I was to
hear about the chief? He was a real good man." *Oh,
Lord.* She swung her face to Miranda's. "And you, too,
Miranda. I'm so sorry. When I heard he'd passed, it was
a real sad day."

"Thank you, darlin'. It happened so fast, and then
Miranda appeared right at the end like some wonderful
guardian angel heaven sent down to keep me going. She
moved me back to Starlit, and now I've got me a grand-

baby and another one on the way." Barbara reached
down and picked up Web, who started to fuss immediately. "Little Web here is actually named after the chief.
Walter Edgar Burrows Casey. Isn't that right, little
man?"

Feeling like her head was spinning, and not entirely
sure it wasn't, Naomi looked back at Miranda, who appeared to be just as surprised. "I honestly had no idea
the chief was your daddy, Miranda. Certainly I would
have said something if I had. But—" She paused and
cocked her head to the side. "Why don't I know you
already?"

"Please don't apologize, Naomi. He moved there after
my mother died and I was already away at school," Miranda replied, then put a brisk, cheerful note into her
voice. "I think we'll just have to get you over for a quiet
dinner while Barbara's here and then you two can catch
up. Right now we're on our way to see Chas and get an
opinion on some wallpaper, aren't we?" She scooped
her son from the inexpert arms of her stepmother and
placed him firmly on her hip. "I hate to rush off, but
I'm trying to scoot in and out between Chas's conference
calls, so we really do have to run. I'll light a fire under
Joe about getting together. I think he's back tonight."

Naomi smiled and said all the right things as she
watched Miranda herd the small group out the door.
Then she let out a breath that she hadn't realized she
was holding, and got in line to order her coffee.

"Hey, Joe. It's like old-home week around here. I
thought you were out of town."

He stopped and turned with a smile as he heard Miranda's voice behind him. That smile froze in place as
he saw who followed her out of the elevator across from
the one he'd just left.

Barbara Burrows, her stepmother and at least a nomi-
nal relative of his because of it—and one of the most

annoying, insipid women he'd ever met. Being in her presence for more than ten seconds usually made him start to itch.

"Hi, Miranda. Barbara, it's good to see you again." He bent down to kiss Miranda on the cheek and seconds later found himself enveloped in a cloud of Barbara's sweet, cloying, dime-store perfume, and sporting a life-sized, hot-pink lipstick mark on his cheek. *Great.*

As Barbara started to babble, he glanced over her head to see Miranda look to the ceiling in a clearly inadequate attempt to squelch her laughter. Reaching into Web's diaper bag, she pulled out a baby wipe and subtly wiped away the lip print.

". . . and I just thought I was dreaming. But there she was, just as pretty as ever. Shorter hair and all grown up and what all, but just the same as the sweet little girl . . ."

He sent Miranda another quick look, one that had his confusion and desperation all wrapped into it.

"Barbara and I just ran into Naomi at Starbucks, Joe," she interrupted smoothly as Barbara stopped to draw a breath.

"Really?"

She nodded. "And it turns out that she grew up in Starlit, Alabama, which is the town Walter and Barbara lived in, where Walter was chief of police, remember?"

He blinked at her, then glanced at Barbara. And the lightbulb in his love-fogged brain flickered on.

He gave Barbara one of his better smiles, and for the first time ever, didn't have to feign interest in what she was saying. "Really? What a small world. Did you know each other?"

Barbara's laugh held a definitely coquettish edge, which was as appealing as long nails scraped along a clean chalkboard. "Why, Joe, you can't live in a town as small as Starlit for ten minutes without everyone knowing your business—"

Jackpot. He glanced at Miranda. "If you have to meet

Chas, I can hang out for a while. I was just going to head out for some coffee, anyway." He looked back to Barbara. "Would you mind walking with me? That way we can keep talking."

"Why, thank you, Joe. That would be real nice."

"Thanks, sugar. I'll take Web with me and go pester his daddy. I won't be but a minute, so why don't I just meet you here in ten minutes or so?" Miranda said, winking at him over Barbara's head.

She turned and headed for Chas's office as he and Barbara turned back toward the elevator bank and stepped into the car the women had just vacated.

It's just some harmless background research, he assured himself. Barbara had worked for the local DA and been married to the chief of police. If the trouble Naomi had gotten into happened when she was living in Starlit, Barbara would have heard about, if not been involved in the case.

No harm could possibly come of it. Naomi might be annoyed at him for a while, but nothing he might learn, particularly something from her childhood—even something felonious—could change the way he felt about her. Whatever she'd done, it was history; that person wasn't who she was anymore. Besides, he was fully committed to proposing to her. To marrying her. He'd trusted her with his company and he was about to trust her with his future and everything in it. A man didn't do that unless he was sure of himself *and* sure of the woman.

"So, you've known Naomi for a long time?" he asked, giving Barbara another smile—the same one he'd used many times to soften up witnesses. And women. It rarely failed him.

"Practically all her life."

She was nervous and flustered, which didn't surprise him, although the fact that he was doing it to her deliberately made him feel a little guilty. Despite the fact that she was technically family, he usually spent the absolute minimum required amount of time in her presence. She bugged the living shit out of him with her incessant chatter, and sometimes it was a real strain to be anything more than polite. At the moment, of course, it was a different story, because the chatter was about Naomi. And her formative years.

"She's a very smart woman," Joe said easily. "I'm not sure what she mentioned to you, but she's here at the company as a consultant. She works with computers." *There's the ball; let's see if you run with it.*

He casually slid his left hand into his trouser pocket and wrapped it around the small leather-covered box in there. His suit jacket covered the small lump nicely, which is why he hadn't stopped at the house to change his clothes on his way from the airport.

Barbara nodded as they stepped out of the elevator and walked past the guard's desk.

"Naomi always was smart. And I'm not surprised she's working with computers. She got interested in them when she was just a little thing, after her daddy didn't want her hanging around the pool and the playground all summer long. He bought her a computer and taught her how to use it, and she just used to amaze us all." She laughed. "At the time, we didn't even have but a few telephone lines in the county prosecutor's office. I think she might have had the first computer in town. And she couldn't have been more than ten years old, as I think about it."

"That is young," he agreed, holding the door open for her as they traded the cool elegance of the lobby for the bright, baking fumes of the street. "It's actually a big responsibility to give to someone that age. I mean, there are so many opportunities for temptation. Even back then, before the World Wide Web was much of a presence, there were still opportunities for getting into trouble by using computers." *Come on, sweetheart, play with me.*

"I suppose there were. I don't really know much about computers, though, Joe. I'm still a little flummoxed by the e-mail on the computer Chas and Miranda gave me," she confided.

Damn. He smiled at her. "I know what you mean. I think the older you are when you start working on them, the easier it is to be confused or intimidated by them," he said in soothing, slightly conspiratorial tone. "But when kids start as young as Naomi did, they grow up with them and the computers become a part of their everyday life."

"I suppose they do. I still just prefer writing letters or using the telephone. It's so much nicer. More personal and all."

He paused. Obviously, subtlety wasn't going to get him anywhere with Barbara. It was time to switch tactics. "I'd forgotten that you used to work for the district attorney down there."

"Well, his title was actually Assistant County Prosecutor back then, but yes, we handled cases from all over the northern part of Baldwin County. Got involved with the odd federal case, too, sometimes," she replied proudly.

That's my girl. "I used to be a prosecutor, too. For a federal agency."

"You did? Well, heavens, I didn't know that. Which one, Joe? The FBI?"

"No, a smaller one called the Naval Criminal Investigative Service. We handled crimes against the navy. I worked in the computer crimes division."

"Oh, my, doesn't that sound like something?"

"It was interesting," he replied with false modesty as he pulled open the door to Starbucks. "But I was always surprised by the age at which a lot of the hackers had started their careers. Some had started even as young as Naomi—I mean, the age she was when she got her first computer. They'd get bored and look for bigger challenges, and eventually that led them to criminal activity." He glanced down at her as they stood in line. "Like hacking into systems that they're not supposed to be in," he finished pointedly and lifted his gaze to the menu. "What would you like?"

"Nothing, thank you, Joe. I just had something with Miranda." Her voice was uncharacteristically quiet, and he spared her a glance. She was looking straight up at him with a concerned and hesitant expression—the kind people wore when they were about to crack.

"Are you all right?" he asked, bending down a little and placing a hand on her shoulder.

She nodded. "What you were saying just called something to mind, is all."

Come to Papa. "Something about Naomi?"

She nodded distractedly, and he let her collect her thoughts while he ordered and paid for his drink, then suggested they sit down while he waited for it. It wasn't until he'd had the first sip and they were comfortably nestled at a corner table, lost in the din of the late-afternoon coffee crush, that he smiled at her again. "I'll bet you were thinking of that trouble Naomi got into when she was—how old was she? Fourteen, fifteen?"

If he hadn't felt some guilt already, the relief that flooded Barbara's face would have put him over the edge.

"She told you about it?"

He smiled and took a sip, neatly avoiding having to give an answer.

"Oh," she said on a sigh. "That makes me feel so much better. I'd hate to be telling tales out of school. I think she was all of twelve. Wasn't she?"

Something clicked on in Joe's brain and he could feel the muscles in his back tense involuntarily. "I'm not sure she told me exactly how old she was."

"Well, I'm not surprised, Joe. I'm sure she thought that you'd just remember. In truth, I'm a little surprised you don't. I mean, it was such a big deal. Although I suppose you may not have been told too much. You must have been pretty young yourself." That flirta-

tiousness was back in her voice and all the fluttery girl-
ishness had returned to her mannerisms.

Naomi had mentioned at some point that she was
about six years younger than he was, so when she was
twelve, he would have been eighteen.

Or seventeen.

An icy hand slid around his gut and he sat back in his
chair abruptly. "Yes, I was."

"But you're so smart and a lawyer and all, and even
in the same field. I just thought you'd have remembered
more about her."

Forcing a smile, he made direct, intense eye contact.
"I'd like to hear what you remember."

She blushed and nearly giggled as she looked away.
"I suppose what I remember most is how angry my boss
was when he wasn't allowed to prosecute her. And I'll
never forget how calm your mother was when she was
telling him that she wasn't going to stand for it."

As he sat frozen in his chair, Joe could see Barbara's
mouth continue to move. All sound had disappeared,
though, obliterated by the roaring silence that filled his
head, the hot, rhythmic pounding that filled his chest.

It made such perfect sense, and explained why she'd
been so nervous and evasive about discussing her past.
And he'd been too damned blinded by her looks to put
two and two together and come up with the right
answer.

Which was, of course, that Naomi was R@ptorGurl.

Cold, steely fury began to seep into him through every
pore, calming his superheated blood and initiating repairs on his savaged ego.

She'd been playing him for a fool the whole way. It
couldn't have been by chance that she ended up on this
project, and it sure as hell wasn't a coincidence that
she'd slept with him. He couldn't believe he'd fallen—
hard—for all that soft, Southern bullshit when the cold,
hard truth was that she'd merely been fucking him over

for the second time. The first time she'd been twelve and hadn't known what she was doing. Now she was thirty-two and knew exactly what she was doing, and she was aiming to do it a third time, probably just for fun.

He felt his back teeth grind past each other. *How could I have been so fucking stupid?*

He'd actually believed all that shit about a leak, never questioning why not one member of her entire team of security gurus had found a goddamned thing despite hitting the networks with everything they had. Never questioning why even the remarkable Miss Connor hadn't found anything until everyone on her team was gone.

Stupid wasn't quite right. *Blinded* was more accurate. Blinded by a smile and a brain and a figure that wouldn't quit, and rendered unable to see that she was fabricating the whole thing. She had access to the offices; she'd probably put the goddamned camera in Trudy's office. And all that high-intensity bullshit about mining the monitoring data. *Running scripts, my ass—*

"Joe? Are you all right, darlin'? You look a little . . . well, maybe we should just get back. Miranda is probably waiting on me, and she has to carry the little man home for his supper."

He blinked and refocused on Barbara, who looked more than a little alarmed as she stared back. He forced a smile onto his face and into his voice. "You're right, Barbara. I'm very sorry for drifting off like that. I just remembered something. I really do have to get back to the office."

When they stepped off the elevator, Miranda was waiting for them. She took one look at his face and didn't say a word. She just raised her eyebrows, scooted Barbara back into the car, and disappeared with a smile and a wave.

He turned the corner and was heading toward his office when he saw Naomi step out of Chas's office, with Chas right behind her.

"Just the man I was looking for," she said with a smile that didn't reach her eyes.

"Imagine that," Joe replied, forcing himself to relax. It didn't work too well, though, because he watched a frown crease her forehead.

Chas glanced first at him, then at her. "I'll see you in a few minutes," he said to her, and walked back into his office, but not before he sent Joe an admonishing glare.

Just wait, big brother.

"Can I talk to you for a minute, Joe? In your office?"

"Sure." He motioned for her to precede him, and didn't bother shutting the door behind him as he followed her.

After a split-second pause, she walked back to the door and shut it and leaned against it. She watched him loosen his tie, her gaze flicking from his hands to his eyes. "I've asked your mother to stay on for a bit. She and Chas are going to meet us in the bubble," she said quietly.

"Why?" He pretended to glance casually at the mail that lay on his desk.

"What's wrong, Joe?"

He looked up, barely able to make eye contact with her, loathing her, loathing himself more for falling for her act. "I asked you a question. Why are they waiting for us?"

Her shoulders went back as her chin went up. "I asked you one, too. They're in there because I've got to talk to the three of you and it's the one place I'm sure we won't be overheard. Now, tell me why you're looking at me as if you wish I weren't here."

"I've got some things on my mind, but they can wait." He walked to the unobtrusive door in the corner of his office and pressed his thumb against the small sensor next to it. When the lock clicked and the door swung open, he met her eyes and motioned for her to enter the small hallway. "After you, R@ptorGurl."

CHAPTER
32

Naomi felt as if every oxygen molecule in the room had been sucked away, leaving her dizzy and unable to draw a breath. She knew her eyes had gone wide, yet the only thing in her field of vision was Joe's face. His beautiful, cold, furious face. His eyes were as hard as chipped sapphires, and his jaw was set like iron. Tension radiated from him, swamping her. Eventually, he shut the door and turned to face her.

"Surprised?" he said quietly. Scorn as sharp and hard as diamonds pierced the word. "So was I. When were you going to tell me, Naomi? Or weren't you?"

She felt her mouth move but no words came out. There were none in her head, none in her heart.

"I guess we can talk about this later. Or not." He pressed his thumb against the sensor again and had to punch in a code this time. When the door swung open again, he waited without comment for her to walk past him.

Pulling herself together had never been such an ordeal, and Naomi only had twenty feet in which to do it. She knew Chas and Mary were sitting on the other side of the wall in the windowless room, and traversing the short, brightly lit corridor felt like a journey from more than one space to another; it felt more like a trip between lives. As if she were crossing a threshold from which there was no return. Which, of course, there wasn't.

When Joe opened the door to the bubble, Mary and Chas were chatting as they sat on opposite sides of the polished oval table. Naomi stepped into the glass-walled room ahead of Joe and greeted them with a forced smile as she walked to the far end of the table. Joe slid into the seat nearest the door.

Her heart was pounding like she'd run a marathon, her knees were shaking, and she was hoping that she'd regained the power of speech. Setting her laptop on the end of the table, she opened it and tapped in her password. She waited until the screen had flickered to life before she looked up and faced the three pairs of eyes watching her, the three neutral expressions that bespoke their experience: investigator, interrogator, intimidator. Cop, lawyer, executive.

Naomi locked her knees in place, kept her arms loose at her sides, and remained standing. "I appreciate you all making the time to meet with me," she began softly, amazed that her voice wasn't shaking. "As you know, my team and I spent a considerable amount of time and effort trying to find your vulnerabilities and exploit them over the last ten days. You'll get a full report of our activities and findings early next week. That's not what this meeting is about." She paused. "You all also know about the spy cam we found in Trudy Barker's office. I've traced that, too, and I'll get to that in a minute. Believe it or not, there's something we need to talk about that's a little more important than that."

She took a sip of water. "Chas, Mary, what you don't know is that a few days ago, I discovered what I thought might be a leak in your networks. Not a vulnerability waiting to be taken advantage of but an active leak. In other words, a deliberately created, clandestine means of siphoning information from your systems for unauthorized transfer to an external endpoint." Their eyebrows rose fractionally. "I informed Joe immediately, of course. Since I had nothing more than an anomaly and a hunch to go on, he recommended that we not say anything to anyone until we found something concrete, one way or the other." She hesitated minutely. "I agreed."

Both his mother and his brother turned to look at Joe with shocked, questioning looks on their faces. He met their eyes with no change of expression, then silently returned his attention to Naomi.

"My findings are not pleasant. You are not going to want to hear them, and I have a real strong feeling you aren't going to want to believe them, but they are what they are. I've spent a large amount of time and effort compiling the data and mining it, and more than twenty-four straight hours looking at the results from every possible perspective. I ruled out nothing." She took a deep breath, which almost seemed to echo over the empty hum in the background. "The bottom line is that Brennan Shipping Industries is, without question, being hacked. It looks like it's been going on since the time your new security updates began to be installed and tested. In other words, for about nine months."

The three Caseys remained silent but not unmoved. Mary's shoulders dropped and she sat back in her chair with a posture that resembled nothing more so than sheer exhaustion. Chas turned to look at Joe, who, in turn, was looking at Naomi with an expression that was pure fury. It unnerved her for a moment, then, oddly, a different source of adrenaline began flooding her bloodstream as her own anger began to bubble up.

"Have you figured out who and how?" Joe asked, his voice tight and sharp. Even Mary looked up in surprise.

After all the extra effort I took to try to clear your name in the face of overwhelming evidence, just who the hell do you think you are to address me like that?

She swallowed the question before it flew out of her

mouth. "As a matter of fact, I have," she replied, and it was a strain to keep her tone civil. "I'd like to explain my methodology as I go along, if you don't mind. I know you'll have lots of questions, and this may help to answer some of them. As difficult as this may be at times, I would appreciate it if you'd let me finish before you start asking questions." She looked down and clicked on the notes she'd made.

"After scouring at first weeks, and then months, of monitoring data for both overt patterns and overt anomalies, I came across some information that synchronized with the downloads from the camera in Trudy's office. It was a classic Trojan horse setup. When that digital-video data reached the server interface, other information was embedded into it. It was from predetermined files, and the video data was very cleverly configured to conceal it. Once hidden, the information was sent as random clusters of innocuously named files to an address at a private domain. Presumably, the reverse procedure was performed on the other end and the information was reconstructed." She looked around the table. "They were small files of varying sizes, but none was so large that it would have attracted any notice. I dug around a bit and found out that the domain they are being sent to is registered to Trudy. She's held it for four years, but it doesn't appear that there's ever been a Web site attached to it. Just some e-mail addresses."

"So the video cam is just a ploy? She's monitoring her own office?" Joe asked, doubt evident in his voice as he leaned back in his chair, arms folded across his chest.

"Yes."

"Why?"

She took a surreptitious deep breath and kept her voice neutral. "It's a security precaution, I figure. She wants to know who's going into her office and why when she's not there."

"Again, why?"

Damn you. She met his eyes, bright blue and searing

her with frigid heat, and threw her caution—quite possibly her career—to the wind. "Because she's the hacker, Joe," she snapped. "And she's set *you* up to take the fall."

Joe blinked and forgot his anger for a moment as Naomi's ridiculous, furious statement registered in his brain. "What did you just say?"

"I said Trudy is the hacker and she's set you up to take the fall," Naomi repeated more calmly, though her eyes had gone nuclear with annoyance.

He let his scorn show on his face. "Trudy Barker can barely figure out her e-mail—"

"It's an act, Joe." Her quiet interruption fell through the air like feathers, scattering in all directions and disorienting everyone. "All good criminals can do it, as I'm sure you know. The reality is that Trudy Barker went back to school five years ago and now holds bachelor's and master's degrees in computer science from UConn. She's also a certified network engineer. A damned good one, in my opinion. She's fooled an awful lot of other good ones for a very long time."

Does she really expect me to believe this crap? "How did you figure this out?" he demanded. "Are you sure the Trudy Barker with the degrees is the same—"

"Joe, Naomi asked us to just listen. I'm asking you to do the same," his mother said firmly, without bothering to look back at him, and he knew better than to take her on. "Please continue."

The anger in Naomi's gaze subsided and she glanced down at her screen again. "I've gotten a little out of sequence, but I'll try to hit just the high points. The domain is ostensibly registered to a Joseph P. Casey in Greenwich. It was a bit disconcerting to see that and it threw me off track for a day or so, I have to admit. Then I started finding other things." She met his eyes. "Things that started to point in the same direction and corroborated the evidence that you, Joe, were the hacker. The monitoring data showed a pattern of e-mails sent daily from one of your user names to—"

He whiplashed to attention. "From one of *my* user names? Just wait a goddamned—"

"Joe," his mother snapped. "I refuse to tolerate these interruptions and I don't care for your language. Control yourself. Naomi asked us to let her finish. Give her that courtesy."

Steam rose in his blood at the sheer outrage of being considered even for a minute as some lowlife scum who would destroy his own company. He leaned back in his chair, rigid and glaring at Naomi, who had regained her poise and now appeared unruffled.

She met his eyes again, and despite his fury, he felt a flash of respect. Her eyes were dark but resolute. She knew what she was doing.

Damn it.

"Thank you. I know this is difficult to hear." She looked at her screen again. "At this point, three things were bothering me. The first was that Joe would be so blatant about using a known e-mail account as a conduit. The second was that he'd send things out so routinely. And the third was that he'd be interested in the video feed from Trudy's office in the first place." She hesitated and gave a slight shrug that was more scattered than apologetic. "I looked for other patterns or trends in his outgoing e-mails, but there weren't any. Against that backdrop, this set of e-mails seemed all the more suspicious. I decided to cross-check these e-mails against your travel schedule to see if they were still being sent when you were away. They were. Are," she corrected herself. "But even when you're gone, they're sent from here. They don't just pass through the local system; they originate in it. Which means they either have to be created and sent by someone else at Joe's direction, or they're automated."

She looked around the room, meeting everyone's eyes before she continued, and Joe couldn't help but feel a glimmer of pride streak through him. She was fucking brilliant. Except, of course, that she had lied to him, and then suspected him of—

"—I finally tried to open one of them to see what they were," she was saying. "The smaller files, which I am assuming held the video data, were tightly encrypted, which didn't surprise me. The larger files, though, contained highly classified material that had been simply cut and pasted into other documents. Before you"—she sent him a warning glance—"inform me that classified files are protected against being copied because of the configuration management application you use to store them, let me assure you that I understand that that's supposed to be the case. But there are ways around those protocols; ways not easy to figure out or attempt, but they can be done if you know what you're doing, which Trudy does."

And so do you, you gorgeous little felon, he added silently, grudgingly.

"So to put it bluntly, criminal activity is and has been taking place for a while." She stopped, glanced down at her screen, then looked at each one of them before continuing in a much softer, almost hesitant voice. "To be perfectly vague about it, in my quest to find the hacker and exonerate Joe, I went on a no-holds-barred fishing expedition using highly questionable practices and some pretty unsavory resources. While nothing I did is technically against the law, it rubs right up against it and is certainly in violation of Brennan Shipping Industries' standard of ethics and behavior, as well my own company's. So if you don't want to hear any more details in order to protect yourselves from potential liability or culpability, I'll understand."

Somehow, he kept his jaw from dropping.

"Thank you, Naomi, but please continue," his mother said quietly, without bothering to look at either of her sons. Chas shrugged nonchalantly and deliberately kept his eyes on Naomi.

God almighty, they've both got bigger balls than I do.
Joe finally met her eyes and nodded.

"First, I ran a credit check on Trudy by borrowing the
authority of the head of Human Resources." She re-
viewed the information on her screen. "Five years ago,
she purchased a small condo in downtown Stamford. I
assumed that it was an investment property, since Trudy
also bought a home in Florida the same year. Then I
ran a criminal background check, just to see what I could
find. And what I found was a whole load of unpaid parking tickets, all issued in downtown Stamford. It struck
me as kind of odd, so I looked more closely. All of them
were issued on weeknights and, when I checked a map,
it turns out all of them were on streets in the UConn
area. That led me to check the graduation lists, and there
she was, twice." She paused. "A scan of the last few
years of her credit card records revealed registration fees
for several high-level computer training courses in different cities, with corresponding hotel and flight reservations. She's also spent a lot of money on electronic
equipment. I didn't find out what she bought, but I can,
if necessary."

From the edge of his vision, Joe saw his mother close
her eyes and take a slow, deep breath.

Naomi must have seen it, too, because she stopped
talking and looked up. "I'm so sorry. Would you like
me to stop?" she asked, clearly uncomfortable at the
reaction her story was generating.

"Certainly not. Please continue." Mary's voice was
hushed, and she didn't open her eyes as she spoke.

Naomi took a steadying breath. "At that point, I figure I'd nailed the means and opportunity part of the
test, so I just started thinking about the motive part.
And, ma'am, after a while, I remembered something you
said," she said, her words more rushed than they had
been, as if she just wanted to be rid of them.

"What was that?" His mother's voice was a wet whisper, and Joe looked up to see her surreptitiously wiping

quiet tears from her cheeks. For the first time in his life, she looked weak. Defensive, undirected anger reared up in him again.

Naomi was still standing at the end of the table, her jaw clenched, her hands flexing into fists, then opening again. She looked like she might start to cry herself. "Please believe me when I tell you how very unhappy I am to have to deliver this news. But the day I was asking you some questions about her, you told me she thought of you as family and that she would never do such a thing to you."

"Yes, I did say that. And it's true. Or at least I thought it was."

"Ma'am, in all likelihood, it is true. She well may have thought of you as family." She paused and swallowed hard. "I think that after a while, maybe, she realized that y'all didn't think of her as family," Naomi said in a voice that had dropped to a painful huskiness. "I know all the good things you did for her; things that you didn't have to do, that most people would never think of doing under the same circumstances. But grief can do funny things to people, and sometimes it causes them to bite the hand that's comforting them, if you don't mind me mixing the metaphor."

"Now you're an amateur psychologist?" Joe snapped, and Naomi brought her eyes slowly to his.

"Not hardly, Joe. I'm just talking about compounded guilt. The deep shame and anger that can build when someone won't let you apologize and get on with it. When, for all the right reasons, they try to make things right, and the truth is that some things are better just left alone. And in this case, because y'all were being so decent about everything for so long, I'm guessing she just finally started to resent the situation, and decided—maybe consciously, maybe unconsciously—to do something that would really make you finally blame her, hate her, and move on, leaving her with her conscience and her pain."

The room was silent except for the low hum of white noise in the background. Eventually, his mother, red-eyed but composed, looked around the table at the three of them.

"I think we have enough evidence to bring in the authorities." Her voice was not as strong as it normally was, but it was calm. "And I, personally, will stand behind your actions, Naomi. Have you contacted anyone?"

"No, ma'am. That's your call," she replied softly.

His mother looked at Joe, then Chas. "What now? Whom do we call? Do we try to detain her?"

"Definitely not," Chas replied firmly, then looked at Naomi. "Does she have any idea that she's been under surveillance?"

"She probably knows or has an idea that we know about the camera. But as far as the rest of it goes, I can't imagine how she would. All of the data I was reviewing was historical, and I was reviewing it off-line."

"I'll get Stamford PD to put someone at the apartment, and I'll have them contact Bridgeport and have them do the same thing at her house. And I'll call the FBI."

"NCIS," Joe said stiffly. "She's been stealing navy secrets."

"How do we keep her here?" Mary asked.

Joe looked up. "I just got back from a business trip. I have a ton of stuff that has to be ready for review by tomorrow. I can keep her here all night, if need be."

"We can adjust her access privileges, too," Naomi said quietly, and all three of them looked at her. She looked straight back at Joe. "Use what you have on hand: your security system. We can revoke her freedom of movement in fifteen seconds and she won't be able to get off this floor, short of pulling a fire alarm."

He sat back in his chair, feeling as if he'd been sucker punched. Again.

"It's a tempting idea, Naomi, but I don't think it's the best option," Chas said after a moment. "Maintaining the illusion of normal is critical. If she tried to go to a different floor and couldn't get there, she'd become suspicious. If she's at all on to you already, she could panic and then all bets are off."

"What does that mean?" Mary asked. "You're not saying Trudy would get violent?"

"I mean that we can't make any assumptions," Chas replied firmly.

"A typical hacker has a big ego, illusions of superiority, and an antisocial streak, Mrs. Casey. They can be unpredictable. Some just admit it and go quietly when they're caught, and some can't handle it," Naomi added gently. "I think Chas is right that we can't make any assumptions about her reaction. There are too many people in the building and too much information at risk."

"But we obviously have to move fast. If we don't cut off her access, information is still going out. If we cut off her access, she's going to notice." Chas looked at his brother. "When does she usually leave for the day?"

"She sticks around until about six thirty to catch the downside of traffic." It was his voice, but Joe barely recognized it. He felt like he was coming out of anesthesia, trying to focus on a blurred world.

"It's four thirty. Do you think you can get anything organized in two hours?" Naomi asked.

"We have to. It's just a matter of who takes her into custody and on what charges." Chas got to his feet. "Let me make a few phone calls."

"Let me." Joe looked over at him, and after a few seconds, Chas nodded.

He glanced over at Naomi. "There's an NCIS office in New London and a Major Crimes unit in Rhode Island. I can send the jet for them. Will you go up and brief them on the way back?"

She nodded; her eyes widening was the only indication that this was taking on a larger-than-life scenario. He looked back at Chas. "Put someone watching her car. One of our guys."

Then he reached for the phone.

"I need to leave," Mary said slowly, and Joe put down the phone as he looked at her. She'd gone sort of gray in the face and suddenly looked old, tired, and very sad. As if her heart were being broken in slow motion.

Both sons were at her side in seconds, but she waved them away. "I'll be fine. You do what you have to do. The company is what's at stake, not me."

"Would you like me to drive you home, ma'am?" Naomi asked softly.

She looked up. "Thank you, but you're needed here. I'll take a cab." Then the last vestige of her composure fractured and she buried her face in her hands, her shoulders heaving with sobs.

Fear exploded in Joe's chest. There was no other word for it; there was no way around it. His mother had never displayed weakness, not like this. He didn't have a clue what to do, and stood there as if paralyzed as he watched Chas help her to her feet, soothe her, calm her, and do it all without seeming to have to think about it.

Mary lifted her head slowly, her eyes still flowing unchecked as she leaned against Chas, his arms encircling her, almost cradling her. "I can't expect any of you to understand it, but this is more than just another hacking. This is nearly a lifetime of trust that has been shattered and betrayed. I can't watch it unfold. She was so young—we both were. I can't help but think I created this," she said, her voice thick with sobs she was trying to restrain.

A moment later, she and Chas left the room.

Joe felt raw inside, not just empty but scraped bare and bloodied by everything that had transpired in the last few hours. A motion at the periphery of his vision broke his trance and he looked down the table to see Naomi closing her laptop. She slid it into its case and left the room, walking quietly past him without so much as a glance.

As the heavy door swung shut behind her, Joe realized that he was alone. Utterly alone.

CHAPTER
33

Naomi leaned against the back of her office door and let the tears she'd been stifling flow unchecked as the reality of the situation sank in. It had felt worse to deliver that news than she had imagined it would. She'd delivered bad news before, even news about hackers and criminal activity, but it had always been to a company's hired executives, who thought of the company in terms of its stock price and benefit packages and their own longevity. Those projects had always retained an element of being a high-stakes game, a challenge that the best, most clever player won. Those projects were about victory and defeat.

This was different.

This was about a family and its values and the legacy of trust it had created; trust that had been twisted and abused beyond recognition by someone beyond suspicion.

This was real and it was very, very ugly.

The look on Mary Casey's beautiful face was unlike anything Naomi had ever seen before. It went beyond pain, beyond grief or shock or disbelief. It was the look of destruction. The look on Joe's face had been worse. It was . . . empty.

It was time to leave.

She crossed the room slowly and set her laptop on the desk. Then, without any hesitation, she began packing things up.

Within thirty minutes, all evidence of her presence was neatly packed into her computer bag and a box she'd filched a week ago from the copy room. Taking a deep breath, she checked herself in the tiny mirror of her compact and repaired the damage she could. Pulling open her office door, she began the suddenly too-short walk to Joe's office. The door was closed, but she could see that Trudy's was still open, so she poked her head in.

Trudy looked up from her computer and smiled. Her expression was guileless and serene, and just a little bit on the ditzy side of sweet.

How could you do this to them? To yourself? Realizing that she was staring, Naomi shook herself and gave Trudy the closest thing to a genuine smile that she could manage. "Hey, Trudy, I just wanted to stop in and say good-bye. I'll be leaving soon."

"That was fast," Trudy replied with a grin.

Naomi cocked her head as Trudy's words registered. Something didn't sound right. "I'm sorry?"

"I figured you had to be giving them the bad news since the four of you were closeted back there together," she said with a laugh. "What's it going to be? Layoffs or just a restructuring?"

As Naomi stood in the doorway, time seemed to stop for just a few seconds. Then adrenaline exploded into her veins.

My meeting was with Joe. She saw me walk into his office. Alone.

She knows about the bubble. And she knows we were all in there together. And she just let me know she knows.

She took a deep breath as Chas's words echoed in her head. *If she's at all on to you already, she could panic and then all bets are off.*

Naomi folded her arms in front of her to hide her shaking hands, and leaned against the doorjamb casually to keep her knees from giving out. She kept the smile on her face and widened it just a bit, and intensified her drawl. "That's some good guessing, but it's neither. I'm not that kind of management consultant," she said with a wink. "By the way, is Joe in his office? I noticed that his door is closed, and when he's here it's usually open."

She glanced at the phone console. "His line is lit up, so he must be in there. Would you like me to buzz him?"

"No, thank you. I think I'll just do the analog version and knock. You take care of yourself, now." Her heart thudding, Naomi kept her pace easy as she walked the few steps to Joe's door and knocked.

"Yes?" came the muffled reply.

She opened the door a crack. "Can I talk to you for a moment?"

Joe's face was grim and didn't change as he nodded. She pushed the door farther into the room and only then realized he wasn't alone. Two men in sport coats and ties had risen to their feet and stood in front of the chairs opposite his desk. She didn't have to see their guns or their badges to know they were police officers.

She slipped into the room and shut the door behind her.

"Excuse me for interrupting," she said, then turned her eyes back to Joe. "I was just talking with Trudy. She knows about the bubble and she knows we were all just in there," she said quietly.

"She told you?" he asked, as if the information came as no surprise.

She nodded.

He returned his attention to his brother and the two detectives. "Okay, what now?"

"We pick her up," Chas said, then glanced at Naomi. "This is Detective Gruber and that's Detective Fiorello. This is Naomi Connor, the security consultant who discovered the hacker and ID'd her."

The detective nearest her offered her a firm handshake while the other nodded with a smile.

"I'm pleased to meet you both." She turned her attention back to Chas. "I have my office all packed up and just came down here to let you all know I'm going to head back to the condo soon. If you would prefer that I stay around for a while, I can do that. I just don't want to get in the way. Naturally, I'll make myself available for questioning."

"Don't leave just yet. Within the hour there are going to be a lot of people who want to talk to you," Chas said with a grim smile.

She swallowed and nodded. "All right. I'll be in my office. It was nice to meet you," she said, glancing at the detectives. She spared a quick look at Joe, who was watching her with a neutral expression.

Well, I guess that's that. Keeping her smile on her face, she left the office and closed the door quietly behind her. Turning around to head back to her side of the building, she bumped into Trudy, who had her back to her as she was shutting her office door.

She also had her purse over her shoulder.

"Heading home early?" Naomi asked, and wasn't surprised when Trudy spun around and landed against the wall with a startled look.

"Oh. Hi. I thought you were meeting with Joe."

"He's still on the phone," Naomi lied.

"Right." Trudy was breathless and wide-eyed, two things most people weren't when they were going home for the day.

Naomi felt her nerves begin to stretch thin as she realized simultaneously that it was up to her to prevent Trudy from leaving and that she didn't know what to do. Stepping backward and pounding on Joe's door could be interpreted as an overreaction if Trudy was only heading to the ladies' room.

You're Southern. Start talking, she ordered herself.

"Well, aren't you lucky, getting to leave early," Naomi began with a smile, deepening her drawl just enough to make herself sound harmless. "I can't believe Joe is letting you leave when he just got back from a trip. He mentioned that he has tons of work to do. I just figured that meant you would, too."

"I, uh, I do. And he's not letting me leave early. I was—" Trudy paused and seemed to calm down suddenly. "I was just heading downstairs for some coffee."

"You know, that sounds wonderful. Would you mind if I tag along? I was hoping to duck out now, too, but he just told me I'm not allowed. I guess he's got more for me to do than I thought. Let's just detour to my office so I can get my purse. That's if you don't mind some company." Naomi held eye contact until Trudy nodded her uncomfortable agreement, and together they headed down the hall.

"I'll just use the ladies' room while you're getting your things," Trudy said in a rush, and veered off down the short corridor to the left of Naomi's office.

Thank you, Jesus. Naomi darted into her office and punched in the number for Joe's private line, praying he wouldn't check the caller ID and ignore the call. After four rings, he picked up.

Before he could say anything, she started talking.

"Joe, listen to me. I only have a few seconds. When I left your office, I ran into Trudy again. I think she was going to make a run for it while I was in with you, but I foiled her plans. She said she was going out for coffee, but she closed her office door and she doesn't ever do that, so I invited myself along," she explained in a harsh, hurried whisper.

"Calm down," he ordered. "You're not making sense."

She let out a frustrated breath. "Look, I *know* I may not be making much sense, but she's making a run for it, and we might be in bigger trouble than I thought," she hissed. "You have to get IT to lock down the critical networks and start searching for logic bombs."

"What? What the hell are you talking about?" he demanded.

She took a quick, deep breath. "When I was looking at the data, I was so busy searching for patterns that I never looked for a digital trip wire. She's way too smart not to have left some sort of logic bomb behind to destroy the evidence. She could have put it anywhere, on any network. She had access to all of them. IT has to freeze things *now*, Joe. Everywhere."

"Where are you?" The annoyance in his voice had changed to urgency and concern.

"In my office. Here she comes. I have to go. I won't let her out of my sight, but you have to move fast. *Lock things down now.*" She put the phone down as she saw Trudy walk past her door.

"I don't know how you've lasted working for him for so long, Trudy," she said with a forced laugh. "He's such a taskmaster. That was him with a few more things for me to do. Still heading out for coffee?"

Trudy nodded slowly.

"Then let's go. I really need some sustenance," she said, rolling her eyes conspiratorially. "I think it's going to be a long night."

Naomi kept up a barrage of mindless chatter as she steered Trudy toward the bank of elevators.

Joe stood there, hands casually in the pockets of his trousers, looking drawn but calm to the point of boredom. His hair showed signs of being raked too many times with aggravated hands and his tie was loosened, but they were the only visible signs that he was tense. He went still when he saw them approach, and that lawyerly, neutral expression slid into place.

"Heading out?" he asked.

"Just for coffee. We'll be back in a minute," Naomi replied quickly.

"I'd like to talk to you," he said.

"Which one of us?" Trudy asked, clearly surprised.

"Both of you, actually. Could you wait a few minutes for that coffee?"

"Sure," Naomi said, as Trudy nodded.

"Great. After you." He stepped aside and indicated that they should precede him down the hall toward his office.

Naomi noticed with surprise that his door was wide open, but it wasn't until she'd followed Trudy into it that she saw the two detectives and Chas standing quietly out of sight in the small area behind the door.

Joe closed the door behind him and stood in front of it as Trudy looked around nervously.

"Would anyone care to sit down?" Joe asked.

No one answered, and Naomi glanced around the room, knowing more things were different than just the tension level. After a few seconds, she realized that the long, low windowsill had been cleared of the antique sextants Joe typically kept there. The desk had been cleared, as well, and the chairs had been pushed toward the corners of the room.

They were taking precautions. The realization that they expected something physical to happen closed in on her, making her break out in a sweat and sending her heart rate into overdrive. A moment later, she felt Joe's hand slide around her upper arm and gently tug. She backed up a step, then he half turned to block her view.

Comprehension dawned slowly, and Naomi locked her knees seconds before they gave out. Joe's grip on her arm tightened. He still hadn't made eye contact with her.

Trudy turned to look at him, nerves and guilt clearly evident on her face. "What's going on? What did you want to talk to us about?"

"Actually, they want to," he replied, nodding toward the two detectives. "Chas, could you do the introductions?"

"Sure. Gentlemen, you've met Naomi Connor. This is Trudy Barker, Joe's executive assistant. Trudy, these men are Detectives Gruber and Fiorello from the Stamford Police Department's Computer Crimes division. They have some questions for you."

Looking past Joe's shoulder, Naomi could see Trudy's head swing wildly from one side to the other as she realized her options were diminishing. Her head remained in the direction of the windows a split second longer than it should, and as Naomi sucked in a hard breath and squeezed her eyes shut, she felt Joe's hand force her ungently to the floor.

"Trudy. No," Chas barked, and the sound of his voice was followed by a heavy thud and a hard crack, then a dull crash.

A gasped cry was overspoken by muttered curses and the sound of grappling bodies. Two metallic clicks silenced the room momentarily, until it was broken by the sound of female sobs.

"You can open your eyes now, Naomi. The windows are made of explosion-proof glass, remember?" Joe's voice was quiet as she felt his hands gently grip her upper arms and begin to lift her up. "Are you okay? I wasn't sure what was going to happen and didn't want—" He stopped.

She opened her eyes as he helped steady her on her feet.

"I'm fine," she said quietly as she tore her eyes away from the warmth and concern in his and focused on the quietly sobbing Trudy, who lay facedown on the floor of his office near the windows, one shoe off, her skirt hiked up too far above her knees. One detective was standing near Chas, discussing something in murmured tones, as the other was talking into his cell phone. Stepping away from Joe, she walked around the desk and crouched down to straighten Trudy's skirt, then slid the woman's glasses back onto her swollen and tear-streaked—but unrepentant—face.

"It was you, wasn't it?" Trudy asked dully.

Silence engulfed the room like a thick fog. None of the men made a sound to break it, and a heartbeat later, Trudy's labored breathing added a rough layer to it.

Naomi nodded. "You're good, Trudy," she said quietly. "The best I've ever come up against." She stopped, not certain what else to say.

"I'm better than good."

"With so much talent, why on earth did you go bad?" Naomi asked after a moment.

"Knock off the high-and-mighty routine," Trudy snapped, her eyes edging toward being wild with anger. "I know who you are. I was here when it happened and I remembered your name. And how easy you got off. You nearly destroyed this company and everyone that worked here. You should be in prison." She stopped for a few ragged breaths.

Her words stung like a slap in the face, but Naomi let her talk.

"What you did was so much worse than what I did, but you still had the gall to come back here, as if you're above it all. Who do you think you are?"

"Why did you do it?" Naomi asked, keeping her voice deliberately calm. "Was it a competition? You wanted to do more damage than I did?"

"You have some nerve asking me anything. You haven't walked away from it. You just think you have. You, of all people, should understand why I did it."

Because I'm a criminal, too. The simple, unspoken assumption sliced through Naomi cleanly, like a white-hot scalpel, and left a gaping, raw wound pulsing with a furious pain that made her catch her breath.

"I've never understood people like you, Trudy," Naomi replied in a voice low with ancient shame. "What I did was by accident. I didn't know what I was doing. What you did was wrong, and you knew it, and you did it anyway."

Trudy looked at her, loathing her. "I wanted my share."

Naomi felt rather than saw Joe stiffen. She glanced up at Chas, whose expression was neutral, except for tight white lines around his mouth. She brought her gaze back to Trudy's face and tried to keep her own contempt from showing.

"So who did you sell the plans to?" she asked evenly, not expecting a reply.

The older woman's face hardened. "Your old friends from Moscow," she hissed in a voice that was clear and pointed and dripping with venom. "They send you their love."

As if she'd taken a blow to the chest, Naomi rocked back on her heels, only to feel Joe's hands haul her to her feet. Taking huge openmouthed gulps of air, she fought the dizziness that was swamping her.

"You have the right to remain silent," one of the detectives began, and at the words, Joe turned her around roughly in his arms and held her to his chest.

His warmth and strength and scent flowed around her, creating a refuge, the only place she wanted be, the one place she wanted to lose herself.

It's too easy.

After a few seconds, she gently disengaged herself and took a step back. Chas had moved to their side and was watching them both with a sad, hesitant curiosity.

She met Joe's eyes for a second, then looked at Chas. "Allow me to introduce myself, Chas. Twenty years ago, I hacked your company," she said simply. "I was R@ptorGurl."

"When's the last time you got any sleep?"

Naomi focused dully on the sympathetic face of the NCIS agent she was talking with. That would be the fourth NCIS agent she'd spoken with tonight, all of whom, oddly enough, had asked her the same questions that the two Stamford detectives had, with a few new ones thrown in here and there. "What day is it?"

The agent glanced at his watch. "In twenty minutes it will be Wednesday."

"Then the answer to your question is Monday."

"I appreciate your cooperation, Miss Connor."

"I'm glad," she said, stifling a yawn. "Please don't take this the wrong way, but how much longer are you going to need me here?"

"I think we've got everything we need for the moment. If I need you, where can I find you?"

"For the next twelve hours or so, I'll be in Stamford, asleep. After that, I'll be heading back to the District, but I'll make myself available to you. One of y'all has my cell phone number. As long as you don't call me before noon tomorrow, I'll be delighted to chat."

He smiled and flipped his notebook shut. "I'll spread the word. I just have one last question."

"Yes, sir?" Her blink seemed to last deliciously long, and she knew that wasn't necessarily a good thing. She forced her eyes open.

"You've been very consistent in telling us where you think we could find the information we need to build the case against Trudy Barker."

"I've tried to be helpful."

He flipped open his notebook again and thumbed through a few pages. "In fact, you've said that you 'guess' we could find detailed information from certain, rather specific sources."

"Yes, I remember saying that. In fact, I remember saying it about four times, Agent Ford."

"I'm Agent Stipple."

"My apologies." She tried to make her next blink last only as long as it should.

"Don't worry about it. So it's just a guess? Each time?"

"Yes, sir."

"Well, I have to ask you, then, Miss Connor, how good a guesser are you?"

She met his eyes and did everything in her power to keep her own open. Despite that, she could feel them start to roll around in her head. "I'm a good guesser. A very, very good guesser. Possibly the best."

"I think we're done here." Naomi sensed Joe's presence seconds before his voice penetrated the fog that had descended on her brain.

She struggled to open her eyes and his face swam into—and out of—focus. "Does that mean I can go home?"

"Yes. I'll take you there now."

"I can drive."

"You walked here this afternoon."

Even though her eyes were definitely closed, she knew he was grinning, at least a little. "Oh."

"Can you walk?"

"Of course."

Nothing happened for a few minutes, or maybe just one, and then she felt a warm, strong arm slide around her shoulders and a warm, strong hand slide around her waist from the other side, and she was gently pulled up from the chair she was sitting on. The arm slipped from her shoulders to around her waist and held her securely to the side of a tall, hard body that smelled of late hours and fast food but underneath it all, just like Joe.

CHAPTER
34

"I really don't know why I let you talk me into this."
Naomi glanced at her mother, who was smiling behind
the flute of Champagne she held to her lips. They were
standing in the last hint of daylight on a terrace facing
the Capitol, part of the glittering, glamorous crowd at
the pre-performance cocktail reception for the season
premiere of the National Symphony Orchestra. She was
trying very hard not to remember the last time she'd
been at the Kennedy Center.

"Because you've been working your fingers to the
bone for the last two months, between taking on that
partnership and dealing with all those lawyers and depo-
sitions and things. I've barely seen you and when I do,
frankly, darlin', you're no fun. When you came down to
visit us, precious, all you did was sleep, and when I came
up to visit you, all you did was work and mope around.
So when this invitation came in, I just had to get you
included."

Naomi kept her smile in place and resisted the urge
to shake her head. Her mother was in her element.
Other than hot white sand fringed with cool blue water,
the thing her mother lived for was high heels and high-

powered socializing. The Washington social scene was her mother's idea of heaven.

"Who are we meeting, anyway? You said it was social, not business," Naomi asked.

Emmaline Blanchard Connor smiled and patted her arm. "Just an old friend. We haven't seen each other in years, and when she called, I was just tickled."

"Who is it?"

"Oh, Naomi," her mother said in a conspiratorial whisper. "Isn't that Warren Beatty and his darling little wife? The one that played that trampy French woman in that movie?"

Save me, Jesus. Somehow, she refrained from rolling her eyes. "That actress is Annette Bening, and, no, that's not her. And that's not Warren Beatty, either."

"Well, I know I've seen his face somewhere."

"Mama, if you don't start wearing your glasses in public, I don't know what I'm going to do with you. That's Tim Russert you're looking at. He's a foot shorter and fifty pounds heavier than Warren Beatty," Naomi hissed and took her mother by the elbow. "Let's go find Daddy. They're going to start flickering the lights soon."

They turned to traverse the length of the elegant West Terrace but didn't make it beyond a few steps. Because there, chatting easily with her father, stood Mary, Chas, and a considerably thinner Miranda Casey. Joe stood next to Miranda, wearing a beautifully cut double-breasted tuxedo on his body and poorly concealed thunder on his face.

Heat and desire swamped her, threading into every cell, settling in every pore.

Sweet Mother of God. "Mama, what on earth have you done?" Naomi murmured as her mother propelled her forward on legs less steady than a Gumby doll's.

"It's about time you put the past behind you, precious. They have."

"I may kill you yet."

"I already considered that, and that's why we chose

this place. The security's good," her mother replied under her breath and through a bright smile.

"Who's 'we'?"

"Mary and me," she replied, and then stretched her arms in welcome to a tanned and rested Mary Casey, who returned the warm embrace.

"Emmy, it's delightful to see you. It's been such a long time. And Naomi." Mary pressed a kiss to her cheek. "It's wonderful to see you under pleasant circumstances for a change, honey."

"Thank you, ma'am." Naomi kept her eyes trained firmly on the two women, but she could feel Joe's eyes burning into her. She was wearing that gown. *The* gown.

"Please. It's Mary."

Naomi greeted the other Caseys; as if by mutual agreement, she spoke with Joe last. He seemed as uncomfortable as she was, which should have made her feel better, but it didn't. She hadn't seen him since he'd taken her back to the condo the night Trudy had been arrested. He'd brought her upstairs and made sure she was all right, and then left with a curt good-bye. The next day, one of his assistants called to say the plane was at her disposal to take her home, but she had already booked a ticket on the train.

They'd spoken on the phone twice since then and had had several e-mail exchanges, but all were strictly about business: One was regarding the report she'd submitted, and the other had been a conversation about her deposition. He'd been decent enough to suggest that she get an attorney and request immunity from prosecution just to be on the safe side. But other than the standard "How are you? I'm fine, and you?" there hadn't been so much as a hint of anything personal between them in two months. Okay, two months, ten days, and nineteen hours, but she really wasn't keeping track.

And now, after all that time, here he was—his hair streaked nearly platinum in places while the rest of him was cast in bronze, his blue eyes stormy and alive, his smile slightly less forced than it had been seconds ago—looking better than he had a right to and obviously intent on making her go weak at the knees.

Well, he can just think again. She squared her shoulders and met his eyes as she leaned toward him.

"Hi, Joe. It's nice to see you again," she said smoothly, kissing him on the cheek as easily—or so she made it appear—as she had kissed each of the other Caseys. She just had to ignore the heady seduction of his presence, the scent of shaving cream and the sunlit sea that seemed to cling to him. She fought the urge to breathe him in.

"You look beautiful," he said when his mouth was near her ear.

Oh, no, you don't, Joe Casey. You owe me one big ol' granddaddy of a groveling apology, and this little Earth girl's not even going to give you a real smile until she gets it.

"Thank you," she murmured, then took a step back and looked toward the rest of them. "What brings y'all to town?" she said cheerfully, probably a little too cheerfully, judging by the subtle look that Miranda sent Chas.

"This," Miranda said with a laugh, and waved a languid hand in the air. "It's my reward for producing the heir and now the spare."

"Congratulations. When was the happy event?"

"Charles Frederick the Third, who that man over there"—she pointed at Joe with a smile—"keeps threatening to nickname Chuckie, arrived exactly on schedule six weeks ago."

"Well, you look divine. Did you bring him with you?"

"No. I pried her away from both of them," Chas replied with a grin, slipping his arm around her narrow waist. "But she's already called home four times, and we only left five hours ago. We have to change the subject right now or she'll be on the phone in thirty seconds. How have you been?"

Seeing their easy, obvious intimacy turned the casual conversation into an excruciating brand of torture for Naomi. A different need swamped her now, the need to be held close to Joe's side the way Miranda was nestled into Chas's, to have his arm around her, his scent engulf her. She forced a smile. "I've been fine, thank you. Busy as all get-out."

"Congratulations on your partnership."

"Thank you." And before she could say another word, the chime sounded. It came as no surprise that the other five members of their party blithely closed ranks and began moving toward the performance hall, leaving Joe and Naomi to navigate the path on their own.

"How are you?" Joe asked so quietly it was almost under his breath.

Still in love with you, damn it. Annoyed, she twitched away the traitorous thought. "Tired."

One glance told her that her bitchy reply had misfired. "Well, it doesn't show. You look dazzling," he said with a smile that was designed to break down her defenses.

"I'm glad to hear it." She kept her eyes trained on her father's fine military posture as it moved through the crowd farther and farther ahead of her.

"I heard that Chas paid you a visit last time he was in town."

She stumbled at the reminder and his arm shot out to steady her. His hand remained at her elbow for a minute—or two—longer than it should have.

"That's right. It was lovely to see him. We had a wonderful lunch," she said stiffly, straightening her back. The slight buzzing sensation his grip was causing in her bloodstream was a complication she didn't need right now. But breaking that contact was something she just couldn't bring herself to do.

"He said you turned down his offer."

"That's right. I like what I do, Joe. And now that I've made partner, it would be hard to leave," she lied.

He actually laughed. "Come on. You'd rather be a partner in a small firm than be our chief technology officer? I don't believe that for a minute."

She lifted her chin. "That's your prerogative."

"You wouldn't report to me, you know. I'm out of it. Or will be as soon as we hire someone. The chief general counsel is retiring next year and I'm up for his job."

"I believe Chas mentioned that," she said through her polite smile. "Congratulations."

"Thank you. Did he tell you that Sarah McAllister is our second choice for CTO?"

She nearly snapped her neck as she swung her head to look at him, adrenaline pouring into her system at his words. His voice was calm and bland, as if they were speaking about the weather or that afternoon's ball game, but his eyes were anything but bland. They were intense and dark, and held a trace of amusement that flicked against her anger, creating a white-hot spark that flashed through her. He saw it, and she watched his amusement fade, replaced by an answering glimmer, and an invitation to deep, dark, lovely sins.

"No, he didn't mention that," she managed to say in a somewhat choked voice. "She's an excellent choice."

"Tell me the real reason you turned it down, Naomi."

Her blood was still running high and fast as they left the crush of the lobby to enter the hallway leading to the box, and she looked away from him as a hot throb began deep inside. "I already have."

"How did you get here?"

She couldn't lie; he'd find out and it would only give him more ammunition. "My parents picked me up," she said tightly.

The smile he gave her was all about bedtime. "Can I take you home?"

"Absolutely not."

"Will you dance with me later?" he asked, his smile widening.

"Not on a bet," she replied serenely. "But thanks for asking."

As she walked into the box ahead of him, she knew he was watching her behind. And remembering that damned hickey.

"How's the Casey hickey?" he murmured as they moved slowly across the dance floor three hours later.

Having her in his arms but furious at him was the most excruciating combination of heaven and hell that could ever be dreamed up, but if he had to deal with her anger, this was the way to do it. They were a respectable distance apart, and neither one of them had done or said anything to draw the slightest bit of attention to themselves, but the tension between them had everyone in their party shooting subtle, and sometimes not so subtle, looks in their direction all evening.

The performance had been okay. He'd managed to keep his eyes on the stage only because that was the least obnoxious way of also keeping his eyes on Naomi, who sat to his left and had actually seemed to enjoy herself. Her eyes hadn't strayed even once from the stage.

Dinner was interesting, with no one on his left and Naomi on his right. Chas had been on her other side and had obviously been under strict orders to ignore her. It was completely out of character for him to do it, but he probably didn't mind too much—not with a finally *un*pregnant Miranda on his right and his nearest offspring three hundred and fifty miles away. As Joe could have predicted, those two lasted for one dance. Then Miranda had made up some pretty lie about being exhausted and they'd bolted for the Ritz-Carlton, where they had a suite.

He glanced at his mother, who was snug in a thicket of cabinet members and ranking senators, and the Connors, who were dancing more closely than he was dancing with their daughter.

"Stop it, Joe."

He looked down into her fiery blue eyes. If they'd been anywhere but at the Kennedy Center with her parents, he'd have hauled her into a janitor's closet three hours ago. "Stop what?"

"We both know what you're up to and I'll tell you right here and now, it's not going to work."

"We're dancing," he pointed out.

"Only because you cut in on my father," she said from behind that tight smile she'd been wearing all night. That pulse fluttering at the base of her neck gave her away, though. Not that he was about to mention it.

"So I have no chance at all? You're immune to seduction these days?"

"I'm immune to you."

You are such a bad liar, Naomi Grace. "Damn. I thought you of all people believed in rehabilitation." He made sure his breath moved just past her ear, which was one of her more sensitive organs, if he remembered correctly. And since he had had nothing better to do for the last two months than remember correctly, he was pretty damned sure he was right. Less than a second later, his recollection was confirmed by the shiver that ran through her body.

"I do." Her voice had gone breathy.

The sound of it did very bad things to his self-control and he was almost, but not quite, relieved when the song ended and they returned to their table.

"Mary, this has been such a wonderful evening. I just can't tell you when I've enjoyed myself more. But it's past time to get these old bones to bed." Emmy Connor, Southern belle emeritus and a charming, if not terribly creative, liar, turned to him with a brilliant smile. "Joe, it has been a real treat to meet you."

"Thank you, Mrs. Connor. The pleasure was all mine." He reached out to shake her hand and was hauled in for a kiss on the cheek.

He regained his balance and met General Connor's eyes. They weren't amused.

"Joe, it's nice to see you." His grip held a hell of a lot more meaning than his words did.

"Likewise, sir."

And then it happened.

"Good night, precious," Emmy said, leaning in to give Naomi a kiss on the cheek. "I know you young people want to stay and have a good time. Y'all look so beautiful out there, like you belong on the top of a . . . Mary, if you're leaving now, we could give you a ride, couldn't we, Tom?" She made eye contact with Joe. "I'm sure that Joe here will see our baby gets home safely. Won't you, Joe?"

Annoyance radiated from Naomi in waves and he fought a smile. "Of course I will, Mrs. Connor."

It was the fastest departure he'd ever seen his mother make from a social event, and when the coconspirators were out of sight, he finally looked at Naomi. "Do you think that was planned?" he asked, keeping a straight face.

She rolled her eyes. "I'm sure it was a coincidence," she drawled.

"Yeah, my mother is good at concocting those." He paused and slid his hands into his trouser pockets. If he didn't, he'd have to touch her, and he knew the time for that was not now. "Would you like to stay for another dance, or another drink, or should I just take you home now so we can get it over with?"

"Get what over with?"

He shrugged. "Whatever it is that's going to happen tonight."

"Or not happen," she added.

"That, too."

Sleep.

Right.

It was a nice goal, but the odds were against her achieving it. Naomi rolled to her right side again. She'd given it ten minutes already; she didn't need to give it more time to know that the only way she was going to get any sleep was if she stopped thinking about Joe Casey. She'd almost gotten good at it over the last two months, and then he had to appear tonight like a mirage.

No.

Like a fantasy.

Every time he'd touched her, it was like being stroked with a downed power line. Nothing on earth could insulate her from the high voltage in their contact.

At first glance, he'd been as annoyed and surprised as she had been. He'd gotten over it pretty quickly, though, and by the end of the night had made it unmistakably clear what he wanted: *her.*

She opened her eyes and focused on the ceiling. The trouble was, she didn't know if he wanted her for tonight, because he was hot and horny and she was there and unattached, or if he had something more . . . committed in mind.

The last two months without him had settled a few things in her mind, and one of them was that Joe Casey was not the guy she wanted to date; he was the man she wanted to marry. And that was part of the problem. She'd begun hearing things about him since the project ended, or maybe she'd just started paying more attention to conversations around her. Either way, his reputation was pretty solid: Joe was a short-term man.

Regardless of who told it, the story never varied. Dating Joe meant good times and happy days, and then he was gone—leaving in his wake not a string of broken hearts, but a long line of seriously annoyed women. *Shallow* seemed to be the descriptor of choice, followed by *insensitive, consumed by work,* and *a geek in a stud's body.*

She couldn't argue with the last two, but the first— those were words she would challenge. The Joe Casey she knew was not shallow. Nor was he insensitive. The look on his face when his mother had left the bubble with Chas that day had nearly ripped the heart out of her. It haunted her, and just thinking about it could make her cry.

That is it. I have had quite enough of thinking.

Refusing to allow herself even a moment to analyze her decision, she threw the covers back, pulled on shorts and a T-shirt, and headed for the door. Fifteen minutes later, she was standing on his doorstep, jumpy and trembling, and waiting for him to answer his cell phone.

Okay, so it's after midnight. He has to be home. There are lights on in the house.

She was about to disconnect when his voice came on the line. He was panting and the sound of it almost drove her to her knees.

He's not alone.

She sagged against his front door. Breath suddenly seemed impossible to find; words were completely out of the question.

"Hello?" he repeated. "Naomi, are you there?"

She closed her eyes and cleared her throat, gripping the phone. "Yes. Yes, I am. I—am I getting you at a bad time?" Her voice came out as a whisper.

"What? No. It's fine. I was swimming. Where are you? Are you okay?"

She almost laughed at the relief that washed over her like sunshine, and pent-up breath left her lungs in a rush. Knees still shaking, she stood up. *Of course he's alone. Joe Casey would* never *abandon a woman during sex to take a phone call.* "I'm fine, Joe. I'm on your doorstep, actually. Where are you?"

"You're here?"

"I can come back another—"

The door opened and a dripping wet Joe—gorgeous, cut, flushed, and breathing heavy—stood in a puddle of reflected light, wearing a towel loosely wrapped around his hips. He snapped his cell phone shut and folded his arms across his chest, biting the inside of his cheek as laughter danced in his eyes. "To what do I owe the pleasure?"

Once again, words failed her. She couldn't stop herself from staring. He was in much better shape than the last time she'd seen him undressed—and he'd looked mighty fine then. That adorable poochy little belly of his was gone, and in its place, gleaming and slick in the glow of the streetlight, were ripples. The good kind.

She dragged her gaze up the length of him and smiled weakly as she met his eyes, holding up the brown paper bag she was carrying. "We need to talk. And I come bearing a gift."

He laughed silently and stepped aside, motioning for her to come in. After shutting the door behind her, he immediately pressed a sequence on the alarm keypad next to it. Then he pressed a light and not overly quick kiss on her lips.

"I'm going to go take a fast shower, and then I'm going to come right back down here. Go anywhere you like in the house, but if you try to leave, you won't get far. There will be a SWAT team surrounding the house in less than a minute." He turned and walked up the stairs, apparently unconcerned about the trail of water that traced his steps in the darkly colorful Oriental runner. All Naomi could do was watch the muscles of his tanned back flex smoothly as he moved.

When he was out of sight, she walked into the kitchen in a mild daze and set her parcel on the counter. She was still standing there, between the island and the kitchen counters when he returned, barefoot, hair still wet, but dressed in a wrinkled blue golf shirt with Brennan Shipping's logo on the left breast and a pair of pressed khaki shorts.

"Want something to drink?"

"No, I'm fine, thanks." She hesitated for a second. "Where were you swimming?"

"In the basement. After my great-grandmother broke her hip, she had the apartment ripped out and installed a lap pool. Didn't I show you?" he asked, opening the refrigerator and taking out a bottle of beer and a bottle of Champagne. "Are you sure you don't want anything? I've got water and soda in here, too. No iced tea, though."

"No, I'm fine."

"So what's in the bag?"

She slid it across the granite top of the island. He looked inside, then looked up at her with a smile that wrapped itself around her like a favorite sweater. "A peace offering?"

Her eyes widened. "Certainly not. I just thought—"

"That it's what you and I do after spending the evening moving in high society?" he finished quietly, and came around to her side of the island.

He was clearly intending to slide his arms around her, so she took two quick steps back and sent him a tight smile. *Not so fast, darlin'.* "No, not that, either. But some of the things you were saying to me tonight have me kind of confused, Joe."

He stopped short. "Like what?"

"The last time we saw each other, you looked like you wanted me to be swallowed up by the earth. And tonight you admitted you were trying to seduce me, but then you left me at my apartment door with a smile and a nod. Not even a handshake." She lifted a shoulder. "I'm not sure how I'm supposed to connect those dots, and I need them connected before anything else happens. I'm just not following your train of thought."

His lawyer face slid into place as his hands wrapped themselves around the bottle of beer and opened it slowly, then he took a long drink. His eyes never left her face. "I've never wanted anything to swallow you up. But I was furious that you didn't tell me who you were," he said simply.

"We established that. But in your office, you more or less accused me of intending to hide it from you forever." She paused for a second. "By the way, could you take that look off your face so I can see what you're thinking?"

He lifted an eyebrow. "Would you like me to open a vein, too?"

She lifted one of her own. "I'll let you know."

A glimmer of amusement pulled at the corner of his mouth, but his eyes were dark and turbulent. He put down the bottle of beer and folded his arms across his chest. "I ran into you about two minutes after I found out who you were." He paused, and she saw a muscle flex in his cheek. "I felt like my guts had been ripped out, Naomi, and I just reacted. I didn't give myself time to think about anything."

"And have you now?"

"Obviously. But I still wouldn't mind knowing when and how you were going to tell me."

She glanced away. "After we stopped Trudy. You beat me to the punch by a few hours, that was all."

"I still would have been furious."

She looked back at him, her heart pounding, the back of her eyes starting to pulse with a telltale ache. "I know that, Joe. And the outcome between us may have been exactly the same, but I would have cleared my name and cleared my conscience, and I would have explained everything. You didn't give me a chance to do any of that." *There. I've said it.* Exhaustion seemed to swamp her then and she leaned against the island, wanting nothing more than to be home in her own bed.

"That's fine for you, but what about me?" he said with an edge in his voice. "What was I supposed to think after you'd cleared your conscience? Did you stop to consider that?"

She closed her eyes. *So there would be no reunion.* The knowledge made her want to weep, but she knew that if she started, she might never stop. "I wanted to tell you from the beginning. There were so many opportunities and I just didn't take any of them. I kept telling myself that I needed to redeem myself first, so I could show you how sorry I was instead of just telling you."

The silence that ensued was long and heavy, and filled the space between them.

"I thought you were the hacker," he said finally.

His quiet words bit her like a prong on the end of a whip, and her head snapped up to look at him. "You *what*?"

"After I found out your identity—"

"My *former* identity," she said sharply.

He nodded once in acquiescence. "Once I found out who you used to be, I put the puzzle together in what I thought was the right way. You found the camera, you found the leak after everyone else left, you knew where to look for clues." He shrugged. "It seemed pretty simple. You create a problem, you solve it, and you're the hero. Redemption in three easy steps."

This is what he believes about me. She stood still for a moment, absorbing the blistering stab of humiliation.

"Interesting theory," she said quietly, studying her nails. "Did you really, deep down, think I was capable of that?"

"I wasn't thinking 'deep down.' I already told you I wasn't thinking at all. I was just angry and had had only about two minutes to process things before I ran into you."

"Who told you?"

"Barbara."

Naomi shook her head. "I should have seen that coming."

"In fairness to her, I weaseled it out of her. I led her to believe you'd already told me."

"I'm not sure I want to know the details."

"You weren't the only one under suspicion, if you'll recall," he pointed out.

"She set it up so meticulously, Joe. I did think it was you. I had to. It's what I was supposed to do," she whispered against a sudden lump in her throat.

"When did you discover that?"

"When you were on that trip to Chicago."

He gave a silent laugh but didn't say anything. He just shook his head and picked up his beer.

She tilted her head toward the bag on the counter. "The ice cream is melting."

"I don't care."

She felt an involuntary smile tug at the corner of her mouth and took a deep breath. "Okay, so let's cut to the chase, Joe. What now? Do we kiss and make up and start over, or do we shake hands and go our separate ways?"

"Neither. Marry me."

She stared at him as his words echoed through her head several times before making a soft landing on her brain. "What did you just say?"

"I should probably rephrase it. Will you marry me?" He dug into the pocket of his shorts, then held out his hand. A large medium-blue square-cut stone in a simple silvery setting rested on his palm. It was gorgeous, even with the little bits of pocket dust clinging to it.

Feeling dazed, she brought her gaze back to his face. "You're serious, aren't you?"

A wicked smile crept across his mouth, nearly undoing her. "Of course I am. Doesn't this look like a serious sort of ring? Big diamond, platinum—what could be more serious?"

Blinking at him twice in not-so-rapid succession was all she could manage. "Well—" She hesitated. "No, I won't, Joe."

His eyebrows shot upward with shock, and he placed the ring on the polished stone countertop between them and stared at her for two full breaths. "Why not?"

She tried to control the trembling. "Why should I?"

His eyes widened as he recoiled from her question. "I can't believe this." His tone of voice revealed more frustration than hurt, and he paused. "Because we love each other."

"Do we?"

He folded his arms across his chest. "You're busting my chops, right?"

"No, Joe, I'm serious."

He frowned, tilting his head in a total lack of comprehension. "What do you mean, 'do we'? Of course we do. You said so that night in the car."

"Well, *I* told *you* that I loved you that night," she said calmly, then raised her eyebrows and crossed her arms in front of her. And waited.

It took at least a full minute before she saw understanding erase his confusion. "Did I ever tell you that I love you?"

"Not as I recall."

"Oh, hell." Rolling his eyes, wearing a sheepish grin, he walked around to her side of the island. "I do, you know. Love you, I mean," he murmured, sliding his arms around her waist and drawing her into a close embrace. He tilted her chin up until their eyes met. "I, Joseph Patrick Casey, love you, Naomi Grace Connor, to the depth and breadth and height my soul can reach."

"Poetry? Be still my heart," she said with a smile fueled by the warmth bursting inside her.

"It's the only line I know, so don't get your hopes up. And I'm sorry I never actually got around to saying it before now. I can only plead inexperience. You're the first woman I've said it to who isn't related to me by blood."

She laughed softly, if only to counteract the hot prickle of tears behind her eyes. "Imagine that. Joe Casey is a virgin."

"Was. Hey, don't you dare start to cry. I'm the one who just lost my virginity. Now, stop talking, or I'll start to feel used," he teased, moving in for a kiss.

She dodged it at the last minute, laughing again as his mouth landed on the sensitive skin below her ear. Heat raced through her veins. "I've got a few more questions, and once you start kissing me, I know I'm going to forget them."

"You're the most frustrating woman I know."

"I'll take that as a compliment. When did you get that ring? It's breathtaking, by the way."

He drew back and reached behind him to pick it up. "My great-grandmother found the stone about fifty years ago. I had it set before I went to Chicago and I picked it up on my way into the office that day." He lifted her hand and slid it onto her finger. It was the wrong hand, but she let it pass. "*After* I flew to Huntsville and introduced myself to your father."

She pulled back, the next best thing to stunned. "*You did what?* Joe, I'd never even mentioned you to my parents."

"Yeah, I found that out. But he turned it around on me," he said with a wry grin. "The second thing he asked me was if you were pregnant."

She laughed out loud. "That sounds like Daddy, all right. What was his first question?"

"Whether I'd already asked you. And by the way, that was your last question."

The moonlight that had silvered Naomi against the dark sheets of his bed had disappeared, not yet replaced by dawn. She lay next to him, warm and wrapped in his arms, wearing a satisfied smile and a big blue diamond. It was the only wardrobe she'd ever need, in his opinion.

"Did you ever actually give me an answer?" he asked lazily, letting his hand drift over her at a pace that caused all sorts of interesting reactions.

"I believe I said no."

"Since I'm well-known for my delicate negotiating skills, I'll give you a chance to change your mind. But first, there's one thing I want to know."

She glanced at the clock and sat up suddenly. "Mercy, would you look at the time? I'm going to be late for work—"

With a laugh, he pushed her gently back to the bed and threw his leg over hers to anchor her. "Not so fast,

Miz Scarlett. What's the story about you and the swimming lessons?"

She looked at him and blinked, then smiled. "What on earth made you think of that?"

"Well, after I ask you again and you say yes this time, we'll have to plan a honeymoon—"

"How about a wedding first?"

"Yeah, whatever," he said with a deliberately dismissive shrug, which earned him a smiling shake of her head. "I was thinking that it might be nice to take the *Mirabelle* to the Caribbean for a few weeks, and then I remembered something else Barbara said. She said you got your first computer after your father said you couldn't hang around the swimming pool anymore." He lifted an eyebrow. "What gives?"

He felt his smile fade as her gaze dropped to his chest. "Bad subject?"

"No, I'll tell you," she said softly. "When Daddy was home on leave the summer I was ten, he came to pick me up from the pool where all the kids in town used to hang out. A bunch of men used to hang around there, too, because it was next to the golf course. We didn't think too much of it, but he heard one of them make a comment about me, and that was the end of that."

Christ. Anger sliced through him. "You were ten?"

She nodded. "In an eighteen-year-old's body."

"Sick bastards."

"That's what he thought. So he bought me a computer to make up for it."

"What did he do to the guy?"

"There wasn't much he could do, right then, anyway." She met his eyes. "It was the local prosecutor who said it."

Joe paused. "The one who wanted to make an example of you after—?"

She nodded. "A few years later, after we'd already moved to Washington, I overheard Daddy tell one of my uncles that one of the happiest moments of his life was watching your mother, with all her high-powered attorneys in the room, cut off the man's, um, options, and hand them to him."

He started to laugh.

"So that's the mystery of the swimming lessons. I believe you were about to ask me something," she said, raising a flirtatious eyebrow.

"In a minute." After a long, slow kiss that left him on the border of delirium, he lifted his head and gave her a lazy smile. "Considering you're already wearing the ring, this might be a little redundant, but will you marry me, R@ptorGurl?"

"She's long gone, Joe," she said softly. "You'll have to make do with plain old law-abiding Naomi."

"That'll do."

A whole new spin on reality from

Jennifer O'Connell

Bachelorette
#1

Sarah Holmes is one of the glamorous young hopefuls on
America's hottest reality TV show. But she isn't just another
bachelorette—she's a married undercover reporter.
And she's about to discover an alternate reality far more
seductive than she could have ever imagined.

0-451-21622-9

Also available from Jennifer O'Connell

Dress Rehearsal

0-451-21399-8

**Available wherever books are sold or at
penguin.com**

All your favorite romance writers are
coming together.

SIGNET ECLIPSE

MARCH 2006:
Lover Eternal by J. R. Ward
Are You Afraid? by Carla Cassidy
Jack of Clubs by Barbara Metzger

APRIL 2006:
Past Redemption by Savannah Russe
Love and Mayhem by Nicole Cody
Parallel Attraction by Deidre Knight

MAY 2006:
Even Vampires Get the Blues
by Katie MacAlister
A Moonlit Knight by Jocelyn Kelley